The most difficult problem for a writer is to get that first novel published. No matter how talented, no matter what writing credentials the writer may have, most publishers simply do not want to take the risk of putting out a novel by an "unknown."

Hence, *Ben Bova's Discoveries*. There's a wealth of talent in the science fiction field waiting for the chance to get their first novels to you, the reader. The *Discoveries* series will present novels by such writers: many of them experienced authors of short fiction or nonfiction, others brand-new writers who have never published anything before.

As editor of the *Discoveries* series, I promise you the same high standards I insisted on when I edited *Analog* and *Omni* magazines: science fiction that entertains you with bold new ideas and high-quality writing.

Rebecca Ore's BECOMING ALIEN is one of the most exciting novels I have read in many years. Not since Ursula K. LeGuin's *The Left Hand of Darkness* have alien beings been drawn with such sensitivity and depth, such originality and power.

I know you will enjoy it too.

—Ben Bova

BEN BOVA'S DISCOVERIES

BECOMING ALIEN by Rebecca Ore
NAPOLEON DISENTIMED by Hayford Peirce

BEN BOVA'S DISCOVERIES

BECOMING ALIEN

—REBECCA ORE—

A TOM DOHERTY ASSOCIATES BOOK

BECOMING ALIEN

Copyright © 1988 by Rebecca Ore

First printing: January 1988

A TOR Book

Published by Tom Doherty Associates, Inc.
49 West 24 Street
New York, N.Y. 10010

ISBN: 0-812-54794-2
CAN. ED.: 0-812-54795-0

Printed in the United States of America

0 9 8 7 6 5 4 3 2 1

BECOMING ALIEN

= 1 =

Floyd County, Virginia

Cap down to his black brows, Warren leaned on his truck, hearing out two men slouched in a junker car—the kind of car those men leave in a ditch after they've done their business. As I came up, Warren said to them, "Well, if you put it *that* way, I'd come up with them pills."

The driver smiled, then asked me, "Tom, you help your brother Warren in the business?"

"Hush, Tom," Warren said. He stared at the truck hood ornament, finally said, "My brother's not in this."

"But he'd be so good as a courier, not quite blond, not quite dark-haired. Can't be much money in four or five hundred hens."

"He's not part of the deal," Warren said, getting the overnight bag out from behind the truck seat.

Drug investors—I tried not to look at them. Did they know he'd been crazy once, me in foster care, the farm almost lost? Yeah, they knew, gave them good leverage.

"And your brother's underage."

"No, I'm sixteen," I said, my face turned down, away from them. I didn't like Warren's drug thing.

Warren asked the men, "And where you from? What's your address?"

"Atlanta's enough. Be in touch with you."

So more and more into drugs for Warren.

While Warren's new Methedrine distributors made pick-ups, I drove off miles through the summer heat, trying to

1

forget that I might come home to find Warren arrested or dead, the truck and Ford Fairlane confiscated. Three weeks after the Atlanta guys visited, I drove up a dirt road, then walked by White's Branch into the woods, trying not to think of jails, school. Warren—so wild and crazy.

The ground screeched like rocks being dragged across rocks. I saw smoke and ran up to a wreck, burning, not a car, but no wings—an odd-looking machine.

A hatch opened. I saw flames behind a man-shape, face twisted bad—wrinkled face writhing and crying. I flashed that he looked weird, but I rushed to get him out and laid him down.

When we heard screams, he sat up and shoved me toward the wreck. *Help them!* The ship sizzled, the screams stopped.

He pushed me again with long bony hands, but now I was really looking at him: dark eyes rolling under bone swellings like bone goggles all around them. He was naked except for pants, them burnt.

Slowly, he raised a hand to his head hair and felt the ash in it. Face hair charred, too, so you could see the skin through it, like on a dog's belly. And face all wrinkled from eyes to pointed chin.

I touched him—not cool like a frog, but bird-hot. Sparse burnt hair covered his body. Then I noticed the eyelashes. Regular eyelashes. Who'd have thought a creature that weird would have regular eyelashes?

When I tried to take a pulse, the creature winced and reached for my hand. He muttered with a tongue that sure looked un-Earthly—dark red, flat-pointed like a bird's, but broader behind the point, real flexible.

No nipples, no navel. Gooky blood oozed out of wire nicks. He was alien, trying to get up.

I held him down. "Easy, whoa, easy," I said, feeling his legs and arms for breaks. The joints and tendons were a bit different, but nothing felt really out of place.

"You're a problem," I said to him, considering Warren's business. "Whole troops of investigators gonna hit this place." *Maybe someone at Tech should help him with his burns*, I thought. He had burnt places all over his back like he'd been struck with red-hot coins and wire.

Alpha extraterrestrialis. Or was that supposed to be *extrater-*

restralus? I didn't exactly want to ask the high school teachers. The first-discovered alien on Earth ever. I'd call him Alpha. The ship hadn't seemed to come out of the sky, though, just twisted out of space, wrecking.

The wreck didn't look like much, other than obviously not a car wreck. The alien looked over at it, then rolled his head to the side and cried. The tears were thick, oily. I helped him up, with my arm around him, and felt his heart thumping in that long torso, webs in the armpits like bat's wings against my hand. We wobbled to the car. I plunked him down in the back seat.

Sitting there, short-legged, the long crooked arms weaving around, Alpha Alien looked drunk. I took off what was left of one shoe. If he'd had a shirt, it'd been totally burned away.

I wondered if we'd see anyone and thought about getting the back seat down so the *Alpha extraterrestrialis* could crawl through Warren's hole into the trunk. But Alph slowly lay down. Only a transit truck could see down into the back seat and one wasn't likely on these little roads, so I drove to the house, resetting Warren's road alarms.

Warren was out, hiding or spending the drug money. In the kitchen, the alien stopped, sniffed. I feared Alpha smelled the chemicals in Warren's tunnels, but the alien got the salt shaker and sprinkled some on his hand, then licked it. He sniffed again and stared at the faucet. I turned on the water and stepped back. My alien guy then saw a glass sitting in the drain.

After drinking, his tongue flopping sloppily inside the glass, the alien put the glass down. Slowly, he sank to the floor. When he covered his face with his hands, I saw the webs running from near the elbow to the chest, wrinkled like crepe paper, trembling. This was so spooky, a web-armed, wrinkle-faced creature shuddering on our kitchen linoleum floor.

Oh, Warren, I thought, *what can we do?*

I put the alien to bed where our parents had slept, and eased off the pants. No asshole and an odd thick cock, I noticed as he helped kick the pants free. I covered him and watched until he was asleep, or passed out.

I'll put the crash stuff in the barn until Warren figures out what to do, I decided.

As I hauled the wreck onto the tractor wagon, soft things flopped inside it. The wagon sides groaned as the thing slid between them. I scared myself with questions: What kinds of aliens were hunting the ship? Was the ship, whatever, shot down?

The ship, looking now like a de-winged small plane, was so far crashed I knew the alien couldn't escape in it. If he didn't get alien help, he'd be stuck here.

Scare questions . . . What did the alien eat? Was he going to whip out that tongue . . . ?

Fears cranked up, with me spooking myself. What were those armpit webs? Why the big wrinkle on its belly and no nipples, unless they'd been burned off? That was worse scary than the awful wrinkled face, the goat slit nostrils, and pointed chin.

No, the alien has absolutely no asshole.

The tractor strained to get the wagon moving, then I drove it off the roads and up through the woods, keyed out the alarms before coming onto our land, and put the wagon in the barn, unhitched the tractor, and closed and padlocked the doors.

I went back to the alien's room. "Tom?" Warren's voice sounded like he was popped in the head a bit. He stood by the alien's bed. The alien yawned, exposing needle teeth, then shuddered.

Warren pulled his hands from his eyes to his nose. Alpha shifted stiffly, as though he was sore from the crash.

"This ain't the time to bring in crazy circus animals, Tom." Warren leaned up against the wall. "Or whatever it is. Anybody know it's here?"

"I think he's an alien, Warren," I said timidly. "He crashed in the woods."

"Bet half the Air Force and all the county saw it coming down. Just as good as killed us bringing it here."

"Nobody saw it."

Warren groaned. The creature looked seriously at Warren, but didn't say even a garble with his own tongue.

"Can't you see he was hurt?" I said.

"Yeah. If it dies on us, you want to explain to the guys who sent it?"

"Was I supposed to let him burn up? Touch him, Warren, he won't hurt you. Call him Alpha, that's what I call him."

"Alph." Warren reached for the creature, kind of rough, and the alien flinched. "Afraid of me, are you?" Warren said, with the voice he used on skittish stock. "Not if you plan to stay in *my* house."

The creature pulled his hand back so that just the fingertips touched.

"Feels hot," Warren said, grabbing the creature's wrist, pulling a bit to test Alph's strength. "Like a chicken. Does it have a fever?"

"Could have."

"Tom, it's the weirdest thing you've ever brought home. Worse than that broke-leg pony I shot and you made a skeleton of."

"And the wreck's in the barn."

Warren sighed. He took off his cap and rubbed his head. "Damn," Warren finally said, meaning the creature could stay despite it being a very bad idea.

"Let's see whose jeans he can wear," I said, " 'cause what he had on was all tore up."

The wreck in the barn began to stink, so Warren told me to clean out whatever rotted in there. I soaked rags in vinegar and went in.

I shoved a rear compartment hatch open. Two charred messes—once live creatures—lay sprawled under the flashlight. One's fingers, bones and dried sinews, tore off on the door handle. It'd died pulling the hatch down, keeping the worst of the fire back from the compartment where I'd found the live one.

I pulled the fingers away from the handle and dragged the bodies out, both bigger than the live alien, but so light. Half the flesh had burned to char.

Warren laid the most complete corpse on an outside table where we'd butchered hogs. He started dissecting the corpse, putting alien meat and organs into Mason jars full of formaldehyde.

"Look, they've got sharp teeth," he said, holding a jaw open with his index finger, flesh on one side burned away to the jawbone. With his other hand, he felt down in the gaping cavity. "And the tongue has a ring of muscle back from the tip." He cut into the tongue with a meat dressing knife. "I'll use carrion beetles to clean off the skeleton. And if the one inside dies . . ."

"Bury the bodies, Warren," I said. "It's the only decent thing to do."

"I wanna see what alien skeletons look like," Warren said. "Bet you're curious, too."

We carried one body to an old log corncrib so flies and beetles could clean the bones. He buried the other one in a copper mine near us.

Back in the house, the creature twisted the bed covers into lumps around his arms. When I went in, he moaned. Swollen veins in the armpit webs throbbed slightly. I washed his cuts with soapy water and sat by him awhile.

When I got up to leave, he dabbed his fingers at me, pinching the air by my hand, so I stayed. As I pulled up a chair by the bed, Alpha shivered. Even though it was summer, I got out a blanket and wrapped it around the alien. He focused his eyes on me, moved his lips a bit, then breathed out a wavery tone.

I clicked my tongue and he clicked back. Remembering the old jungle movies, I pointed to myself and said, "Tom."

He pointed to me and said a sound with only the ghost of *Tom* in it, the tones, maybe, like he had the tune, but not the words. Then he touched his shoulder and went, "Hwu-ing."

I tried to imitate what he said. The alien huffed, touched his shoulder again, and made another different call, bell-toned. I tried to imitate again, but just made him agitated.

Like Vietnamese, I thought, having heard from Warren that Asians built their languages from tones.

I shrugged my shoulders; Alpha shrugged back as if he was testing shrugs for meanings. Then he wadded the blanket up and put his arms around it. Rubbing his face against the bedclothes first, he closed his eyes, then the breathing shifted, slowed down.

I sat on the chair, creaking the cane seat from time to time, until Warren came upstairs smelling of chemicals and solvents, his sweaty hair tumbled down his forehead. He felt the creature's face, around the eyes. Still the alien slept, just bird-singing once when Warren touched a wire nick.

Finally Warren asked, "Did you see anything in the paper about the ship? About a fireball yesterday?"

"No, like I said, Warren, it didn't come *down* from any-where. Popped out of the rocks and air all twisted and burning."

"If anyone comes checking, that thing's got to go."

"Warren, he's sick. And he can't talk."

"Can't?"

"Can't. What he tried to do with my name didn't make any sense at all."

"Maybe it's like an alien space monkey." Warren pulled back when the alien turned in his sleep and reached his arm around Warren's leg. He put the alien's arm back on the bed. "But we don't send out space machines without tracking them."

And the ship was still on the tractor wagon in the barn. "Warren, let's get rid of the ship."

He smiled, with a funny twist to his face. In a little flat voice, he said, "Tom, it's not a hallucination, is it? Just too much, especially now." *The Atlanta people.* He clinched his jaw and hands, then said, in a more regular voice, "I ought to disable anything odd in the ship, in case they're tracking it. Then we'll dump it down an old copper mine up-county."

"It stinks inside, Warren," I said. "And those metals might be super-hard, too."

"Those monster metals ain't that tough. It crashed."

The blood drained out of Warren's face as we slithered inside the ship, dragging tools and two trouble lights on long cords. The stench was awful.

The aliens built with weird screwheads, but Warren hung up one of the lights and filed down a steel rod to fit.

He slid forward, unscrewed a panel, and shone the other light in. "Don't look or smell too different from other wrecks I've worked, Tom." The veins and tendons popped up on his hands as he fussed with the screws, unhooking all the electronic stuff he could reach. "Reminds me of 'Nam," he said. Finally he pulled off a panel with geared knobs and liquid crystal displays on it.

Snip! Warren cut wires behind the panel, the noise star-tling, metallic and harsh, inside the ship. After sliding the panel aside, he reached down into the hole and twisted. I heard weird soft clicks, then Warren pulled out a black metal egg-shaped thing a foot long, with gold lines twisted all over it.

"Heavy," he said. "Bet this is navigation equipment, ship sensor computer, lots of little curved plates stuck to it before I pulled it free."

We saw a shimmering place, a liquid crystal display, in the skin of the egg-shaped gadget, which turned colors that looked like a map, from space, of America. The colors spread until the shape of the continent disappeared. Lines appeared out, but nothing like anything I'd seen on a road map. Has to be a location device with a map on it, I thought, not sure I was happy for Alpha or not.

Warren knelt in the alien cockpit, hefting the egg-thing, then he looked a long, long ways out of his eyes, through me, as though he was staring out into space, looking for that alien's planet.

Back in the house, I rolled a map measurer wheel around the gold lines on the metal egg. Warren thought he could figure out what frequency the aliens used if the gold lines were antennas.

"Not antennas . . ." Warren said, going for a Bausch & Lomb ten-power magnifying glass. He looked at the lines and said, "Whatever, it's beyond me." He took the egg to his room.

After lunch, we cut up the rest of the ship with propane torches. From the pieces, you'd never have known the wreck was exotic, from space. Just hunks of metal, fused silicone and plastic.

When I went in to see Alpha the next morning, he sat up, hunched over. His eyes looked filmed. I decided to give him a bath. When the tub was ready, I reached for his upper arms and he pulled back, but then touched my eyebrows with his long skinny fingers and leaned against me. *Not the idea*, I thought, uneasy about him touching me. I wanted him to stand up by himself and walk to the tub.

He finally followed me and seemed to understand what the tub was for. I helped him into it, then washed his back while he brought up a palmful of water to sniff, taste. Gently, he took the rag and soap out of my hand and scrubbed his long crooked arms, around his armpit webs, and behind his ears, which were rounder than a human's, but convoluted inside just the same.

Then he pursed his mouth a bit, rounded his lips between the two biggest face wrinkles. Warren came in and said, "Sorry-looking cuss, ain't it?"

"He's smiling," I said. "I think."

"It looks like it's going to kiss someone."

"Well, purse your lips like that—let's both do it and see what he does," I replied.

We both pursed our lips like the creature. Alpha looked startled—same expression for man, dog, or alien—wide-eyed, head tossed back. Then he leaned toward us while we slipped back into human grins. He smoothed out his lips and touched my mouth, then tried to move his thin lips back into a smile like ours, but finally pulled the lip corners with his fingers.

Warren slipped out and came back with the big black metal egg we'd gotten from the ship. The alien oo'ed and reached out tenderly for the egg. Warren held on to it while Alpha traced his fingers around the gold lines.

The alien breathed in little gasps, touching the map place on the egg, then gently stroked Warren's wrist, muttering little singsong tones.

I reached down and took his pulse. "He's running over two hundred beats a minute."

"Yeah, he's happy to see it all right. Now we know to get rid of it," Warren said, lifting the egg out of the alien's hands, "les' they bring our government with them."

Alpha seemed so cheerful after he saw the egg. Each morning, for the next few weeks, he ate eggs and butter for breakfast, dressed in a cut-off pair of Warren's pants, and followed me around as I gathered eggs and ran feed bags up and down on the trolley in the center of the chicken house. But he could only wear socks on his feet because he had more heel bone than humans, and only four toes.

Warren wondered about that and cleaned the chaff off the skeleton. Weird to see the huge space for the eyes, the bone eye-socket shields. Alien, not like the biology book's human skeleton. Warren twisted the leg and foot bones around, then said, "That big heel is a twisted toe bone."

He brushed more chaff off, beetle grubs in it, and grunted, disconnecting the bones and putting them in a sack.

Warren said, "I know who told the Atlanta investors about me. If aliens gonna hit on anyone, that guy, he's out in Bolinas now, he ought to be hit."

So Warren and I took the egg up to another dealer Warren knew in Roanoke. The Roanoke guy called the California man and asked him to hold some computer goods, hot programs in a military shell—sure there'd be a market for it. The Californian settled for 30 percent of the gross and fifty dollars a month holding money.

"Just keep it cool for me," Warren's Roanoke friend said, then Warren reached over the guy's shoulder and clicked down the phone cradle. I recognized Warren's special smile—twisted on by willpower, nothing in Warren's eyes but sheer calculation.

Three days later, Warren checked the creature's leg cuts, going up and down each leg with his hands, twisting a little, while Alpha gripped the bedclothes with his narrow hands, looking, eyes as squinty as they'd go, at the top of Warren's head.

"Fit to work, I'd say," Warren said. "The chicken house at first, since he eats enough eggs, until I see how tame he's going to be. He's got to learn to hide from strangers."

The alien nodded at Warren, not a friendly nod. Then he looked at me, shrugged, and touched the back of Warren's hand, very lightly.

The next day, I took Alpha with me to milk. But when he saw our old milk cow, he walked his funny rolling walk up to the cow and began prodding her milk veins. Then he moved forward, palpated her neck, wrapped his long arms around her shoulders, and bit into her skin.

She flinched, but didn't knock him away, so he bent over and pumped blood out of her neck with that flat tongue of his. Then he wiped his mouth, just like a man would have, flicked his tongue out to clean his lips and wrinkles. Then he oo'ed at me.

The cow stood stiff-legged, jerking her eyes around to show white every now and again. The alien held the nick closed with his fingers until the clot formed. When he was satisfied that the cow had stopped bleeding, he turned back and touched her udder again.

The cow cocked a leg, lashed out, but the creature ducked as though he was used to stock, talked to her in that singsong voice, and bent down to milk the udder.

No milk came down—the cow was too nervous—so I massaged the udder and finally milked out a dribble onto the alien's skinny palm. He sniffed and tasted, seeming somewhat dubious. Then he flipped his tongue out and fluttered the milk into his mouth.

So the alien drank blood and milk. I woke suddenly one night. He stood by my bed, a faint chlorine odor in the air. My heart bounced, then beat fast. The creature slowly reached for my hand, touched it gently with just the pads of his fingers. I sat up in bed, and pushed his hand away. The floorboards creaking under his bare feet, he cried softly, two huffing sounds.

Alpha looked lonely, not dangerous. He stroked my upper arm and stepped back.

But I saw his reflection in the mirror over my dresser—alien, burnt skin growing new hair on his back—and wanted to lock the creature up, before he got me with his sharp teeth and that blood-pumping tongue.

He took my hands, pulling me to the kitchen where he found a pencil and stared at me as though asking *where's paper?*

I got him paper. He sat down awkwardly at the table and began to draw a broken outline of one of his kind. Then, where he'd left blanks in the first outline, he fitted in another creature all twined with the first. He drew others, a soft knot of sleeping bodies, aliens with closed eyes, and closed his own eyes, brimming full of tear oil.

His kind slept in heaps and he was lonely, not out to get me. I took the pencil out of his fingers and sketched a human, not as finely drawn as his, sleeping alone. He stared at the paper.

Then a brindle cat waltzed up, milk beggar that it was, and rubbed against the alien's legs. Alpha picked up the cat, sniffed its mouth, and oo'ed. I managed to sketch out a figure with a cat sleeping in the crook of its knees. The alien's forehead twitched, then he bumped his elbow against mine and went back to his room, carrying the cat.

During the next week, Alpha gathered a heap of cats to sleep with. I suspected he bribed them with eggs.

I spent hours watching the alien draw precise drawings, done as though he laid a vision on the paper and was just tracing lines to make his visions visible to me.

Strange buildings and plants appeared on our Terran drawing paper, with stranger creatures walking among them. The alien looked sideways over his fuzzy shoulder at me and added another figure, almost human. He pointed from it to me and oo'ed. *Me*. But my face was distorted. I pointed to my real face and then to the paper, *draw me*. He touched the top of my head, then my clavicle, and started to draw.

He drew me as though I was part alien—the grooves between the mouth corners and the nostrils exaggerated, eyes bigger—but recognizably me.

Then Alpha drew a creature chunkier than a cow, with ropy flesh in the neck, giant veins, then another beast, drawing herds of them, over and over again as if he wanted to make them alive with his pencil.

Eyes heavy with the oil he used for tears, he laid down the pencil. I picked up the drawing of me among the alien buildings. "Do you miss those creatures?" I asked stupidly.

September came. Odd to leave the alien and Warren, walk to the road, and wait for the yellow bus, thinking of planets in space, how I'd never thought about them much before.

Then classes, where I knew too much for my kind, and the kids all knowing what Warren did, at least the bad ones, and the good ones avoiding me lest I tell them. A teacher from New Jersey, all bearded and full of goat milk, wanted to pry into my serious local-colorfulness; the other teachers ignored me best they could.

Days when we needed groceries or feed, I drove to town and played Space Invaders at the video arcade, the bumpa-bumpa music going while I missed shots. I wondered if I ought marry the girl who'd got me in bed when we were fourteen, short and messy as that was, and run away.

But what would happen to Alpha? So I went home to our real alien, who was a flop as an invader. And he and I tended the chickens, scooping feed from the trolley, then coming back down the long shed gathering eggs from the wire cages. If a car came up, he hid, like Warren trained him.

At night, or in the late afternoon when I wasn't delivering eggs, Alpha questioned me through his drawings. He had a sign, like)(, for questions. He drew a mother and child and put the)(sign after it. Parents, dead in our case. I drew two figures lying down, shrouds over them. He drew)(again.

I walked him out through the twilight to the family graves. He looked at the ground, the stones, and looked back at me with his chin tucked down, hands limp at his sides. As we went in, he stroked my ribs with his knuckles.

At first Alpha couldn't see what was on the television, even though Warren'd rigged an antenna that got channels from Greensboro to Roanoke. Finally he took out a ballpoint pen and drew dotted lines across the paper real quick—heavy and light. When he got to the bottom of the paper, I saw that he'd drawn Warren.

He got up, shook the drawing beside the picture tube, and looked at us, oo'ing. *Yeah, TV tubes have little lines of dots in them that make up the picture*, but I didn't know he had to learn how to make them out.

Each night before we all went to bed, Alpha and I went outside. He'd look around, the muscled tongue trilling so high-pitched I could barely hear it and Warren couldn't hear it at all, but the cats came running, rubbing around his legs as if to tell him they were here, even if his people weren't.

Then, one night, Warren made sure we stayed up late, to watch some horror movie he'd seen before. The alien sat by me on one of Warren's red leather sofas. Warren slouched on another, drinking whiskey with ice.

When the aliens on the screen landed and the humans ran off screaming, Alpha stared at Warren, then got his drawing pad. Kneeling, thighs spraddled out, in front of Warren, he drew the egg with all its gold wire tracery, and the question sign:)(.

I froze and looked at Warren. The alien lay the drawing on Warren's lap.

"What egg?" Warren said, even though he knew Alpha couldn't understand English. He slowly tore up the drawing. On the television, humans were shooting aliens.

Alpha looked at the screen, then set his shoulders back and rocked on the balls of his feet, staring at Warren. Warren laughed and threw the little bits of paper into the air. "Thing, you want your egg? Tom, turn off that space movie, it's giving Thing bad homesickness."

I quickly switched off the TV. Alpha looked from me to Warren, then rubbed his eyes with the back of his long hand.

Warren said, "Heard from Roanoke that strange folks in California asked around about the location device. I wanted this one to see what we humans do to bad aliens."

The alien singsonged at Warren, an unhappy song. Warren rose off the couch, took one skinny hand, and pulled it down to the floor. Alpha gave a sharp cry but bent at the waist and knees, let Warren guide his hand.

"You stand in my clothes," Warren said as he forced the alien to pick up the paper, "eat my eggs, and you want to bring the whole universe down on my farm? Egg gone. Tom, you said he knows *yes* and *no* from head moves, didn't you?"

I nodded.

Warren held out his hands as if he was cupping the egg between them, and shook his head no. "No. No."

The alien stepped back and threw out his arms, crying out one strange sound, the tones almost like *no*.

"No," Warren said again.

"Nuyngh," Alpha replied, crumpling to the floor.

I started toward him, but he scrambled to his feet, wrapped his arms around himself, and ran stumbling to the room we'd put him in.

"All since you showed him the egg, Warren," I said, "he's been expecting his people."

"Fool. I just wanted to know what the egg was."

The next morning, Alpha lay sprawled in bed, the webs spread out, his body cold. *Dead*, I thought, until I held my finger on his throat, and felt the vein throb once, then again five seconds later.

"Warren!" I cried. Half naked, barefooted, he rushed in and laid his hand against Alpha's throat.

"Dying," Warren said. "Just as well."

Alpha stayed tranced out the rest of the day, no colder than five degrees above room temperature, heart going twelve times a minute.

While I sat with the cool, stiff alien, I wondered if his people made movies about beating off hordes of attacking Earthlings.

Warren and I didn't say much to each other all weekend, expecting those spaced-out heartbeats to finally stop.

But Sunday, the alien's pulse beat a little faster. At breakfast Monday, before I caught the school bus, Warren said, "You gonna trust me not to barbecue your alien or what?"

"He's upset. He could have had hope . . ."

"I don't want some space freak dividing the family. You trust me to take care of it if it wakes up, or not?"

"Okay, Warren, I trust you won't hurt him more."

"What do you mean, 'more'?"

"Warren, I'll miss the bus," I said, gathering up the books I needed and stuffing them in my pack.

"Well, don't miss the damn bus. The Atlanta guys're upping my production schedule, by way of threatening to break your legs, but I guess what happens in the basement's no damn concern of yours."

At lunch, I called Warren on the school pay phone in the hall. "How are things?" I asked him.

"Cool," Warren said.

"Cool?" I asked.

"Yeah, cool, just like you left it. Okay. You've got school business to tend to, don't you?"

"Yeah, physics."

"Chemistry'd be better use," Warren said. "Bye now."

I hung up, wondering if Alph was still alive, or if Warren'd said that to keep me from worrying. Then Roose Dexter came by and asked, "Them hens gonna keep you too busy for baseball again come spring?"

"Yeah," I said. "Them hens." And I walked off to physics class, wondering how my buddy alien got from wherever to here.

"Can't go faster than light?" I asked. "Won't we learn ways around that?"

The little-guy teacher took off his glasses and wiped them clean on his shirt. "Well, Tom, mass would be infinite at light speed, so you'd need infinite fuel. That's the universe. Can't go faster than light. The stars are out of human reach."

I knew that wasn't so. "No way?"

"I realize what this does to your science fiction fantasies, but right, no way."

Bullshit, I thought, and Alpha is from creatures smarter than us, but we're killing him, Warren and me. I pulled out a bit of knife blade from my wallet and started cutting on my desk.

"Tom!" the teacher cried out, looking nervous, because I was taller than him, and country-built from heaving chicken shit and feed.

"Right, sir," I said, hopping up to hand over the bit of knife blade. Doesn't do to take a good knife to school, so I grind down something I find broken, whittle with it.

Then algebra—so beautiful and inhuman, math problems, without taints of human social bull. But today, the numbers just jerked around in my mind.

When I got home, the alien still lay on the bed, but his arms were sprawled different. "Alpha?" I said, and his chest jerked. Slowly, he pulled his arms close to his body, then spread them slightly. The veins throbbed and he pulled his arms close to his sides again, and shivered violently.

All the cats who'd deserted him when he was cold started back in as Alpha moaned and shuddered.

Maybe he'd like a hot bath. I drew him a tub, then mixed some hot salt water in a glass as he climbed, still quivering, into the tub. Alpha took the glass in his palms and lay back in the water, sipping the hot salt solution.

Warren came in. The alien gasped, spread his arms, veins pulsing in the webs, and started to slow down his breathing, but I called to him and pushed his arms down against his body.

Warren touched the strange pointed chin. He said, "You were okay until you asked about the egg."

Alpha levered himself out of the tub with his long arms, found a towel, and dried off. He looked at both of us, and wrapped the towel around his waist. Strange to see him tuck the end in, just as I did. He beckoned us to follow him to the kitchen. There he handed Warren a knife and raised his head, baring his throat.

Warren slowly touched the creature's throat with the knife, saying to me, "Maybe he wants it. Maybe he's going crazy."

The alien looked little and sickly, his long arms quivering, goosefleshed under the hair. Warren slowly lowered the knife and shook his head no.

The alien then wrapped the towel tighter, found his paper, and drew a circle with funny splotches on it. From where I sat, the circle looked like an Earth map, but he'd drawn it upside down and fuzzy. Then the alien drew two eggs, one smashed. And the question sign,)(.

"Warren," I said, "he wants to know where the egg is, smashed or not."

Warren grimaced. "Doesn't give up, does it?" He pointed from the undamaged egg to the circle, running his finger around the whole circle. "Still on this."

The alien wrapped his arms around himself, webs strained over his chest, then drew the egg on all the continents, then in the oceans. He drew another circle, put Europe and Asia on it.

Laughing a snappish laugh, Warren pointed at the egg in the ocean and shook his head. "Okay, space thing, the egg's on land. I ain't gonna tell you any more."

The alien sighed, gave Warren the knife again, tried to wrap Warren's fingers around the hilt. Warren shook his head, said, "No," sharply.

Alpha leaned down, laid his head and arms on the table top. Warren took all the map drawings away and turned back to scratch Alpha's fuzzy back. Alpha pushed Warren's hand away, got up, and walked to the door.

"Follow him, Tom," Warren said.

I went out and saw the creature sprawled on the porch, arm web spread to the sun, those eyelashes, so much like ours, beating down tears.

A grey tabby mewed and bumped the alien's nostril slits until Alpha sat up and cuddled the cat while it licked around the creature's eyes.

For dinner, the alien melted butter and pumped it up with his tongue curled into a tube.

When the school bus stopped to let me off, I saw Warren standing, waiting with a "don't talk" smile curved into his face. The bad guys on the bus grinned at Warren. Hands deep in his corduroy pockets, he didn't react, just waited until the bus pulled off down the road.

"Your alien's gone. Stole my day pack," Warren said when the bus had pulled farther down the road, "couple pounds of butter, eggs, jar of honey."

I wondered if Warren'd hurt or killed the alien. He saw doubt turn my face and pulled his fists out of his pocket. "Really, Tom, I didn't hurt it. Creature bollixed the alarm. Right smart creature, but . . ."

"Did he take a gun?" I asked as we walked back to the house.

"No," Warren said. "I checked."

"Gonna get cold tonight," I said.

"Maybe we'll get lucky. He'll die and rot to bits in the woods before human or thing figures out where he was, or what he was," Warren said as we stepped up onto the porch.

The cats had left, too, but around dinnertime, I saw the big grey tabby slink back, then her favorite black tom, followed by others, all ears back, tails low. After dinner, I went to feed them and saw a little yellow cat limping. When I saw it worry its hind leg with teeth and tongue, I realized it'd been shot.

Alpha'd been shot, too—I knew it. Warren said, "I'll go to town and see if anyone's seen anything."

Warren heard plenty. "Folks thought one of the hippies got the jump on Halloween, going off like a monster and carrying cats around. Your star-buddy got all the way to Pannell Knitting before old man Hendricks used bird shot on him.'' Warren took his jacket off while I got a fire going.

"He'll freeze tonight," I said, setting the kindling on fire, "this late in October.''

"Better he be dead, and not linked to us. I keep thinking how he can't talk, but the bastard sure can draw, faces and maps.''

Warren was right for Warren, but I slipped out about midnight, leaves crunching like little bones under my feet. When I was good and away from the house, I turned on the flashlight, kept it low, looking for tracks, broken twigs, but the night was so cold and dark. About two miles out, I realized how hopeless searching was and went back to the house. Coming up to it, I saw lights.

"Damn, Tom," Warren said, putting his Uzi machine gun aside. I gaped at the Uzi—I didn't realize he had such weapons around.

"If I had an ultrasonic dog whistle," I said.

"Get to bed." He stood over me, skin tight around his eyes.

I didn't sleep and heard Warren fussing around until dawn. Sunrise, he stepped out on the porch, and said, "Damn you, stupid.''

I got up, threw on a robe, and went out there. The alien, legs bloody, sat on the steps.

Warren peeled his day pack off Alpha's back. Alpha opened his arms and moaned, then curled down, scrabbling at his legs as though the bird shot itched. "Tom, take care of him," Warren said, heading out for the car.

I spread papers to catch blood around a kitchen chair, then helped Alpha. He'd walked at least fifteen miles since he'd snuck away—socks worn off, heels bruised bloody. I wiped up where he'd put his feet and then gave him water.

Better get all that bird shot out, I decided, going to the bathroom for tweezers. When I worked the tweezers around in a shot hole, Alpha jumped, so I held the first pellet up for him to see. He rolled the shot around on his palm, then touched my shoulder gently. I moved the tweezers back down to his legs. He said, "Dus," for *yes*, but kept his hand on my shoulder and squeezed when the tweezers got particularly painful. Finally, I thought to ice the holes to numb them.

After I helped him to bed, the alien grabbed me and just held on, alien heart going faster than a bird's, hot body up sideways against me, ribs rolling against my ribs. I could have pulled away, but realized how utterly alone Alpha was, so I sat, stroking the alien's shoulder, saying quiet dumb things like, *we'll both escape, find an alien biologist, speculative guys like Carl Sagan.*

Me just babbling—the alien really stuck here.

His heart finally slowed down, but not so much that he chilled off again. When he yawned, I saw that dark red tongue curl, tiny nipping teeth gleaming. So human, so Earthlike, to yawn, but such an alien mouth. He arranged the bedclothes in lumps again and called the cats, who hopped up on the bed to check him out.

The alien slept, the cats curled against him, their finer fur blending in with his leg and arm hair. He moaned after a while, kicked a leg free, unsettling the grey tabby, and shifted the pillow against his belly.

I realized I'd missed the school bus.

I said, "Why don't we just drive it up to D.C. and drop it off with the Smithsonian?"

Warren was cleaning his hands and clothes after working in his bunker. He looked up from the sink and said, "I suspect, if it can navigate around in the dark like it did last week, it would figure out where we kept it, even if we locked it in the back of a truck."

"He'll go nuts without any of his kind."

"Dogs and cats don't go nuts, do they?" Warren asked. "And you cut school for a couple days." He draped his wet shirt over a chair and leaned up against the refrigerator. "Don't trust me with it, do you?"

"Both of us can keep an eye on him better, since we know he wants to get away."

"Suppose it could run a vacuum pump? Weigh batch chemicals?" He sat down. "Having that creature here is weirder than having a nark snooping. What might it tell, if it got to the government or back to its people? Tom, I've got quite an operation under this house. You haven't seen it in a while, have you?''

''I make you lots of methane,'' I said, ''with the chicken shit. And you've bought a whole ton of cement.''

''Couple tons,'' Warren said. ''let's take you down. I'll set up the air-disturbance alarm in the outer rooms after you lock the alien in. Maybe it's time you got in the family business, paid for your pet here. I need all the help I can get now.''

''Are they squeezing you?''

''Squeezing?'' Warren grunted. ''They sent me this. Post-mark Atlanta.'' The photo was of a dead man, legs crushed. As I stared at it, Warren threw some switches in the kitchen. ''Seen enough?'' he said, taking the photo out of my hand. We went down the basement stairs—copper-clad rungs wired to 220-volt house current—knock anyone snooping dead off the rungs. In the basement, Warren climbed onto a small front-end loader and moved a section of the wall—not a false cement front, but a real cement-block section about three feet high. Behind the blocks was a tunnel.

Warren and I crawled along in the tunnel and finally stood up in dark that smelled medical, bitter. A switch clicked and I saw retorts, a vacuum pump, and bottles of chemicals under one bare light bulb.

Two huge props began turning, sucking the stale air away. I guessed he'd vented the bunker through a couple of old tobacco barns. He cut on another light and the one we were under went out. Under the second light, I saw a pill-making machine, with its press lever and the pistons that squashed Warren's illegal powders into aspirin-sized tablets like honest medicine.

''That's the tabber and the mill,'' he said. He spoke of his equipment like it was some sexual woman. ''Best pull on a dust mask in here,'' Warren said, reaching for two on a rack beside the machine. Should have done it early, I thought, my heart racing, mouth just a bit dry. Warren's eyes crinkled above his mask as though he were smiling.

Then, after Warren pressed about fifty pills to show me how the machine worked, we walked back the way we'd come, lights dying behind us. When we got to the crawl tunnel, Warren took both masks and hung them up.

''I've worked on this for fifteen years and no baby monster

is going to threaten it. You get awful moral about drugs, but we've got expenses, mortgage, school for you later.''

My head buzzed with a thousand questions, but they got tangled before I sent them out to my tongue. Finally, I managed to say, ''But speed, Warren?''

''Helps kids get through school,'' he said, grinning at me. The grin dropped away instantly. ''They buy it, whoever makes it. I'll quit in two years.''

''Will the Atlanta people . . .''

''I'll sell this, split your share, then we can settle some-where better, California, Oregon.''

I went to unlock the alien while Warren re-set the alarms, ran the juice through the ladder rungs again.

''Warren,'' I said, ''please use the respirator down there. Over time, that stuff'll drive you crazy.''

''Over time, life'll drive you crazy. If you gonna drop out of school for that thing,'' he said, pointing a cold fried chicken leg at Alpha, ''can you help me make quota?''

''I'll help you. We'll teach him to help, too.''

''Better kill it and dump it somewhere.''

''You told me the Army had devices that could smell out a man in the jungle. What if we killed it and found out its people could track it even years later?''

''So you'll help me?''

''Yes. And get him a respirator, too. Speed might drive him crazy.''

I went back to school on Monday, wanting to be away when Warren worked the alien in drugs for the first time. School was cold, big mental freeze-out of little me.

Nobody said anything particular. Lunchtime I went in the cafeteria and found myself alone at a usually full table.

School'd always been weird, though. The local teachers'd told me the only reason I tested high 90s percentiles on those California achievement tests was my ''sociopathic lack of test anxiety.'' Crook's nerves, they wanted me to think, so I wouldn't know I was really smarter than the good kids.

And Warren might work the alien to death if I didn't help. Drop-out time, I decided.

*   *   *

Neither Warren nor the alien was in sight when I got home, just a bunch of anxious cats, so I fooled around straightening feed sacks in the barn, and worked myself up madder and madder. Wasn't cute like girl geniuses the teachers loved to save. No, just a gawky country boy.

Since I didn't know when Warren and the alien would be up, I opened a can of beans and made a bean pot to set on low heat, ready anytime. Then I tried to read one of the books I'd got from the library, but ended up looking through the alien's drawings—the buildings set off in space somewhere, with me drawn among them, or at least me as the alien saw me. Maybe the aliens wouldn't be bothered if I was smart for human.

About six, Alpha came into the kitchen, holding the respirator mask in his hands, eyes with the pupils tiny although the light wasn't bright. He hissed and showed his teeth as he gave his arms and face a thorough washing. I handed him a towel as Warren followed him up. The alien took the towel with a snap of his wrist.

Warren grinned. "He didn't like it, but he worked. Must have dealers all over the universe, or he doesn't like the taste."

The alien's eyes quivered. I felt ashamed. He stared at Warren and nodded a hostile nod.

"Damn, Tom," Warren said, "I don't hog-tie folks and shoot 'em up with heroin."

"Sure, Warren," I said, feeling hideous. "It's a service."

"Damn straight. Keeps us from getting killed by those Atlanta guys."

The alien, eyes still quivering, started cutting up the sink sponge to fit around the mask. I guess he wanted to block all the dust. His fingers trembled, and he dropped the scissors once. Warren was right—Alpha was either drugged or knew what he'd gotten into.

While Alpha fixed the respirator to fit him, Warren and I ate beans.

"So what happened in school today?" Warren asked, most relaxed.

"I quit. You need help, and I want my share of the farm eventually, too."

"School folks didn't think much of me, either," Warren said. "We'll be a pair."

"I was bad to test high. Didn't fit in with what they expected."

The alien finished gluing sponge on his respirator and got out his eggs and butter. He fried them up, then drank a glass of thawed deer blood before leaving for his room, carrying off a Mason jar with lid and screw seal.

"Be easier if he spoke English," Warren said, "but then I'd always wonder if he was some trick infiltrator."

The alien went along the bookshelves in the living room with his head straight, not cocking it to read the titles the way a human would. He pulled down novels, encyclopedias, Warren's hunting magazines, staring at the illustrations, and shoving each book back. When he found the tattered Rand McNally road atlas, he trembled over it as though he'd found secret messages, so Warren took it away from him.

Alpha found the atlas again and brought it to the kitchen table. He drew the question sign on the United States.

"He wants to know where the egg is, Warren," I said softly.

"I'm gonna burn that damn atlas," Warren said, putting it by his chair.

When Warren went to the bathroom, I got the atlas and quickly drew a little black egg on the West Coast, in California.

Nostril slits twitching, Alpha touched his shoulder and my shoulder, and pointed to the map, circling with his long finger. I touched the map in the Virginia mountains.

Alph seemed to know the distances involved—he sighed. Like a human sigh, with exasperation in it. I felt awful.

"Stop, Tom, you can't help him."

Singsonging at Warren, Alpha drew two pictures: one of humans running from an alien like him, the other of humans touching elbows with the alien, side by side. On the first drawing, he drew himself getting shot that night before Halloween. Then, just like a nervous human, he got up and paced.

Warren raised his arms as if holding a gun and said, "Blam!"

The alien flinched and cried out.

Warren grinned. "He knows humans don't like him from getting bird shot in his legs. We're the only nice humans there is." Picking up the drawing of the humans screaming and running from an alien, Warren shook it in Alpha's face.

Alpha went rigid and hissed at Warren. When Warren grabbed his elbow, the alien's head hair rose like a cat's and blood veins swelled, then collapsed in the web of the arm Warren held. The alien tried to jerk away, but Warren grabbed a handful of web and twisted.

Warren shoved Alpha away. The web skin bled red weeping crescents where Warren's nails had punched through. "Tom, you tell him where the egg was?" The alien stumbled, then ran for his room.

I tried to explain, softly, "I just indicated California, didn't . . . I don't know the town anyway."

"We're humans, he's not. Stick with humans. Shit, Tom." He came up to me, took my head in his hands. I was afraid he was going to hit me, but he just held my forehead against his. "I need all the help I can get."

I dropped out of school, and the state abandoned me to Warren. *To hell with humans,* I thought, the day I realized no school people were ever going to try talking me back.

The next time Warren was gone, the alien sat me down at the table and drew pictures of us crossing the country, of me among aliens, all of them friendly, hugging me.

No, I shook my head.

The alien tried to make me nod yes, holding either side of my jaw. "Yus," he said. I stiffened and brushed his hands away. He got out the map book, drew a car, and dragged it across the United States map. Then he took my head again and tapped my face with horn-colored nail tips.

I shook my head again. He stared down at the map. Then he began writing, the script going up and down the paper, first up, then down, squiggling pencil lines. Obviously agitated, he singsonged to me.

"No, baby, we just can't do it," I said, but . . . The hair on my thigh skin stood up. It'd be easy. I could escape this drug mess. Warren'd come home with too much money for quick deposit in his banks, so he'd have lots of cash around until he eased it all into his accounts. But stealing from my own brother?

The alien flipped to the map of California, stared at it awhile, then tapped Berkeley. He looked across the table, talking to me in his language, low breathy sounds and trills.

I want to be a star people's biologist, I thought, but not one that cuts up people. I wanted to be able to talk to Alph, really talk, not just draw pictures and signs. I wanted both of us to be safe.

After I set the house alarms, we both spent all afternoon wrestling up sheets of roofing tin onto the hen house and nailing down a new roof. By four, we finished the job, both of us sweaty, fingers all tin cut and dust in our hair. Alpha mimed turning on faucets and washing and oo'ed a bit.

Then after we washed and ate dinner, him drinking down some thawed blood, Alpha wrote some more of his north-south-north squiggles and packed his writings away in double Mason jars. Then he found a claw hammer.

What was he doing? He began pulling up floorboards in his room. But when he saw the sub-flooring on top of the concrete slab, he must have realized there wasn't room to hide his jars there. He turned to me with his face wrinkles all hanging loose, questioning.

I helped him bury his double jars of strange script under an old corncrib floor. After we tamped the dirt back and laid a few stones down, Alpha marked the doorframe with alien scratches.

Then we went in, and he drew a little car, found the map, cut the little car out, and ran it along the map from Virginia to California.

I shook my head slowly, and he drew a picture of himself lying, stiff, eyes half opened, a fly on one eyeball.

Dead.

His nostrils bellowed in and out. I must have smelled like agreement. We both sat trembling on the floor.

Then, as he watched me intently with those dark eyes, I pantomimed sleep and waking five times. Say five days to get to California, I really wasn't sure.

But what could I do in California after the alien went back to his own people? I shook my head at him. "What about me?" I asked him out loud.

He picked up the drawing of him dead and held it in front of his face, just under the eyes.

Slowly, I tore the drawing up and threw the scraps away, then touched him.

He reared back, hissing, singsonged furiously at me, his pupils tiny, head hair erect. Scared, I jumped back. Then he reached slowly for my face. When I ducked, he beat his twisted-toe heels on the floor and chewed at his hands as though he was gnawing splinters out of the base of his thumbs. When he reached for me again, I let him touch my eyebrows, and I smoothed down the hair over his bone goggles.

He got up and turned on the TV. He watched all evening until some midnight space flick came on. When the humans started running, Alpha screamed, his chest heaving.

I turned the set off and let him go to bed with his cats without bothering to lock him in. *Why did Hendricks have to shoot him when he tried to get away from Warren?*

Warren came back from a drug run and stared at the alien, who'd come out bare-chested onto the porch. "You don't lock him up?"

"He knows other humans would be scared of him. So he stays with us."

"Well, with you dropped out of school and him, I've got help enough," Warren said. "They want me to make about ten thousand pills a week, plus tab another ten thousand Quaaludes. But I also heard some Atlanta investors threw one drug-tabbing operation to the Feds."

The alien shivered a bit in the cold, early November. I wondered about leaving Warren with this mess, traveling cross-country in dead winter. We'd have to cut out holes for the webs in the alien's clothes. He needed warm clothes. And food—what if someone caught us?

I got Warren's other bag from the back of the camper.

"The Atlanta people know I've got a brother, but they sure didn't mention the spare help." He laughed as though having an alien helping was one thing he had over on those Atlanta investors. I got scared for Warren, too.

Alpha, after a quick look at me, gestured to Warren, wanted him to see all the work we'd done on the chicken house. The moonlight glinted off the new tin roof, off the methane tanks, and the compressor squatting low and dirty between the tanks and the chicken house wall.

"Hell of a lot of work," Warren said tiredly. I thought he was more referring to what he had ahead of him than the shed we'd roofed. "Damn eggs, damn pills, both a bitch to market."

The next morning, two guys drove up in a big Ryder truck with mud-smeared plates and unloaded another pill-making machine.

Huge, anonymous guys, one black, one white, feed brand caps low on the foreheads and enough dirt on their faces to mask them. Their voices seemed to shift accent with each separate short sentence that they spoke.

"See," Warren said to me, "they're helping out." His hand shaking, he signed a receipt for the machine.

"Don't sign anything, Warren." I saw the curtains at the alien's window flutter a bit, as though he'd been watching. Warren handed them the receipt and looked at me as though he was stoned, doomed, or both.

The guys from Atlanta took the receipt and drove away. Next day, we unbuilt the machine and re-built it in the bunker.

Alpha stopped the machines just as Warren started them, the powder mill and both pilling machines. The alien, one hand cupped over the powder mill switch, lips pulled back so the little teeth glittered, pointed from me to the respirator, and back.

Warren sighed, went upstairs, and came back with a gas mask for me, which was hot and clammy, but it worked.

I'd never before seen Warren take bossing from man or beast, but now he had a whole mess of bosses.

At Thanksgiving, Warren went over to Galax to spend the holidays with a woman he knew. As soon as he was gone, the alien started drawing again, me with a human woman, among aliens. I wasn't sure if they shook hands in space the way he was drawing them, or if he was using the Earth gestures to make me think I'd be at home in space.

I stopped his hand, and drew Warren getting shot by a black guy and a white guy.

We sat there a long time, at the kitchen table, with cats

mewing at our feet. He hummed low in his throat, first drew a black man and a white man shooting us all, then three skeletons, two not quite the same as the third, as though he guessed what our human bones were like under the different flesh.

Yes, we could all get killed. I heard the road alarm finally go off, the clock buzz of it, and burned the drawings in the sink. Horrible drawings.

The alien went *"blam"* with his lips, so real I jumped as though a shotgun had gone off, expecting to hear pellets rattling against the walls until I realized he'd spoken it.

Then he stepped up behind me and rubbed the backs of his hands against my shoulder. I knocked his hands away and said, "Don't tempt me." He pushed his knuckles, hand curled slightly, against my chin, then walked away fast, as though very frustrated.

The alarm stopped just as I got out the shotgun—Warren must have missed disconnecting the override, but he'd gotten back to it.

The alien and I fixed the turkey, then Warren came out of his room, red-faced. His Galax woman wanted him to quit the drug business, now. "She doesn't approve," he said. "And she sure the hell doesn't understand what they'd do to me."

All of us were bone-jerking tense. The alien began pacing, rocking his torso over his short bowed legs, spreading his arm webs, then pulling his arms around his body, the membranes stretched tight around himself. He spread his arms again, as if he turned hot and cold, or didn't know which he was, cold or hot.

Warren, his eyes on the turkey that he was slicing to bits, jerked his chin at Alpha, who stepped away from the table, hands hooked behind his neck, the long arms fitted up against his sides. "Gonna be weird," Warren said, "when the Atlanta people get tired of me, and the law finds your alien here." He started to laugh, then turned an angry red.

"If you hadn't expanded your damned operation on Alpha's labor . . ."

"Shut up, Tom," Warren said. "It was way the hell over before that. And the guy in California dumped that damn locator in the ocean. *He's* none too happy. He shot a man with thyroid eyes snooping around where he kept the egg. And he didn't get it killed. Other people took it away. Aliens after us." Warren grabbed a turkey leg, bit into it, and choked, coughing the meat out into his hand. I guessed he hadn't stayed long enough to eat in Galax.

After dinner, the alien watched Warren drive off, then turned to me and went "*blam*" again, just like a shotgun. Then he curled up on the sofa and beat at the armrests with his fists, hissing and singsonging, eyes quivering.

"Warren," I said at breakfast soon after that, as nonchalantly as I could, "why don't we get the Fairlane tuned up, the battery's getting old. Get it in shape in case I have to come after you in Atlanta, or something."

He looked up at me, his eyes red-veined, fork with egg on it in front of his unshaved chin. Quaaludes and speed—crank it up, crank it down. Quaalude-slow this morning, he stared at me blankly a long while. Finally, he said, "Sure."

At the sink, the alien turned back to look at us. He came back to the table, glass of blood and oil in one hand, plate of our eggs in the other, and oo'ed slightly.

"You're using, Warren," I said. He'd always dabbled, but he wasn't stable enough to do a whole lot of speed. And here I was, going to abandon him to the drug investors. I felt guilty, but God, I had to get out. Save Alpha. But seeing Warren using hurt—he was my brother.

"Have a lot of work to finish," Warren said. "Alien here doesn't seem to mind the push, and I don't force the load on you."

All I ran was one pilling machine, and I felt doubly guilty, to be making drugs, to leave so much work to them. Triply guilty, to be plotting to leave.

"Sorry," I said.

"I'll get you a new battery, tune that old Ford up. Must be boring all the time with some weird creature who can't even say *boo*."

Alpha had made himself a flat straw out of a Coke bottle he melted and fussed with over the gas stove and now he had it stuck deep in his throat, pumping up the blood and oil mix, breathing in and out all the while.

Hadn't noticed he could breathe when he drank, before.

Alien, very alien. Could he and I escape and leave Warren, who'd lose everything, maybe even sanity or life, to anonymous guys with dirt-masked faces?

Or should I turn the alien over to the government? Sure, turn Alph over to the Air Force—him prisoner for life and the Atlanta investors still after Warren and me. The alien had already drawn up the best plan: kidnap some girl and leave the planet with the friendly aliens, if he hadn't been lying with that old yellow #2 pencil.

Flat lot of good #2 pencils had done me all my time on Earth. Me high-percentiling the achievement tests only made teachers think I was thief-stock cool.

"Thanks," I said to Warren, who didn't seem to have noticed that my pause had been rather long.

While Warren went out for groceries and a new car battery, Alpha and I worked in our respirators, both weird-looking beyond the ordinary with the breather snouts and shadowed faces under the harsh light of the bunker, working between earth walls shored up with chicken wire and two-by-fours.

On a machine like in a factory—nothing romantic about drug-making. Damned machines whumped down the pill powder while I cleared the stupid little pistons and adjusted the powder flow. Stomp that pedal, old obsolete cranky machine.

The alarm went off, then stopped. Warren.

The alien watched from the porch as Warren drove up and parked. Smoke came off the engine block, so Warren said, "Think I'll drive it about, see if it needs more work, or if the oil's just got to burn off."

Alpha, up on the porch, fidgeted, almost dancing. Suddenly, I thought of how stupid, really, the escape plan was— where exactly were we going? I hopped up on the porch and caught him by a web, rudely, then shifted my hand to his elbow and led him inside.

Alpha embraced me, so excited, and brought out the atlas again.

How, I wondered, was I ever to understand them in space? I drew me speaking, using a little balloon for the words like a cartoon. Then the alien, with a balloon full of song notes. Then his question sign.

He drew me and a balloon with an exact copy of the word

"Executive" in it, copied from the top of the legal pad. Then he drew a box, "Executive" going in and scribbles in his own writing coming out. *Translation machines?*

I heard the Ford coming back and cleared up all the peculiar drawings before Warren could see them. All the rest of the afternoon, the alien chirped and koo'ed, acting pert when Warren tried to make him load the ball mill faster.

"Damn, Warren," I said, "I'd rather take getting shot than doing this forever."

"Hush, Tom. Your little buddy's quick on tones. Don't you encourage his fussing. Thought I'd broke him good."

"Damn machine's gonna jam."

Yelling, muffled voices in a haze of speed dust, Quaalude powder. Worse than factory work, buried underground working. Warren reached into a bag and took another pill, swallowed it down with a beer, and began staring down the basement tunnel as if he'd heard something. *God, his hair's turning grey—I hadn't noticed that before.*

Then he looked at the alien and they both jerked their heads down, not *nodding*, not at all friendly.

The alien wanted to leave *now* and kept shoving little drawings of the Fairlane at me when Warren wasn't looking. He must have stayed up late, drawing little cars on paper scraps, filling his pants and shirt pockets with them.

He wore shirts in the cold, slit from elbow down to the waist for the webs, which he kept close to his body except when he reached out to hand me one of those little drawings. Then the web would dangle out, raw and cold looking.

Carefully, when Warren was out, I checked for inside alarms and searched for Warren's money. He'd hid it inside his stereo. I only found it because the screwheads looked a bit too used and the stereo hadn't worked in years. Who'd have thought someone would mess up a thousand-dollar stereo and tape deck for a stash, but the stash was around $20,000. I took $5,000, trying to persuade myself it was my money, too. And it was, really.

While I found the money, the alien, eyes glittering, watched *Dr. Who* and sang to himself, spreading his arms periodically, blood pulsing into the web veins. Warren came back about fifteen minutes after I'd taken his money and said he was going to deliver pills to his Atlanta connection tonight.

As we got set up to pack the pills, Warren gave us both plastic surgical gloves, which didn't fit Alpha well. He managed to cover his fingers, though, and we all scooped pills into double plastic bags, then dropped each bag into a barrel half full of chicken shit. Warren showed the alien how to top off the barrel, and then we soldered the barrels shut.

Two barrels of pills. Warren got the camper-back off the pickup and laid down planks so we could roll the barrels into the truck bed. Didn't look like much, just a couple of chicken-shit drums for some organic farmers.

We watched Warren drive off, me thinking about the guys who killed over the drug business, Alpha dancing around, glad to see him go. The alien and I re-set the road alarms after Warren passed the electric eye, then started packing.

Alpha got the shotgun and shells from Warren's room. We had a TV show on, playing loud to keep me a bit distracted from what I was doing. The alien came up to the screen, watched the humans a bit, then raised the gun, grinning his alien grin. *Blam!*

After I realized he hadn't actually blown the set away, I took the gun and shells away from him. He danced around me, flipping his elbows out, whacking me with them.

Warren had fixed the Fairlane so you could flip the back seat down and get to the trunk. Once we'd gotten the back seat out, the alien could ride up front most of the time, but could hide in the trunk if he had to, or when we stopped for gas and groceries. I thought we'd be better off to drive at night, sleep off the road during the day.

So. I sat in the car, an alien beside me, night coming on, the ignition key pushed in the slot, cartons of eggs and suitcases in back. Both the alien and I trembled. He opened the atlas and pointed to Berkeley. Maybe, I thought, some scientist could figure out how to understand him.

My hand, as though it'd grown an alien-sympathizing brain, turned the ignition key before I really wanted to. Then, remembering the teachers back at high school, I dropped one foot down on the accelerator, the other on the clutch, and shifted—*Bye, Virginia, we're history.*

= 2 =

Steel Things, Steel Places

We'd escape to the alien buildings in Alpha's drawings, abandoning pilling machines jammed on nasty drugs and photos of men with crushed legs in envelopes postmarked Atlanta.

The alien reached over the seat for the shotgun and shells. Softly making fired gun sounds, he stuck his long index finger through the trigger guard.

Damn! I stopped and pulled the gun out of his hands. The alien watched very intently as I broke open the breech, saw it was empty, and closed it. He reached to take it back, but I shoved the gun as far as I could through the trunk hole.

As I re-set Warren's road alarm, the alien drummed his fists on the dashboard, then got a shotgun shell, holding the shell delicately in his long fingers, the sparse fur on his knuckles picking up highlights from the inside lights.

The sooner we got off county roads and onto the I-81 going west, the safer I'd feel. Warren—I knew it was irrational— could have spies watching on Rte. 8.

The alien began to sing to himself.

About a half mile farther, I saw a black mass pull out of an abandoned house's driveway onto the road.

My headlights hit it.

Warren's truck!

I wondered if I could jam it on and get around him, but fence posts, high banks crowded me.

"No. No. No."

My God, Warren's in the truck, I thought for a second

before I realized it was the alien, imitating Warren. The alien shook his head vigorously. He'd learned *no* from Warren.

I said, "Sorry," and stopped the Fairlane.

"No." The trembling alien spoke exactly like he'd said the other *no*'s, precisely the same tone. He began climbing over the seat, to hide in the trunk as I'd drawn that he should do when we were around strangers.

Now the beating. I turned and drove back home, parked close to the house, and started crying on the steering wheel.

Warren's pickup almost rammed the Fairlane. He came out of the cab white-faced, jabbering. "If you'd waited another hour, I would have gone on, but you were so obvious, so damn fucking anxious."

Slowly I got out of the Fairlane. "Where's the alien?" Warren asked. "Where's the monster? You shit, Tom, my only brother, sneaking out with an alien monster, blood drinker." Warren yanked the keys out of the ignition and bent them against a stone. When he reached into the car again, Warren's voice faded. "Sweet Jesus."

I moved toward the car. Warren said almost calmly, "Stop, Tom, it's got a shotgun trained on me."

"Not loaded," I said. Then I remembered the shell the alien fingered, how he'd watched me open the breech. "Wait! Could be . . ."

As Warren backed away, the alien crawled out over the seat, with the gun crooked in his elbow, muttering soft *blam*s. The creature was crying. He said again, in Warren's voice, "No," and raised the gun up, finger not quite on the trigger, head and shoulder hairs standing up.

Seemingly forever, both stood in the truck headlights. Then Warren, reaching for his boot pistol, rolled into the darkness. The dark flashed, the little crack of the .22, not the big .357 magnum.

The alien screamed and dropped the shotgun. He braced himself against the car and began talking hoarsely in his own language.

"Warren, are you all right?" I asked.

"Yeah, I got him."

"No," the alien said. "No." He reached down and spread a hand over the wound, then began trying to walk to Warren.

I caught him, and he pushed my hands against the wound, like wet hot meat, and collapsed.

"Bring him in the house," Warren said. He held the door as I staggered in, the alien weighing almost as much as me. "Put him on the kitchen table, strip him." Warren left me while I did that, the alien softly crying, hands fluttering, touching my eyebrows. Warren came back with a first-aid kit and a syringe.

As Warren heated morphine and water in a little copper pot Mom'd used for melting butter, the alien drew in the air with his hands, then grabbed me, and looked around until he saw the pad. I got it for him, and he drew me with the aliens and looked at me.

Exhausted and crying, I nodded. He wrote more on the drawing, then drew me giving the drawing to other aliens who looked like him. Then he quivered, the blood oozing from his chest.

Warren drew up a needleful of morphine and palpated the veins in Alpha's inner elbow. Alpha tried to touch Warren's face. "He's got veins, almost like us," Warren said, slipping the needle in, drawing blood into the syringe.

Before Warren could inject the painkiller, Alpha sighed and went utterly limp. His heart didn't beat again, even after five minutes, ten.

The eyes clouded up, the fingers stiffened. "He's dead," I told Warren.

"They're hunting us," Warren said. "Aliens'll find us and kill us. I didn't want him dead. Honest. Tom, I'll hide him good, but if the other aliens come, I'll preserve him for autopsy. Maybe they can regrow him. Why did he die like that when I was trying to help him?"

Warren was too spaced out to deliver the pills, but they had to be delivered, or it wouldn't be just aliens all over us. I drove down to Wytheville and found the black guy and an Oriental waiting by a Ryder truck.

"You late," the Oriental said as we rolled the drums from one truck to the other.

"Had problems at home," I said.

"You brother's using," the black said. "Not good."

I shrugged and got back in the cab. "Where's the money?" I asked.

They threw an attaché case at me. I looked in it. They had probably shorted me, but what the fuck could *I* do about it. The Oriental guy smiled as they started the truck up.

When I came back, the alien's body was gone, and Warren was huddled by the fire muttering, "Can't trust nobody no more." Speed-talking, I thought at first. But he stayed incredibly jumpy after the alien died, as though someone—drug people, aliens—would get revenge on him. "But the body will prove me innocent," he said, " 'cause I didn't shoot to kill," looking up from the fire with eyes that seemed trapped between smiling and screaming. "He'd have lived if he'd been human, hurt like that."

The work we did for the Atlanta investors piled up, what with Alpha gone, hard for me to make the egg route and help Warren under the hill.

Then one day I came home to all the county cops, some Feds, the IRS boys, and eight photographers snapping cameras at everything.

"Shit, shit, shit," I said, beating my fists on the steering wheel. One of the local deputies, a former high school baseball pitcher, cuffed me and led me aside.

"Who did us?" I asked. A gun went off, muffled sound, inside the house. A guy in regular clothes came running out, screaming about tear gas.

"Aw, Tom, the Feds found them an informer in Atlanta. Your brother'd signed a receipt for a pill-making machine."

Crazy Warren. I never knew whether speed warped his brain or whether he'd brooded himself crazy over possible vengeful aliens. Whatever, he was under the house waging his last war.

"Tom," the deputy who'd cuffed me said, "I can take you into town now."

"Want to see what happens to Warren."

They finally got him out, both him and deputies all bloody, two deputies shot some in legs and arms, but the law'd worn body armor when they went after him.

"He probably won't die, Tom," a medic deputy said.

*   *   *

So I went to jail, in handcuffs and leg irons like a real badass, while Warren rode a helicopter to the hospital in Roanoke, screaming about aliens from his stretcher.

Cold steel bars with painted cement floors—light bulbs protected by wire grids. The deputy said, "If you'd give us all the egg money and the milk, my wife might be able to take care of your hens and cow."

"Is Warren alive?" I asked as he turned the key in the cuffs and shook them off.

"Yes, but he's out of it. Crazy."

The cell toilet was open, with a sink by it. "Yeah, let your wife take care of the hens and the cow. Cats, too." Hoss, the town drunk, grinned up from a bunk as he fiddled with his cock under his greasy overalls.

Every morning, they made us mop with Lysol, then fed us plates from the diner, cold by the time someone walked them across the road.

Jail breeds bad daydreams—when I wasn't ducking drunks or hearing various deputies and prisoners brag about where their cocks had been, I sat in space fantasies, hours and hours of Alpha's drawing imagined almost real.

While Amos, a big black, wrestled a deputy over the Valium vial, I dream-walked around those alien buildings, with Alpha. If only we'd waited a bit longer that night.

The judge asked, "Tom, why'd *you* get involved in this? We could have arranged foster care, even if you hadn't said what Warren did."

I shrugged in my cuffs and said, "Warren needed me."

They took into consideration my age and the influence my brother had over me. So I spent time in Camp 28, in a sheet-metal dorm full of men at night, walking the roads picking up trash during the day.

Jail and prison were both hideous, dumb and stinking. Steel bars, steel mesh got into my soul. *So this is what I am, a felon, with about 90 percent chance of returning.* Just before I was supposed to enroll in a prison carpentry class, I got put out on probation.

I was lucky; Floyd County didn't hang charges over me to keep me away from my own farm. But when I wanted to go back to school, the high school told me to study at night with guys out of jail like me and real dumbass dropouts.

The teacher laid it out slow and easy, as though he dealt with bobcats.

I turned eighteen under court supervision, and wondered if I'd ever get used to being a criminal. At night, I'd dream about the alien, mostly as a friend, sometimes haunting me, his skinny body surrounded by cats.

I heard a knock on the porch door one afternoon and saw a stranger there, man with big eyes, in a tee-shirt and baggy jeans. Not a black man, I thought uneasily. Maybe Indian, with that coarse shaggy hair.

"Can I look around your woods for mushrooms?" he asked in an accented voice I couldn't place. "My name is John Amber."

Undercover law. A spate of them checked on me over the past two years. *What's the use of keeping him off?* "Sure, you won't find anything."

Then I noticed the old cats, who'd stayed on after Alpha died, checking this stranger out, so I followed him into the woods, quietly.

He stood staring up the hill, a lump under his chin vibrating. I couldn't hear anything; the cats ran up to him. When he saw me, his knees flexed slightly and shoulders got rigid. *Alien, just like Warren feared.* Maybe made over into human form—the face seemed stiff. I dropped my hand to my boot knife and said, "I guess you came about your friends."

The man-thing turned, and asked, "Where are they?"

I'd thought when I first saw him that he must have eye trouble—big eyes, like Bette Davis has. Like the human-looking thing the guy who had the egg had shot . . . "Two died in the crash. My brother . . . I tried to get the little one away." I had a memory flash of Alpha handing Warren the knife.

The alien with the man's face said, "Are they all dead?" Not completely like a man's body. The flat chest . . . that's why I thought it was a man.

I nodded.

Its shoulders rocked back and forth, breaths heaving in and out. "Even Mica? He was alive after the crash."

"Mica? His name was Mica?" Slowly, I eased my hand back toward the boot knife, while the cats did cat-figuring and slunk off. The alien cried, murmuring in that strange tongue that Mica (Mica, strange to know his name now) couldn't teach me. I felt guilty. And terrified. "Are you the one who was shot in California?"

"My true son is dead, then?" The alien looked at me, and I froze my arm where it was, halfway down my leg. "What happened," it asked, "to the others? They also were my kin. And you shoot, keep us from the location device, play cruel movies. If you touch what you're reaching for . . ."

I said, "The ones killed in the crash we've got bones of. How come you look human? How can you speak English when he never could?"

"Surgery made us look like you," the alien said. "I asked to be made the dominant sex. I couldn't stand being considered one of your females."

Us. The alien crouched, muscles tense, eyes level with mine. Something cracked a twig behind me. The alien looked over my shoulder, then back to me with a twitch of the lips.

Two others, like a black girl and a blond man, both moving wrong for humans, stiff-faced, came up brandishing chrome things I suspected were guns. The black woman—looking one, about five foot two inches tall, with impossibly high tits, like a demon sex cartoon, slid the knife out of my boot. "Vicious xenophobes, Cadmium," she said to the blond guy, who was a bit shorter than me. "They stay still if you put the point here," she added, putting the knife point under my chin.

I thought, *I'm dead.*

"Don't do that, Rhyodolite," the blond said. The black-girl one oo'ed slightly, obscenely, and lowered the knife.

They took me back prisoner to my own house. "What about Mica's body?" the John Amber one asked me, eyes quivering, oily tears rolling down the human-styled face. They all had big, big brown eyes with lopsided whites.

"Warren preserved him. He hid the body, so you can do an autopsy and know that we were trying to help. He pulled a shotgun on Warren. My brother shot in self-defense. He tried to treat the wound. Mica could have lived."

I opened the door and went inside between the John Amber one and Rhyodolite, the fake black girl. The blond one and Rhyodolite sat me down on the living room couch while John Amber called a number on my phone and asked for Room 18, then said in English, "You can join us now."

Aliens looking like people terrified me, since they had to be trickier than the first one seemed to be. "You found the egg, then?" I asked. "I didn't tell Warren to send it away from here."

"We found it," the little black female-shaped Rhyodolite said, "after one of your kind shot Black Amber. It told us everything."

"Black Amber? Not John, then. I heard one of you was shot when you tried to find the egg. I'm so sorry."

Black Amber sighed. Her hand moved over her stomach. "So vicious," she said through her human fake mouth. She'd shaved her face, but the stubble growing back was inhuman, thin face hairs like Alpha/Mica's.

"Can I use the bathroom?" I asked.

"I'll take you," Rhyodolite said, following me to the john, holding that gun-like instrument dead steady. When I finished, the alien pulled out a cock.

"God," I said, "do your women have those?"

"I'm small. Female human fit better," he said as he pissed thick stuff like Mica'd done. "Being among hostile aliens pisses me off, too."

We all sat around the living room—them waiting for the others to arrive, me numb. Rhyodolite, his face rigid, held his chrome space gun out, a flat bell facing me. His arm lay flat on the coffee table and his head drooped, as though he was exhausted. The arm and fingers had been considerably shortened.

"The egg lead you back here?" I asked.

"The people who tried to keep us from it caused unnecessary delays," Amber said. She leaned up against the blond one and closed her oil-smeared eyes.

Finally, we heard a car drive up. "Cadmium," the Amber one said to the blond, "make sure it's the Barcons." The blond one went out and came back with two others, a different kind, who looked like stout Negroes with straight hair, if you didn't look too closely. Both were taller than me, one about six foot four and the other just a shade shorter. When I looked closely, I realized how different their jaws were, how thin their lower faces were for such a spread of nose. And no dent between the nose and lip.

"Is that what you really look like?" I asked.

"Yes," one said after they looked at each other, "except for seasonal hair. And this." It spread out a hand—six fingers.

The five aliens talked to each other in what seemed to be two different languages.

"What are you going to do to me?"

"We Gwyngs don't kill sapients, but the Barcons can," Black Amber said.

"Mica drew a shotgun on Warren."

She didn't answer for a while, then said, "Gwyngs don't kill," as if I'd lied to be cruel.

That night, Black Amber and the other two Gwyngs heaped together on the bed where Alpha/Mica had slept. Squirming around, crying, they left oily patches on the sheets and pillowcases. I tried to bump elbows, but Black Amber stiffened, and bobbed her head with that attack nod—like I'd seen Mica/Alpha bob his head at Warren. I backed to the door and asked, "He and I couldn't figure out at all how to talk to each other?" Somehow, that she could talk English seemed a mockery—if only I could have talked, really talked to Mica.

"It's a fake tongue manipulated by two skull computers." She poked it out—like a human's tongue, not flat and broad—then pulled it in and kept looking at me out of that almost human face, but her eyes were so alien.

In the living room, the rawboned black Barcons watched television while I sat in a chair, unable to sleep. A space horror film came on about midnight. *Alpha . . . Mica hated to see those*, I thought as I got up to turn it off, but a Barcon took my hand off the dial. My skin crawled to have six fingers touch it.

"I wasn't afraid of just one alien," I said defensively.

The smaller one said, "Our Federation used to get very upset with xenophobes, but we're gentler now."

The other Barcon stretched and said, "Well, he's not irrationally xenophobic. The Gwyngs do want to bruise him."

"What kinds of aliens are you?" I asked.

"Barcons," the biggest black said, "and Mica and these

are Gwyngs. The closest thing you have to us is bears. The Gwyngs evolved from marsupial bats, let another animal carry their young in its pouch.''

As we watched the show, I told them about *The Day the Earth Stood Still*, so they'd understand we didn't always make aliens out to be the bad guys. ''The alien was a saint from space.''

The two Barcons made rough coughing sounds. The big one turned to me and said, ''Holy from space? Xeno flip-flops.'' They wiggled their noses at me and each other and talked their language again. I heard something made out of almost human sounds. It sounded like *Karst*.

''I'm awful tired,'' I said. And I was scared, so scared.

''We're more tired than you,'' the smaller one replied, ''and not a little frightened ourselves to be among xeno flip-flops. Very tiring to be among a species with extreme ideas about us.'' The one talking was just a little bit smaller than the other one, but with wider hips. Female?

Slowly, I got up and as slowly got a blanket out of the closet. The bigger Barcon yawned and followed me to the closet, looked up at the quilts stacked on the top shelf, and pulled two down. I started for my bedroom, but he said, ''Bring your sleeping things in here.'' Together, we dragged in the mattress and moved the coffee table so it would be in front of the couch.

''You will sleep tonight,'' the smaller one said, grabbing my arm and pressing a needled cube against it. I half about fainted onto the mattress. When I woke up, the taller Barcon was asleep in the other's arms, but the one awake nodded at me. *Space cops, have to be space cops.*

In the morning, we all got up, stretching muscles cramped from being slept on in unfamiliar ways, and went into the kitchen. The Gwyngs, already in there, sucked on lumps of butter. Black Amber took the teakettle off a burner and nodded tensely at me. I knew Gwyng nods were hostile.

The Barcons talked to her and all three Gwyngs pursed their lips and koo'ed that giant demented dove noise I knew was their laugh. I supposed that the big black Barcons had just told them about *The Day the Earth Stood Still*, because Rhyodolite lipped off, ''Bunch of xenophobic-philic twitch brains. Why should we save your nasty species from atomics?''

"Look, I quit school to help Mica," I said.

"You failed," Black Amber said.

I looked hard at the Gwyngs for traces of the alien I'd known. Black Amber was wider-hipped than most human men, but heavier in the shoulders than most women. Surgery, or her natural body shape? Rhyodolite was delicate. With longer arms and shorter legs, Cadmium could have been Mica's brother. Not Alpha, Mica.

Cadmium, Rhyodolite, and Black Amber—Gwyngs. They'd probably kill me soon.

Black Amber slumped in a chair with a teacup in her hands. She looked at me through almost human eyes as she drank whatever was in the teacup. *Tea.* I noticed they had brought alien tea bags.

"I know where the bones of two of your kind are," I told her.

"Have a Barcon go with you," she said. "I can't . . ." and her voice broke.

We went out to the barn where the Barcon immediately fitted the skull bones together. Then he looked closely at the finger bones, pulled out a plastic bag and put the bones in it, then sealed the top. "Evidence," he said. *Oh,* I thought.

The other aliens stepped out on the porch. The little black-girl one, Rhyodolite, pulled out a gun gun, a .357 magnum.

Black Amber took the bones out of the Barcon's hand. We all went inside where she put the plastic bag on the kitchen table, reached in, and pulled out bones, crying again.

"Are you . . . you going to kill me?" I asked.

"*We* don't kill sapients," Black Amber said, lips tight, tucked in as if their fullness embarrassed her. "I want my true child's body, the remains of the others, pieces of the ship. Despite what you did, we found the emergency recorder. So stupidly vicious." The fake mouth twitched. "No officials know?"

"No," I said. "Warren didn't want them around." I felt sick as the other Gwyngs took Black Amber in their arms.

Humans were the monsters . . . they were the monsters . . . My brain twitched . . . my breathing was ragged, like the alien's after Warren shot him. I stared at the aliens, half expecting their human-shaped flesh to run off their bones. But even the bones had been re-worked.

The Barcons put one skull on the kitchen table where it glared at me with its big eye sockets and thin V'ed chin. One Barcon examined the fingertip bones with a magnifying glass, then said, dropping the bones back in the plastic bag, "Definitely burned."

"We didn't mean them any harm," I said again. "Even Warren tried to help Mica in the end, but he died anyhow. Of shock. We didn't make the ship crash."

The Barcon touched the skull plate over the left ear hole and stared at it. I noticed that it looked plastic. "We hear the last sounds from this," the Barcon said. "Computer."

Rhyodolite, the black face strangely stiff although tears dripped off the chin, stroked the arched bone, thicker than in a human skull, on the outside of the eye hollow.

"We want to get Warren," the blond Gwyng, Cadmium, said.

"He's insane now, in a jail hospital," I said.

"How convenient," Cadmium replied.

I slowly stood up. "I'll give you Warren's map. He hid Mica's body in an old copper mine." Mica's three kin and the shorter Barcon went off with the map in their human car.

I sat with the other Barcon and finally asked, "Does this happen often, a ship crashing?"

"Not precisely a ship. Often enough the transformation geometries crash. Their field collapsed in transition. How did you manage with a Gwyng for so many months—so social?"

"I liked him being friendly."

"You, your small predators, dogs, cats, social squirming all day, all night. Yet xenophobic." The big alien, all dark on the couch, muttered more in its own language and I felt I was more a thing to be watched than a person.

"I miss him. We were going to go to California together, look for the locator egg."

The Barcon drew back, startled. "He . . . of course, he couldn't explain exactly. Do you think we watch you?"

In California, I realized, there was an alien safe house, like spies have.

Then he said, "The Gwyngs are almost lethally empathetic with each other."

"I liked him because he wanted me to come to space with him, but you're not friendly," I told the Barcon.

The alien just sat, not replying, in a house built with drug money, with another alien's skull on the kitchen table. Finally, I turned on the TV and exposed more human follies on the six o'clock news.

The aliens' car, the left door removed, came back with a big wooden crate wedged in the back seat. My guard and I went out on the porch to watch the others put the crate in the barn.

After the Gwyngs put the crate up, the Barcons rigged up a net of one-inch cables in a thirty-foot circle. Sighting to the horizon, tightening wires, testing voltages, hooking cables in and out of our house current, putting black and white boxes in and out of the electrical circuits, the aliens fooled around for a good three hours before the smaller Barcon spoke into a microphone.

Enough more time passed for them to hook in another box, test it, take it out, and put in a box that finally was satisfying.

Black Amber, wearing some of Warren's old clothes, came over to me. Taking my wrist gently in her fingers, she found my pulse, which gave away my heart's humping. "We always leave," she said, "accounts hidden from untrustworthy people. If he left accounts you know about, then he trusted you. Despite . . ."

That last word was bitten off. Despite what? "Yeah," I told her, "we hid his diaries and drawings really good. He did a drawing even as he lay dying. I was only a kid when he was here, still in regular school."

"Did you tell others?"

"No. Even the law didn't find the diaries when they busted us."

"You're under legal supervision here. Why?"

"I helped Warren with his business. Your kin, Mica, did, too."

She dropped my wrist and raised her hand to sniff the shirt sleeve.

The air over the cables turned blue, shimmering, and a small spaceship, more like a diving saucer than an aerodynamic plane, popped into the blueness and thumped down on the cables. All the lights flashed off and on as though lightning had struck a transformer somewhere. Then a ship light flooded the barn with a greenish yellow glare.

"Rector's man Tesseract," Black Amber said, sounding less than fully satisfied. "He's been studying your kind."

The creature who came out was nearly human—taller than the Barcons, a *big* alien with a crested skull, bald pink skin over the bone ridge, coarse hair either side of it, heavy jaws, like an ape-man, but he wore a tunic and pants. As he climbed down from the machine, he looked at me and smiled, lips tightened back, not pursed. If he'd had a skull like a human's, I could have thought he was a giant Mexican. The lips parted to show big teeth. At least he and the Gwyngs both had five-fingered hands.

"Tesseract. Former pilot, good in space math," explained one of the Barcons. "Represents the Academy and Rector in this investigation. He knows xenophobia very well."

The investigator.

Rhyodolite hugged his breasts and then looked down at them as if he wasn't used to having flesh hanging there. "And he and his wife," the little black Gwyng said, "regard the rest of the universe as the prime source of intelligent pets. Ahrams, that kind . . ."

Cadmium said something sharp to Rhyodolite, who shut up as Tesseract came closer. Over six and a half feet tall, and massive, Tesseract had a very disconcerting twinkle to his eyes. Whatever he was, he spoke the language the Barcons spoke. The Gwyngs jabbered in Mica's bell-tone language and I felt horribly outside it all.

"Well, let's get on with the investigation," Tesseract said in good English. "One is insane after shooting the sub-cadet Gwyng Mica. The other said the killing was an accident."

"Not altogether an accident," I said, "but Mica had a gun aimed at my brother."

Tesseract looked at Black Amber.

"Near-technological planets are most unpleasant," she said. The black human-looking Barcons went into the spaceship and came back out with a stretcher on wheels, not much different than an Earth-style ambulance stretcher.

"Can you bring him back to life?" I asked the larger Barcon as we stood in front of the crate.

"Perhaps if you froze him properly, before tissue damage." He touched the box. "No." They pried up the top boards with an alien crowbar.

Inside I saw the big heavy plastic bag that Warren'd heat-sealed, and inside the plastic, Mica . . . Alph, all dead and wrinkled up, paler than he'd been in life, veiled by the plastic and embalming fluid, naked.

The big Barcon slit the bag with a scalpel. Black Amber twisted away from the two Gwyngs who tried to hold her back and reached for Mica's body. She was too weak to lift it onto the stretcher herself, so I helped her.

As cold formaldehyde soaked my clothes, I felt the dead-meat feel of the corpse in my hands and shuddered. The Barcon pulled Black Amber's arms away, then wiped the body gently, speaking to it a little.

"He says Mica was smaller the last time he examined him," Tesseract said to me, pulling me back.

Black Amber passed her hands over the dead face, the bullet hole in the chest, then back to touch that broad mouth which curved thin-lipped around the short muzzle. Her fingers stroked the armpit webs and trailed out to the arms, twining her live fingers with his long, cold dead ones.

Cadmium and Rhyodolite, stiff in their fake human bodies and faces, worked her fingers loose and pulled her back from the body so that the Barcons could take it into the ship for the autopsy.

Tesseract took me back into the house. He was amazingly strong—I couldn't have run if I'd wanted to. I ached from fear as though all my muscles were strained.

"Calm down," he said, sitting me down in a chair and kneeling beside it. He rubbed the skin over his skull crest and said, "I guess that's rather hard to do."

"Black Amber asked about records," I said. "Al . . . Mica and I buried some in the corncrib."

Tesseract said something in alien to the Gwyngs. Black Amber glared at me and went back to Mica's room, but the others turned around and went back outside.

"And something else, if you'd let me go to my room," I said, thinking about the drawing Mica had given me just before he died. Tesseract raised himself off his knees and held my elbow as I took him into my room and found the drawings. The law'd ignored it, probably thought I'd drawn some space fantasy myself. The big alien took them in his hand and said, "Do you know what these mean?"

"One was the last thing he did."

"Would you want to go with us? Do you know what we'd do with you?"

My heart pounded. He put his hand on my chest and sighed. "Not so dire. He wanted you to be a cadet as you weren't as xenophobic as other humans. Little Mica precadet. Very interesting for a Gwyng."

I sighed, and he took his hand off my chest, patted me gently on the shoulder, then took the drawing and called the gun-happy Rhyodolite up to guard me. "I need a shower badly," I said.

Black Amber came out of the bathroom herself and spoke alien to Tesseract as she dried off her phony human body, not bothering to cover either the fake cock or the real fur-rimmed pouch slit, like a wide navel—an unreal shameless body to her. It made me a bit angry, until I saw the bullet scar below her ribs.

Tesseract answered her and she began bobbing like a turkey cock, furious. The singsong speech turned to hissings.

"You told her Mica wanted me to be a cadet," I said.

"Yes," Tesseract said. "Now go take your shower."

In the shower little Rhyodolite prodded me with the gun to turn me around, bend me over. "One of the ones who shits," he said as if having an anus was a defect.

"I'm sure you knew that before," I said. What if they'd seen pornographic movies from space, us unknowingly naked before aliens? Horrible to think about that.

When I came out, Black Amber stared at me with those big eyes as one of the Barcons took a plastic bag of Gwyng bones to the ship. She finally asked, "Why should Mica want *you* to take his place with us?"

"We tried to escape Warren together. I wasn't sure what he planned to do with me once we found the locator. But I guess he did have plans for me, after all." I remembered how I'd been afraid he was just using me and felt guilty.

"Your brother is a criminal," she said, a quiet voice with a buzz saw in it.

The two Gwyngs and the big skull-crest guy, Tesseract, gently led Black Amber back to the room Mica'd used. I let the Barcons put me back in my room and heard them tape the windows and slide wedge locks in under the door. I got into bed and stared at the ceiling, lights still on. *They'll make killing me look like an accident, or suicide.*

When I woke up, the smaller Barcon watched me from a chair. *Funny jaw*, I thought again, *too many bones in it.* And the bones around the eyes, the eyes themselves slanted, like a wolf's eyes, not like human Orientals. And the six fingers on each hand. I wondered how they could go around in public looking like that. But then humans didn't expect aliens to go run around in public.

From the sun on the floor, I knew it was well toward noon. I'd slept a long time, but I didn't feel drugged.

After I dressed, I went into the kitchen past the humanoided Gwyngs, who looked at me as though I really was an amazing horsefly.

Black Amber handed me a bowl of scrambled eggs and raisins. *Too much salt*, I thought absently, before I looked closer and realized *raisins and eggs!* Smiling probably a bit too grimly, I ate the eggs as if nothing was wrong with them.

"When do you have to be inspected by your legal people?" the larger Barcon asked.

"I've got to go to see him in three days."

The aliens gave me about half an hour to eat and get really awake, then Tesseract called us all to the living room. I smelt court when I saw how they'd set up the furniture, and almost balked at the door. Tesseract sat behind a table with alien machines on it, strange contraptions in battered aluminum-like boxes, as though they'd seen lots of travel.

So, then, the Barcons on the couch were the expert witnesses and the three Gwyngs on the other side of the room were prosecutor and jury. I worried about the defense.

Instead of asking us to rise, like I expected, Tesseract played his hands over a keyboard real fast. A machine spoke for him in English, introduced himself as an investigator for the Federation of Space-Traveling Systems.

Yeah, last time I'd just been up against the Commonwealth of Virginia. The machine spoke next in two other languages, the birdsong Gwyng one and what Tesseract and the Barcons used.

Tesseract said, through the machine, that he had been

authorized to deal with emergencies, deaths and wills of
Academy officers, cadets, and pre-cadets. The Gwyng called
Mica had been a pre-cadet assisting two others when their
ship failed, sub-catastrophically, and space-holed to a planet
with a sapient culture approaching space competence in some
sectors, but with xenophobic reactions, as earlier monitoring
teams had recorded.

Then the bigger of the two Barcons told us the skeletal
remains showed burn signs. From the skull computers and
Mica's own reports, the Barcons determined that these Gwyngs
were killed when the twist friction caused supplies and ship
metal to ignite.

I sat like an ice person while this went on. The Gwyngs
stared at me, eye assault.

The whole planet Earth, I thought, *is on probation*.

The big Barcon twitched his jaw in some funny way, as
though some of those bones were jointed different than the
jaws of all the rest of us. He hit one key on a machine, which
began printing and speaking the autopsy results:

Initial injuries appear to be well-healed cuts
and burns on the body. This correlates with both
accounts given by the planet species natives
and by Mica in his reports. A second series of
less well healed scars resulted from injuries
caused by small lead projectiles, one of which
was recovered from the left calf.

Subject showed fat loss consistent with a period of lowered metabolism and some mineral
deficiency. The subject was taller than he'd been
at his last physical examination, and showed
muscle development consistent with manual labor.

Subject had been shot in one lung, which
seemed to have precipitated a shock death within
less than one hour. The lead projectile wound
was not necessarily fatal. Subject appears to
have died due to possible misapprehensions about
an injection of a local painkiller, residue of which
was found at an injection site near the arm
joint.

The examiners feel that if subject had attempted

to fire a projectile weapon at the planet species
natives, he had little or no understanding that the
results could be lethal. However, since weapons
of this type can be lethal, the defensive reaction
on the part of the senior native was not unwar-
ranted. Both natives seemed to have tried to help
subject following the shooting incident.

Avoiding alien eyes, I stared at the printout as the machine
sprayed out other translations.

"Mica willed his position in the Academy to this human,"
Tesseract said. "If we don't take Tom off-Earth, we'll have
to destroy his memory or credibility. Tom, we won't kill you
or your brother."

Black Amber said, "Brain-wipe this one, and his crazy
brother, too."

Brain-wipe sounded extreme, a death inside the body. *Gonna
steal my body or my mind.*

"Rector Karriaagzh will decide," Tesseract said with a
grin. He added some alien words that Black Amber hissed
over.

Tesseract sent a message pod back on the cable net and we
waited. A wait in a house full of aliens.

When Monday came around and I was dressing, the male
Barcon handed me a stiff leather belt. As I put it on, I
felt two little wires prick through my clothes and skin. I
climbed into one of the aliens' rental cars with the Barcon,
who checked the car dash as thoroughly as if the Toyota
had been a spacecraft. He turned the ignition key delicately, head cocked. I directed him toward town and the
courthouse.

"What do I call you?" I asked.

"Barcon. We don't share names."

"That won't work well in the sheriff's office," I said.

"Sam Turner, then," he said stiffly.

As we walked in, the deputies stared at the black guy, and
he looked from them to me, slowly.

"Got you a new lawyer, Tommy baby," one deputy called
out, "or is the man investing?" I walked on with the alien to

the probation office. The probation officer, Mr. Jenkins, waited.

"Who's this?" Mr. Jenkins asked.

"Sam Turner," I said, using the big Barcon's alias. "He's thinking about buying some of my land."

"Well, he'll have to wait outside if he's not a lawyer. And your land's tied up now."

The Barcon put one hand to his waist. *We got you covered*, I knew he meant.

"Nah, he ain't mah lawyer." Pile on hick, I thought, let's just get Jenkins and all the aliens listening in behind the wires relaxed, and let me be unbuzzing, loose. Not nearly electrocuted by my own nervous tension. The Barcon left the door open a hair when he went out.

"Jobs?" Jenkins said.

"What's the use in trying to find jobs? I'm an ex-felon, no civil rights. You ought to come out and see the place." *Oh, please, care enough to come by.* "I manage on chickens. I'll give you a couple dozen eggs, free."

My belt shocked me and got hot over my spine.

"As long as you keep making the egg deliveries." *Oh, shit, but the damn aliens know now from other than me that I've got to get the eggs delivered.*

"Yes, sir. All I ever wanted to be was an honest farmer."

"But you're talking of selling land? I realize you got used to easier money, but it's up to you. Society has helped you all it can."

"Yes, sir," I said. "But . . ." I felt like my spine was on fire. I shut up.

"And if you leave the county without permission, it's jail if I see you again. We were very lenient to allow you back in the county after what you were involved in."

Sam the alien grabbed me with a wrist lock as soon as I opened the door to leave. When we got to the car, he asked me to explain myself.

"Human psychology," I said, feeling sick. "If you tell people to drop by, they won't." I wished I'd hinted I was being held hostage by drug people, get some human police out to the farm. But probably the wires in the belt would have given me a "heart attack" there in Jenkins' office.

His nose wiggled. After he started the car, he asked, "Might we not stop for canned mild alcohol solution for drinking? Beer?"

Son of a bitch thinks this is funny. "You drink beer? When you're on a mission?"

"Autopsies are hard work—cutting delicately, looking at tissues, chemicals. Horrible smells. Sawing skull open and finding shock." He paused, then said, "And so much contact all the time with Gwyngs and xenophobics."

When we stopped at the Hop-In, the big alien headed for the beer display and stared at it like an amazed man.

Back to the farm, Sam the Barcon went off with his female and the beer. They came back hours later, drunk, wiggling their noses like crazy, watching all the other aliens, all of us, as though we were odd-tempered exotic bugs.

Black Amber nodded tensely at them, but they just shook their nostrils at her. She glared over at me, huge eyes rolling by the small human-sized eye holes.

"No, ma'am," I said. "I'm sober as a stone."

"Tried to escape us," she said. "I hope you test out to be only marginally sapient. We'll rip out your memories then."

"It's just a test," the big Barcon said as he sat me down under that helmet. But I didn't trust him.

The smaller Barcon turned a knob after the helmet came down. Thousands of little wires pricked my scalp, and they strapped my head tight to keep the trembling from pulling the little wires loose.

A test? I watched their six-fingered hands working dials. "Close your eyes," the female said. When I closed my eyes, I saw a test pattern—a blue cross on a white field. Then the Barcon twirled a dial and told me to keep my eyes shut and describe what I saw as best I could. The test pattern started jumping around. I opened my eyes, and the Barcon pulled back a lever.

"Keep them closed."

"Are you going to take out my memory now?"

"I told you, no." The Barcon scratched her nose and looked annoyed, if that's what a tightness around the lips meant. So I kept my eyes closed, still expecting chunks of my life to rush out on their electricity.

The pattern rotated to the right, stretching and curling its bars and shifting colors. Then it rotated to the left, up, down. Finally, it wavered and the lines simply couldn't be described. When I saw gold starbursts and red flashes, the alien told me to open my eyes. She cranked the needles out of my scalp and unstrapped my head. I was surprised that I wasn't bleeding, but they'd been tiny little needles. Still nervous, I ran back over my memories of the last two years and found them almost more vivid—Mica/Alph dying on the kitchen table—than I would have wanted.

"High cadet average," the Barcon said slowly, index finger tracing lines on a computer's flat screen.

Black Amber looked at me and said, "How did you do it?"

I shook tension out of my wrists and forearms. "I score real high on human tests. No test anxiety, teachers claimed. But I guess I'm just a bright guy because I sure was damn tense this time."

The Barcon's nose wiggled as she handed me a towel to mop off the sweat.

"Whatever the test, I don't want you on Karst," Black Amber said. Her human body, especially her head, looked distorted, as though the flesh were trying to heal back to Gwyng form again. "You'll remind me that Mica died horribly, in great fear."

When Tesseract came in, they all talked alien awhile and the Barcons led Black Amber off. "Come see the transport," Tesseract told me.

I hadn't been in an alien ship since Warren and I stripped Mica's wreck. The aliens had padded the floor and walls with rubbery stuff and set chairs contoured for various species near black glass display panels. Tesseract motioned for me to go through a door.

A small compartment—the autopsy room, just a little bigger than the table. Mica's corpse lay so cut up I could barely recognize him. I shuddered, pitying him, scared for myself.

"Would you pledge on his body that you meant him no harm?" Tesseract said, a small box, probably a recorder, whirring between his hands.

"Yes, and . . ." I was about to say, *I'm not lying to get*

the space academy gig either, but did I have a choice in that? Or did I even want that, with Black Amber hostile to me?

Tesseract bent his head forward a bit and waited. I didn't know what to swear by—the head was opened, the body cavity. The shoulder, I decided. So I laid my hand on his cold wet shoulder, the stench of formaldehyde almost crippling my lungs, and mumbled, "I never meant to hurt him, or let Warren hurt him. I would have saved him if I'd only known how."

Tesseract said, "We will teach you." The box stopped whirring. Me wondering and afraid, we stared at each other across species and star distances.

Tesseract left the next day in his little ship. The Barcons left and came back. "We told Mr. Jenkins we were social workers and psychologists," the female said, "called in by relatives who thought you were going into the same craziness that got Warren."

Black Amber koo'ed like a giant demented dove. Bat bitch was as sensitive to emotional undercurrents as Mica'd been.

I still made my egg contracts, driving to Christiansburg with one of the Barcons first; then the Gwyngs went with me, always with the belt on, an alien on the trigger box.

"Tom, we need to stop and get beer for the Barcons," Rhyodolite said during the second trip. "They complain about being stuck with us."

We stopped at a store where I could cash a check, and I got out with a black Gwyng and a blond Gwyng, both dressed in jeans and hippie shirts, alien enough for Christiansburg if they *had* been what they looked like.

One of the locals asked, "Black girls better, Tom?"

The woman-faced Rhyodolite placed a smile on the false lips and said, "No, I'm with this blond man."

Another old boy, in dirty overalls, red clay clotted on his steel-tipped shoes, looked around the store carefully and asked me, "Law off your tail yet? Know a man needs a good helper."

The Gwyngs, six-packs in their arms, looked at us.

"No, I don't make 'ludes no more," I said loudly.

The girl-faced Rhyodolite started to pay for the beer, but the clerk asked for I.D. Cadmium leaned over with adequate plastic. As we started for the door, the old guy in the steel-tipped shoes said, "No offense meant."

I nodded curtly, almost like a Gwyng.

"What was that about?" Cadmium asked.

"Illegal business everyone expects me to get back into. I hated it, hated what it did to my brother."

"Poor little xenophobe," Rhyodolite said.

"I'm not a xenophobe."

"Prove it," Rhyodolite replied. "Play with us."

We didn't go straight to the farm, but drove up to Roanoke where the Gwyngs bought a carton of science fiction books and a dish antenna and electronic gear.

Under human fluorescent lights, I noticed where they'd been cut to make them look human, almost saw the forms they should have had.

Alone for a while in the Sears store, I stood unwatched behind some stoves. Rhyodolite flipped from channel to channel in the television department while Cadmium was outside loading socket wrenches and a soldering iron on the truck. *Now*, I thought. *Now what*, some crazy part of me responded. *Save my species? No, they could have exterminated us earlier if they wanted to. I'll save myself.* I was just an ex-felon on Earth. Other humans were xenophobic nuts, and I wasn't like them. I'd take the space gig.

Cadmium, who'd come back inside, touched my arm. "I'm coming," I said.

The young Gwyngs rigged up the TV something awful. Reception came from all over, like cable. At night, bored and tense, we watched re-runs of *M*A*S*H*, *Buck Rogers*, and anything else if they couldn't find a war movie or space flick to make humans look bad.

Finally, a few nights later, we got bursts of patterned interference on several different TV channels and the Barcons went out to re-spread the landing grid.

Signals from the ship took hours to reach us, blurring the TV programs in flashing patterns only Gwyngs could read.

"Now," Black Amber said after two days. The Barcons trudged out to the barn while the Gwyngs continued watching

TV. The ship's transformation into our space flickered the house lights.

We froze. Finally, we heard the Barcons and Tesseract talking as they came up the porch steps. One of them knocked on the door and I got up to open it. "More polite this way?" Tesseract said. "May we come in?"

"Yeah," I said. "These people have been driving me nuts."

"And we haven't been made comfortable either," Rhyodolite said. "They have legends of dangerous bats."

For the last three egg trips, the Gwyngs had collected heaps of stuff that showed how we imagined aliens. The living room looked like fifteen-year-old science nuts had invaded: boxes of sloppy soldered wires and chips hooked to the TV, science fiction and flying-saucer books flopped all over the carpet, beer cans and E.T. and Wookies models on the tables. The Gwyngs looked from Tesseract to the stuff as if they hadn't collected it themselves and oo'ed.

"Still," Tesseract said, stepping over one of the boxes, "the Rector wonders if we should contact this planet as an experiment. They'd love our technologies."

"Mica wanted me to take his place at the Academy. If you contacted us officially . . ."

The other aliens looked at me as if I'd been a rude child. Black Amber nodded and began to clench her fists, but Tesseract eased his fingers between hers and gently opened her hands, talking softly to her in alien. He'd wanted my reaction to that proposal, I realized, so he spoke in English.

"If your planet is contacted," Tesseract explained, still rubbing Black Amber's hands and elbows, "then we would take home government candidates before we took legacies."

Great, if the universe met Earth, I'd still be a parolee, busting hump on mortgage payments and Warren's and my fines.

Black Amber spread her lips, stared an eye-stab at me. Black Amber's in a bind, I thought. *Black Amber, you allow contact—you keep me out. But you'd hate to see us killer xenophobes in your Federation.*

Silent and tense, we hunched over our laps, sitting in the living room. Finally Tesseract said, "Black Amber, is this really impossible for you?"

"They shot me, they killed Mica. Hideous species. Contact would be stupid."

"Tom," Tesseract said, "I'll have tea with Black Amber, then talk to you."

Black Amber and the big crested alien went into Mica's old bedroom. I remembered Mom and Dad going in there to talk in private, and how little I felt then. The same now. The two Barcons heated water, then suggested that the younger Gwyngs and I go tend the layers. We loaded feed onto the trolley, them helping me, not saying much, and gathered the eggs and washed them.

When we came back inside, I heard Black Amber crying in the bedroom and Tesseract's low voice. My hands got cold and tingly, my mouth sticky.

"Black Amber hates losing," Cadmium told me. Finally, Amber and Tesseract came out, Tesseract stroking her side gently. Black Amber's eyes looked glazed.

Tesseract spoke softly to her in alien, and she went back to Mica's old room. While the Barcons made more tea, Tesseract asked me where we could talk privately. "Warren's room," I suggested, the farthest from Black Amber.

After I closed the door, Tesseract walked over to the window and looked at my garden. I'd just plowed it two weeks before they came.

"You should understand about Gwyngs," he finally said, sitting backward on a straight chair, chin to chair back and legs around it—the way Warren sat. "Gwyngs work harder to be alive than almost any other sapient. Twice they crawl into pouches. You know what a marsupial is? The true mother's pouch, then a host mother's pouch. And Mica was Black Amber's true son. Once they leave the pouch host, life for them is easy, very social. No Gwyng expects death before brain rot, unless the Gwyng goes insane, which to them is premature senility."

"Oh."

"Mica was nearly insane, by their standards, before he died."

The Barcons brought in a strange un-Earthly tea. I felt more relaxed after I drank some, then realized it was drugged. *Well, this is it*, I thought. Tesseract waited for the tea to loosen me up. I felt tranced, worried as hell, but the body odd, like the fear didn't register. Slowly, I lay back on the bed.

"So Mica was her baby?" I said. "I remember when I was five and Warren was a god."

"I met Mica once," Tesseract said. "Charming for a Gwyng."

The tea loosened hideous memories: the shotgun noise, the gunshots, Alph/Mica crying on the porch, legs full of bird shot. I rolled belly down and mumbled, "I miss him." I almost forgot Tesseract wasn't human, then looked at him and saw that crest, skin and flesh over a bony skull ridge, the big jaws. "The tea's drugged," I said.

"For relaxation purposes," he said.

"Sure," I said. "It doesn't make me feel . . ." I started shaking with sobs, missing Mica worse than I thought, missing Warren. Tesseract touched me, and I pushed him off and asked, "What was in the tea?"

He stared down at me, eyes hazed slightly, and I remembered he'd drunk tea with Black Amber. *What a universe!* I wondered what came next, then he stood up, stretched, reached at the ceiling curiously with his fingers. Smiling, he said, "This tea is difficult, but we have better teas."

I said, "I'm sorry I didn't get him away. Was he really going crazy? Warren said cats lived among humans and didn't go crazy."

"The Gwyngs are unique sapients." He sighed. "We try, in our Federation, to smooth over the differences, but . . ."

I cut in, "Cadmium says Black Amber doesn't like losing."

"Be kind to her. You'll spend some time together while we turn her back to Gwyng-shape. We'll do it at the observatory station, since she's dominant for a Gwyng and would be uncomfortable in your shape among her own people."

But what did becoming-a-cadet mean? Later that afternoon, I got Tesseract away from the others and offered him a beer, if he could drink on duty. He smiled. I smiled, and we drank together in the kitchen while the Gwyngs and Barcons loaded their souvenirs in the ship.

"Very strange business," I told him as he leaned back against the kitchen counter, sipping beer like a real man. "What do cadets do?"

"You smile almost like we Ahrams do," he said. "Do you come from tree-dwelling stock that evolved into walkers who had to become intelligent to protect their awkward locomotion? Very social, but with sexual activity constant, high male aggressiveness, at least before intelligence became a major factor in social organization and technology?"

"Yeah, and another teacher said God made us out of clay." He hadn't answered me as to what cadets do. That was, I realized, a kind of answer. I wondered how much Mica had really liked me.

I got in touch with Warren's lawyer and sold Warren my share of the farm with life tenancy rights for me. The trip to the lawyer's was quick—then I felt truly cut off from Earth, a stunning feeling, as though I'd been flash-frozen. Later that day, I sold all the hens and the cow, knowing if Jenkins heard, we'd have to rush.

Tesseract took me aside. "The xenoreactiveness of your species," he told me gravely over another alien nerve tea, "might be latent in you. Our two Karst languages have similar slang terms—'xenofreak' in English, more or less. The Academy warns all potential cadets. Someone brought a few of your species to Karst several hundred years ago. Most are primitives in a reserve. If being a cadet is too stressful, or if you hurt one of us, you'll have to go live with them."

I drank his tea, feeling it slow me up a bit, but not quite like pot. "I could just go plain crazy, like Warren," my tongue said despite me. Not the best answer, I realized in the following silence. "But aren't we more alike than not," I asked, "if this tea affects both of us the same way, and you didn't even evolve here?"

"How do you know it's affecting me the same way? The Rector thinks we're all inevitable expressions of one universal mind, but you should see *him*."

"What does he look like?"

"Big Bird, like on *Sesame Street*," Tesseract said, sounding slow and sloppy. "With fingers," he added, wiggling his own, "instead of wings."

"*Real* alien," I said, feeling conspiratorial, ape to ape. "Not more or less normal-looking, like us."

Tesseract smothered a giggle in his big hand, then looked at his teacup and said, "I drink too much of this. But all you little alien cadets . . ."

"What else?"

"Black Amber's been promoted to Sub-Rector. She demands an apology, in public, for not escaping with Mica. And she wants you to learn a more educated dialect of English. I could teach you."

I nodded.

"If you can't manage our language, we'll have doubts about your sapience."

Fast, very fast. We packed: clothes, books, VCR machine, tapes, and the rest of the cultural relics. Then the Barcons raided the refrigerator for food samples. I brought several plastic razors, wondering if any other species shaved their beards.

One of Mica's cats who'd stayed to play with the search crew rubbed up against Black Amber as she unhooked the VCR from the TV. "Did this one know Mica?" Rhyodolite asked, reaching over to stroke it. Black Amber picked up the cat, which went snuggling limp and purred. The alien rubbed her face against the cat's mouth and spoke to it in Gwyng.

"She says it should evolve into a wonderful sentient," Cadmium translated. "Reserved enough on first contact, then genuinely friendly."

I said, "I guess they'll go wild again."

Black Amber looked at me as though I'd showed her my hideous alien-shooting side, then spoke in Gwyng to the Barcons, who picked up the cats and checked under their tails. The male Barcon went out, to the ship, I supposed, and came back with something like a pencil-sized cattle prod. "We can fix," the female Barcon said.

Yowh, right to the balls. My own balls shrank up in sympathy. So three Earth cats, the freshly sterilized male and two females, went with us.

When the Barcons began packing up the cable net, I noticed the Gwyngs twining together and dabbing out with their feet. Tesseract said, "I promise I'll get us out of the well and into the net without a geometry failure."

We went on board ship. No windows, nothing. How long was this going to take?

"Put your suitcase under the bunk," Tesseract said as he sat down with a steel cap on his head, wires leading to a computer with flat displays, not liquid crystals, something better. He squeezed his eyes closed and sat there for several minutes, then asked, "Ready?"

We all sat down, then the ship lurched.

"How long will this take?" I asked.

"We're ten light-hours out, at the first switching point. Wait until the station crew checks the airlock," Tesseract said, "then we can get out in the station and stretch. We'll be here awhile, Tom, so you can meet the crew. They've seen months of your television, but haven't ever met a human before."

I heard clunking on the outside of the hull. More aliens who traveled millions of miles in no time flat. Superior aliens. "Where's the john?" I asked.

Tesseract got up and swung a small basin down from the wall, looked at me, and adjusted it to fit. My bladder jammed with all them looking. They were amused.

The airlock doors slid into the walls and I stood there gaping up at two big hairy aliens. *That's what Barcons look like with the hair.* Black coarse hair, like, well, almost like bear's fur. They talked alien at the guys I'd traveled with, then one said to me in English, "We keep the station rather cool. Less parasites that way."

"Get me out of this body," Black Amber said as we went with the new Barcons into the station. "Most painful body I've ever been molded into."

I was surprised at how roomy the space station was, but it didn't have windows except two thick ones in a little observatory room. Instead, the aliens had walls of holograms: all kinds of landscapes, even cartoon holograms, composite holograms of impossible landscapes. And the walls without holograms were carpeted or covered with semi-hard plastics, which deadened all sounds. The furniture wasn't fixed to the floor either.

Tesseract showed me to a room bigger than my bedroom at home. "God, the station is huge," I said.

"People live here for long terms. We don't want social friction. So space enough to avoid each other."

He unfolded my bed, a mattress attached to a shelf hinged to the wall, while I checked out a padded tube, like a cocoon sofa, covered in a funny cloth almost like velvet. The inside was obscene, squishy. "Gwyngs love that," Tesseract said as he watched me scramble back out. "Reminds them of the pouch, I guess."

"I wasn't expecting that stuff inside," I said.

"You might want to be left alone for a while, but if you don't, tell me." He showed me a flat pressure switch on the wall above a marble-sized intercom pickup so I could call them. "Or just come on out."

Desperate for privacy, yet not sure I really wanted to be alone, I nodded. "And the toilet adjusts," he said, pulling the wall toilet out just like the one on the ship. "Tilt it to suit."

I smiled grimly. He touched a wall stud and Maybry's Mill popped out of a wall, but I felt almost physically ill to see something from home. "No."

"Would you prefer New York City?" he said.

Maybe, I thought, nodding very slightly. The wall began playing a reconstruction flat movie from some TV show, a weirdly edited New York. "How do you turn it off?" I asked.

He showed me and I sat there, alone, after he'd left. Suddenly, I felt like a microbe in vast space. Very tired, I crawled into the bunk.

The next day, after I shaved, Tesseract introduced me more formally to the other aliens who watched us humans: no names for the Barcons, which seemed odd, and various chemical and rock names for the others, more Gwyngs, just like Alpha/Mica, the same webs, funny goat nostrils. Only one Gwyng spoke English.

All the Gwyngs wore pants like gym pants and vests with deep sleeve holes. The Barcons just wore pants. Either the Barcons were all females with breasts on the lower trunk, or both sexes had tits.

While Black Amber went through surgery, I wandered around the space station, turning off holograms. All that alien scenery made me nervous: funny beach houses made of woven planks, carved stones marking a tunnel in front of a glacier, alien jungles. In all of them the light seemed wrong. But when I left each room, I switched the hologram back on, so the aliens wouldn't complain.

The next day, I went to the hospital room to see Black Amber, who lay wrapped tightly in plastic film. *She's a big Gwyng,* I realized, seeing her now with the legs and arms back to normal size and comparing her to the other Gwyngs at the station.

Tubes went through the plastic at various points—eyes, nose, mouth, shoulders. Some flushed liquid over her skin and drained it off, plastic pulsing. I thought how this must hurt, worse than gunshot. She rolled her eyes toward me, slowly, as though the tiny eye muscles were freshly re-stitched.

Her face wasn't so wrinkled, but I supposed that was post-surgery puffiness. I couldn't see her tongue, but she raised her head and I saw the muscle lump under the chin.

So much like Mica. I ached for all that surgery she'd gone through, in and out of human form, the gunshot, trying to get her son back.

A Barcon took me by the arm after a few minutes and led me out. "She isn't in any danger," one of the hairless ones who'd been on Earth said. "We stop the pain. She's been through it twice before."

One of the Barcons, a few days later, decided I needed something to do and asked me to help tend Black Amber. Unwrapped from the plastic, she lay under covers pulled up to her nippleless chest, two triangular heating pads ready beside her to warm her webs. On her lap, she held a machine with five finger-operated toggles, like little chrome joysticks. "I hate humans," the box said for her. "Conditioned by the gunshot, deaths. And your hatred of aliens."

"Out of all you met, they were all bad?" I asked, holding up a glass of Gwyng formula with the broad straw they used.

She twitched her fingers against the language machine's joysticks. "Maybe," the machine said for her.

Taking care of her was eerie, as though she were the large ghost of Alpha/Mica. The two others in human face visited her, but stood off, as though the surgery and her weakness made them nervous.

"When the Gwyngs feel comfortable around Black Amber again," Tesseract told me, "we'll have a formal ceremony, investing her in her new Sub-Rector's uniform."

"Why don't they feel comfortable around her now?" I asked.

"Gwyngs can't stand weakness," he said. "I guess since they live so densely in their colonies, they had to isolate the sick to avoid illnesses wiping out a group. But they don't get sick often. They trance out to escape social friction, but otherwise they're healthy and totally social."

Isolation seemed to distress Black Amber, who called me to her room a couple of times. But when I came in, she stared at me and didn't speak. Once she said, through the machine, "Still a monster, I see."

As she got better, she exercised with free weights and I spotted for her. But otherwise I was bored, among the static holograms. "Teach me your languages," I'd ask, but all the aliens refused, saying that would interfere with the language operations.

Finally, the Gwyngs tussled and Black Amber beat them all. "You bluff bone-breaks," Cadmium accused her.

She looked at him and koo'ed.

"So we're ready to go back to Karst," Tesseract said, watching Gwyngs squirming bodies together, Black Amber top Gwyng, social again.

Black Amber came out in a green uniform embroidered with real gold bound up in the piping around the neck and sleeves. Her body and head hair, freshly washed, picked up red highlights. I still saw scars on her face where the Barcons had re-built it, but the puffiness was down, the Gwyng wrinkles deeply grooved from her nose and eye corners. *Slots for air when she presses her face against a blood animal*, I realized.

"Pre-cadet uniform," Tesseract said, handing me a pair of baggy white pants with wrap strings, a little hand riveter to use for making string holes, and a white tunic that came down to my knees.

Black Amber silently showed me how to fold the pants front, where to put the rivets. Then she bumped elbows with me for the first time, and oo'ed, just a little.

Tesseract said, "Welcome, Pre-Cadet Red Clay. Mica gave that as your Academy name."

"Being a cadet is not a delight," Cadmium said.

= 3 =

Reframing Sense: The Language Operations

There's no sense of distance with space gates. Instead of bumping dozens of light-years from gate to gate, I might have been in a boxcar, being coupled and uncoupled in switching yards. The Gwyngs, frustrated after getting me instead of rescuing their own, slumped together and stared at the walls.

At a gate a light-day from the Academy and Institutes planet, I heard more radio chatter in alien languages, clunking sounds against our ship. Tesseract led me through a grey plastic tunnel as we switched to a dual-drive ship.

"I want normal space time," Black Amber said with the box. Steel slabs pulled back into the walls.

Tesseract turned off the cabin lights so as not to dim the stars. "There's Karst's sun," he said to me. "Looks tiny out here." The Gwyngs looked out briefly and went to the bunk room.

Around the sky, I saw huge puffs of stars and glowing gas. In the near space, tiny space-suited figures worked around hundreds of space transport pods, from small one-man diving-bell-like units to huge round container vessels as big as moons. Welding torches glittered like dust motes.

"Black Amber wanted a week on reaction drive, but since she's asleep, I'll get us a bit closer quicker," Tesseract said. He closed the shutters, and sat down at the controls. We lurched again.

Then Tesseract cut off the gravity to let me float, pulled back the shutters, and rolled the ship slightly. Under us, I saw the curve of a big planet with a ring like Saturn's. We drifted closer and I saw lumps in the ring—coarse rock cobble. Tesseract talked to another alien and waited for the time-lagged replies.

"Always charming to see someone see space the first time," Tesseract said as he started the rocket drive. "Most of us see the emptiness as a nuisance, not part of the structure. But for you, all this is powerfully charming, yes?"

"Oh, yes."

"It's still the universe that built us, even if we evade its distances with our agile minds."

While I was still staring into space, the Barcons came in. "We've got to continue working out your biologic," the big male Barcon said.

"What do I call you?" I asked.

He looked at me without changing his expression. Tesseract smiled. "Ah, Barcon, he has to have a name. Human nature."

"S'wam."

"The Earth alias, plus the Barcon form for male," Tesseract explained.

"We don't get too close to our medical subjects," the female Barcon said stiffly.

I followed the Barcons to the medical bay where S'wam punched tiny holes all over my back, dabbing each with a different chemical. "We need to know what chemicals to use when we operate on you for language."

"Operation for language?"

"When we put in the skull computer and make space in your language center for new languages," S'wam told me as he rolled plastic film over my sore back.

I was going *what* inside my soon-to-be-violated skull.

"I'd spray to ease the sting," the female Barcon said, "but we want pure reactions. We'll wait until we get to Karst before doing brain tissue biopsies. Sleep now."

"I'll try," I managed to say. The cats squalled in their boxes. Was I just another exotic pet, I wondered, and how could Barcons be confused with blacks—slanted eyes, skinny jaws with too many angles, noses that wiggled.

In the bunk room the Gwyngs were sleeping, twined around each other, Black Amber in the center. The Barcons pulled down a narrow bunk for me on the wall across from the Gwyngs' large pallet.

"We brought human drugs and beer to make you sleep better," the female Barcon said. "We are all very tired and want you to be passive."

"Some drugs and beer are dangerous."

"Aspirin?" the male Barcon said, handing me a cold beer and a couple of little white pills that looked exotic in this environment.

"Thank you," I said, sipping the beer, swallowing two aspirins. "I'll sleep better now." My back ached. "Good night, S'wam."

"No real night here. Sleep."

I lay down on my stomach on the bunk and looked for the covers, but all I saw was a little rheostat that made the space warmer or cooler. "Okay," I mumbled.

I looked back at Black Amber, whose face showed thin scars in the dim crosslight. Tesseract came in and I whispered to him, "I'd be more comfortable with a sheet."

He handed me a cross between a sheet and a blanket, made of paper, then crawled into his own bunk, big body twisting under a similar sheet. *But they aren't like paper, exactly,* I thought, *they don't rustle.*

Quiet, disposable alien sheet. I could hardly relax under its strange texture, but finally I dozed off, dreaming of deer mocking wolves. Waking with a jolt, I saw the Barcons together in a bunk, softly murmuring to each other. Tesseract was gone, but the Gwyngs were still sleeping.

Must have woke me when Tesseract changed shifts with the Barcons, I thought. I slept again and dreamed horrible murky dreams about a cat who shot at me. Finally, I woke up again, turned up the rheostat-controlled heat, and lay there, afraid to look at the aliens right away.

"Can I see your back now?" S'wam asked as soon as I stretched. I almost rolled over, but remembered my back just in time, so wiggled out, trying to keep from bending that sore skin. The Gwyngs had gone, but Tesseract was asleep again now, snoring faintly, his mouth open, big teeth faintly visible. I pulled on the white pre-cadet pants and, sweating a little, followed the Barcons to the medical bay.

S'wam let me see my back through mirrors. Three test

holes that had begun to itch looked red, while four others had turned black. S'wam ran a tickling rod around the seven messy punctures and washed out the holes, cleaning out the dead flesh. His mate finished up with little suction cups that sprayed and drained each hole.

"Well," S'wam said, "we now know how to kill you." He checked off boxes on a chart and spoke his language into a dangling microphone, then re-sealed the cleaned areas, which felt very sore now. "You like space? You must see this," he said.

This turned out to be an ice planet, so close it filled a third of the viewport. The Gwyngs stared at it without talking. Fractures in the planet's ice glaze splintered sunlight into colored and white flares.

So beautiful. "You also find it beautiful, Black Amber?" I asked.

She looked at me and back at the planet. "Lungy see'ng i," she tried to say. Then she waved her hand at me, not wanting to leave and get the English-speaking box. "S'oos be." She moaned.

Lucky seeing it, supposed to be. Earlier, I'd noticed hand signals that seemed to be for *yes* and *no*. I raised my fist and said, "Lucky seeing it, yes? You nod the fist like this for *yes*?"

She grabbed my head and covered my mouth. I held myself still against those long bony fingers, feeling them squirm over my lips. Her other hand twisted my hair. As the ice planet slowly drifted away, Black Amber pushed me roughly away from her.

Then she found a writing pad and wrote to me:

> Signal agreement by cupping the hand *slightly* and bringing it down. Do not make fists at us. Do not. It is supposedly lucky to see Ichrea on an incoming flight. Hideous to have you here and not Mica.

I read the note and looked up; Cadmium closed his left hand and made a fist, pumping the fingers. Then he opened his hand under my nose. Even with it surgically adjusted to look like a human hand, I saw a hole at the base of the thumb, wet fluid around the hole. I sneezed—my eyes watered.

I cocked my elbow and puffed my armpit at them. Cadmium jumped for me, biting at my armpits.

"Stop. Now," the female Barcon ordered, grabbing us in her massive hands. I trembled.

Rhyodolite said, "Cadmium isn't sure of human challenge signals."

"He made me sneeze."

"Odd or even," S'wam said.

"Odd," Cadmium quickly replied.

"I punch the computer for a random number. If odd, Cadmium apologizes first. If even, you." S'wam touched buttons on a console. The number was odd.

Cadmium caught his head just about to bob and said, "I apologize. I thought you insulted the Sub-Rector."

I said, locking eyes with him, "I intended no insult. I'm alone here." Because I felt my lips begin to quiver, I looked away first.

"I think," S'wam said with a big sigh, "I should take another look at your back." In the medical bay, he took my chin gently in his hands and said, "Move slow."

He unwrapped my back, put stronger solutions in the test punctures, then re-plasticized it. I noticed when S'wam turned to go that he didn't walk like a black man or a white. The medical bay door closed behind him. They're all aliens, I thought as I looked around me. *And I can't go back.* The only familiar object was a mirror. I went over and looked at myself—I needed to shave. *Maybe I can talk to Tesseract, if he's awake.*

There's no handle on the door. I was sure they'd locked me up, but when I moved closer, the door slid into the wall. In the bunk room, from the back, Tesseract looked human enough: same shoulder muscles, curve of the spine. Big, though.

I asked, "Can I talk to you?"

He rolled over and yawned hugely, exposing giant nut-cracking teeth. Alien, broad-skulled with that bald bone ridge on top, thick jaws. I felt faint.

"Are you okay?" he asked.

"No," I said. He reached for my hand and we both felt me tremble. I sat down, gripped the chair arms hard, afraid they'd cut off the gravity and let me float off into space. "I'm lonely. I'm scared." When I heard myself, I got worse scared. "Xenofreaking?"

"Little carnivorous ape, if you were xenofreaking, you'd be screaming with your back to the wall, not trying to talk to me." He sat up and pulled on a top. "But you're almost as intense as the Gwyngs."

"Do I make you nervous?" I asked. The universe, I thought madly, will be fair if I make one alien a little nervous.

"Yes. Come let me make you tea."

"Keep talking to me in English," I said.

Tesseract spoke continuously. "Have you read Jane Goodall and other human writers on chimpanzees? We consider that you might be chimpanzees 'writ large,' so to speak. Very flexible, can be social, can be independent. You should be able to survive this better than most primitives."

By the time we reached the eating bay, I felt foolish. Cadmium came in and Gwyng-talked at Tesseract, who answered curtly in the other tongue. I just heard the Gwyng, couldn't look at him, and was glad when he walked back out.

"He's nothing like Mica," I said, sipping an alien tea.

"Mica was terribly promising for a male Gwyng," Tesseract said.

Black Amber came in next, eyes rigid in her skull, gaze fixed on me. Tesseract talked to her while I, stupid and primitive, cycled between terror and anger at a million miles a minute.

"I guess," I said, daring to interrupt them, "if you wish for the stars and get them, you run a risk." The tea hit then, and I leaned my drugged head down on the table. "Strong tea, Tesseract."

A thin finger rubbed down my neck. I mumbled to Black Amber. "I'm sorry you got hurt. I didn't want Mica to die."

Rhyodolite and Cadmium stuck their heads in, fake humans looking more and more ragged as their bodies struggled to grow back proper Gwyngs. I felt the tea coming back up.

"Could they stay back a bit?" I said. "They make me more uneasy than you do." *Stupid, stupid,* then another quiver shook me. Tesseract said something and Cadmium and Rhyodolite went out.

It's like a damn parade, I thought when S'wam came in shortly after. The big Barcon moved around behind me slowly, one hand on my shoulder, to look at my back. He shook me a little, then went out and brought me a small green pill.

"Muscle tension like a computer misprogramming itself—or feedback in a microphone. This relaxes, can't hurt with Tesseract's tea," S'wam said. "Take it if you like."

"I don't want to be alone." I took the pill with more tea. "But even with Tesseract here, I am alone."

"I'll talk English with you until you fall asleep," Tesseract promised.

"I'm glad S'wam didn't grab me and give me a shot."

"Too much taking away control already," S'wam said as he patted me on the shoulder, just missing the test holes.

I sat, afraid I'd collapse if I stood up, but then finally decided to look out the viewports. Aliens surrounded me. When we got to the chairs by the viewports, I saw the two sort-of-human Gwyngs already there.

"Are you all right?" Rhyodolite asked. I nodded. "A human male," he said in sleaze tones through the black-girl face, "showed me how to make humans feel better."

Oh, no, I thought, afraid this was going to be sexual.

He came over and stood behind me, rubbing into the tops of my shoulders and neck muscles with his shortened fingers. "Tesseract," Rhyodolite said, "if Red Clay had fur, you'd like doing this."

How do dogs stand it, that never see another dog all their lives? I felt like a smart puppy dragged into a world of super-intelligent bats and bears. But between Rhyodolite's massage and the little pill, I felt my muscles loosen as though they'd been stretched gently.

"Well, it's finally getting to you," Tesseract said as I halfway fell asleep. "You want to lie down on the bunk?"

I blinked and nodded. He helped me up. "Am I really primitive? I scored high average for a cadet."

"It's not your theoretical capabilities. It's what you're used to."

"Do we shock you? Are you more civilized?" He sat down by the bunk. I felt my face and said, "I need a shave. I can't stay awake." My eyes closed as he began explaining pre-cadets, swearing in, legacies, but I'd absorbed as much as I could and went to sleep fast.

I slept on my back and didn't even notice. No dreams.

Some time later, I heard humming. Rhyodolite and Cadmium, bodies twined together, stood by my bunk, the lumps under their chins vibrating, grown back despite all the human transform surgery. Their weirdness was almost comic this morning. I pulled on my pants and blinked at them, then reached for my toilet bag. The razor was gone. "Did someone take my razor?" I asked, suddenly a bit chilled.

They pushed me up between them and rocked me sideways. "Don't worry about it," Cadmium replied.

"Your web armpit is really smelly, Red Clay. If you wave it again when my nose is fixed, Cadmium and I both will be really upset," Rhyodolite said.

"Try not to be a human animal stranded among us," Cadmium said. "Be Academy. Species after Academy, after the Federation."

"At least," Rhyodolite said, fake tits pressing against my side, "that's what cadets are *told* to believe by the boss monster."

Finally, my sore back woke up. "Hey. The places where they stuck me."

Rhyodolite said something in Gwyng and explained, "Means red clay covered with aliens."

"Where is my razor? Who's the boss monster?"

"Meat-eating-ape, Tesseract said your ancestors defeated something like his," Rhyodolite said. "So perhaps he's afraid for you to have these hair-slicing things."

"Can't have it. Suicide precaution," Cadmium said. "Come see Karst from space. It will make your face hair seem insignificant."

Karst hung in space like a green milky marble, glowing. I wished I'd seen Earth from space.

Sitting at the controls, Black Amber moved a chrome stick—I heard gas hiss through the hull and the ship pivoted. The disc expanded, filled the viewport, and we swung into nightfall. As we passed over, I noticed the land was mostly vacant, no lights like pictures of Earth from orbit. "Nobody down there?"

"The Federation needed a neutral multi-species city, but a city takes a whole planet to anchor it," Tesseract said. "So we built a planet about five thousand years ago, baby planet.

Twenty million people live in Karst City or around it. Still room to expand.''

When we swung around to day, I looked at Karst City through a telescope. Three rivers, one glittering silver, the others green and broad, ran through the city into a huge bay with more built-up area wrapped around it. In the bay, I saw floating ships that might have been space liners. I was thrilled, a little scared. ''Was the Academy responsible for building this?''

''Academy and Institutes,'' Tesseract said.

''So big,'' I murmured.

''Mos Eisley, it's not,'' said Rhyodolite.

But why did they take my razor? They worry too much about this xenofreaking. What was I supposed to do, run amuck with a plastic safety razor? As I put on a fresh uniform, Rhyodolite kept sneaking touches of the stubble. *Perhaps they want to humiliate me?* I refused to believe I could commit suicide with it.

''Next time, we'll only know Karst languages, and you'll have a computer plate in your head,'' he told me. ''And we'll hear your tongue mess up in Karst for one-step-at-a-time brains.''

Cadmium spoke up then, ''Just remember, 'refugee' in Karst I comes from 'dump heap.' We picked you off a dump, didn't we?''

''You two look like wax dummies left in the sun too long.''

''You look like a stinky-arm human being,'' Cadmium said.

''Cut it out,'' Tesseract said.

''If he can't learn, we'll send him to the fat-in-tea drinkers.''

Tesseract said something curt in alien to Cadmium. ''You okay?'' he asked me.

''Sure.'' But I fluttered inside as he asked. ''Is there anyone I salute when we leave the ship?''

Tesseract touched my shoulder. ''Look, right now, you could crawl off the ship naked, and no one would think much of it. You aren't considered sapient until you learn Karst languages.''

''Did I leave Earth for some sort of massive alien put-down?'' I was pissed off, and afraid. Were they right to treat me like a fool?

''I know your people are quite technological, paleo-electric era, to borrow and shift English terms,'' Tesseract said. ''When you can write in Karst, thank the Rector for the appointment.''

A bell rang—Black Amber pulled on a headset with a microphone dangling in front of her muzzle. She spoke Gwyng into it, then reached up, her vestigial webs straining against her uniform sleeves as she pulled a short lever to close the window shields.

''These landings are so archaic when we have gates,'' Cadmium said as he belted himself into a chair. Tesseract helped belt me down in another chair.

''*This* is primitive?'' I said, gripping the chair arms as the ship shuddered and groaned. Then we changed course again, a fierce hiss, weight lurching to the right. I felt vibrations through the seat as Black Amber pulled down three knife switches. Suddenly I weighed a ton.

The viewport shields parted. A huge, fabulous city, all cut stone and dark wood, swooped by. I'd never expected a space city to look old. Faceted glass, polished metal building trim and caps, copper roofs, then bushy green parks swirled by under us.

We shot over and landed outside the city on one of the runways I'd seen from space. A huge whomp came from the ship's rear, and I was thrown way forward against my straps.

''So I'm not on Earth,'' I said.

''Would you like a sedative?'' one of the Barcons asked.

''No.'' The aliens didn't need to sedate this country boy; I was dazed enough and just sat while Tesseract undid the chair straps. Then I walked unsteadily to the viewport and looked out at the alien trees.

Green. More green. And the flowers bloomed in regular flower colors, faded and wilted now—I'd skipped spring. The buildings looked like airport buildings, despite being completely on another planet. Just all these aliens around.

''Are you okay?'' S'wam, looking like an African growing fur, asked.

''Yeah. The plants look green.''

''Chlorophyll and hemoglobin here, too, like all the Galaxy

we know about. Very economical to evolve—biochemical brothers. Come out. You can see more.''

I stepped down a rickety aluminum ladder, feeling light, not sure that was a different gravity or shock. Tesseract and the Barcons talked to each other in alien, nervously, I thought. The Earth cats squalled in their boxes as Black Amber and the two still raggedly human-looking Gwyngs off-loaded them. Cadmium looked really weird in full light with Gwyng fur tufting up on his blond man's body, short fuzz instead of stubble on his face.

Eerie, I thought, and started laughing.

"Don't,'' Cadmium said, his human face contorted with Gwyng concern. S'wam knelt beside a medical-looking bag.

"You aliens worry too much,'' I said, getting myself under control as S'wam brought out the injector cube. "No,'' I said, gesturing him back.

Aliens went about their various jobs, hardly bothering to glance at me. *Refugees land here every day*—that helped calm me down, but I was a bit pissed, too. I was the first human—no, not the first. Other human screwups lived on some primitive range. Barbaric me, whose brother shot an alien, was no surprise to these space sophisticates. A few looked over and moved their faces slightly. I blushed for my beard stubble.

Two curly-coated short aliens drove up in an electric cart and loaded it with baggage and cats, then drove across a runway that was non-shiny black, smoother than asphalt without being plastic-slick.

"We have a ride waiting,'' Tesseract said, "and the Gwyngs are very tired of looking human.''

Karst's sun shone in its blue sky, and aliens walked around as if spaceships landed every day, on that strange-surfaced runway which was dusty, little particles of dirt that looked just like Earth dirt, stirred by a breeze that felt no different from any Earth air. But I felt like I was being mildly electrocuted, all my muscles jangling.

Tesseract led me into a reception building where he got a tag for my wrist before we all climbed into something that looked like a commuter bus, grey and green paint peeling over the electric engine. While we were going down an expressway in what had to be a warehouse district, I fell asleep. I don't believe they drugged me.

Tesseract shook me awake later and said, "Here's the hospital where you'll have the language operations. Go with S'wam and the Gwyngs. I'll see you later." I looked up and saw a big building, like a short-armed concrete cross, lots of stories, lots of windows. All the passing alien shapes ran together in my mind. S'wam, the sort-of-human Gwyngs, and I got off the bus and went inside.

The floors were covered in *something* like linoleum, but closer to rubber, noiseless underfoot. We walked to what looked like a nurses' station with a waist-high counter and terminals, flatter screens than most Earth computers, and a drug trolley locked to a post.

Cadmium and Rhyodolite joked around with a pug-faced nurse who hunted behind the counter for our records. Really pug-faced, like a dog, and dark-skinned, she made me feel vaguely sick.

Rhyodolite finally asked the nurse for something, probably a phone, since she handed him a metal rod with flat discs on either end. He adjusted it to fit his face. Ah, like the toilets, I thought, as he talked. Then he gestured to Cadmium with a cupped hand and told S'wam and me, "Our own operations are scheduled here. We'll be in touch."

As they walked away, the Barcon handed the nurse a plastic card. She pushed it—I guessed it was data on me—into a computer, punched some keys, then handed S'wam back the card. He moved me toward the elevator.

Shit, we had to wait for it just like any other elevator. S'wam asked me if I was okay.

"You all look alien enough, but the sky's blue, the dirt's dirt, and the trees are green. We've got plastic. We could build a landing strip like that. It looks like Earth here." I trembled a little. "But I feel lighter."

"Denial is very soothing," the Barcon said as the elevator door slid down. He gently took my elbow and pushed me in.

"It goes up like an elevator," I said. *Utterly too late and too far away to be scared*—my life was way out of my control now.

On the sixth floor, we got out in a huge meeting room, with eight doors off to the side of one wall. I saw tall shiny black aliens, short fuzzy aliens, aliens with knees that bent backward, aliens with bones in funny places—skull crests, real sharp cheekbones. Fuzzy big aliens, fuzzy little aliens, naked-skinned aliens . . . until my mind jammed and refused to classify them any further.

Most were relaxed. But six acted like female kittens in first heat—wide-eyed, keeping lots of air in the old lungs. We were the ones here for the language operation.

I nearly freaked, looking at aliens being scared. Then I spotted the eighth of us, with an Ahram translator like Tesseract. He shielded her—a human-looking, female-looking, good-looking woman. Maybe another human, from Europe?

"Let me talk to *her*," I said to S'wam.

S'wam talked to her translator and said, "She's rather sedated. But you can try. She may look like you, but she's not the same species. Very primitive planet."

She smiled at me delicately, eyes not quite focused. I smiled, almost stroking her with my eyes—she was very delicate—four foot ten with a head almost too big for her body. Her mouth bent funny on the face, different.

I blushed again for my stubbly face and asked S'wam if I could come closer. S'wam talked to her translator, who asked her in a guttural language I couldn't imagine her speaking, but she answered back in the same burrs and gargles.

"You'd be welcome. You don't look like a nightmare," S'wam said with a flick of his nose.

I stepped closer, feeling her body heat. I didn't want to know whether she'd saved Karst people while I'd failed. She reached for my hand, her five fingers twinging between my own. Both of us having flat fingernails with white tips seemed miraculous. She widened her eyes at me. I ached to go skinny-dipping in all that warm blue.

Then something really alien walked into the room—an olive and brown bird guy with soft-looking hands and scaly arms, here to welcome us. S'wam translated as the bird spoke. "He says now that we are to show you to your rooms."

The translators fanned out behind us, ready to catch anyone who bolted. I remembered Tesseract said we weren't considered fully sapient until we knew the languages. S'wam reached for my elbow, but I said, "I won't run off. Let's get settled in. Then I'd like to get away from the crowd for a while."

S'wam showed me through the third door from the right into a small room with two foam mattress beds. I sat down on one of them and wondered how long I had until the operation. Another pug-face came in to show me sheet samples. S'wam suggested, "Pick a fabric similar to what you slept on at home, not something exotic." We could get harder or softer slabs, and the platforms went up and down on chromed posts. Some sleep high, some sleep low, I thought, dazed.

A flat TV screen hung from the ceiling so anyone on either bed could watch it. Just like a hospital on Earth, I kept thinking. I got a weird feeling that these aliens were special-effects aliens. Before this idea set hard and drove me crazy, I decided I'd better see the stars, and asked, "S'wam, is there somewhere to see the sky?"

"Not an unusual request," he said, gently but firmly taking my upper arm. We rode the elevator up to a roof garden.

"Could you turn off the roof lights?" I asked.

"Can't switch off global clusters."

Huge star clusters hung up in the gaudy sky. Colors spun shimmering, not twinkling, from the largest stars. And two moons—crescents in that Karst sky.

I was the only human . . . not quite the only human, but I saw this all for my own first time. This was the sky Mica'd drawn.

"Where's Earth?" I asked. The whole trip flashed through my mind as S'wam shrugged. I was here, alone. Shivering, I said, "We can go in now. I know where I am."

The aliens put me to sleep with a pill. In the morning, S'wam woke me up and said, "I leave now. Tesseract will be in later. A health person will give you a shaving razor or remove all the hairs permanently. Then they will feed you breakfast before they anesthetize you."

"Anesthetics after breakfast?" He looked at me furtively and left.

I wanted to follow my human routines, so I asked for a razor. They gave me a battery-operated electric one. After I shaved, I looked and looked at myself in the mirror. A human face. Then I went out and looked at all my alien colleagues. I didn't look any more freaked than they did.

By the wall near the nurses' station, I saw a low table without chairs, with spoons and glasses on it as if we'd eat there. One of the Barcons brought in a cart full of pillows and handed them to us. Then I saw a pug-faced nurse push in a steam table. The Barcons herded us into a line and panto-mimed that we should each take a tray.

The little almost-human girl, so tiny and blond in pre-cadet white, stared at her breakfast as though it had insulted her. As I tasted the grain cereal and fruit, I thought, alien but good. The fruit was like strawberry citrus something.

Another girl-like alien, very shiny black with delicate fea-tures and a too-pointed nose, ate like a robot, jerking the food to her mouth while her eyes twitched.

The others were either like Tesseract or Barcons, close enough, except for one almost like me, but ashen-skinned with larger ears.

Then, another alien, taller than me and shiny black, sat down by the black female, who immediately reached for his hand. They were both the same height when they were seated. Mates, had to be mates. They stopped looking at the rest of us.

Finally, just to be talking, I asked the little blonde, "How long before we can talk to each other?"

The blond girl smiled and spoke back in her incomprehen-sible garble as though she'd understood me perfectly. Soon the whole table jabbered in alien languages, desperately talk-ing as though the coming operations would cut our tongues out. A Barcon medical team surrounded the table and mobbed us as translators tried to calm everyone down. A Barcon grabbed me from the rear, holding me by the elbows. Tesser-act came in grinning. "Time to move on," he said.

I laughed, then started shaking. A Barcon pulled the blond-girl alien around so she couldn't see me, while the Barcon holding me stared at me as though checking for emotional plague.

"Too scared to go through with it?" Tesseract asked very gently.

"Tranquilizer okay?" I managed to get out. If I chickened out, they'd just turn me loose on the primitive range. After this operation, they'd educate me the way I should have been educated back home.

"Fine," Tesseract answered. The Barcons injected most of us with a hand-held thing like half a telephone. The two black mates twined around each other and were taken out together, unsedated. The air began to shimmer.

Little White Princess watched the hysteria with blond disdain until she keeled over in a faint. As the Barcons laid me on a stretcher, I saw others bend over her.

Last thing I remembered, they put a fat tube down my throat. *So much for breakfast.*

My head was wrapped in plastic. A Barcon leaned over my bed and spoke. I tried to answer in English, but . . .

No English! Gone! I grabbed the Barcon as though I could shake my English out of him, but he eased me back down on the bed. When he spoke again, I babbled nonsense back. My tongue was sore and what I said was totally meaningless, but he looked pleased.

So I babbled while the staff only spoke to me in Karst I. Familiar aliens without names talked while I imitated their sounds. Alien gentleness and drugs made the business only marginally bearable.

After five days, I picked up some really basic Karst I—and would hold on tight to S'wam or Tesseract when they visited, begging "don't go" and "no, stay."

S'wam went when he wanted to, but Tesseract often stayed until I made a grammar mistake. In another day or so, I knew pronoun parallels and joined the others each morning for lessons in the common room.

The eight of us began to talk like three-year-olds. Before a month passed, we mastered the grammar, but we still used rather childish vocabularies. Adult pride took over as most of us recovered from conceptual shift disorientation—sedatives helped a bit—and we began more formal language study.

The language had executional categories of concepts. Concept of computer-as-mental-design and its specific execution at the nurses' desk. The light had names for its angles, for the places the sun took in the sky. Connections formed between alien gestures. One minute, the Karst language seemed more real than English; the next like an arbitrary alien code that trivialized my human emotions even after the Barcons stopped blocking off the English in my brain.

And I noticed the little blonde was still sedated. She sat in a chair when the Barcons forced her out to be among us, and stared grimly at the wall. We all tried to talk to her, so finally she began learning, clumsily, to fend us off.

"What did the monsters do to me?" she asked me one day.

"They re-turned on the brain plasticity we'd had when we were babies. So we could all learn to speak Karst I well. We're going to be diplomats, I think."

She squinted her cold blue eyes and fleered her lips back off the pointed teeth. *Alien*, I thought, backing away.

Refugee. A funny, hurtful word. The root in Karst was *refuse/d, set aside*. The little blonde, whom the Academy named Calcite 2, and I were refugees.

Three sapient bears, like slender Barcons, but less hairy and much more friendly, came to the hospital. "Hello, Red Clay 5 and Calcite 2," the male said in Karst I, speaking slowly, "I'm Shir and my female is Gerris. We are support-class people. This is Klip, our oldest son. You are to live with us now and learn more about Karst customs."

They'd had previous experience with refugees, the female, Gerris, said as they showed us to the transport stop in the hospital's basement.

We walked through a tunnel lit with softly glowing panels and waited for the train. When I looked down the tunnel, I couldn't see tracks, just hoops of cables. Then the train came floating through the hoops, swaying slightly in mid-air, and my nape hair began to rise.

"Magnetic train," Gerris explained. We waited for the train to settle, then got on. The cars were molded sections of grey opaque plastic, a little dirty, with clear windows. Gerris showed us how to adjust the stools.

The train rose gently. I looked over at Calcite. She had her eyes closed tightly, throat muscles in spasms as though she was strangling screams back.

We got off underground and took an elevator to the bus stop, where we got into a red bread-loaf-shaped bus with the number equivalent to Earth 8 on it. "This will always get you to our neighborhood,'' the mama bear Gerris said, "red number 8 bus. Keep your pre-cadet wristbands on, and you can always get a free ride home.''

Calcite looked out the windows, her small face heavy, and said bitterly, "Home?''

The house we lived in was plain, no strong sense of being for a particular species. Both of us had our own rooms, with a tub in mine with new pipes leading to it. I still shaved with the electric razor, but this one worked better than most Earth electric razors.

Calcite and I left the house each morning and walked. For a couple of days, me pretending she was human, we explored the neighborhood. On most corners, aliens had put up statues. By the sculptures were covered benches where we'd huddle together and watch all the strangeness pass by.

Bench sitters, by custom, were ignored, so nobody looked back at us. Like we're invisible, I thought. *Or they don't want to look at us.*

"They're not too odd,'' I said to Calcite. I'd expected really exotic things, but all these guys walked on two legs, had two arms, head on top, none larger than a really big Earth basketball player or smaller than Calcite. "If I grew out a full beard, I'd be as exotically haired as any of them.''

"Some have feathers and beaks,'' she said. "And look at that one. It bends its knees backward.''

Mammal, in loose baggy pants, but the knees did bend toward the rear. Totally ignoring us, it stopped and waited for a bus. Calcite stared at it until the bus came and it stepped up. Face was funny, too, expressionless, but ridged with muscles.

Calcite said, "I confuse myself with this language. This planet stupid, makes me stupid with heat.''

I didn't think it was too hot or chilly, except some mornings were cool when the wind blew down from the mountains, which were visible like an alien Blue Ridge on clear days, off to the west. "Sorry,'' I said.

"My language,'' she said, slumped on the park bench, eyes not looking at anything. "I can't think as we did at home. This Karst language—I distort myself.''

"Like refugee meaning *trash kid*?''

"Worse,'' she said, giving me a quick look. Her own

rough language accented her Karst regardless of the work done on her speech organs, and her grammar was poor. "You and I will be put in a zoo. Or sent on most dangerous missions. These monsters—so civilized they don't need to be brave. They find primitives who'll take risks for them."

"You saved a bird?" I asked, embarrassed that I'd failed to get Mica back.

"We sent out prayer rockets to impress service classes, who had no idea our technological people weren't magicians. A bird crew brought one of our prayer rockets back to us."

"I thought they were only supposed to approach new species who had gate capacity," I said.

"We knew no space tricks," she said. "The bird . . . I ran away with it. I killed for it. I didn't think they were demons or gods; *I* understood that. I can't make . . . even you, refugee. You speak this vicious code better than I."

The house had a video room, with a flat-screen TV and a round plastic holograms tank, except that someone had scratched it and the images wobbled.

One day, in the video room, Calcite asked, with sad boredom in her voice, "What do you look like, Red Clay?"

"Come on, Calcite," I said in equivalent Karst slang.

She grabbed for my white tunic top and pulled up. My armpits, all that hair, startled her. "We do not have such tufts of fur in our arm-body joints, freak."

I pulled the tunic back down, but she grabbed for the pants. "Yeah, and what do *you* look like?" I asked, wrestling with her.

"One who bears babies. Are you truly intact? A fertile male?" She pulled my lips back, touched my teeth. "Our intact males have bigger teeth there."

"Nobody's messed with my balls, but I wouldn't be fertile with you."

"I should get you some teeth, false ones, except I'd know. Big male teeth are so exciting." She quit trying to pull down my pants and began trembling. Her other language clouded her Karst again. "Let's kill and eat these *shchargree*."

"If I were back on my planet," I said, "I'd be just another ex-criminal. Aliens saved me from that."

"This language code en-stupids me inside my own head.

Do you know what happens if you refuse language operations?'' she asked.

"I wanted to be able to talk to them."

"I asked. If you can't speak Karst languages, these monsters don't consider you intelligent. My bird showed me those who refused, who couldn't learn. The non-Karst speakers are loose in fields, allowed to come into Karst City when they learn 'better habits' . . . Genetic samples. The Barcons manage their fertility."

She took my head in her hands and stared at my face. I saw a fine line of fuzz around the lips that angled down toward the chin, no dip under them, and the pupils were slightly oval, not round. I thought about horses with mule babies and pushed her away. She crumpled up, holding her knees against her little breasts, staring at the wall and shuddering.

"I can't adapt," she whispered.

After three months, the bears took us both back to the hospital for the computer implant operations. The other six were also back. Since the operation, they had learned about Karst and Karst I in species houses with their own kinds.

As I recovered from the terrible post-operative head- and earaches, I realized, hearing Gwyngs talk, that the machines that replaced our left temporal bones didn't translate Karst II directly into Karst I, but transformed the Karst II patterns into a whispery voice speaking sounds we had to learn to hang meaning on. Sometimes, the Gwyngs clicked their tongues—a moist clink sound—and turned on a computer function that made us see images in our minds' eyes.

Karst II speakers bothered Calcite. "I hate them, whole different mind fields," she said. "To make me hurt like this. The machine garbles more than the machine interprets."

"The one I wanted to talk to most is dead," I told her.

"Talking to monsters is stupid," she said.

Over the next couple of days, Calcite developed pneumonia but refused to rest. Instead, she paced the ward, stopping to stare at a mirror by the nurses' station, then looking back at us and shivering. All the other sapients seemed to expect that I'd know how to help.

"Aren't they both the same?" I heard someone whispering as I walked toward her. She stopped pacing and turned around to face me.

"Calcite," I began. Her mouth opened wide, impossibly wide, and she lunged teeth-first at me, almost a dive at my throat. *The mouth, so wide, teeth glittering.*

We ended up rolling around on the floor, me trying to grab her, push her away without hurting her. Finally, a Barcon got her by the back of the neck. She didn't kick or scream as they led her, glassy-eyed and rigid, to bed.

While the Barcons tended her, I heard one of those birds with hands lecture on the damn computers.

"Basically," he told us, "the computer transforms distinctive features since Karst II slices perception differently and uses echo-location mapping structure in communication."

Fucking unreal to hear this lecture with Calcite going nuts. I was surprised to find I thought that in English.

The bird spoke Karst I and Karst II, both accented since the birds couldn't take Barcon brain re-building. Lucky him, I thought. A Barcon handed the bird a note and he cut his lecture short and went to Calcite's room.

She was the only other refugee in the batch and, even knowing I shouldn't, I identified with her. "Can I come in?" I asked from just outside her door.

"Why not?" she said. "All the other monsters are here." Her face was mottled, propped up with pillows.

"I had no idea you'd take the cultural transition so hard," the bird said. "You seemed so bold."

"I'm a savage to you. Dumb," she told him.

The bird looked at me, feathers puffed up on its face. "Don't die. This male seems to be doing well. He'll miss you."

"He's another monster. None of you will miss me."

A Barcon reached for her with an injection machine. "Yes," she said, fending it off with her arms, "force me better and make me your pet. Red Clay, they'll do it to you, too. Refugee, stinking refugee."

The Barcon held her down for the injection, leaning against her. Calcite tried to bite him, unhinging her jaw like a snake. The Barcon flexed his nose as he backed off, the job finished, and said, "We medical people are never fully appreciated."

Calcite tried to scream as she slumped off to sleep.

One of the Barcons looked up at me, trembling by the door, and said, "Don't identify with *her*, refugee. Her kind eat each other."

Two Gwyngs, thin lips pooched out into oo's on their muzzles, scars around their nostril slits and eyes, came to see me in the hospital a few days later.

"Rhyodolite! Cadmium!" I recognized something about them even though I'd last seen them looking rather rattily human. Cadmium had yellow streaks throughout his sleek short body hair and on his head hair, even in the thicker fur over his eyes, a brown and yellow pied Gwyng.

Neither spoke English anymore.

"(In-two-rotations/days) you/refugee Red Clay with us leave (unless you/we make other choice)," Rhyodolite said, or at least my computer said for him in its whispery little voices.

Weird computer—it gave me sensations, complex modifications in ~~overlapping ghost voices and brain images~~, a visual of other humans, Asiatics maybe, and a certain sense of reservation on the Gwyng's part. *Boy,* I thought, *Gwyng intelligence sure is different from humans'*.

"I'm supposed to come with you and learn how to understand Karst II at Black Amber's?" I asked, wondering how the computers in *their* skulls would get what I said across.

They oo'ed again.

The day Rhyodolite came for me, Calcite screamed at all of us in her old language. When no one understood her, she, with her tiny body, shoved the tall black female. As a Barcon came toward her with a drug cube, she backed up and froze, trembling, against the dayroom wall.

"Red Clay," she screamed. I started toward her, but the face twisted, baring her teeth. A Barcon stopped me and swung me around to Rhyodolite.

"Red-Clay-with-social-problems," Rhyodolite said, rocking me side to side.

"I'm not like her. Not primitive," I said.

"Cute," Rhyodolite said as Barcons immobilized her under a net.

"She wasn't my species."

"Xenofreak. Not-you, on ship, you were nervous/maybe tired-silly." He looked at me and oo'ed. "Species difference/no problem for sexual stimulations."

"What happens to her now?" I asked.

A Barcon answered, "She wasn't fully sapient as she couldn't use all the grammatical structures. As you've had some space shock symptoms yourself, Red Clay, I recommend a mild tranquilizer. Rhyodolite, don't socially mob him Gwyng-style."

"We are not socially obsessive and you (anti-social, isolated) should(not) talk/gossip," Rhyodolite said.

"Don't shit in my ear, Gwyng," the Barcon replied.

Gwyngs. Tropical islanders with blood-pump tongues, they lived by the ocean. As we drove up, I recognized the houses from space station holos—walls of planks woven together like baskets—but nobody there had told me those were Gwyng houses. Behind the houses, animals grazed. *It will at least be calmer here,* I thought.

Inside Black Amber's house, Gwyngs, elbow to elbow, lay around on foam mats covered with squishy fake hide. Or they squirmed into tube sofas, two or three together, koo'ing.

Little Gwyngs and the three Earth cats came and cuddled up to me. And I was eager, with my touch-crazy ape hands, to stroke them—the familiar cat fur, the strange feel of the Gwyngs' smooth stiff hair and thick skin.

"Black Amber's busy (in her room) with dispatch box (today's)," Rhyodolite said, "but when she finishes/stops, she'll ask to see you."

The Gwyng adults hanging around the house memorized my features, then went on squirming together, chatting in Gwyng languages my computer couldn't transform. Finally, just as I was about to ask Rhyodolite if he'd show me the beach, Black Amber came out and said, "We have no fixed mealtimes, so your food is in our food storage room for your self-service. Red Clay, not much personal time (don't care to give any)."

At least, that was what the computer gave me.

Black Amber, a major Gwyng official, fussed with visitors and dispatch boxes all day every day. Periodically a bell rang and she went into a private office, built of metal and plastic and set in the house like a giant safe.

Most mornings, some Gwyng kids and I walked on the beach, followed by the pouch-host animals—motley creatures like cows crossed with rhinos, or long-legged hippos with Holstein skins. Gwyng kids clambered over them, sliding into the pouches if they were small enough.

The bloodstock animals, varicosities dangling like ropes under their neck and shoulder skins, stayed more aloof. Some of these were milked like cattle, besides being blood sources. I helped the Gwyng kids with the milking machines and the electric blood drainers—nothing primitive about that.

And in the strange basket-woven houses, with floors that bounced gently underfoot, I saw screens that played odd fast-shifting patterns.

"Black Amber, your TV set seems to be broken."

"Not vision electric pattern, but/more pattern of understanding," she said. "News language." She looked up at the screen. "Gossip/social babble."

"You can read that?" I asked.

"Even (I personally/not all Gwyngs) holograms/light interference patterns."

She stared at me—what, I wondered, did she see? There was a sparkling distance about her, the scars and the glossy dark fur with reddish undertones. "What-do-you know about savage female-placental (who xenofreaked)?" she asked. Her hot thin finger dropped on my wrist, right on the pulse.

"Her people sent ships up, to manipulate their lower classes."

"Farce to attempt/force contact with species-without–space drives. But perhaps/because since I am (just) an Under-Rector, the bird sneak-changes policy."

"*What* happened to Calcite?" I asked. "If Calcite's caught in some Karst infighting . . ."

"Hush." Black Amber took her finger off my pulse. "Skull computer gives depth/complexity from your speech. Better than your Ang'ish. Emotions complex."

Then she scooped up an Earth cat, who'd purr for whatever scratched behind its ears.

Black Amber refused to sponsor me at the Academy, so I waited for another sponsor. Tesseract visited occasionally, to teach me proper English and speak Karst I with me. "Some days," I said in English, hearing that my voice tones weren't quite human now, "I think I'm just a live souvenir you picked up off the Blue Ridge."

"You can't go back."

"What about Calcite?"

"We might send her back. Her people aren't as sophisticated as yours. The whole incident would fade into myth."

"They'll kill her," I said.

"She's not fully sapient."

"Being murdered would hurt her just the same. Didn't you test her before you brought her to Karst?"

"The bird was desperate."

She was right, I thought. They liked refugees because our stunts indicated we'd keep stunting on, brave little half-sapients, saving them. "So she dies."

"*Tom* Red Clay, she isn't dead, just out of the Academy. We might find a primitive species to put her with."

When he left, I stripped to shorts and went down to the beach.

Karst's beach soothed me. Funny, because I'd never been to any ocean on Earth, but this alien water sent me noisy waves full of shells not much different from ones I'd seen at school. Beaches and waves had to be alike on all planets—sand, waves and wind, shells. A row of white bird-things flew by, flying the same as birds. I sat down in the swash where the waves slid back, searching for shells that looked most like Earth ones.

Rhyodolite came down after me—I suppose Tesseract told him I'd been worried about Calcite.

"Shells," I said, "the same as Earth's."

"Growth by mathematical series," Rhyodolite said, dropping down in the wet sand beside me. After we'd watched the waves a bit, he asked, "You miss/yearn sexually for the Calcite (a bit animal)?"

"Not really sexually, but she isn't an animal, you know." I shuffled through a heap of small shells looking for spiraled ones.

"Don't identify with her. We might misjudge you." He looked over at me, face wrinkles in deep shadow from the sun, nostrils faintly quivering as he breathed in and out.

Somehow he'd gotten sand on his little chin. "I have been forced (mildly) to be a sneak-sex-getter," he told me earnestly, maybe testing me, trying to get me to reject him. "I am small for a Gwyng. On your planet, Black Amber took sex-period suppressants, not me. One year. Then she was shot. Barcons and Cadmium came. No chance after Cadmium."

"Isn't she like your mother or sister?"

"No. I was given to her as nymph. Hard loss to have a small body. Larger the Gwyng female/more social power. Small males play forever."

"Oh." I didn't know about this confession. He was about five-two, Earth measure. But he was wiry—worked out with weights, ran, swam, played a weird ball game. I was lonely for ball games. "Could you teach me hazzard?"

He didn't answer me as he paced a bit on the beach, body rocking over his short legs. Then he looked at the surf before sitting down beside me again. "Xenofreaked placental female Calcite is not xenofreaking now (more or less)." His thin fingers rambled through the sand, pounced on a tiny clam, split the two shells. After eating the clam, Rhyodolite asked, "You interested (in *any* way)?"

"She doesn't make me feel less lonely."

"Introducing to own species coming," he said, seemingly satisfied. "Black Amber has arranged."

Whatever he was, flanked by Barcons, sitting with raised shoulders in coarse brown wool robes, he wasn't American. I hoped he really wasn't another human, but I knew he was, maybe by smell, body posture. His sweating face looked almost like an American Indian's. Stocky, Asian? His hair was bound up in cloth-covered cords.

Black Amber looked from me to him, her lips loose, then pursed forward.

"You're 100 percent congruent in proteins and DNA, RNA," one of the Barcons said, "so you both are the same species. Red Clay, if you can't stand the Academy, we'll give you tools so you can try to make a place for yourself in their society. We thought we'd introduce you now."

The human stared at me as if Karst I were gibberish. "Own kind," the Barcon said to him. "Fresh family. Breeding permit."

"No," he said firmly in hideously accented Karst I.

"Yes," the Barcon said. They weren't arguing about the same thing, I thought.

The man stared around the room, at the lights even, as though he'd heard about places like this. *Yeah, and it's just as bad as he'd thought.* "We sell to *Bon*, won't take spy-*Bon* in. Want women for him, don't you?"

"*Bon* is root from their language for demon," one of the Barcons told me.

I felt my face go hot. "Look, I want Academy training, not to get cut loose into some primitive tribe."

The human stared at me. "We are not primitives. We are the only true beings here."

"Sounds *just* like your people," Black Amber said. She oo'ed, almost koo'ed, but pressed her thumb against her chin lump and spread the other fingers over her muzzle, her eyes sparkling maliciously. He stared at her, not comprehending, but perhaps picking up on the mocking tone. She buzzed a little picture of me in his clothes into my brain.

"I won't go," I said.

"No, but some contact might be more comfortable for you," one of the Barcons said.

"I'm not that," I said. "Even if he is *human.*"

The man smiled a nasty smile, eyes very narrow, then he pulled back against the sofa, as if waiting for these creatures to turn him loose.

"Perhaps," a Barcon said, "moving males from social group to social group is difficult. Maybe easier to move females."

"*My* daughters are not for sale," the man said.

"There are others in the west side of Karst City," one of the Barcons replied.

I asked, "When did they come here, anyway?"

"About five hundred average planet cycles ago. They need fresh DNA," the other Barcon said.

"Demon, take me away from this," the man said, standing up, arms bent slightly at the elbows, knees flexed, ready to die if need be to get out of this room.

"We can bribe some of them to take you, if you don't prove capable of Academy work," the biggest Barcon assured me as they led him out. "They're poor enough."

* * *

I felt bad enough before Rhyodolite brought Calcite, dressed in brown, to Black Amber's house. Brown, I figured, was a non-status color here—the Oriental and she both wore it.

"Oh, I think I remember you," she said. "Weren't you kind once?" Empty eyes, no *Calcite* there. Filed-down teeth gleamed when she smiled. A face shifts when memories go. *Like a zombie*, I thought, unable to speak to this body before me, a corpse tricked into living. She looked hurt that I wasn't answering her. Mind-wipe *was* getting clubbed dead from inside the brain, and I was glad my brother was safely crazy in the Veterans Hospital.

Rhyodolite took her hand and led his pretty little zombie inside. Blood rushed to my cock and head and I felt absolutely dizzy.

"Don't do that to her, *man*," I yelled at him.

He flexed his hand almost into a fist, a Gwyng gesture like our middle finger.

Black Amber didn't like the girl being there either. The Gwyngs screamed at each other in languages my computer transformed into squalls I couldn't put meaning to—other than the obvious sense, the quarrel.

I liked Black Amber better for yelling at him, and even better for sending Calcite away.

Rhyodolite didn't walk with me on the beach that day. When I came back, he was down on the floor, other Gwyngs nipping at his armpit webs.

"*Serves you right, you son of a bitch*," I said in English.

He was too socially mobbable by other Gwyngs to stay angry long with aliens who didn't tease-nip him. The next day, he sat down beside me on the beach and said, "Do you understand/accept?"

"No," I said. "You're a loser among your own kind, aren't you?" We sat in the sand digging up little clams no bigger than my thumb joint to eat raw there on the suddenly chilly beach. "You people plan to rip my brains out, too? I'm just a junk kid myself. Waiting. Waiting."

"You don't eat your own kind, do you?"

"She was a *cannibal*, wasn't she? Well, she was better off . . ."

"No. Reason (by her example) why we must avoid primitive planets. Too much shock, to them."

"What about me?"

"Want to prove yourself?"

"Sure."

"I am going to/want to return to active duty almost immediately-to-soon. You want to space-hop (punning image) with me, pre-cadet? I am capable (financially and in terms of authority) of sponsoring pre-cadet (for later cut in planet trade shares)."

"Who do I have to ask?"

"Black Amber and the Rector's Man. Better/tentatively superior than you being bored/lonely here (when I leave anyway). Cadmium would come with me, but he's training."

"And?"

"They've assigned me to train a bird cadet. Better to have you to keep him away from me." He paused and got up off the sand, dusting it out of his fur the best he could. Then he hunched slightly and said, "Don't remind Black Amber (semi-dangerous to you now) of Mica."

"I remind her of Mica every time she sees me."

"Perspective problem/locked pattern sight. Out of vision, then pattern can shift. She may accept you as her cadet finally."

"*Oh.*"

"Red Clay makes noise indicating perception?" Rhyodolite koo-chuckled. Then he leaned over in the surf to take a drink, knuckles down, knees bent, the muscle hump where his jaw met his throat bouncing up and down. In his left vestigial web, I saw a faint crescent of bruises where the crepe-like skin running from his shoulder blade joined his upper arm.

I touched the bruises and asked, "Calcite?"

He flinched. *Hurrah for her, nailed him despite brain-wipe and all.*

= 4 =

Xenophobia Variations

Courteous and grave, the bird folded scaly forearms across his belly, and said, "I'm Xenon 7." The bills, like stiff lips, immobilized his face—no facial expressions. When he unfolded his arms, his black cadet's uniform slid awkwardly off his olive shoulder feathers.

Avoiding the creature's brown eyes, Rhyodolite shuddered slightly and said, "Tom, put his bag up."

Xenon's hand was soft as a human's, softer, I noticed, when he passed his bag to me. I stowed food cases and clothes bags, then we sat inside the ship while the ground crew loaded it on a net for gating.

Those trips I was the junior flunky: twist that dial, mix Rhyo's space food formula, develop this chip fast—the computer's flinked, and flinked computers kill. In the monotonous cargo stations, each lit the same, each heated or cooled to the same temperature all over the Federation, the bird cadet stuck close to us, nervously.

But Rhyo was edgy as though neither of us were a good shipmate. He'd brought a kitten along to sleep with, but some sleep periods, the black kitten would ignore Rhyodolite and play with the bird's feathers, thin and long like cock hackle all over. "Tom," Rhyodolite would ask, "catch it for me so I can sleep." The bird would lean back, sighing, from the cat, no expression on its beaked face.

One stop before Carg, a newly contacted bird world, Rhyo got wonked on drugs, and alternately giggled at us and wept until we reached Carg Station.

We took on new cadet candidates there, nine birds, bigger than Xenon. They goggled at our bird, Rhyodolite, and me as though we were all equally strange.

Aloof in his operator's chair, Rhyodolite watched them through a drugged haze, but one came up to him on backward-bent legs, feathers puffed slightly, head weaving from side to side. "Need (we all) Karst practice," it said, in slow and roughly aspirated Karst II. "We must memorize sounds/sonic maps/drawings since mammal doctors can't/won't work skull computers and learning drugs for us."

Rhyodolite hit all the gates fast and dropped into pre-landing orbit, hardly giving us time to strap down for re-entry. After Rhyodolite landed and shut down the ship, all the birds, including Xenon, climbed unsteadily down the ladder. Slumped in his chair, Rhyodolite flexed his nostril slits, staring out a viewport. Representatives of the two other Federation bird species helped the new cadets onto buses. "Xenophobe, yourself," I said.

"Things like those used to eat (and may not have stopped) little (image of a bat walking upright, wings spread for balance). Like crawling-rib (snake image) for you?"

"I don't hate *snakes*, crawling-rib creatures."

"No lethal intentions toward birds (from us). Just armskin/flight nerves/web muscle jumps."

"The Rector's a bird. Does this complicate the tension between him and Black Amber?"

As the last pre-cadet who'd flown with us hopped up the bus steps, Rhyodolite said, "The Rector is my nightmare. Bird-possessed poor me."

"Black Amber?"

"Hush/stop prying."

After reporting in, Rhyo and I took a black bus, with a Gwyng squiggle on it, back to Black Amber's.

The next morning, I tried to explain Frisbees. Odd, to be lonely for Frisbees, I thought as Rhyo lathed down some plastic the way I'd described.

On the beach, I tossed it to Rhyodolite. Rhyo koo'ed hysterically as he caught it backhand, then threw it up over my head on a great boomeranging loop. I turned and caught it, then saw Black Amber coming.

Brooding in gold and green Under-Rector's clothes, she

trudged through the sand, dark eyes on the Frisbee. Then she said, "Rhyodolite, first contact mission. Come (abruptly/now) talk (with me)."

"You (Red Clay and Xenon) can't come on this," Rhyodolite said. "Dangerous."

After Rhyo left, Black Amber slept with cats, went into Karst City on business, and avoided me. Tesseract came four times to improve my English, bringing books so technical I knew only in Karst how to explain the diagrams. And I preferred to talk in Karst. English made me homesick.

"Interesting book here, Tom. An American astrophysicist's theorized a space gate. His aliens—holy from space again! But your people are thinking."

"I miss Rhyodolite," I told Tesseract. "But he's not much of an officer, is he?"

"He does better with mammals than birds."

Two weeks later, Rhyodolite opened the veranda door and said, "It was horrid." Black Amber slingshotted herself out of a padded tube with both hands, koo'ing, weaving her body back and forth as soon as she stood up.

Rhyodolite stumbled to her. She tucked him up against her side and brushed her muzzle along his lip corners and eyelids. Twined together, they talked in a Gwyng language my computer couldn't slice right. She led him to a pile of floor cushions and both, trembling, sank into them.

"Are you tired?" I asked him.

"Dead-body-eating-ape question. If the gravity well/trap we'd set hadn't been there, they would have gated into their sun. Now most upset to find they must share the universe. Xenophobes like you."

"I'm not such a xenophobe," I said.

Black Amber cradled him and nibbled his hands, then said, "Federation needs drug traps/automatic sedation of ships caught in the gate nets." She nodded to the air as she spoke, a long big campaign of the Under-Rector's—avoid or drug primitive stupids.

I slunk off to bed, a refugee.

The next morning, while Rhyodolite and Black Amber slept with cats and baby Gwyngs, I answered their phone. A deep voice asked, in rough Karst II, to speak to Black

Amber. When I said she was asleep, the voice switched to Karst I and said, "Tell her it's Karriaagzh."

The bird. "Certainly," I said. I went into the Gwyng sleeping room, touched Amber gently, and said, "The Rector's on the phone."

She stretched and froze, then slid herself free of the Gwyngs' tangled limbs, wrapped cloth around her pouch and genital slits, then came out.

Nodding slightly, she listened to the Rector, then hung up with a deep head bob. "The Rector will come (self-invited) to the house soon," she told me. Then she nibbled her palms and went back to the sleeping room.

About an hour later, when a medium-sized grey electric car pulled up, Black Amber, in a pink shift that bared her webs, came out to the steps. Shouldn't she wear her uniform? I wondered. The web veins were distended, and the air smelled of alcohol. I looked closer and saw that her webs were damp, as though she'd tried to cool them off.

Without help from his driver, the Rector unfolded himself from the seatless back of the car—huge bird, moving slowly. He cocked his head sideways at Amber and bent his hocks. If he'd stood erect, he'd have been at least eight feet tall.

Black Amber, blocking my way, stood on the stairs so she could look down at him. One leg dabbed out toward him, twisting, as though she was fending him off. Are they going to attack each other? I wondered.

"Rector Karring'cha, we mistook/misunderstood (due to family preoccupations) when you were coming (deny evasion). Would you (female talking to male) come in and (hide your feathers) discuss (paying attention to *me*) the problems we've had with first contacts? Last mission badly handled."

No expression on the bird face—bony ridges shaded his yellow eyes. The arms twitched, though—arms longer than most aliens', then grey crest feathers ruffled and rose as he listened. *She's insulted the hell out of him.*

He was scary, huge, impassive, grey feathers clamped tight to his body. I kept looking at him—feathers covered the blade-shaped upper arms but tapered off to scales on his lower arms and to yellow skin on his hands and fingers. He smoothed his thigh feathers and shuffled his strange shoes.

Those yellow eyes found me sitting by a piling. I ducked

my head a bit, then flushed that he might think I'd nodded hostilely. Karriaagzh slowly blinked at me before looking back up at Amber. "Black Amber," he said in Karst II, "my respect for you/r opinions, but life and space (both) have risks. If you(r species) wishes to avoid first contacts, I will most eagerly assign you (and every Gwyng) to safer duties."

Black Amber kicked the air. She jerked her foot back and shifted her weight onto it, but the foot still twitched. "We do not leave our own to die in space or on primitive planets. Federation policy/rule centuries before we landed you/refugee, bird Rector."

The Rector looked at me again and twitched his beak sideways, as though preening the air, then cocked his head, not looking back at Amber, his gaze drifting away from both of us.

"My apologies, Rector," Black Amber finally said. Her fists clenched.

The Rector looked at the fists, then locked eyes with Black Amber. She trembled; he raised his crest high.

Then the giant bird sighed as though he should have given up on this bitch long ago, lowered his crest, and got back in his car.

After the car pulled out of sight, Black Amber smeared fist gland secretions furiously on the stairs and railing. I wondered if she hated being afraid of him.

Rhyodolite slept through the Rector and Black Amber's meeting. His superior officer called him that afternoon with Karriaagzh's side of the conversation. Rhyo jerked the phone away from his ear, bobbed his head at the earpiece several times, then pulled the receiver close, screaming, "No one, not *any* sapient *ever* accused Gwyngs of cowardice," and hung up.

"That's too much," he said to me. He walked—almost lurching—down the stairs and wiped his fists over and over where Black Amber'd left her own anger secretions earlier.

Gwyng kids started using the side and back stairs. The other Gwyngs up and down the beach stopped visiting until the smell faded three days later.

Relentlessly, Black Amber had Tesseract train me in proper

English. Yet she refused to be my sponsor, or help me find one.

I begged Rhyodolite to take me away on his next mission, dangerous or not, just to get away from the house. For about eight days, no flights, nothing. Then the Academy had just the flight.

Three years earlier, a search ship picked up a probe coming through recently gate-charted space near a planet-orbited sun. Karst traced the orbit back to the fifth planet.

Now the observation team, which had been watching the system since the probe was discovered, spotted nuclear launches from high planet orbits. One was in a trajectory that would take it out of its solar system altogether.

Rhyodolite, myself, and the bird cadet, Xenon, could volunteer to pick up that probe.

Rhyodolite said, "Lots of ambiguities about that assignment. Sure you want to go?"

"Of course." I wasn't going to be more chicken than a Gwyng.

"With that web-shuddering bird again," Rhyodolite said. He sucked his hands and explained, "We're going into *their* solar system. Our gate capacity should/may be able to outmaneuver them, but it's their system."

When we arrived at the ship, Xenon stood stiffly by its bags as though waiting for a reprimand, the breeze ruffling those long olive hackles.

"I-could-tell-you-were-sober-and-reliable and other lies of the Galaxy," Rhyodolite muttered under his twitching nostrils as he swung himself through a hatch. He lowered a gangway, and we came on with the baggage. The ground crew loaded the whole ship into a huge transport globe, called a cargo belly.

The cargo belly dropped us at the alien planet's observation station.

For the first time, I wore a space suit and floated around in the sky, tethered, while I helped string up gate/gravity cables.

No up. No down. To give myself some arbitrary point of reference, I decided down was Rhyo's little triple ship.

When I re-entered the ship, Rhyo was sitting in a chair, Xenon hunched down on its hocks beside him, both computing the geometry for a jump near a gas-giant planet where we'd intercept the satellite. Xenon would lean forward to explain calculations, and Rhyo'd shove the computer board at him. A little almost-dance with them.

As the station crew positioned our ship on a net, Xenon got the computer ready to generate a shipboard field to catch us while Rhyodolite looked at me and squeezed his nostrils shut.

We popped back into space/time in the right orbit and Rhyodolite and Xenon congratulated each other.

Suddenly, the artificial gravity went out. Making incomprehensible Gwyng noises, Rhyo shoved toward the radar controls as Xenon and I shot up, startled muscles pushing us off the floor.

"No, no, no," Rhyodolite said as the radar screen went crazy from interference—radar bouncing from a wall surrounding us was impossible.

"Open the port," Xenon said, its legs flexing in the air as though it was trying to get its balance, scaly fingers gripping a handhold.

Rhyodolite opened the port, but looked at us. Xenon and I looked. We were surrounded by huge ships, whose people knew about gravity nets, because we were floating between two of them.

Rhyodolite finally glanced out, pulled his nostrils open and shut a few times, and hauled himself to his seat. "Not (definitely not) supposed to be a first contact mission," he said as he wiggled into the chair and pulled a lap strap tight. Then he looked at us bleakly and said, "Prepare to be boarded. Not completely lost until we die."

"What do you do to prepare to be boarded?" Xenon asked, legs flexing faster, as though it was running in air, feathers bouncing up and down.

"No muscle moves, no words. Strictly psychological preparation (due to ridiculous policy)." Then he said, almost to himself, "No checks for lumpy gravity and active gate interconnections anymore?" His fists almost clenched and he said something in another Gwyng language, its analog hissing in my computer.

"Were we set up? To force a contact?" I asked.

"I don't know (who . . .)." Stabbing a glance at Xenon, Rhyo continued, "If these trap-setters are not birds, spread arms loosely from sides. This is rumored (no bets) not to be any mammal's attack gesture.'' He reached for the radio and said into it, ''Immediate danger of being boarded. Need higher mass to get us out of their gravity trap. Seven hundred thousand mass measure should do it.''

Xenon, beak gaping, took in a hissing breath. Our ship lurched sideways, and Rhyodolite and I gasped, too.

''Can't we talk to them?'' Xenon said.

''Say in what? We don't know (but who'd tell a Gwyng these days) what system they (animal/non-sapient) have for radio/video?''

''Só?'' I asked, asshole puckered, biting my shorts. ''So?'' I suddenly realized I was almost hysterical.

''We go back (hypothetical) and ask for better research.'' Rhyo's fists were spasming curiously. He finally nibbled at the anger juice, his arms lifting out from his sides, the web veins pulsing. ''Bird hideous, couldn't take Amber's complaints.''

Two space-suited figures floated toward us and looked in our ports. Suddenly, we got lots of gravity. *Wham*, the bird and I hit the floor. Rhyo sagged in his chair. The bird whimpered, an odd sound coming from something that large.

While we lay pinned, we heard aliens fussing around our airlock. The gravity eased up, so Rhyo reached for the control panel and cycled the lock, muttering, ''Xenophobes, come in. Come on. We'll be nice prisoners.''

The two figures outside the viewport continued to watch us.

''Rhyodolite, I certainly hope they use the same air as we do.''

''Red-Clay-covered-with-aliens, if not, they'll kill us because we tried to poison them.''

''They use the same air,'' Xenon said.

''You know? We get odd people/creatures in our forces these days,'' Rhyo said, opening the inner door.

Five heavily armed space-suited figures swarmed in. I felt naked beside them. This has to be a test, I thought numbly. *I wasn't trained for this*.

Hackles erect on its neck, Xenon shrieked. Two aliens went to the floor, prone, guns aimed. The three others slowly knelt. The bird half danced back a step. The central kneeler fired.

As blood and stuff splattered me, I flinched. Rhyo, still strapped in his chair, said, "Your kind of ape."

I looked at the guns aimed at me, faces shadows behind the helmet glass.

More aliens, in uniforms, not in space suits, came in. They were horrible caricatures of human beings: eyes rounder than mine and blob noses. Curved jawbones left no point to the chin. They had darker skin than mine, coarse straight hair on their heads, but hairless faces, except for eyebrows and eyelashes. Their joints bent funny.

Rhyo spread his arms, web veins pulsing, and said, "Impossible. I'll wait." He gasped a few times, then slumped. Like Mica, playing possum, I thought. *But they'll think he's dead.*

A sweating alien approached me. I spread my arms out a bit and went rigid, seeing Xenon's corpse sprawled out on the floor. Two aliens held guns on me while the sweating alien stripped me, even took off my wrist tag.

Leaving me naked and quivering, the aliens carefully unstrapped Rhyo. He slid to the floor. They laid him out and looked at me. I started crying, tried to stop.

A medical character came in to take Rhyo's blood pressure and check his heart. Having obviously caught one beat where he expected ten to twenty, the alien leaned back on his heels, looked at me, and pointed from Rhyo to Xenon's body. I thought the alien was asking if Rhyodolite was dying, dead. I pointed from Rhyodolite to me, meaning, *no, alive.*

The medic broke a glass ampule under Rhyodolite's nose, but Rhyodolite wasn't coming around.

The aliens also checked Xenon, but he'd been very dead from the first. They went through the ship, looking at me from time to time, seemingly a bit more embarrassed with each weaponless locker they checked.

My kind of ape. I was freezing, utterly naked.

Finally, one of them came up to me and spoke a couple different languages at me. I said, in Karst, "We only came to see about the satellite we thought you launched to go out beyond your solar system."

The alien pointed at the computer and said, "Fluist?"

"*Computer,*" I responded in English. This language thing hadn't worked with Mica, but if they had Karst I–type minds, we might be able to understand each other. I'd teach them English—didn't want them badassing around space luring other Karst speakers into traps.

"Kampootir. Fluist."

They seemed to be understanding. Okay. I stood trembling as they wrapped cloth around my waist and loaded me down with chains. "Fluist?" I said as they cut the computer out of the ship with torches and whirring metal saws.

"Fluu-ist."

"Fluu-ist," I repeated again.

"Hum."

"Tom," I said, wiggling a finger at myself. "Tom." *You guys don't know how bad it can get if we can't communicate.*

"Tom," the alien who'd stripped me said, then pointing to himself and all the others, "Yauntry."

"Yantry?" I tried.

"Yauntry."

"Yauntry."

"Hum," went the Yauntry.

I wasn't sure if *Yauntry* was nation, species, or squad name. Abstractions get you into trouble.

What ugly assholes, I thought, trying to blind myself with fury, as they led me into their ship and put me into a cell after taking off the chains. No windows, unpainted metal walls, one light bulb on all the time under a wire grid. I got furious, which abruptly switched to fear. *Jail again and nobody to talk to.* I had to shit, from terror. There was a bucket in the cell for wastes.

After the ship moved around, gas hisses and all, two guards came in, grabbed and re-chained me, fixing my hands so I couldn't raise them above my waist. They stood back and a grey-suited guy came in with a glass of water. I moved toward him to take it, but he pulled back and said, "Huh-na."

I waited. "Hum," he said, putting the glass up to my right hand and watching me bend my head down to my chained hands, contorting for a drink. I wondered why the fuck didn't he hold the glass for me if they wanted me chained.

He did take the glass then, and held it while I sipped, and finally put a hand on my shoulder to steady me.

"Gwyng hum?" I hoped rising tones implied a question. He asked one of the guards for something, got a metal tag that unlocked my hands. Then he handed me a drawing pad with a felt-tip sort of marker, too blunt to stab with.

Like with Alpha/Mica, I thought. Suddenly very afraid, I drew Rhyodolite. I pointed to myself and said, "Tom, alive. Yauntry alive." Then I touched him slowly and said, "You alive."

He flinched. The guards stirred.

"Huh-na," I said, waving my hands, then I drew the dead bird, saying, "Bird dead." I pointed back to the drawing of Rhyodolite and looked the Yauntry official in the eyes.

He pulled out a pocket recorder and played a tape of all the things I'd said when they first trapped us. After looking at me for a long moment, the alien said, "Ging alif-dad. Tom?"

I looked up at him. He pointed to himself and said, "Edwir Hargun." Sounded almost human. Xenophobes, too. My kind of ape.

He unchained me and shut the cell door. Through the walls, I felt the ship twitch as it accelerated.

For two days the aliens fed me rations from our ship: mine, Rhyo's, the bird's, and changed the waste bucket, but left me otherwise alone. I spent those days trying not to go mad. Terrible questions rose in my mind: *Was I working for the good guys or interplanetary thugs? Had we been set up?*

The ship twitched again as it began to brake. On the bunk, I gripped the mattress edges until we were down.

Three aliens put leg irons and a waist chain with manacles on me. As I went out, blinking into their nasty sun, I saw Rhyodolite lying naked and chained on a stretcher. *Think hillbilly,* I thought, *think survival.*

Black Amber is right. We must be more careful.

Then an alien covered Rhyodolite up to the chin with a blanket and felt his wrinkled little face.

Others draped my handcuffs with towels as they jabbered to each other, then one bent and took off the leg irons. "Thanks," I said. He looked at me, then at the others, and shrugged.

As I walked where I was led, camera lenses glittered in the alien air. I could imagine the headlines, "Alien Invaders Captured."

Edwir Hargun offered me food while the soldiers tried to sneak my handcuffs off so the cameras couldn't catch them.

The food looked like cheese. I kept my face still and reached, slowly, for it. Camera aliens crawled around, butted into each other, lifted lens machines high in the air. Hargun tightened his lips; it seemed a smile to me.

Another headline came to mind: "Wild Space Beast Fed by Local Dignitary." He watched while I tasted the curd stuff, feeling blood rush up under my beard stubble.

"Tom," he said. I looked at him.

The press aliens went absolutely flat-out wild, and the guards tried to chain my hands again, but I said "huh-na" and hung on to my cheese. A curve-jawed devil stuck a microphone in my face, holding his body as far away as possible.

Speaking in respectfully toned Karst, I said, "You are a stupid bunch of shitheads, shooting down an innocent diplomatic ship that picked up your cannibalistic fucking decoy satellite. Rhyodolite should piss in your cheese."

Aliens with microphones asked gibberish questions, but I just said "huh-na," like no comment, and started crying. *If Rhyo dies . . . ,* I kept thinking, imagining Black Amber's face, needle teeth bared. *Someone set us up, because she was nasty to the Rector.*

Edwir Hargun watched me so closely I wanted to hide. When the guards chained me again and hustled me into the back of an armored vehicle, he sat just in front of the steel mesh and stared at me.

What shits, I thought, trying to prop up anger against rolling panic, but then I raised my eyes to that weird alien face, round green eyes and round jaw, an otherwise almost Oriental head. Short blobby nose. Edwir Hargun flinched back as though I was coming at him through the mesh.

No beard, although he had wrinkles around the eyes enough to look to be about forty. And the head hair didn't look cut. And his jaw was wrong, damn wrong.

We pulled down a car tunnel. Hargun watched as the troops unloaded me, then disappeared down one corridor as I was led, again, to another cell. Jail, forever, whether I was on Earth or among aliens.

Panic, no point to panic. If I pulled my hands down against the waist chain, I didn't shake. *Horribly embarrassing panic.* Shoving my hands down, I grew light-headed and stayed on the verge of fainting for what seemed hours, in a cell with neither windows nor bars, just dull grey concrete walls lit by lights shielded by milky plastic.

The floor had a smelly slit in one corner—the toilet. I hobbled to it and managed to get the cloth they diapered me with away enough.

Finally, Edwir Hargun and several guards brought in parts of the computer and navigation instruments, still showing the digits from the satellite trajectory calculations. "Computer?" he said, pointing to it. Then he held up another instrument— the space-holes topology generator. I didn't know what to call it in English, even though I knew in Karst.

Then he noticed that all I had on was their stupid loincloth, and sent me out with two guards to shower. As I stepped out, they handed me a pair of my pants and a towel.

"Thanks," I said.

Hargun said, "T'nks," and led me to an office with a table. Still no windows.

An alien guard brought food while Hargun drew a grid of blocks, eight across, eight down. He drew three little squares above the grid and put a single figure beside them, then drew nine squares and put down two digits. Then he passed me the pad.

Base eight, I realized. They never learned to count with their thumbs. I began sketching for dear life and Rhyodolite. These creeps couldn't push us around; we represented over a hundred planets. Ten squared, ten down, ten across.

The pencil tip broke, flew off the pad. One of the guards started as though I'd tried to assassinate Hargun with a pencil tip, but Hargun said something and put his hand on my shoulder. *Steady, boy.* But his fingers squirmed to be actually touching this thing that I was.

I jerked my shoulder. Hargun leaned back and beckoned for another pencil. *Jesus, Tom,* I thought to myself in English, *maybe he's trying to be nice.*

After I wiped the sweat off my hands, I roughed out schematics of a sun and planets, then pointed from the schematic to the blocks of ten down, ten across. *A hundred systems, don't you understand?*

My hand was hot and cramped from the fierce drawing I'd just done so I swung my fingers to cool them. My eyes started tearing up again. Hargun smiled stiffly. "*Don't smile at me*," I said in English. He held out a packet of amino acids and minerals Rhyo had mixed with oil and water for space rations.

"Rhyodolite, hum," I said. "Tom, huh-na." I pantomimed water, pouring in the crystals, then said, "For Rhyodolite."

I gestured drawing and Hargun gave me the pad. My hand shaking, I drew a ship with bowl-jawed people on it, Yauntries, then different kinds of aliens greeting them. All the aliens smiled, whatever their real happy facial gestures. Hargun slowly reached for the drawings and left.

The guards brought in cloth tape and pantomimed that I should measure my legs, wrists, and waist, and mark each measure with chalk. I pantomimed bathing. "Hum, hum," one said as though I stunk. Other than my stubble, I got freshened up and dressed in clean alien clothes.

Then Hargun came back and led me to where they'd stashed Rhyodolite.

Cool, taking his occasional breath, Rhyodolite lay on a thin mattress—his arms chained. As Hargun and I stood over him, the guards brought in his uniform, ration packets, and water.

I touched the chains and said "huh-na" vigorously. One of the guards looked at Hargun, who must have signaled in some way, because the guard took off the cuffs. Rhyo's arms dropped stiffly back to the bed as though the juices in his joints had congealed.

The aliens backed off. Rhyodolite didn't move. Hargun said, "Tom, Rhyodolite, *weskiyo, hum,*" and gestured to wake him. *Weskiyo* must be "get him up" or "wake him," I decided.

If and when Rhyodolite woke up, I figured he'd want to get warm, so I got the drawing pad back and drew a pan of water over fire. Hargun said something to a guard, who brought back a two-inch-thick metal rectangle about eight inches square and a pan. Kneeling on the floor, I poured water into the pan. Hargun reached over my shoulder and pushed a green square on the metal rectangle. These people were more sophisticated than Earth people, I realized with some dread as the metal warmed up on top. "*Thanks,*" I said in English.

Hargun smiled. I smiled back and put the water on to heat. Then I rocked Rhyodolite gently from side to side without lifting him, calling his name. Hargun watched for a while, then motioned to the guards. When they moved in, I grabbed the mattress and said, "Huh-na, huh-na."

The guards stepped back and I drew a little picture of Rhyo under heavy covers. A guard sighed and went out for a blanket. Hargun pointed from the blanket to the hot plate.

Ah ha, an electric blanket. He wanted me to put it over Rhyo right away.

I found the pressure switch, thinking I could use their things even if they were more sophisticated than Earth stuff. *I bet these individuals didn't invent this either.* Before I put the blanket on Rhyodolite, I wanted to see how hot it'd get.

"*Go out,*" I said in English, waving them back with my palm. Edwir Hargun smiled and, after much alien jabber, the guards went out and watched us through an armored window in the door. Hargun put the palm of his hand toward me.

Play it by eye, I thought as I raised my own hand tentatively toward his. Our palms touched—the skin felt just like human skin. Hargun looked away from me at Rhyodolite, then back to me, staring at my face. Slowly, he raised his hand and touched my beard stubble. They don't grow beards, I realized.

Finally, Hargun left me with Rhyodolite. Metal bolts slid from door to doorframe while I sat by the unconscious Gwyng, talking softly to him in Karst I. I wanted his company so badly.

Finally, he shuddered and rolled to his side, shivering. I stood up to block the window in the door. One of his long-fingered hands flopped over the side of the mattress.

"Rhyodolite, I tried to tell them we're part of a hundred-planet federation and that we want to meet them. If you understand, move your little finger."

"Red-Clay-idiot," he mumbled. "Fingers cold/stiff."

"Rhyo, Rhyo." I sat down beside him. He turned his head, looked at me out of one big eye, then shuddered again. Floundering, he tried to sit up.

"We're still captives, aren't we?" he said as I propped him up against the wall. Hargun and the guards came in. "Yes, I can see," Rhyodolite said, then, "Red Clay, I need something hot." I mixed his ration mix with the water and brought it to him.

Rhyodolite sipped some, then diluted it. "Next time," he said harshly, "leave me asleep until the rescue team arrives. Where are we?"

"On their main planet, I think."

Another blue-suited alien joined the crowd standing around us, back at least three feet. Then he and Hargun stepped up to us, hands extended.

"What do they mean by that?" Rhyodolite said.

"Sort of like touching elbows," I said, "maybe. Hargun didn't act upset when I touched palms with him."

"Hurgoon, a name already. They *are* your kind." Rhyodolite oo'ed a bit and gave them ten like a black girl.

The alien officials looked a bit startled.

Rhyo slumped, breathing fast. "Hold me, Red Clay, but don't pin my arms down. Causes panic in situations like this."

I held him; he still quivered. "You're not warm enough," he complained.

"They brought an electrically heated blanket," I said, reaching slowly for it. *Lots of aliens subject to panic here, including me.*

"No, could be too hot."

"*Huh-na* is local for *no.*"

"*High-nu* blanket. You know I'll mess up their local if I try to speak it." He tried to sit up, still shaking. "More hot water."

After I poured it for him, the guards tried to move me out, but Rhyodolite fell back as if he was going to hibernate again. Hargun, looking very nervous, sent the guards and the other blue suit out. When the door closed, he stared at the window, then looked at us as if wondering what weird and unearthly attack we'd launch. I suddenly felt hurt that he didn't trust us more.

"You must have been his first alien," Rhyodolite said. He pursed his lips and watched Hargun through barely parted lashes as the second alien official returned with an organizational chart.

Hargun pointed from himself to the chart, from his companion to a niche above that, and finally from the window full of guards' eyes to a lower level. Then he pointed from me to the chart and circled various sections with his finger.

"Red-Clay-crawling-with-aliens, the asshole planet's mono-governmental, probably military,'' Rhyodolite said. "Some-one surely knew that. Military planets are . . .''

I could imagine. So I pointed from me to the same level Hargun indicated was his own, then from Rhyo to a higher level.

Rhyodolite's mouth got weirdly contracted and all his wrinkles got deeper. He drank more hot water, wrapped the electric blanket around his shoulder, played with the controls, and said, "Red-Clay-asshole, get me something to draw with.'' I gestured drawing to Hargun.

Eyes averted from the aliens, Rhyodolite took the pen and pad gently from Hargun and drew some fantastic high pyramid of an organizational chart, with the hundred planets, drawing it from the bottom, in full detail, like a TV scanning in a picture. Then he drew in a huge fleet of ships.

After he handed the drawing to Hargun, Rhyodolite lay back and tried to hide his mouth in the electric blanket. The second blue suit left with the drawing and Hargun leaned against the wall near the door and stared at us.

Rhyo bit the mattress, then turned over and spread his arms, koo'ing. Hargun jumped for the door. Rhyodolite saw him and shuddered. Slowly, Rhyo got up and pissed his thick stuff down the corner slit, then he climbed back on the mattress, pulled the electric blanket around himself, and went to sleep. Both Hargun and I checked his pulse and watched his breathing. Just asleep.

The guards came back in and escorted me out.

Back in my cell, bolts still went into the lock sockets. An hour or so later, the guards wound the bolts back and brought more food from the ship, mine and the bird's. I shuddered, remembering the bird's blood and guts hanging out, and set that food aside.

Edwir Hargun also brought in other things from the ship and asked me my words for them. I picked up my electric shaver and turned it on. Hargun called for the guards while I began shaving my stubble. They realized I wasn't hurting anyone and watched.

After I finished, Hargun touched my chin, feeling for the jawbones, and slowly reached for the razor, took it back, and quickly handed it to the guards.

They didn't let me too close to the rest of the gear after

that, but morning and night for the next few days, the guards handed me the shaver and pantomimed shaving, urging me to keep that face hair off. Perhaps, then, I looked more "normal."

Hargun took me for walks inside the prison grounds, but otherwise, I was left alone for several days while they worked with Rhyodolite, communicating through drawings.

Sometimes, Hargun was angry when he came to my cell, and I wondered what Rhyodolite had done.

Finally, guards led me into an office where Hargun sat behind a desk. He rose up from his chair slightly and reached across the desk to offer me his palm, which I touched gingerly with mine. When the aliens brought Rhyodolite in, Hargun twisted his lips, but still extended his palm to *that*.

The Gwyng clenched his fist before laying out his skinny palm. The base of the thumb glistened.

Hargun blew out from his nose, sneezed, and my own nose twitched. Rhyo's lips stayed flat and tight, wrapped firmly around his little muzzle. Hargun frowned and reached for Rhyodolite's hand, but the Gwyng tucked it in his armpit web.

Hargun looked at the strange flap of skin and fleered his lips off his teeth. I shrugged an apology. Smiling back at me grimly, Hargun opened two files and began looking from one to the other.

Rhyo hopped up on the desk to see for himself. Hargun firmly sat Rhyodolite down in a chair, holding the little Gwyng as far from his body as he could.

Then in Karst I, so garbled I could barely understand, Hargun said, "Your people we contact. They teach language."

"My computer can't deal with that," Rhyodolite said, eyeing Hargun sourly, "but I get the idea he might think he's speaking a Karst language."

"He said they contacted our people, or that our people contacted them, and they taught them some Karst."

Hargun showed us a photo, taken inside a space station like the one I'd seen near Earth. Yauntries and various Federation types—mostly Gwyngs and Barcons—sat in front of terminals.

"Holy from space," Rhyodolite said. "The Federation got the bird-killing apes to meet with a Federation linguistics team."

Then Hargun smiled more broadly and showed me a more

official Federation rank chart than the one Rhyodolite and I'd cooked up. I shrugged.

I got paper and pen off Hargun's desk, slowly, because Hargun seemed quite nervous. And I drew Xenon's body the way I'd last seen it.

Hargun sighed deeply and couldn't look us in the eyes. He fumbled for Karst words, but his vocabulary didn't cover what he wanted to say. "Karst has . . . body . . . now," he finally said. "We are made to be sorry. You go back."

Rhyo got out of his chair, walked his rolling walk up to the desk, stared at the drawing and at me, lips tight over his muzzle. Hargun pressed his head with his fingertips, then patted Rhyodolite and smiled slightly.

How did the Federation get the Yauntries into that space station? I wondered. Threats?

Hargun walked us back to the cell block himself. I gestured that I wanted to be with Rhyodolite, and he allowed me to stay.

"The bird," Rhyodolite said faintly. "I . . . (not satisfactory) my attitude to/with birds, but . . ."

"I'm sorry," I said, leaning against Rhyodolite. He turned and stared at me, then his eyelids relaxed and he curled up in a ball against my shins, staring away from me at the prison's grey concrete walls.

"We'll get out soon," he said.

Late that night, with Rhyo curled up against me and asleep, I lay awake in the Yauntry jail cell, feeling the Gwyng's breathing, eerie, eerie, all of it.

In the morning, Hargun came in with guards who gave us clothes. *Uniforms, Karst uniforms!*

I dressed, watching Hargun. His face seemed drawn, tired, the thin ring of eye whites faintly bloodshot around those weird green irises.

Rhyodolite finally pulled himself out of sleep and relieved himself in the toilet slot. Then he stripped off the prison pants and washed what he could with the drinking water before putting on his blue uniform.

Hargun stared. I'd seen Rhyodolite's cock before, but wondered if he was being insulting to strip in front of us.

"Now you go to Karst," Hargun said as soon as Rhyodolite was dressed.

I was surprised at how relieved I felt. We went with Hargun to a blue Yauntry car, paint like polished enamel, which took us to the airfield where we were first brought down. This time, the airfield was almost deserted except for a Federation transport on a gate net. Two Barcons leaned against it.

As we got out of the car, one Barcon came up and looked Rhyodolite and me over, as though we might have been changed in Yauntry hands, infected by some weird sapient brain parasites.

Hargun, in his own language, said something to the Barcons. One translated for us, "He asked us to tell you that he was as kind as he could be."

Hargun looked at me and said, "Hum, Tom?"

I remembered the bird dying, the chains, then an image of Mica and Warren rose to mind, shotgun and pistol, and I said, "Hum, Edwir Hargun," holding out my palm toward him. He took my hand and put it on his shoulder. The transport opened and a Gwyng looked out nervously, then koo'ed when he saw Rhyodolite. We stood there a moment while Rhyo fell babbling into Gwyng arms.

"They said the shooting of the bird cadet Xenon was an accident," one of the Barcons said.

"No," I said, "it wasn't."

"Well, they get forgiven for it, either way," the Barcon said, "since we were in their planetary system."

We climbed into the transport, Rhyodolite and his Gwyngs and me without any of my own kind. A Barcon brought me a cold beer. I sucked on it, then continued describing the attack, over again, how the squad of men fired on the bird.

Rhyodolite freed himself from the other Gwyngs and came over. He said, "The bird jumped. Then they fired. Red Clay, they were scared."

"Xenon was scared, too," I said.

One of the Gwyngs wrinkled her face and hugged me. "Rough business for a pre-cadet."

Too exhausted to say more, I slumped into a crash chair. Turning my head slightly, I saw Rhyodolite get engulfed in a hot wiggle of Gwyngs.

"Piss on their cheese," Rhyo said, and koo'ed until he choked.

* * *

Black Amber and the old hawk Rector Karriaagzh, both fully uniformed, looked like we'd interrupted a serious conversation when we arrived at the Karst landing field.

"See," Karriaagzh said in Karst II, "your Rhyodolite survived. The Red Clay refuge-seeker survived. Only one of my parallels died, and he showed fear first."

Black Amber massaged her hands.

"Food, new clothes, sleep," Rhyodolite said.

Black Amber held out a cadet's black uniform to me. "Still want it, Red Clay?" she asked.

"I earned it." I sounded tougher than I felt.

Amber and Rhyodolite koo'ed. The Rector pulled out a pocket screen, punched a display up, and said, "You need the cadet training, although I suppose you did as you thought you should."

"What did I do wrong?" I asked. "Were we set up? We weren't supposed to be in that kind of danger."

The Rector said, "Unless we tell you to resist or lie, never do it. The dangers of first contacts are exaggerated, but fear magnifies your xenophobias."

Black Amber looked as though she wanted to explain more.

"But I'm a pre-cadet. It wasn't supposed to be a goddamn first contact. Sir, they killed one of us."

"Red Clay, your job is to stand still and be non-threatening. Not that we want our cadets killed, but a species which has murdered one of us can be extraordinarily contrite, if we don't react with hostilities."

So I hadn't earned a medal, I thought as I put on the black cadet uniform. "Who's sponsoring me?"

"I am," Black Amber said.

I watched her smooth down the hair on the backs of her hands, then said, harsher than I'd meant to, "You still want the public apology?"

The Rector stood up over me and rubbed his beak through my head hair. Black Amber flinched, then said, "We'll discuss that later."

Back at the Gwyng beach house, Rhyodolite melted a pint of butter and slurped it up with a broad oval straw and his funny tongue muscles.

I asked him, "What will the Federation do to species we contact?"

"We tame them," he said. "Good trade contacts develop. Sometimes more of us die."

I put my head down on my arms and bawled.

= 5 =

Breaking Down to Common Mind

Barcon mopped us cadet initiates with reeking gook to strip us bald except for hair or feathers around our eyes. After I washed the hair down the shower drain, I shivered, naked, with nine other freshly de-haired males. One of them, slit-nosed with grey skin, blew alien powder at my crotch from a hair-dryer-shaped blower. "To keep from chafing," the alien said, handing me the blower so I could spray dust on him too.

Bitching about how this de-hairing hurt our dangling balls, we climbed into our black uniforms and went to an old building for the convocation. I looked up at the prism windows and beams of blond wood with dark grey veins that looked positively un-Earthly.

Of course. The wood *was* alien. About a thousand novice cadets shambled in, gawking at the hall, each other, and the old grey Rector Karriaagzh, who stood in a hooded pulpit—like a Jack-in-the-pulpit blossom. Suddenly, I realized we'd had pulpits with hoods on Earth at one time.

All the aliens tried to find seats suited to their joints and leg lengths, but settled for what they could reach as Karriaagzh turned on a sound system and muttered harshly into it.

When his crew of mixed teenage aliens settled down, Karriaagzh, his grating accent suddenly very impressive, welcomed us in both Karst languages.

"You have duties to an ecology of Mind that goes beyond species," Karriaagzh said intensely. "In your oath, you will promise to obey Federation officials and protect all known sapient life, but your duties go beyond that. Academy before species, Federation before Academy, Mind above all.''

Beside me, a dark alien with a flat face and tiny round ears muttered, ''He believes this accident that we are has some big ultimate meaning?''

Karriaagzh continued, ''You think a five-thousand-year-old institution is permanent? I come from a species with ten million years of history. Not one of its institutions lasted more than half a million years. If you don't maintain the ideals and goals of the Federation, it *will* wither, random death will claim it.''

''His species is dying out,'' the alien beside me whispered, not terribly impressed, although I was.

We all stood to pledge our lives and energy to the Federation, then stood looking at each other until black-clad cadets with gold shoulder stripes led us out in groups of ten by stumps of ancient metal and stone walls, by centuries of buildings, to the dorms.

My group went through absolute mazes of hallways. Every hundred yards or so, the senior cadet spoke a name. A bald alien, race and sex disguised by the baggy black uniform, went into a room. Some left their doors open; others closed them instantly.

''Red Clay.'' I walked into my new room, feeling vaguely like a prisoner in the black uniform. No underwear, absolutely bald, I felt my legs, my dangling genitals, my arms, as I'd never felt them before, as raw skin.

It was an odd room, three alcoves, each raised by one step, around the central square. Two alcoves, each the size of the central square, were off to either side, but the central alcove stuck out into a courtyard. The courtyard alcove bed, mounted on a frame that traveled up and down on smooth metal posts, was at ceiling height. I went closer.

A naked bird, with a beak like pointed lips, glared down at me, and said, ''You mammals make me look terribly ugly.'' He pulled a sheet around his shoulders, but I got a solid eyeful—raw pebbly skin, yellow, like a plucked chicken.

Absolutely correct, ugly, but I didn't look great either. ''They want us to all look alike. At least as much as possible.''

The bird fluttered membranes vertically across its eyes. ''We never went around in such fabric things.''

"All the other bird species do. Even the Rector."

"Lactating monstrosities forced them," the bird muttered, reaching for the bed's controls. As the bed slid down the metal wall posts, I backed away. The bird stepped off the bed, straightened his backward knees, and stood up about six and a half feet tall. His breastbone poked out like a dull machete.

"What's your name?" I asked. Surely, he wasn't dangerous?

"Granite Grit," the bird said, awkwardly pulling on his blacks. Each foot had three club-like toes. *Granite Grit*, I thought, staring at those huge clawed toes, *sounds like a fighting-cock line.* "And the Academy calls you?" he asked.

"Red Clay." *Like the Rector says, forget species. This is just a beaked guy, who hates lactators, your roommate for God knows how long.* "You like your bed?" His foam slab was very thin, covered with a pebble-textured plastic.

He gestured yes, the Academy gesture with the hand tossed back. *He seems rougher than Xenon.* I felt vaguely guilty.

"Why did intelligence develop?" the bird finally asked despairingly.

"To protect big heads on poky bodies," said a new voice in Karst II, the third roommate. He looked like a chunky Gwyng, but with nostrils on a cartilage structure, a real nose.

"We," the bird said, "aren't poky." He stared down at the third alien like a great horned owl looks at a frantic blue jay.

"I don't think intelligence has really developed yet," I decided, remembering humans and Yauntries.

"I'm Gypsum 8, born on Karst of Ewit stock," the creature said. "Who are you (both)?"

"Red Clay," I said.

"Oh, that refugee connected with the Gwyngs." He decided intelligence certainly hadn't developed on my planet, I thought. The Ewit turned to the bird. "And you?"

"Granite Grit."

"From Carg?"

"Yes."

"Hey," I said to Granite Grit. "We flew you in."

The bird inspected me with his dark reddish brown eyes, moving his face skin in odd waves. "The flight was difficult. The Gwyng-thing is hostile. Would not practice the . . .

language with me." He climbed back onto his bed and retreated ceilingward.

"Odd. An unsocial Gwyng," the Ewit said. "Well, I have
Karst friends here that I must see." As he wandered out to
talk to more civilized beings, I thought I'd have left, too,
except I'd get lost. Hell, I *was* lost.

Some weird bears bustled in with three sturdy computer
consoles, followed by a blue-clad ape-stock officer, who
asked, "Where are your roommates?"

I pointed to the bird bed. Granite Grit looked down, the
junior officer flinched, and Granite slowly landed his pad at
floor level.

"The other one," Granite said in Karst II, "isn't here. We
drove him out."

"Gypsum, Karst-born Ewit—he knows these consoles.
We've got one Karst II and two Karst I boards, or would you
rather have a Karst II board?" the alien, who looked rather
like me but not really, asked the bird.

Granite said, in Karst I, "I'd be just as happy with small
segment linear for written." Those transparent vertical eyelids flicked across his eyeballs again.

The ape-alien said, "All right," as the bears put the console in Granite's alcove. "The computers and mass storage
unit linked with your terminal can switch architectures to give
you different hard-wired systems. Don't try much parallel
pathing; the system could go sentient and start arguing with
us. Your board can be placed on your cubicle wall here," he
said, indicating plates inside the alcove, "or here," indicating floor plates in the central common area. "They operate by
voice, keyboard, or light pen. Keep the printer filled with
paper, in the hopper, here, and thread it, like this."

He opened a side panel. A stack of paper, fanfold, sat
there, feeding up into the machine. All that showed on top of
the console was a slot.

"Give me your hand," the junior officer said, "and I'll set
you up. You log on by hand pattern."

Granite got off the bed and placed his hand, with opaque
brown nails like arrowheads, on the key-in plate. The junior
officer delicately etched its outline with an electric scribe.
"Just put your hand inside the lines. If it grows, call us and
we'll re-key you."

One of the bear-like techs added, "We're leaving a manual with each console. Other cadets have survived it."

They set us up and went *bye*. The manuals dented our foam pads seriously—thousands of pages, plastic-covered monsters. The bird lifted off again for the ceiling, muttering about rude mammals. I abandoned the manual and opened the closet-like cubicle beside the bed.

Exactly like the bathroom in Floyd, I thought, until I sat down on the toilet and noticed it was lower, but not uncomfortable. Fitted into the space with the toilet was a tiny shower with sliding doors and a weird basin, just big enough to wash my hands in, with a dial for water temperature and a lever to cut the water on and off. After I relieved myself, I considered how they'd fitted all this in a box so small I could touch the walls each way. Mirror over the basin. I still looked human, but a bit ugly.

Back out, I opened the humongous computer manual, trying to find out when and where we ate. I could ask for things in plain Karst, so I called up the day's schedule. About ten screens scrolled by, the start of a schedule for over fifty thousand people, before I escaped and got something simpler, the first-year cadets' schedule.

We had meals scheduled. I was getting hungrier and hungrier, but had no idea of where to find the food. *Maybe this is the first test. You couldn't pull a map, you starved?*

The map finally came up with a little "you are here" sign, and explained that I could adjust scale or relative schematicity by twisting knobs to the right of the keyboard.

By twisting the knobs enough, I went through the Academy architectural data in cross section. I guessed I could use the tallest buildings to figure out where I was, so I slanted things at a 45-degree angle and pulled a paper copy.

Just curious, I rolled the schematic/information density knob until the screen showed full color and detail as sharp as a photo. I pulled another print which looked like a Kodachrome. *What about video games?*

"Hey, Granite Grit, come down and take a look at this!"

The bed whispered slightly on its columns as it sank. Granite took one look at the map, pointed to a building, and said, "Three buildings away—food."

We went out, trying to orient ourselves by memorizing

door styles, plants, windows. The bird's walk was almost running for me.

At the cafeteria door, each alien spoke his or her name into a talking computer. The bird was told to go upstairs. Granite Grit actually looked alarmed when I got a different assignment on the ground floor. Then I realized I had the maps. "I'll meet you here," I told him.

I found table Ah-zha 104 and saw table companions that ranged from Gwyng-looking to almost human, all with relatively dark skins except for one piebald, who looked diseased.

"You like cushions?" the most human-looking one asked.

Cadets, I noticed, could sit on cushions or stand to eat, like Gwyngs. My tablemates were on cushions.

"Cushions are fine," I said, not wanting to be fussy. I'd got the place with the menu screen, so I read and punched for all of us. The selections were . . . arrgh, so many options. I finally ordered a baked-to-coagulation bird, fruit, baked grain meal leavened with yeasts, and two random vegetables.

A live waiter brought the food. "Status," the piebald murmured. We weren't just bald adolescent sapients, we were Academy cadets. Machines served the masses.

As we ate, we silently watched each other. When I was almost finished, I looked up and saw my bird roommate scrambling toward me.

"Red Clay, could you loan me your map or come back with me to the room?"

"I want to walk around," I said. "We've got a free afternoon."

Granite's skin tried to wriggle non-existent face feathers. I held out the building floor plan. *Shit*, we're only three buildings away, I thought.

The bird stepped toward me, took the map, and danced back, studying the map. We walked outside together. "I think the dorm is that way," I said, pointing. Granite moved back and forth in little hock-lift steps, then twitched as though he were trying to shrug out of his clothes.

"I'd walk with you, Red Clay, but I'd feel odd."

"*Oh, sure,*" I said in English. "Good-bye, Granite Grit," in Karst.

* * *

All afternoon, I explored the campus, navigating by the eleven high towers.

As I walked through the strangely scaled gardens between the other buildings, I saw they varied weirdly. Almost too close together, the buildings crowded each other like alien competitive plants. Some looked like ultra-modern Earth buildings except lichens had crumbled their stones. Others looked ancient, with a touch of Aztec, but were only half finished, alien construction crews guiding stone- and brick-laying machines.

Bits of old walls poked up here, there, looking melted and glazed, rough seats for new little cadets, freshly stripped of hair.

By accident, I found a maze of name-covered walls—not labeled on my maps—fifteen hundred years of names in Karst I and II characters/glyphs. The oldest walls were stainless-steel slabs. The newest were thin granite, so polished I saw my face in the stone behind the gold inlaid letters.

Near the end—Mica, posthumously promoted to cadet. Third from the end, Xenon.

Like the Vietnam Memorial, I realized, suddenly numb. *All these names are of cadets who died in service.*

Nine dead between Mica and the bird. And two dead after the bird—I stared back and forth from Mica's name to the bird's, suddenly feeling even more prisoner-like. *Cadets sure die a lot.*

Walking backward, I came to a huge cluster of names three hundred years earlier. Some big attack? And heat so intense that the walls melted?

I walked slowly back to Mica's name, reading names, clusters of dates. "Oh, Mica," I said, leaning my forehead against those gold inlaid characters, "why did you want this for me?"

When I got back to my room, Gypsum was out, and Granite had tucked himself up high. Transliterating as best I could, I asked the computer for the file on Yauntry. The machine printed back **Species, first contact; Species, language; Species, continuing observations; Species, biology** ... I chopped it and asked for a 250-word first-contact file.

First contact with Yauntry was initiated by linguistics study team 189123, Karst I, following

disappearance of a satellite recovery team. The linguistics team approached Yauntry ships in space, retreated as per standard maneuver. Yauntry ships made no aggressive displays, but followed Academy ships into a protected gravity net massing in excess of 100,000 unit masses. Academy ships exceeding the number of Yauntry ships pulled out of presumed detection range. Linguistics study team members attempted to contact the Yauntry ships by video. Earlier research indicated the Yauntry broadcast in horizontal double sweep and reverse lines set at 512 lines per visual unit, indicating a possible base 8 numerical system. Broadcasts in this visual format were sent and received. Typical contact films opened communications. Once communications were opened, queries about the missing search team survivors led to quick release of Cadet Officer Rhyodolite 10 and Sub-Cadet Red Clay 3. Cadet Xenon 7 had been accidentally fatally injured in initial contact confusion.

Yauntry people are moderately xenophobic and have demonstrated theoretical knowledge of space drive, although They had not built space-driven vessels or worked out near-star geometries at the time of initial contact. They accepted a study team and are possible candidates for admission into the Federation.

See also Biology, Behavior, Language . . .

Oh, I thought, I wasn't a very significant part of that. I wiped the text, not bothering to print it. Then I transliterated "Earth":

Files not available to this terminal.

Okay. Instead, I asked for a 20,000-word printout on sapient biology, introduction. Cadets died for this, I thought as I fumbled with the fanfold paper. Gypsum came in, giggled, and showed me how to bind sheets with the console. "Insert here," he said, shoving the paper into a slot in the console's lower left side. The machine spat the sheets back bound and trimmed.

"I tried to get material on my own planet but they told me the files weren't available on this computer," I said.

"I can get around those system locks," Gypsum said.

The bird's bed whispered down the wall rails. "Perhaps you could help me?" the bird asked hoarsely. "I need to find out who manipulates who here."

Granite and Gypsum bent large craniums over Granite's computer while I read that indeed intelligence probably developed to protect awkward, large-skulled animals.

By sunset, both Granite and I seemed mildly confused, and I went out to eat. Our table display had a note for me—Black Amber would see me that night in my room.

Before Black Amber arrived, skinny bear-stock guys took our furniture orders. I asked for a wall lamp over my bed, cushioned chairs, and a table for my alcove area. They suggested a desk and two storage chests. And shelves.

"What will the cost be?" I asked.

"Free, need any decorations?"

"Yeah, a huge blown-up photo of Earth showing North America in the center." Surely they could get that.

Granite Grit ordered hard cushions, elbow leaning pads, and a low table—bird furniture. A full-length mirror for his wall. And a partition for his alcove.

"No partitions. When you've gotten to know each other, you should talk about the central area."

"What about a music disc system with earphones and room speakers?" Gypsum said quickly.

We agreed to the music system.

Black Amber stood in the doorway with a little oo on her muzzle. "Red Clay (come). If you've finished." I thanked the furniture guys and followed her out.

We walked under building lights and the stars, with her headed for something, not just walking. After about a quarter mile, I realized we were near the memorial walls. "I saw Mica's name on a granite slab."

She stopped and turned toward me, her huge eyes looking oiled in Karst's dusky night. An eddy of air ruffled her head hair, which seemed puffed up. "Ah, Cadet," she said. We sat down on stones that looked glazed in patches. When I fingered the glaze, she said, "Attack on Karst eight hundred years ago. Easier then."

"So you lose cadets now in ones and twos, rather than by hundreds?"

She leaned against me—bat-sapients have no social distance. "Red-Clay-with-flecks-of-Mica. One of mine."

I couldn't be a Gwyng, I thought. My body stiffened. She said, "Oh," and stood to stretch slightly. "You were concerned about Rhyodolite when the others held you?"

"Yes, very," I answered.

"The Academy tested him with a bird (I can't explain, sounds/seems xenophobic). I don't want Rhyodolite to be demoted. I lost Mica, but you tried to help, against your own." She touched my chin with the back of her knuckles, and oo'ed faintly. We walked on to the memorial walls. With her left hand, she traced Mica's name, each finger writhing as though scorched by the gold.

Sapience requires an excess of 10 to the 10th neurons per 70 kg. of body weight, I read. Putting the printout aside, I checked my messages. Rhyodolite left word that I could skip dinner since I was invited to a First Contact Party. Dress in best blacks, be very good for ape-eating ape. Rhyodolite 10.

How am I supposed to behave? Granite Grit, muttering in bird, was soldering his own chips to the console motherboard. When Gypsum came in, I told him about the party.

"You're not socially ready for that," Gypsum said.

"My friend said, 'Be very good for ape-eating-ape,' " I told the Ewit before heading out the door to a sapient-behavior discussion.

After flunking the chemistry placement test for Cosmic Geophysics and Chemistry, I went down to the physical activities building. Being a cadet got you a choice of bathing suits: brief-like, tights-like, or a whole body suit. I chose briefs, wondering what had worn that pair before me, and belly-flopped with the rest of my new de-haired crazy gang.

When I came back, balls half chafed raw, to my room, Granite Grit, perched high, was quizzing Rhyodolite about the computers. Rhyodolite, one leg twisting anxiously, stood in the common square—both bird and bat being fantastically polite. I noticed Rhyo's feet were booted in what looked like Gwyng-fit European bully marching boots.

"The boots, Rhyodolite? They look like Earth boots."

"Yes/but heel re-done. You like?"

"Weird. What is this party, anyway?" I noticed his dark blue sash with medals and badges.

"Terribly important people come to see the first-contact people and new aliens. You'll start your banner," he said, touching his sash. "Hurry, change."

I winced and held my legs apart. He looked at me and tore up a sheet, making me a little loincloth pouch for my genitals. "Hurry. Didn't someone/Tesseract tell you to watch naked skin against skin?"

"No," I said, trying to tie another strip of sheet around my waist.

"Dust." He went into my toilet cubicle and came out with a powder which helped.

As I put on my dress blacks and shoes, I asked, "So this party's for those who didn't end up on the memorial walls?"

"Red-Clay-fool, don't. Forget Mortuary Walls." He looked at me and sniffed. "Your web glands stink."

"How do I get deodorant around here?"

"Ah (don't worry about that now)." He glanced at the bird. "Show no teeth in facial gestures—can be misunderstood by drunks. Don't discuss senior guests afterward."

We scurried out, Rhyodolite chattering almost too fast for my skull computer to transform, about drugs. Drugs?

"You know," I said, "Black Amber almost wants to adopt me now."

He stopped short and blinked at me from his wrinkled face, with his own oiled eyes—suddenly very alien. "She is very Gwyng-minded—Gwyng-planet-raised (unlike me/Cadmium). She is allied to live things, against death."

We climbed into Rhyodolite's three-wheeled electric plastic egg and drove up to a two-story stone and timber building with much glass—both plain and crystal cut—the Rector's lodge, on a hill just inside the Academy grounds.

This alien party, I realized, wasn't going to be anything close to a bunch of drunks with a string band.

Under the main porte cochere a small servant alien took the car away while a terribly nervous pre-cadet checked us off on a terminal.

A Barcon, only furred in patches, but thoroughly groomed, took us through a velvet tubular hall into a large room. He pointed to the food tables. "Any guest can eat these, although they might not digest all the proteins." The Barcon put a finger up to its ear, listening to a plastic speaker in its ear tube, then left us, saying, "Recreational drugs come in key-out boxes—explain to Red Clay, Rhyodolite."

Weird alien sitting instruments filled the room—upholstered body gloves, loft seats with attached ladders, pillows, straw mats on low daises, and couches. Around these, on these, moves crested, naked-skinned, furred, feathered, or wrinkled aliens.

"Rhyodolite, I don't know these people. Stay with me."

"Wonderful," Rhyo said, putting a thing like a brown pancake on a plate. "Cadmium and surprises will be here."

"What are you eating?" I asked as Rhyo fitted his fingers with tongs like artificial nails. He gave me a taste off the fingertip tongs. *Cooked meat juice.* My mind went *oh.* "Fried blood?"

"Good?" Rhyo asked. He began clapping fried blood cake mouthward.

I wondered if any aliens used forks and found a short curved knife—shorter blade than a butter knife, with a slight spoon to the blade. The fried blood hadn't been bad, so I dished up some for myself.

Black Amber and Cadmium walked in, bumping each other gently. She wore a green and gold tunic top with bloomer shorts, and soft slippers. Rhyodolite grabbed her shoulder and sniffed her. Black Amber thumped Rhyo's right thumb. I had no idea of what sniffing and thumping meant, so, lips pursed into an embarrassed oo, I looked down.

Black Amber pushed my head up with her knuckles. I thanked her formally for sponsoring me. "Since I'm not used to this kind of party," I added, "I'd welcome advice. I know no one here except three Gwyngs."

"More acquaintances here than you expect," she replied.
"You called up the Yauntry contact account. Perhaps not
flattering to rate only a line." She dropped her hands from
my head. "A smile for you." Her fingers pulled up her
mouth corners. "Mechanical, but up-lips for us means something different. But your test was awful."

"I knew I flunked it. How did you find out so soon?"

"Computer."

Boy, those computers. I hadn't realized how closely the
computer let her monitor me—what I read, tests, reports from
lecture leaders, gym.

"The Yauntra report was scandalous," she said, handing
me a greyish brown sash. "But you must give him (Yauntry)
this as he gives you yours."

"What?" My bowels lurched as two Barcons marched up
with a Yauntry between them.

Edwir Hargun.

He stood grey-faced with a black sash in his hands, dressed
in brown Academy-style clothes. I raised his sash while he
looked down and moved his arms stiffly so I could fit it over
his shoulder.

"Your Federation knew only one Yauntry," he said in
stumbling Karst I, "to call out by name. Our *Encorals*,
leaders, made me go."

I bowed my head and let him put the black sash over my
shoulder. Then Hargun turned to Black Amber and the other
Gwyngs. "I was brought to Karst. A hostage, perhaps?" he
half asked. "I am terribly sorry about Xenon."

I looked away from all of them, as I thought about
Xenon trying to be friends with Rhyodolite. Why was Rhyo
so rude? Because birds with wings ate bats once. I said
slowly, "We feared you would shoot us, also," and looked
up at Hargun.

He caught my eyes then for a second. I looked at his round
jaw and short blobby nose, almost like a cartoon character's
face, but I couldn't remember the cartoon. Then I had to look
away. *He's so afraid*.

Hargun found a plate and one of the short knives and
dabbled up bits of alien food. Standing beside me, he groped
for vocabulary. "You seemed . . . so angry." He rubbed

small folds at the outsides of his eyes. *Ah, that's what makes his eyes look so round.* Obviously wanting to say more, he said, "No one here really knows my language."

"Why did you let us go?" I wondered if the Yauntry version differed from the Karst version.

"No weapons on you. Other ships did not hurt, but sent electric pictures." He sighed, frustrated with his minuscule Karst. "And you . . . so young, despite the strange *s'kos* face." He smiled faintly at me and said, "Satellite stealer."

Rhyo cocked his head and said, "Ah, the flesh-eating apes can talk to each other, but don't translate that, Red Mud, or I'll imitate vampire tonight." He buzzed a visual through the computer—little bat with a human face and fangs like miniature tusks.

"The one who spoke was the one your people captured with me," I told Hargun.

Hargun turned to Rhyodolite and said, "Your Federation is an enormous thing to fight. An intimidating alliance of mammals and birds."

Black Amber looked sharply at Hargun. The Yauntry smiled back as though his face had turned almost to glass.

Rhyo pulled Cadmium aside and talked some Gwyng language to him that my skull computer couldn't work out. Cadmium, annoyed, bobbed his head, bounced his pied body against Rhyo, and plunged off into the crowd. Wrinkles deepening, Rhyo looked wistfully after him.

Black Amber extended her fingertips to Hargun as she moved her body forward in a fluid roll. He started to touch her palm with his, but she only allowed her long, furred fingers to brush his, knuckle to knuckle. "Please explain," she said to me, "that Gwyngs are more sparing of friendly hand gestures than former brachiators/tree creatures."

I added that he shouldn't nod at Gwyngs either, since they tended to do that when they were annoyed. Rhyodolite nodded slightly and tried to edge Black Amber away from us. She arched her body at him and raised her brow fur. Both went off into the crowd and left me with Hargun.

"Are they angry with me?" Hargun asked.

"No." I looked around and noticed lots more Barcons than I'd been aware of—all blended into the background. The two who'd brought Hargun up to me stood behind us, observing, not socializing.

"Wonderful at your age," Hargun tried to say, "to know about strange . . . people." He stared down at his shoes as if he'd run completely out of vocabulary.

Why did the Gwyngs leave? I wondered.

The room noise choked off as the old bird Rector Karriaagzh entered, yellow hawk eyes with fierce bone ridges swaying over the rest of us.

Hargun turned and stared at the Rector. Man, Karriaagzh was one truly impressive and alien alien for a space novice to see. Hargun murmured, "Your regulator?"

"More or less."

"Birds regulate you? Now I understand . . . a bird's death." His voice trailed off as Karriaagzh stalked closer, dressed in russet with real gold worked through the cloth.

I was too awed by Karriaagzh and didn't catch until later the implications of what Hargun said.

The Rector's uniform was undone to show some of his ridged breastbone—his comment, perhaps, to us mammals that he was different. Disdaining entourages, alone, he moved with backward knee strides through the crowd.

Slowly, talking his way from alien to alien, he made his way to us. "Red Clay Tom, you aren't such a xenophobe as Black Amber feared. Edwir Hargun, *shiwi-la, hum, u* Federation-*bhlu*. I hope my Yauntro is not too impossible."

Hargun's eyes went hugely round, almost like balls, and Karriaagzh eased back and bent his knees, to make himself less tall. The bird gave us his whole attention—neither eyelids nor nictitating membranes moved. Karriaagzh breathed in rhythm with Hargun, first quickly. When the bird breathed slower, Hargun's breaths slowed, too, as though the bird'd hypnotized him.

My mouth opened a little. Karriaagzh moved his facial feathers and said, "I would like both of you to be at the tale-telling later."

As the bird moved on, Hargun's eyes tracked him. "I know people who spoke for . . . a . . . people."

"Diplomat?" I suggested. "Representative."

"Bird-like things should not be able to speak Yauntro. And I didn't come with full . . . not my idea. But I know a master. This . . . grasping for words fools me. Difficult to seem sapient without proper words.''

Karriaagzh, having gone through the crowd like a master politician, stepped up on a dais and said, "First contact takes courage and initiative on both sides. We honor our guests tonight.''

Hargun trembled slightly—xeno reaction, I thought. His Barcons eased him up against a wall, so aliens couldn't crowd in on all sides as they came over to congratulate us.

"Stay with him,'' one of the Barcons told me. "You know him from the contact.''

"And you have so many amino acids in common,'' the other added.

Hargun braced his body against the wall, tense, ready to fight if necessary. Where was Tesseract and his calming teas? I'd thought of Tesseract when I saw another Ahram enter the room, with a Gwyng, both dressed in handspun tweedy clothes. The alien crowd whispered, "History Committee.''

Black Amber suddenly appeared by my elbow and moved me toward the slow chatty path they took through the crowd.

"Is this?'' the other Gwyng said to Black Amber, indicating me.

"Mica's legacy, Red Clay. Red Clay, this is History Committee Member for the Gwyngs Wy'um.''

"History Committee Member, I am honored to be here tonight . . .'' What should I say to this bipedal bat whose hand was sliding up and down Black Amber's stomach? I didn't know what the History Committee was, but these guys arrived late and grabbed more attention than Karriaagzh.

The other History Committee Member, the Ahram, with reddish skull crest skin, smiled. "Cadet Red Clay, I'm History Committee Member Warst Runnel, of the Ahrams, like Tesseract, no?''

Wy'um sniffed the air delicately. Black Amber blinked slowly and showed Wy'um a little glass capsule. I felt tension in the air, as if some illegal drug was in that vial, ready to spin brains when cracked and sniffed. He oo'ed. The Ahram's crest skin flushed even redder, and he looked at Black Amber as though she were a whore.

Black Amber stared me into silence and thanked them, saying she'd see them both later.

Then the History Committee aliens moved on.

"Who," I asked Amber, "were they?"

"History Committee determines Karst and Federation policies, holds us together with good history. Wy'um S'fee I'e is the first *male* Gwyng to hold the position." She raised her brow hair slightly and twitched her lips, then headed over with her rolling gait to the food table.

Look, I told myself as Black Amber eased away, you speak the language—mingle. So what if the Barcons wanted me to stay with Hargun. He made me nervous.

I looked for other cadets, but black suits were scarce. Finally, I spotted a young female ape-type, with multi-colored head hair, like a punk tri-colored collie. *Why not,* I decided as I went toward her, *she's shorter than me.*

Funny chin, no dent between it and the bottom lip, even if it's not rounded like Hargun's, I thought. Her face and nose angles were a bit broad, but the eyes were okay, getting quizzical as I stared. "I guess we're two of the youngest winners," I managed to get out. "I'm Red Clay."

"Topaz 17. I understand your species is new here. First contact and first contacting, all so suddenly."

"Yes. Was anyone hurt on your first-contact team?"

"No, we prepared well. I even dyed my hair to look less alien to them."

"Is that . . ."

"No, this is my normal color."

"Usually, are there casualties?"

She looked around, then said, "Most first contacts are accidents—if we'd planned, did radio approaches first, we'd have fewer dead."

My first impulse had been to imagine sunglasses on her with that weird hair, but now I mentally jerked off the imagined-on shades and gave her professor glasses, so serious. "Right," I said.

She smiled. "You were with Rhyodolite 10?"

"Yes."

"He uses Gwyng-heat scent poppers for sexual arousal with non-specifics. Watch him around your women."

"Little glass poppers?" I asked.

"So he has them tonight."

"No, Black Amber . . ." Suddenly I realized I'd almost

said too much, but I covered up, saying, ''. . . told me about them.''

She moved away from me, suddenly bored.

Alone again. I saw Hargun staring at me.

But in the middle of this alien party, I thought about me—here—a parole breaker. Yeah, I should have asked my parole man if I could have gone star-hopping.

I relaxed and realized how tense I'd been. No Gwyng was gonna bite my neck; no Barcon planned to microtome me down to slide specimens. And Hargun was at *our* party now.

But Rhyodolite had abandoned me. That runt—hard to find such a tiny Gwyng in the crowd, but finally I spotted Cadmium's blond streaks. Rhyo was with him, back at the fried blood. As I came up, Rhyo oo'ed and grabbed me, offering me a chunk of blood cake on his fake fingernail.

''He'll eat it,'' Rhyo told Cadmium. I obliged.

''Would he eat it with honey on it?'' Cadmium asked.

''Sure. He'll drink it raw with honey. After all, his species invented cow juice oil.'' Rhyo poured a glass of watery blood and looked for the honey. Cadmium had an oo poised on his blond-streaked face; his wrinkles tightened and shifted.

I gagged on cold blood and honey. Rhyodolite dipped his fake nails into a stoneware jar and pulled out a grub.

''No, Rhyodolite,'' I said, trying to sound firm, not hysterical. ''I didn't dish it up. You go ahead and eat that yourself.''

''But, Red-Clay-with-maggots-crawling-on-it, I don't like this flavor.'' Rhyodolite nodded to the grub as though it had annoyed him. But Rhyo had a little oo poised on his muzzle.

''Let Cadmium eat it, if you've injured it already.''

''I tell you, let's feed it to the alien Y'ngtree. The one you were with. So polite. *Ewing Haring*. So stupid,'' Rhyo said as he waved the grub around.

''Rhyodolite-with-a-sexually-delinquent-pouch-mother,''Cadmium said as he took Rhyo's flailing wrist and guided the grub to his own mouth. ''You know Red Clay isn't a real person and won't eat proper food.''

''Don't you bats ever eat vegetables?'' I asked.

''Clots the cock. Makes webs stink and shrink.'' Cadmium asked, ''Didn't that happen to you?'' They chattered in Gwyng talk I couldn't follow.

''Red-Clay-with-blushing-neck,'' Rhyodolite said. ''Relax.

I'll show you the Rector feeding a toilet. Black Amber said they've discussed/argued about first-contact procedures half day. When the bird gets tense, he relieves himself . . .''

"A female cadet said we approach slowly."

"Topaz, my mission," Cadmium said. "Very good ideas. But neither Black Amber nor Karriaagzh approves. Too many new aliens for Black Amber. Too few new birds for the Rector Karriaagzh." He coughed out the bird's name.

But I wanted a tomato. Where were the vegetables? Where were the big vegetarian guys? Ahrams couldn't disappear in the crowd like a little Gwyng.

"Stay," Rhyodolite said. "Made you honorary Gwyng and you don't appreciate it."

But I'd spotted some Ahrams and plunged into the crowd.

"Okay," Cadmium said, "we'll watch you."

While I ate raw vegetables, the Gwyngs commented on the downright perversity of stealing food from the lovely cows who would so willingly turn all this rubbish into milk and oil for me.

"And there he goes," Rhyodolite commented, "biting into another vegetable sex organ."

Then they saw something. Cadmium picked up the platter of red and yellow things, and said, "Follow . . . follow," hustling the platter and me upstairs into a turret room with a huge bay window facing the city—traffic glitter and starry sky visible through black tree shapes.

Cadmium and Rhyo deposited me and the vegetables by the door and cruised casually up to Black Amber, who greeted them again with full sideways body slams. The Gwyng History Committee Member, Wy'um, stood right by her, flicking his eyelids up and down. Rhyo and Cadmium glared at him.

Karriaagzh stalked in and settled slowly on his hocks—an odd sight, the body resting on the upper legs. The Gwyngs moved away from him.

A short bear-type alien eased its way through the crowd with little soft hoots, passing out oily or alcoholic drinks. Karriaagzh took a glass, opened his beak, and flung the liquid in.

People had heard that the big guys were here and the room filled up fast. Edwir Hargun and the two other alien ambassadors hung back beside their Barcon translators. Warst Runnel and another Ahram with a cup of hot tea in his hand came in. Tesseract?

Yes. He came up, seeming mildly dazed by some nice abuse substance, and said, "So space wasn't so horrible that you turned down your blacks."

"Do I call you Tesseract or Rector's Man here?" I asked, not sure of the etiquette. "Black Amber's introduced me to History Committee Man Warst Runnel and the Gwyng History Committee Member."

Warst Runnel smiled. Tesseract looked at him and then back to me, saying, "Black Amber's only on pheromone suppressants, isn't she, the bitch?" He slurped a bit of his tea as he spoke, and his skull crest reddened. "Call me Tesseract here."

"Edwir Hargun, the Yauntry representative, thought the Rector was very impressive."

The two Ahrams exchanged broad grins. Tesseract said, "I told you to think of him as the *Sesame Street* Big Bird. But he is impressive on first sight. And he doesn't age. When a Rector is seventy, one expects signs of change. Same ideas for decades— wants to expand—link all intelligence in a huge mental conglomerate."

"Big Brain Bang Theory," Warst Runnel said. "Karriaagzh loves contacts. But we can't drag primitive people into the Federation. Too intimidating."

Tesseract added, "Bundle the universe right up. Many terrified primitive cadets, many Rector's People and Barcons hurt or killed by xenophobes. Like the Calcite you knew, Red Clay. Right?" He traded his tea for a cold drink off the little bear's tray. "A fabulous creature, our Karriaagzh. Loves legacies. You keep doing the crazy things that got you in contact with us in the first place."

"I didn't do anything right. I just tried," I said. "And you, sir, were very kind to me on the ship."

"I'm still kind. Listen to gossip. It's almost 88 percent correct. Wonderful living here, on Karst, if you avoid sudden walls."

"Memorial walls?"

"Ah, Warst Runnel, Mica picked well. Sharp refugee. Red Clay, don't you just love the intrigue? Like Black Amber's body bribes."

"No. Mica should be here now."

Tesseract's crest skin flushed again. "I'm sorry, *Tom*. And not all those names died on first contact, either. Some people kill across species lines years after first contact.''

Warst Runnel moved off, closer to Karriaagzh. Tesseract put down his drink and took a deep breath. He sighed and picked up a vegetable slice off the plate I held and ate it. "I am sorry. Gwyngs are conservative, don't want expanded contacts, but they're probably making planet landings to leak technology to their primitive parallels. Karriaagzh is rigorously moral, but he'd sacrifice any of us to his dreams.''

I edged away from Tesseract and stared out the window. Looking at the thousands of suns out there, I shivered a bit, feeling isolated, then turned back to the party.

Black Amber was in a hanging seat with counterbalance weights touching the floor—as high as she could go. Under her, the Rector was stretched out on a mat and cushions, lying on his back like a mammal, weirdly, all eight feet or so of him. He propped himself up on his elbows as though they were furniture he could lean against all night.

Wy'um attached another swing seat to a pulley ring near Amber. As he rose toward her, pulling himself up, the two senior Gwyng officials blinked slowly, little oo's and quivering nostril slits on their faces.

Heat? Not like a dog's or cat's, but something *was* going on. The young Gwyngs and Karriaagzh stared at them. Warst Runnel, who seemed totally unaffected by the Rector's almost reptilian length on the floor, asked, "Don't mind, Rector, if I step across you?''

"Go ahead." The Rector took another drink from the liquor tray, tossed it down, and re-folded his arm behind him. When he saw me, his crest lifted a bit and he wiggled some face feathers, but then the crest went absolutely slack, feathers slopped off to one side, as though the liquor hit his brain right then.

Tesseract sat down under Black Amber's swing chair, while I found a place for myself near enough to hear, but away from the power guys.

Once everyone was settled, Karriaagzh said, "Would one of our guests tell us an origin myth? I always like to see how Mind works in a new species.''

Two of the new aliens said they'd rather hear our myths first, but Edwir Hargun, perhaps bolder because he'd held

Karst people captive, moved away from the sheltering Barcons and said, "I'll try to tell my myth."

"Is it of life or time?" Black Amber singsonged from her swing. Karriaagzh translated to Karst I for Hargun.

"Life, I think." Eyes down, Hargun groped for words in our alien language. "Start. Our planet was hot. The waters dense, thick with . . . chemicals. Air physics shook these waters and chemicals until they . . . made chains. Chains chained other chains. First, chains didn't use the gas that burns with another gas to make water, gas that aids fire. But other chains made this gas and poisoned out the first variety of chains, except for airless places. Not exactly chains." He made spirals with his hands. "Other chains turned to use this fire-gas. Skins developed, and ate the earlier chains . . ." Hargun broke off, sweating, and sighed. "I'm sorry I don't have the words in Karst for my story. We have much to study of Karst on Yauntry, lest we become like the non-fire-gas chains."

"This is the theory of the accidental jarring together," Karriaagzh said, straightening and tightening his face feathers. "I don't approve of this theory. If life came from things being jarred together, then life could be jarred apart. If we are just accidents . . . I prefer to think that life is matter's inevitable expression. All matter drives toward live, for sentience, sapience. We're chemical mobiles, what all sulphur, hydrogen, carbons long to become." Karriaagzh paused and stared at Black Amber until she squirmed, hanging in the air like she was.

Hargun slowly turned red. "Black Amber," Wy'um said in Karst II, "perhaps you should tell a Gwyng tale, having been born on our home planet. We should be reminded of what we lose if we civilize our new contacts too quickly." Wy'um seemed the most sober of the lot.

Amber hooked her arms around her neck. Longer than human arms, they fitted nicely, curved to her sides. If she'd hung upside down, she indeed would have looked like a bat. Her eyes unfocused a bit, then she chanted:

Time began between footsteps, with awareness of walking. Time reached backward to the black Giant Death, whose face no one sees, but who eats the children of Time and Space both.

. . . Time is the giant we walk inside, but Death, his great father, tracks us. Death catches those who stumble, those who lose their time . . .

No one translated for Edwir Hargun and the other aliens for a while, then one of the Barcons seemed to explain Amber's story quickly to Hargun in his own language. The other new aliens sat watching our faces.

Black Amber continued,

As we, warm, moved and made steps in Time, Death had found our tracks. The Gwyngs gambled with Death, to stop him, but forgot what Death was, the first terrible chill of him behind the ones crawling across Space. So Death lured the Gwyngs into gambling again. They lost, but Death promised to be greediest before Gwyngs stepped on two feet to make Time solid, or to wait until Memory dissolved, leaving only Death coming behind, when the people were feeble, searching for the black inside of Space again.

She paused. "Hard to tell it in Karst II, and I think you don't understand Time if you think in Karst I. In the real Gwyng, we have it all in three linked patterns. We see a universe most of you are blind to: sound structures, light-sky-patterns. Like when the sky patterns, the planet rolls to night. But you're blind to that, aren't you?"

"And you have no concept of history," Karriaagzh said.

"We've learned," Black Amber said. "But Time-future is a very odd concept."

"For you," Karriaagzh said in Karst II.

Hargun's Barcons weren't translating this.

"Gwyngs aren't inflexible," Wy'um said. "Now Karriaagzh, your people worshipped the future and spent all their energy (as a life form) leaving messages to it. You [emphatic] tell us your tales. We will see what kind of thing you are."

Karriaagzh stared up at the Gwyngs as though sizing them up as meat, then took another drink. After he gulped, he thought a moment, then said, in Karst I, "I'll tell the story of a man who invented gunpowder." He continued on in Karst I, speaking slowly:

Two thousand years after paper writing began, Azzark sat in his family estate. The juveniles crested up, the scholars translated the old words, the barely fledged fed the babies. But his enemies gathered to destroy Azzark, his records, and all his lineage, so the future would hold no trace of him.

He called on his lineage in sleep and intoxication. Day and night, Azzark called on his lineage, through dreams and old writings. Then in his dreams, one in shaft-broken feathers said the lineage would guide him through rocks and trees of his home. The rocks and trees of his home would save him.

Azzark asked trees what he should do. A half-burned tree in his stove by the young babies, a half-burned hard tree and a baby spoke beyond reason and years—"Powder the trees caught between wood and ashes."

He went to his herds where the juveniles spread yellow rock dust against mites. He knew the dust melted and burned, so he took it back and slept with it dusted through his head feathers. The ancestor spoke in his dreams and said, "Azzark, this rock and the half wood/half ash make an ink to write you in history if you add salt that is not a salt of the ocean." Azzark sent juveniles to a salt cave for baskets of salt–not-salt-of-the-ocean.

And Azzark made his air ink with fine milling stones and built an iron pen, to write *Azzark* forever with thrown steel nibs. And Azzark was revered and remembered for 4 million years.

Karriaagzh twisted his face feathers near the joints of his bill—his smile, I guessed—and said, "Azzark didn't realize that gunpowder had been invented in several locations on our planet thousands of years earlier."

"I understand *that* fable," Edwir Hargun said hotly.

"No," Warst Runnel said to Hargun. "Karriaagzh, the Federation is large and intimidating. Now you've told these newcomers a fable that makes you sound militaristic. History proves that military solutions don't work across species lines. The Academy and Federation want to help species trade peacefully. And besides, didn't all your history tie your species up in knots?''

Karriaagzh's feathers bristled. Instantly, he sprung upright on his hocks, bouncing slightly. He stuck his fingers between his mandibles, in the joint corners, and champed down. Slowly he took his fingers out of his mouth, raised his head, lowered some of the feathers, and said carefully, ''Individuals do die. Species do die. Mine will die out relatively soon. Two of the species which founded the Federation are already extinct. We might have different biologies, different moralities. But intelligence does converge, despite . . . no, *through* all our diversities.''

Trembling, Karriaagzh nestled down on his hocks and withdrew from the party, off in some mental space.

Nobody moved or spoke for a terrible number of minutes. Then Tesseract coughed. Karriaagzh slowly re-focused his eyes and imitated Tesseract's cough. Tesseract nodded—a signal had been exchanged—then drew the alien ambassadors aside.

Cadmium and Rhyodolite reached for Black Amber's ankles, talking to her in Gwyng, not Karst II, but she kicked them away and batted her eyelids more at Wy'um.

''Red Clay (come/where are you?),'' Rhyodolite cried suddenly. ''Distract us.''

I pushed toward them as they stepped nervously by Karriaagzh, who gaped his beak lips slightly at them. Rhyodolite flinched, but Cadmium twitched his irises.

''Back downstairs,'' Rhyo said. ''Fun is over for us.''

We started down the stairs. At the bottom, Hargun turned from Tesseract, and looked up at me with his grey alien face, with those green round eyes. He was the captive now—I remembered very clearly what being a captive was—from both Virginia and from Yauntra.

''They don't do physical violence,'' I said, as simply as I could. ''And the people here are more than weird non-Yauntra-looking creatures.''

''More to damage than simple physical beating,'' Hargun said.

Rhyodolite edged between me and Hargun, toddling down the stairs in his re-built jackboots. Hargun stared at Rhyodolite's hands, then at the wrinkled wide-eyed Gwyng face, and said, ''The rude hands again. Two others plotting tonight, both in *wyn*.'' He mimicked the eye blinks.

Wyn must have been Yauntro for *swing* or *heat*. For a second, Rhyodolite stood four risers above Hargun, astonished, then he said, "Stop!"

"Why? We killed your bird and you don't charge us like real . . ."

Rhyodolite cried an almost ultrasonic shriek. Tesseract, when he saw Rhyodolite's throat tense for the cry, swung Hargun around so that Rhyodolite kicked into Tesseract's massive side, not the Yauntry.

I caught Rhyodolite before he tumbled down the stairs, stood him upright, and held on to him. "You don't understand," he said, forgetting that Hargun literally couldn't understand Karst II, "we die for this stupid Federation. Nerves/guilt."

"Edwir Hargun, the Gwyngs aren't very happy tonight," Tesseract said. "Had you asked, I would have suggested that you avoid them." He rubbed his side and added, "Rhyodolite, maybe I should punch you an asshole."

"That refugeeing Y'ntee," Rhyodolite said, "shot my cadet. Bird death/guilty pleasure."

Greyer than ever, Hargun stood trembling beside Tesseract.

"Separate them," a serving bear said with great exasperation. "It's hard to feed you creatures when you're fighting."

"I thought you said your Federation wasn't violent," Hargun said to me.

"Tell him that kick wouldn't have killed him," Rhyodolite shrilled, trying to shrug me off. "Tell him he stinks all the time, like all apes."

"*Should I let Rhyodolite go?*" I asked Tesseract in English.

"*Okay,*" he said. "*I'll watch him.*"

When I let loose of Rhyodolite's arms, he slumped down on the stairs and put his hands behind his neck, arms at his sides, just like Black Amber had done when she sat in her swing. "Too many new species, all at once," he said. I rubbed his shoulder a bit, ready to grab him again.

Cadmium came down and Gwyng-talked to Rhyodolite, moving him off the staircase. Then he said to me, "Black Amber is making us edgy tonight, but I can't explain."

"She showed Wy'um a glass vial, and someone said she was in heat."

Cadmium shrieked softly at Tesseract. Tesseract nodded

stiffly, anger a Gwyng could read. Hargun said, "You told us we could return to our planets tonight."

"Tell Hargun I'm miserable/sorry," Rhyodolite said. He nibbled at his thumb bases, then offered his hand to Hargun, who just stared at it.

"He apologizes," Tesseract said. "He nibbled any anger secretions out of his thumb glands. Their politeness gesture is to touch fingers lightly."

Hargun said, "Piss on their cheese."

After the alien ambassadors left, Rhyodolite, Cadmium, and I went back to the food tables. "Sorry, Red-Clay-mobbed-by-aliens," Rhyo said, "such a tense night. Black Amber and Wy'um (pre-mating) want to argue down Karriaagzh . . ."

Cadmium said, "Stop, Rhyodolite-nasty."

But Rhyodolite continued, "Black Amber and Karriaagzh will/must continue their ritual argument. Then the bird will feed the toilet—his way of kicking out tension."

Cadmium said, "I've seen him feed the toilet, Rhyodolite. No interest."

"Red Clay is impressed by the bird/vulture."

"I don't need to see him dead drunk, throwing up in the toilet," I said. I was impressed by any creature so alien, so isolated, who could live among the rest of us. I, at least, knew of another couple humans tucked away on some primitive range. But Karriaagzh was *drunk* tonight.

"Not drunk throwing up. He feeds his baby-bird-faced toilet. In the main facility for males. Like sex/body pleasure," Rhyodolite said.

"Where are these facilities?" I asked, since by this time I needed to use a urinal myself.

"More spectacular male facilities you've never seen," Cadmium said as they led me to the door. Rhyodolite hummed and flung it with his shoulder, banging it against a door stop.

The huge room echoed from water falling. Some males spray into waterfalls—here were quiet falls and bubbly falls—whatever your alien bladder craved.

"Without running water," Rhyodolite said, "some people would void in a sink."

Sand boxes, holes in the tiled floor, posts that smelled

slightly. "Some species," Rhyo said, after whoofing and closing his nostrils, "need to leave marks."

Holes in the rock walls and fake tree limbs. In the center of the room, I saw rows of open toilets like Earth's toilets, but with different angles and heights for different posteriors—plastic, not porcelain. And for the shy, closed stalls.

Cadmium rolled a rheostat to dim and brighten the lights. I was almost too amazed to piss, but went over and used a waterfall while Rhyodolite and Cadmium used fake tree holes.

"I'll watch the meat and tell you if I see the bird chunk up," Cadmium said before he slipped out.

"This is the bird's," Rhyodolite said, showing me a toilet—red inside with a red lid—set so someone inside the stalls could see it in the basin mirrors.

We looked at each other. "Too many species," Rhyodolite said, sitting down on the floor. "We pollute/warp each other. You usually do not void in waterfalls. The Rector-bird should never lie on his back. Too many new aliens, even for the bird (but he won't admit it)."

"And Gwyngs usually don't kick nervous aliens," I said.

"Ah, Red Clay, I never had a cadet of mine killed before. Worse it was a bird (almost good . . .)." He sniffed his thumb glands and washed his hands. "Punishment for kick comes."

"Could you go back to the Gwyng planet?" I asked.

"Bored there with babble about sky functions and plastic collections. Terrified of accidents on missions. Life is a paradox, no/yes?"

"What species uses each of these things?" I asked. He walked me around, explaining.

Soon Cadmium stuck his head in and said, "The bird Rector gulps meat. He has his special stones in his gullet."

Rhyodolite dragged me into a closed stall as Cadmium withdrew. We both waited, peering through cracks at the mirrors.

Eventually, Karriaagzh came in, crooning softly. The front of his neck where it met the body surged and his crest swayed from side to side as he balanced unsteadily on his huge legs. He seemed to stare once into the mirrors—I ducked back.

Rhyodolite was right—the bird got off on this. I guess sapients had to get pleasure from feeding their young this way, or else no 10 million years of history. Why get your beak all messy throwing up into a baby unless there's pleasure in it?

Karriaagzh swayed, hands massaging his crop, dangling his tongue, reflected in all the mirrors. Rhyodolite motioned for me to climb up to the stall top, but I thought surely the Rector would hear us.

Oblivious, the Rector bent over his toilet, crest feathers dangling around his eyes, and ran his hands over the bowl. He heaved rather solidly into it—one time, two times, three. Between heaves, he murmured to "baby hole," in ironic tones.

Then he reared back to stare at the toilet bowl before vomiting out a more liquid vomit. Slowly, he raised up on his legs, closed the toilet lid, and flushed.

Rhyo and I slid down into the cubicle. I heard a beak strop itself on wood, then rustling paper and running water.

Then a huge tearing sigh filled the place, as though all the air in his bones, if he had hollow bird bones, rushed out through a tight, hurt throat. That sigh sounded so lonely and painful.

Then I looked over at Rhyodolite. His face was rigid, wrinkles carved of coal; his fingers were arched and twitching. He turned his head and stared back at me with bat eyes, animal-dumb.

After Karriaagzh stumbled out, I said softly, "Rhyodolite?" I watched his throat, his legs, those curved long fingers with the hairs standing on end.

Slowly, intelligence re-entered his eyes. "I am very tired of your human boots," he said, as though Karriaagzh's strange performance at the toilet happened weeks earlier. "Need drugs. Time to blow neurons/nerves to cool black space." He dropped to the floor of the stall and added, "Barcons have a drug for Gwyngs that makes awareness of species differences go/merge/blend. Like bird fantasy of all alike. Unfortunately cuts motor control."

Before we left the male facility, Rhyodolite rinsed his webs with alcohol and held his arms up, spreading the webs to let the alcohol evaporation cool them. "Drugs, drugs," he muttered as he stood there, arms out, "tasty drugs."

"How safe are these drugs?" I asked.

He oo'ed faintly.

* * *

When we pushed our way by blithering aliens to the drugs, we saw Cadmium standing belly against the table, throat lump contracting slightly, almost throbbing. He was staring at a grey box, like a small copying machine with a glass plate and mirrors under the glass. "You put your hand here," Rhyodolite said, pointing to the glass, "and speak your cadet name and I.D. number, and the drug number, so."

A Barcon behind the table said, "We hear you need some 496 very badly, Rhyodolite."

"I'll cooperate."

"496 blurs species differences? That's the drug?" I asked.

"Illusions of oceanic togetherness," the Barcon said, preparing the dispenser box. "You also, Cadmium?"

"Haven't used any drugs for this quota period. They can be scary, but this time, yes."

"What for me?" I asked. "I want to party with them."

By some Karst variation of 2 A.M., Rhyodolite, barefoot at last, took off his uniform top and began his best vampire imitations, rolling his eyes so I could see how huge they were under the lids and skull protrusions.

Too bad, I thought, Gwyngs wrinkle so early, show old age in babyhood.

Waving his webs—like diagonals of black crepe paper—Rhyodolite clicked his teeth at my neck, hooting. I sank to the floor, laughing, but still not so stoned that I'd dare point out that five-foot-two-inch vampires looked silly. "How nice, Rhyodolite," I finally managed to say, "that you've changed into something almost human."

The tri-colored girl I'd talked to earlier came up. "Help me," she ordered as she pulled out a piece of plastic with what looked like round Band-Aids in it. Cadmium and she began talking seriously as he applied one of the sticky circles to her inner elbow.

Wonderful drugs, I decided. "No aliens here, just a lot of protoplasmic ooze," I told Rhyodolite.

"You're doing nicely," he replied.

Life fuzzed up and soon I was riding with Cadmium, the tri-colored girl, and Rhyodolite in the little two-person electric car. The Gwyngs kept saying *things*—squares, oblongs,

funny swirls. I didn't know whether it was the drugs or the
way they were babbling, cutting visuals on in my skull computer.

Finally, Rhyodolite said clearly, more or less, "We must
swim."

"Swimming in the gym would be boring, Rhyodolite,"
Cadmium said, "when we have a starlit pool."

"But, Cadmium, the gym is open. For Jereks and other
night pests—but if I saw one now . . ."

"Get suits for swimming. Officer's card."

The girl shrugged and looked hard at me while Rhyodolite
climbed all over himself getting out of the car. He came back
with four male brief suits.

No, lady, I thought in English, *I won't touch you. Best we
could do would be make a mule*. Thinking that reminded me
of Calcite and cut my drug high, but the mood rolled right
over and we were four great guys having a great time together
on a super planet.

And besides, I knew in my bones that the girl'd mastered
fighting styles humans couldn't have imagined even in Japan.

So we swam under that glowing alien sky—*stars so red
and blue I can see them up close*.

"I wish (sometimes)," Rhyodolite said, floating on his
back, "that we could be like this with each other forever. But
the drug spoils the brain. Maybe Karriaagzh's brain self-
generates a safer illusion drug than this—Barcons should
check."

"Shut up, Gwyng," the girl said, swimming around us.

For decades, it seems, we floated in the starred liquid, four
people together. I said, "I wish Karriaagzh and Black Amber
could do this together."

Rhyodolite dropped his legs and turned in the water to look
at me. "Horrible to come out of it the next day, have double
sense of birds, friendly terrors. I have enough guilt."

Eternity in the floating stars, until Rhyodolite wanted to
touch the girl's breasts, explaining earnestly that he had
breasts once, but he doubted Barcon fakes felt like the real
things. He sounded more lonely than horny. "Just let me
place a little fingertip on one?"

"Time," Cadmium said ominously, "is coming back. (Painful) tomorrow patterns the sky."

As the planet turned to face the sun again, we all dressed,

dripping wet, in our uniforms and sashes. And then we looked at each other, in low-angle sunlight that accentuated the differences between us. My nerves jangled from the hangover, from sleeplessness.

More and more brutal light. Rhyodolite managed to drive—fortunately few other cars were out. The girl-alien sat on my lap, her leg muscles squirming as though she was trying to sit lightly. She yawned and grinned at me, her eyelids bouncing up and down—short dense eyelashes in two colors of hair.

At her dorm, she crawled off my legs and climbed over Cadmium to get out. "Watch your pouch kin," she told Cadmium in passing.

I managed to fall out of the car when we reached my dorm, and sat on the pavement laughing at the weird creatures who'd driven me home. They started koo'ing, then Cadmium punched Rhyodolite in the shoulder to get him driving again.

As my roommates were getting dressed, arguing about what it meant that I wasn't back, I walked in, shedding uniform, headed straight to bed.

The bird wanted to see my sash. I'd left it in Rhyodolite's car. Arggh. My computer spoke, "Red Clay, sleep until noon. Then physical education evaluation, remedial chemistry, and English classes . . ."

Damn Black Amber, I thought, driving the bed ceilingward, wrapped in Karst's best imitation polyester sheets. Gypsum set an alarm, I noticed, as my eyelids started sticking shut.

After the Barcons finished running me on a treadmill collecting my carbon dioxide or something, after various aliens condemned me in chemistry, and after Tesseract's erudite English chatter about Charles Dickens and his specific significance as a human explainer, I came back to my room stiff, half woozy, to discover the furniture had arrived. Minus the Earth-from-space shot—something about planet chauvinism.

Instead, they'd hung a large photo-poster of a little mouse with almost-human ears. "It's a tree shrew," Gypsum told me, his face twisted with humor, "your most distant traceable kin."

Old Tree Shrew made a nice accent—humble beginnings, like the old log cabin photos people'd have in their mobile homes.

And Granite Grit's mirror had arrived. He took one look at his quill tips and hung a sheet over the mirror, "until I look pretty, with full feathers."

Gypsum stopped teasing us about kin and mirror long enough to bitch about the laser discs that had come with the music machine.

Old Shrew seemed to look down at his distant cousin with anxious wonder.

The next morning, I made a VCR tape for Warren to let him know I was alive and okay, so he could see it once he was out of the crazy house or prison.

After I made the tape, Black Amber sent a message to me over the terminal: No public apology for you or for Rhyodolite. You will go to Yauntra as a linguistics team observer/trainee. Not immediately. You need more polish. Black Amber, Sub-Rector, Academy and Institutes.

Yauntra—damn Yauntra again. Being a cadet or officer was real serious, I realized, not a game. I began to read Federation history, trying to figure out those wars that left melted wall stumps.

= 6 =

The Other

One morning several weeks later, Black Amber grumbled at me over the computer phone about my academic progress. I lay in bed, half listening, checking out the plants in the courtyard—especially the bush with narrow prickly leaves, like a dieting holly, and the pillow shrub. From week to week, they grew at each other as though they were going to duel under the alien sun.

Terribly lonely, *alienated*, you might say in English, I became a cosmic book buster, but it was a harder school than Earth's. No class lasted longer than a week, and some were condensed agony, diurnal cadets going sleepless lest we miss some fantastic conceit blazing through a crepuscular alien brain at four in the morning. But I hardly saw anyone again after a class.

"Rhyodolite and Cadmium now have the same rank, since the Yauntry complained," Black Amber said through the computer speaker. "They went off into space."

Not into it precisely. The gate system avoided the tedious empty spaces and cosmic rays by hopping right from Karst to other gravity nets—instant alien, in no time at all. "The computer *tried* to show me gate math, once when I asked," I told her sleepily.

But I was good at comparative anatomy . . . I found out that Gwyngs have disgusting sex lives. They go into season—like Black Amber at the party, only she was tamed down by some Barcon counter-pheromones—like cats or dogs. And the females like being pregnant as much as they can get, because for a Gwyng, delivery is like coming.

"Red Clay? Are you listening?" Black Amber said.

"How did the thing with Wy'um work out?" I asked. The babies, smaller than kittens, just head and arms and a tadpole-like tail, crawl hand over tiny hand up the sensitive stomach hairs. After a pouch host has had its own litter, the Gwyngs take out some of the pouch host babies. Mother Gwyngs make their little Gwyngs, crawling and dying, go up into that cow-rhino beast.

"We were merely trying out your morality."

And the female goes into heat until she's pregnant again. Gwyngs.

The senior instructor had said, "If they were successful with every parturition we'd be outnumbered by Gwyngs in a hundred years, all of us."

Barcons, on the other hand, mate for life and tend the babies together, both parents giving milk. One instructor was a Barcon.

Weird stuff.

"Work harder in chemistry," Black Amber said again and signed off. She never came to see me, just bugged me over the terminal.

Three times a week, I worked out in the gym as the Barcons prescribed—mostly with free weights since designing machines for over a hundred different species would be impossible—all the different ranges of motion, tendon insertions.

The gym was a long hall with mirrors and video displays on the walls. Some Karst II species used ultrasonic feedback, but I just watched the mirror and the monitor and tried to move as I should.

Furry and remote, Barcon instructors prowled around. Once or twice a week, one would come up and move my joints through their range of motion.

The hall was cold, about 50 degrees American. Some species had no sweat glands. Other aliens, even if they did, exercised all bundled up.

Sometimes the barbell collars were wet, and the whole gym rank with un-Earthly odors.

We all watched each other, but nobody was friendly.

Granite Grit took the cover off his terminal, filing down a rod to fit the screws like Warren did.

"Is there any information not available to your computer?" Granite Grit asked me.

"Can't get anything on Earth on my terminal," I said, not paying much attention as I tried to figure out why Amber'd scheduled a Gwyng ceremonial game session for me.

"Could you ask some questions of your terminal and I'll ask mine of Earth?" Granite said, moving his bed down to floor level.

We tried, but the computer got very coy: Accesses to all computers in this area are cross-restricted.

Lifting his hocks high, Granite went to his cubicle for components. He tried to fit them in my terminal, cursing in bird with his nictitating membranes half covering his eyes.

"Stop," I told him. "I need my terminal for study."

I got back up in the biology program and hammered on. "Does studying and work all the time bother you?" Granite asked.

"Sure," I said. "But . . ." He'd come over to the central area and when I looked at him, he sank down on his hocks and twisted his hands together.

He looked so concerned. Shit, I was lonely. But tomorrow I had hateful remedial chemistry, a whole lab of it with three instructors, so I switched programs, studied while Granite Grit tried to fit a scanning wand system to his terminal. Finally, I went to sleep tangled in valences, bonds, weights, and coils and coils of carbonaceous matter.

The next day, I came back to find camera units fixed to all our computers.

Gypsum said, "You sneaking shits," pivoted on his heel, and thereafter only came to the room to sleep.

As I watched some weird Gwyng exchange of small pebbles in patterns I couldn't follow, I wondered what Black Amber would do if one day I didn't go through the schedule. Just stop for a day, fool around. What did they do here for playing hooky? Maybe they'd throw me out on the primitive range? *Yeah, and maybe I don't give a shit.* I never saw

Black Amber or Tesseract after the party—weeks, months maybe, had gone by.

So the next day, I ran the track, ate the alien breakfast, and went down to the lake where we'd swum stoned, alien differences obliterated. Great drug, I thought, they need to improve it so we can dose out every day. I'd seen a fish jump then, so now brought a pin and string. Grubbing under some rocks, I found a live alien thing—like an earthworm but with a crown of cilia. Reddish brown. I threaded it on the bent pin.

The bass-sort-of fish came up with a bulging belly. As I grabbed it, I felt squirming inside, and silver babies fell out and swam away, or flapped on the bank.

God, even the fish are alien! I threw the mama back and trembled.

Under trees with tiny silver-bottomed leaves, I sat, then lay back and napped restlessly, as though I could dream my way back to Earth's familiar jails.

After my nap, I wandered over to the memorial walls and found a new name added. Looking at the names, I stood, trying futilely to put my hands in non-existent pockets. A cool alien wind tapped my face and shuffled plate-size leaves until they squirmed on their almost muscular stems and rolled up. Damn alien tree didn't want to shade me.

Mica's name wobbled as my eyes filled with tears—not crying for him. He wasn't getting teased for being a hick. Same bullshit as before, for what? The chance to let aliens shoot at me? Some glory for less than five dollars' worth of gold on a granite wall.

Maybe, I thought, I should volunteer for some really impressive mission—go down in altered face and foul the horrid plots of some truly offensive alien.

And live.

But I didn't heal fast enough, I'd been told after my medical evaluations here.

Goddamn stuck here, hungry, with all the hassles. I thought about going for lunch, but I'd be back on the computer. They might catch me before I ate. I had a few vending machine tokens in my tunic pocket, so I walked hunched down to a building with snack machines, watching so I could turn if an alien I recognized came by.

All the weirdest aliens were out today—one bird, then

several pug-faced ones like the hospital receiving clerk, pairs of Barcons who walked like the secret lords of us all. A Gwyng female strutted by, trailed by three Gwyng males with nostril slits clapping open and shut.

And here I was, eating alien crackers filled with unsweetened jelly that was maybe poisonous to me.

All afternoon, I walked from one courtyard to another, up by the Rector's glass and stone lodge, down by the main gate where I saw alien peddlers out beyond it, over by each of the main towers, stopping to sit on stumps of fried ancient walls.

Even with all the towers, I finally got lost, but found the lake around sunset, planet roll-around time. *I surrender!* I went back to my eating hall.

I was so hungry. The crackers hadn't been enough for all my walking. "Where have you been?" a tablemate asked.

"Out," I said, punching in my choices.

Code flashed across the table display. A Barcon came out of the kitchen area, headed straight for our table. "Cadet Red Clay, I will walk you back to your dorm."

"I'm so hungry," I said, almost whining.

As my tablemates looked from him to me, the Barcon replied, "You may finish your meal."

I almost choked on the food when the little bear brought it. The Barcon stood, waiting. As I got up, the Barcon moved in close behind. "No trouble," I said. "I'm heading back for my dorm."

I walked across campus, trying to pretend I wasn't aware of the furry giant following me. The Rector's Man Tesseract and a hugely angry Black Amber were waiting at my room.

"He appears anxious, but not excessively so," the Barcon said. Tesseract looked relieved, but Amber re-grouped her face muscles toward disgust. Tesseract sat down in one of my chairs, looked from her to me, and smiled faintly.

"Did you have fun?" he asked.

"No." I sat down on my bed and began to finger the controls.

"One shouldn't throw out schedules unless one is going to have fun, Cadet Red Clay," he said.

"Yes, Rector's Man Tesseract," I said, not trusting to smile myself. We all paused there a moment.

"I want a pass for Red Clay tonight, so we can see what

happens to those who can't/won't cope with our system,"
Black Amber finally said.

"Black Amber, I read that you tried to introduce him to the
primitives," Tesseract said. "Red Clay, we seem to have
similar ancestors, if that's kin of yours." He looked at the
Old Tree Shrew poster on my wall. "Males of your species
find it hard to fit in with a new group?"

"Yes, Rector's Man Tesseract." I looked at Amber, whose
face twitched toward an oo, very slightly. "I'm sorry I
ignored my schedule today, but I was so tired. I just keep
studying into the night. I don't know how I'm doing—*no
report cards*. I feel stupid in chemistry. People make fun of
me, my planet, my species. I don't have friends."

Black Amber sat down. Tesseract began, "Red Clay, you've
picked up the necessary basics of comparative sapient behavior. Considering that you've had to learn all new terms and
you lack the chemistry, you're doing reasonably well in biology. The gym observers have made no complaints. Your
reading shows an interesting curiosity. Unfortunately, the
computer shows you do nothing but study. No dances, gallery
visits, casual discussion groups . . ."

"I'm a *goddamn* refugee."

Black Amber looked from the Tree Shrew poster to me,
then said, "Tesseract, I *do* monitor my cadet's progress.
Cadet, are these studies too difficult/demanding for you?
We'll bring back more of your species if you are a successful
cadet here. I met several prospects for your breeding/social
group when I was on your planet."

"What do I need the *dumbshit* chemistry for?"

"You need the chemistry to understand weapons classes,
astronomy, biological and medical systems." Black Amber
was bloody implacable.

"Yes, chemistry, then. But what kind of English do I need
to know anyway?"

"My dear Red Clay," Tesseract said, "how will your
people like to have their species represented by a *hick* when
they finally come to space? Your English has improved."

"I speak with an alien accent, thanks to all the surgery.
You're alienizing my English even more."

"Red Clay," Black Amber said smoothly, "a slightly alien

accent would be more desirable (sexually/socially) than a backward one.''

''*Oh-fucking-kay*,'' I said.

''But your reading is a trifle disorganized,'' Black Amber continued. ''Thank you, Tesseract, Quad-duty Barcon, I'll deal with him now.''

''He has done well for an isolate,'' the Barcon rumbled as it turned to leave. Tesseract winked at me and followed the Barcon out.

''*If you have my future Earth friends picked out, then I suppose you have some fucking aliens to shove down my throat, too*,'' I said to Black Amber in English.

''I can easily get a translation of that,'' she said, drawing back from me a little. ''I have an excellent memory for random-pattern sounds: 'If you have my future E'th frientz pigged out, then I suppose you h'v some fuckin aliens to shove down my thoroat, too.' You should tell me what that means.''

''You have my Earth friends picked out? Who do you plan to have as friends for me here?'' I asked more calmly.

She looked thoughtful for a Gwyng. ''Cadmium should be back fairly soon. Rhyodolite had a rough time and isn't on Karst now.''

''I'm not a Gwyng, you know.''

''Yes, you've made that clear/plain with traces of obnoxious behavior. But I want you to be perfect of your kind. I will take you to see something tonight. Academy failures live there if they can't get passage home.''

Thinking of Calcite, I said bitterly, ''Why not? It's been an awful day. Nothing could make it worse.''

We drove in her car, the one she'd loaned Rhyodolite the night of the party, me sitting grumpily beside her as we left the campus, passed some Institute buildings in stone and glass, and then headed north up toward the slums.

To me, coming from the rural dumps, Karst's back streets—plastic windows and streets with ruts in the plasphalt—weren't so bad, being well lit with heavy grates over vapor lights.

Then I noticed a young slick-skinned officer grab the crotch of a furry female in a short tight tunic. She reached into a bag she had slung over her shoulder and pulled out a glass ampule. *Arousal pheromones.* "*She* couldn't handle her classes," Black Amber said as the blue-clad officer rumpled her head fur and led her away. "Or her ancestors couldn't."

The bright lights dangling from the tough chromed poles suddenly seemed garish. Black Amber looked for one special horror among all the aliens hawking stuff from the sidewalks or out of the little ragged shops.

"Unsuccessful of your kind," she said, pulling up to the curb by some people dressed in coarse wools and cheap synthetics. The men looked up—they were like the man who'd been dragged in earlier to meet me. These humans led heavy-furred creatures with humps and strange horns—not quite cows. Never saw a cow that furry, or carrying packs, either.

One of the men spat down on the sidewalk in front of Black Amber as he passed, leading his beast.

"The sapients smell just like you," Black Amber said. "For centuries they've wandered between the hills and Karst City. Free trader families, also your species, sell grains, milk oils, and weavings for them."

"They don't like me already," I said.

"Ah, but some of their women might," she said. "They think they are in hell. We try on occasion to train them."

"Why don't you people clean this slum up?"

"Deal with your studies better, then you can become a City Committee member and reform this area yourself." She started her car. "Perhaps we should hire you a female."

"*Damn you*, Black Amber." I looked back and saw one man point to the car. The others laughed. "You want me to fail? Get shot by crazed aliens if I don't?"

Black Amber didn't answer. She closed her eyes and squeezed her nostrils shut. But when we were close to the Academy, she said softly, "You can go to a more remedial chemistry class."

After a terribly silent ride through the Academy grounds, she dropped me off at my dorm and didn't look at me as I closed the car door.

The Ewit was furious at both Granite and me. "Both shits for roommates/forced to take," Gypsum said. "Gwyngs watch the refugee; Jereks the bird. Horrible."

The bird lowered his bed and stepped toward Gypsum,

huge threatening steps. ''Listen to your milk-piss speaking tapes, monstrosity, and leave us alone.''

''I can't bring my friends to this room,'' Gypsum squalled in Karst II.

''Shut up, mouse, or I'll eat you.''

I asked my terminal for the survival rate among cadets, wondering again what I'd gotten myself into:

> Out of five contact teams and linguistics mis-
> sions, generally one member will be held for
> questioning or interrogation for more than five
> days. Casualties range from one to three individ-
> uals, including non-official actions, per three mis-
> sion years.

Terrific.

The next morning, Tesseract, through my computer, invited me to a three-day visit at his country place. Rather than sound desperate, I asked if the weekend after the four-day rotation would be fine.

Low-rent chemistry, one step away from patched plastic slums. We were all embarrassed to be there, ill-educated first-generation cadets and refugees. The teacher was a thin gentle fuzzy who seemed weary the whole class period. Chemistry, I realized by the break, was a lot like drug-making— that's probably why I hated it.

That night, Gypsum was out as usual, so the bird and I moved in on the music system.

The bird and I went through the music tracks, me hating some he liked okay, Granite hating some I could stand to listen to, but both agreeing on the hideous.

Granite went back to his cubicle and came back wrapped in a sheet, even over his head. He scratched some around his ear holes, then began to play some cuts over and over, teaching me what to listen to in weird un-Earthly stuff.

''They think I'm likely to mess up,'' I said, ''because the only others of my species here are savages, or something.'' I wished I had some mountain music here, or some blues like black church people do on the piano between hymns.

''Pressures may drive me insane,'' Granite said, sitting

down on his hocks, with a cushion for his elbows. "Some hideous force controls this Federation; I must identify it." His naked skin shuddering a little under the sheet, he put on another disc. "My planet . . ." As the music played, he closed his eyes, first the nictitating membranes, then the regular eyelids, from the bottom up.

I asked, "Your planet?"

He hissed, "Yes, hush." When the songs stopped, he stayed down on his hocks staring at the disc player, staring at it. "Red Clay, are you ever afraid? Seriously afraid."

"Of here?" I asked back. "Like I joined an army and didn't know people got killed doing contacts?"

"Of me?" He turned his head toward me, beak tucked down, brown eyes open wide. Pin feathers had sprouted around his ears. Then he slowly stood up, beaked head over me, and dropped his sheet.

We stared at each other. "A little," I said.

"Well, now I'm ugly. You should see me when I've got feathers. They're beautiful."

"What's it like, growing feathers?"

"They tickle—bigger coming in than your hairs. I have a stone in my toilet cubicle to scratch against." He raised his head slightly—more relaxed?

"Could I see?"

Granite shrugged one shoulder. "Yes, if I can see your toilet cubicle." He wrapped the sheet over his shoulders again.

"Sure."

His was weird—a dust shower with ultraviolet lights, a slot in the wall. I guessed he was like a Gwyng or a chicken and didn't separate shit and piss, just backed into the grey plastic depression around the slot.

He did have the same small basin with the mirror over it—Karst standard, always with the water temperature set on the dial. He liked his hot.

I looked inside the shower at a rough black stone like a five-foot-tall pumice footstick. He'd rubbed skin flakes off on it, and even bits of feet scales, arm scales. I wondered what the ultraviolet lights did.

We both came out almost embarrassed—at least I was.

"Don't you get cold from the water shower?" he asked.

''They gave me a hot and warm control.''

''Ah, I'd like that for the dust.''

''Bet they'd do it if you asked.''

''You're more their kind of alien than I am.''

''Karriaagzh?''

''Problem with non-hard-wired brains—they mop up influences, go weird. As a bird, he's an imposter.''

''I sure don't think of him as a mammal.''

Granite sighed and stalked back to his bed, rode it up high, then had to come back for his home-planet music disc.

Gypsum abandoned the room except to sleep, so Granite Grit wrapped up in a sheet each evening and played music, sitting like a humongous nestling, his scaly elbows propped up on a red-lacquered stand.

''You seem sad,'' I said one day after hearing the same home music disc over and over.

''I was forced to come here.''

''Oh.''

''Let me test your ears on this,'' he said. ''I can't go out without the hateful uniform.''

I turned off my display screen and sat cross-legged on the other side of the music player. He stared at my legs. ''How did you fold them?'' he asked. ''Show me again.'' I stood up and sat back again. ''Very strange. What this music does is twine pitches in our scale. I hope you can hear the entire sound range.''

He taught me alien bird music, and I was not so lonely. But, four nights later, another bird, olive and brown like Xenon, came in with two Barcons. Granite hunched down, clinging to his sheet.

''We need your help,'' the other bird said. ''Another one of your species, Academy name of Sulphur . . .''

Granite got up with a hop-spring from those backward knees. ''You didn't come for me then?''

''We don't deal with conflicts between species and Federation,'' a Barcon said. ''Can you help us with Sulphur? He's xenofreaked.''

Granite dropped the sheet and pulled on his black uniform, saying, ''Don't report me for not wearing . . .''

"Hurry," the Barcons said, their hands on his sloping shoulders.

Granite was gone until after uniform change hour. When he came back, I saw a huge bruise beside his beak. He didn't say anything, but brought the bed down and stripped his uniform off, disappeared into the toilet cubicle for a while. His shoulders were bruised, too.

When he came out, naked, he collapsed, awkwardly, on his bed and flicked his nictitating membranes back and forth across his eyes, not bothering to raise the bed. A clear fluid drooled off the tip of his beak.

"What happened?" I asked. Granite gestured no, and drove the bed up. I heard his fists slamming against the mattress, over and over.

Gypsum came in and asked, "They tell him not to stuff his computer full of spy chips?"

"Leave us alone," I said, "or I'll beat your ass if he doesn't."

"I'm moving completely out," Gypsum said, headed out the door.

In the morning, Granite shook under sheets—I saw his yellow-skinned hand convulsively gripping and twisting his thin sleeping mat. I pulled on my pants. "Granite?" I asked, going up, but keeping back some.

"Mammals have squishy minds," he said.

"Granite," I said, "you need help?"

"Couldn't the Barcons be quick in their killing?" He stared down at me with eyes half covered by membranes, like a sick cat.

I didn't know what to do, so I typed in my computer that my roommate was shaking and not getting out of bed, accused me or mammals in general of poisoning Sulphur.

The computer flashed: Enter cadet name and general type: I typed Granite Grit, bird.

"Sulphur . . . lost control," Granite said, "utterly. All aliens terrified . . . we, too, aliens, not feathered. The Rector came . . . held him down while the Barcons . . . The Barcons were sorry."

A chip voice came out of my terminal: Is Granite Grit able to communicate with other species?

Granite almost stopped breathing and stared at the machine. I said, "Yes, but he's upset due to what happened to his con-specific." Then I said, "Granite, can you communicate?"

"Mammal brains. I want to go outside the wall, run, just run."

Barcons will be over, the computer's voice said.

"No!" He tore at the mattress with his scale-backed hands, breaking his fingernails back to the thick part.

The voice of the computer changed. "Red Clay, this is Tesseract. We can excuse you from classes if you think you can help Granite Grit. Barcons will not enter the room. See if you can bring him to the Rector's complex."

I was a little under six feet and not sure how my muscle insertions compared to the bird's. "Granite, I can't drag you out. If you don't want to bring the bed down, I'll have to tell them I can't help."

"I'm scared. I don't understand mammal thinking."

"When I was coming here from Earth, I got scared like this. Come on with me. If you faint, I can't hold you up."

Tesseract spoke again through the computer, "Red Clay, what's happening?" The bird jumped.

"Don't talk out," I said. "And please give me time."

"I suppose I'm a nuisance," Granite Grit said, hands on the bed control, but not bringing it down. "Can he promise me that the Barcons won't dose me with the drug that paralyzed Sulphur?"

Granite's computer whirred. I read, We will be more careful.

"They'll be more careful. Do you drink tea? Tesseract'll make you a nice cup of tea at the Rector's office. He gave me tea on the ship." I spoke softly, still not getting too close to him.

"Don't talk to me like I was . . . one in down."

"*For Christ's sakes, get your bird-ass down here then*," I said in frustrated English. I realized he was worse than a bit nuts, and an alien who outweighed me. "Look, I want you to be all right."

"We're trapped by the Academy. Zoo sapients."

The computer whirred again. Tell him that if he comes in and talks to us, we may, stress may, give him a pass to run outside if he allows us to accompany him. Us can be you or Barcons, whoever he feels comfortable with.

I had the machine print this out and went to hand the paper up to Granite, who reared back, glittering eyes narrowed. I flinched, turned my head sideways so he couldn't blind me if he struck.

"Red Clay!" He sounded almost shocked. One of his hands went up to massage around his beak while the other one took the paper from me.

"Don't rear back like that. That's the way birds on Earth do before they peck."

He shuddered. "I didn't realize." Then he straightened himself out on the bed, legs tucked neatly under his body, and read the printout. He looked horrible—bruised face and body shaking. "I'll go," he finally said. His hand clutched convulsively on the controls as he lowered the bed. He fished his uniform out from under a wad of sheets on the floor, and sighed deeply before dressing.

"Tesseract, if you're still listening," I said, "he's coming with me."

"Great, Barcons will follow."

Granite hissed something in bird that ended in *Barcons* and sat down on the floor, breathing hard.

"Would you rather go in a car?" I asked, wondering if he'd go claustrophobic. I wanted to touch him, but I was afraid to get too close just right now.

"Less embarrassing than having Barcons trail me across campus," he replied, pressing his hands flat to the floor. His emerging quills went erect.

"The Barcons will drive. We'll send a car. See them outside your door," Tesseract said.

Granite shuddered and slowly levered himself off the floor. I saw muscles in his arms twitch. "Can Red Clay come with me?" he asked Tesseract through the computer.

Pause.

Long pause.

"The Barcons outside your door will make the final decision on that," Tesseract said.

Skinny muscles quivering under his bruised skin, Granite

looked at me and said, "I'm ready." He looked like he was prepared to die, the haws slack in his eyes.

We walked to the corridor and saw four Barcons slouched against various walls, one with a speaker/talk button in his ear. Swarms of dark bodies, fuzzy skins, other student aliens gawked, hurrying by fast.

"You're Granite Grit?" the Barcon with the speak/talk button asked.

"Yes," he said sadly, "that's what you call me. I'd like a ride to the Rector's complex, please. And I need Red Clay's company."

The Barcon reached for Granite's elbow slowly, but the bird's head reared back. "We'd prefer that you accept some light sedation," the Barcon said, "not what we gave Sulphur. We would not have hurt one of you deliberately while your species was under investigation."

Granite closed his eyes and pushed out his arm, holding it out stiffly with his other hand. He had a twitch above one eye, just like a human with a tic. "Please don't make it lethal," he said. "You four could drop me if you wanted. Not without injuries. I could kill . . ." Granite shut up, still holding his arm out, braced against the other hand.

"We want no more accidents. Your group seems very drug-sensitive."

"I saw. Still you want to sedate *me*."

"Maybe if I came," I said, "he'd be calmer."

Granite opened his eyes, looked at me, and said, "Red Clay must come."

"Red Clay, sit in front. Granite Grit, you might shock out from fear if we inject you now. Sit in back between us."

We went out to the Barcon's car, a green mini-bus with a plastic carapace. Granite looked inside before he awkwardly stepped into the back, his hocks not quite fitting in on the seat. "Maybe we should have walked," he said, closing his hands tightly on the back of the front seat and twisting around between the two Barcons.

I reached back and stroked his fingers, feeling little scales on the first-finger joints. He clung harder to the seat. His eyes squeezed tightly shut, the muscles around them jumping.

We weren't headed for the Rector's lodge. I wondered if the Barcons were taking Granite straight to the infirmary. He felt my fingers tighten on his and looked at me. We pulled up to a white-tile-fronted building with chromed pillars and black wood trim.

"Infirmary?" I asked.

"No," the Barcon with the com ear button said.

"It's not the lodge."

"No, office," the Barcon answered. Me picking up Granite's nervousness, we walked into the hall. Granite looked at his naked feet as if he wished he'd worn his bird shoes. His nails tapped the hardwood floor like little pony hooves.

Stairs. He went up them sideways, as if terrified of losing his balance. At Tesseract's office a scared Gwyng showed us both into the room where Tesseract was sitting behind a stout desk. Granite looked around at the seating instruments, saw a high padded stand, and jumped on it. Tesseract slowly got up from his desk and sat in an armchair.

"Would you feel more comfortable," he said to Granite, who trembled on his perch, "if Tom Red Clay left?"

"No."

Tesseract, one hand stroking his skull crest, looked at me with dismay, then watched Granite while Barcons waited in the doorway. Granite plucked the stand's padding nervously with his broken nails, tensely crouched on his hocks, not down on his breast.

"Help me," Granite finally said. "But no drugs."

"Your species finds life here difficult," Tesseract said calmly. "I think your government asked a lot of you. What can we do to help?"

"Stripping us of feathers, putting us in mammal clothes. You have open sex organs. We don't."

"Don't rip the seat cover," Tesseract said. "Could you trust us? Last night we heard another of you make some terrible threats."

"You know what we've been doing here?"

"What you've been trying to do, yes. That's not at issue now. You need help for this anxiety. Then we'll talk to your home planet officials."

"Your rector was an isolated bird. I don't know how he survived." Granite Grit looked tragic, eyes half covered by membranes, beak dripping.

Karriaagzh came up to the door and leaned against the

frame, crest fully erect and bent up against the frame top. "Because I had to. Pull your shields back."

Granite blinked fast and opened his eyes quite wide, shields back. Brown eyes with that ugly bruise under one of them—Karriaagzh's were a baleful yellow. "I survived," the bigger bird said, "because my race was dying and I had to link it with others who'll carry our memories and intelligence forward."

"Rector, what force holds this Federation together?"

"Curiosity, trade links, the need for peace. Any race that can work the translocational geometries is impossible to kill off. Try and in a thousand years the species becomes utterly ferocious. So the Federation was founded." Karriaagzh's crest settled and his face feathers relaxed. "So, Granite Grit Ahlchinna, what makes *you* most uncomfortable today? Not your species, you?"

"Not being able to run and catch things."

"What about the little aliens who think you plan to eat them? Make you nervous?" Karriaagzh then noticed me. "What is he doing here?" he asked Tesseract.

"I'm his roommate," I said.

Karriaagzh's head went back on what must have been a longish neck under those feathers. "Black Amber's," he said in Karst II. "You were to be tested with a bird after your misbehavior with Xenon. Well, this bird had his own agenda, didn't he?"

Granite Grit said, "Rector, I wanted Red Clay's company. He's an oddity among these people also."

"And didn't spec a thing while you frinkled the computer." Karriaagzh dipped into Karst student slang then.

"I'm not an informer," I said.

"Rector," Tesseract said.

Granite looked back at me and settled down on the high perch, not poised ready to jump anymore.

"Other species have learned to trust us," Karriaagzh said.

"Rector," Granite replied, "even you are alien to me."

Karriaagzh asked, "Do you itch?"

"Yes," Granite Grit said. "Very difficult to go through fledging again."

The grey crest flicked. "I have something for you," the

Rector said. "Tesseract will get it from my office when you've settled down for his tea. His teas are not deadly."

"I suspect we all should have some tea," Tesseract said, sweating a little. He pulled out an electric pot and two mammal cups and a bird cup with a short spout. "And do you want any, too, Karriaagzh?"

The crest went up slowly. "*I* don't need it," Karriaagzh said and went back to his office. While the water was heating, Tesseract closed all the interconnecting doors.

"I don't make Federation policy," he said to Granite, "I just try to keep the students alive and studying. Tom Red Clay is coming to my house this weekend. Perhaps you would like to come along, too. We live near farmland and hills. If you're calm enough, I think you could run there. Maybe later, we'll bring a small group of your species to the farm."

Granite watched Tesseract's hands tremble slightly as he poured the tea. "You work under the . . . Karriaagzh."

"Yes," Tesseract answered. He lifted the lid of the bird cup and filled it with the tea, then looked at Granite Grit and dropped another tea bag in for a little extra strength.

"Like a zoo with intelligent specimens," Granite said.

Tesseract smiled. "Precisely the way I describe it." He took the tea bag out and handed Granite his cup.

Granite took it with both hands and looked at the spout, then tested some of the tea against his wrist. "You're not afraid of him?" he asked Tesseract.

"I'm not afraid of him as an archetypical predator from ancestral dreams. I have . . ." Tesseract shut himself up, but he looked strangely at me. Then he grinned.

The bird said, "I hope you know, sir, that birds aren't put at ease by what you mammals call humor."

"I remember. Don't, however, try to be too dignified. We find that hilarious in any species, even our own."

The bird shot Tesseract a glance that needed no specialist in behavior to analyze, then poured tea down his throat. I almost smiled. Then Granite put the cup down and covered his face with his hands, which looked diseased, oozing patches around the scales, as though he'd been picking at them. Tesseract said, didn't ask, "Still shaky."

"Yes," Granite mumbled, words slurred against those rigid lips.

"Tell me, Granite Grit," Tesseract asked softly, "what do I look like to you?"

Granite looked up and said, "A giant lactating monster."

Tesseract sipped his own tea then, and asked, "What do you feel like in mammal clothes?"

"Ugly." Granite drank more tea. "I don't want my body to be seen by my people like this—gross, naked. To die like this . . ." Some fluid dripped off his beak tip and Tesseract slowly got up and handed Granite a napkin. Granite wiped his beak and continued, "I don't want to die in a naked ugly skin. Please let me run. I feel so jumpy."

"What if you panic while you run? We'd have trouble catching you without hurting you."

"I won't panic. I'm not panicking now."

Tesseract's intercom/phone lit up. He answered it and went back to his desk, going "um, um, yes" into the mouthpiece as he rifled through a desk drawer. He came back with a vial of little blue pills and shook one out onto his palm. "I'd feel better if you tried to rest now. The Barcons swear this would be safe for you. Another one of your guys . . ."

Granite's eyes went wide. Tesseract moved toward him slowly, saying, "Mild, not like the injections. A muscle relaxant. You're twitching all over."

Granite held out his hand and gently took the pill off Tesseract's palm, looked at it, and looked back at Tesseract.

"In three days," Tesseract said softly, "you can run and Tom can follow you in a land cart or on a riding beast. It's all right, just swallow it. You can run rather fast, I suspect."

Granite swallowed the pill as if he didn't care if it did kill him or not. Tesseract talked on in a soft monotone, "The Rector has beaten some of our smaller cars . . . you're shorter, but I suspect you also run fast, have endurance. Bipedal is good for endurance, cuts speed a bit. I always enjoy watching your kinds run. And I've heard you'll be very colorful when you're in mating feathers, if it's polite to talk about that. The sight of you running then will be quite special. You duel for females, and females duel for you, I've heard, except that there are genetic considerations."

Granite was having a bit of trouble holding his head up. "If you don't mind," Tesseract added in a less hypnotic tone, "I'll go to Karriaagzh's office and see what he wants to give you." Tesseract slipped out and came back with a squeeze bottle. "Makes feathers come in easier. He uses it himself—it wasn't responsible for his feathers coming in grey. That was an earlier Barcon mistake."

"I can rub it in," I said. Granite's eyelids blinked—lower feathered lids swinging up, which made him look fragile. "One of the Gwyngs did this for me when I was nervous, but without the lotion." I poured the oil stuff on my hands and eased his uniform off his shoulders. The skin was mottled red in patches, bruised where the other bird had hit him. I saw the new quills coming in, and, when I smoothed on the lotion, I felt them like matchsticks under the skin, which was looser and thicker than I'd expected. Even deeper were nervous bunchy muscles I couldn't massage hard for fear of breaking the quills.

Having quills in the skin roll under my fingers was the oddest sensation—alien, yet . . . The tips bristled against my fingers, but the bulk of the lengths were still under the skin.

"Go with the way they're growing," Granite said sleepily. The skin softened as I rubbed in the lotion and the muscles under the quills quivered and relaxed. "I . . . don't . . . get . . . out . . . in . . . the . . . sun . . . enough." I helped him off the perch. He stretched out one arm and leg, then stretched the leg and arm on the other side, stumbling against me. I felt the quills twitch against my hands when I steadied him.

As Granite settled to the floor, Tesseract slumped in his chair, put his own tea aside, and sighed so deeply that I, remembering my own panic time, was embarrassed. "Did you sigh like that when I went to sleep after my xenophobic reactiveness?"

He smiled, sighed again, and said, "We'll take him to the infirmary now."

"Is his friend going to live?"

"He's paralyzed. We've got him on a respirator. As soon as we've gotten the other birds stabilized, we'll make a decision."

Tesseract got up and knelt by Granite, who was down in a heap on the floor, and tried to rouse him. Granite mumbled a complaint in bird language. "Okay, my friend," Tesseract said before calling in the Barcons with a stretcher.

Karriaagzh checked on us again. "Maybe a hot oil bath

would be nice for him now." He sat down bird-style by Granite and touched the other bird's bottom eyelid, which flicked. "I don't remember much of my first days here, but I do remember itching."

Granite shifted around as the Barcons lifted him onto the stretcher. Karriaagzh added, "Security must talk to them now, before all panic, but keep in mind they have their honor, loyalties." The old bird ran a finger around the other bird's ear holes and added, "Also, check for mites."

While the Barcons tended Granite, monitoring him while he slept, I went on to deal with my schedule as best I could.

When I came back to the infirmary, a Barcon directed me to the showers. Granite was standing bare-skinned under a hot water spray, nictitating membranes covering his eyes, huddled over while Barcons scrubbed him and rinsed. Then they covered him with hot oiled towels and led him to a bird leaning cushion. He propped his elbows on it and drew his haws back and looked at me.

"Mites," he said. "And xenophobic reactiveness."

"They must have survived in the facial feathers," one of the Barcons said, "then went down to feed on the new feather tips. If your feathers are messed up, it isn't our fault this time."

The Barcons were testing miticides on another bird, but for Granite now, they'd use lots of hot water and soap.

"Always something," the Barcon concluded. "Now we've got to check all the bird kinds for mites, but probably only this kind has them. Among them, I bet they're epidemic. Such stress they put themselves under."

Granite said dismally, "We must seem rather like a joke." He stared at me, flashing the third eyelid again vertically across his eyes. "We have special mite powders. But Red Clay's crew seemed to be in too big a hurry to ask for all our equipment."

"I'm sorry. Rhyodolite was boss on that one."

The Barcon was incredulous. "Sent a Gwyng to fetch birds?"

"I'm going to tame that Gwyng the way I've been tamed," Granite said.

"I don't believe you'd be able to tame a Gwyng, bird," the Barcon said. "That's a hard-wired reaction."

"In a sapient, there shouldn't be hard-wired reactions," Granite said.

"We'll have to fumigate your room, so you both can stay here. You can get your schedule through our computer for duration. Someone will tell your other roommate." They led Granite by the elbows to another room; I tagged along behind.

"That Ewik won't be coming here?" Granite asked.

"Is that xenophobia or is that something personal?" the Barcon asked with a wiggled nose.

"Personal."

"He'd rather not associate with us," I said.

"Well, we'll let him seek other quarters, if he wants."

Granite gestured assent and crouched down in the oily towels. The Barcons gave me a little electric heating cup full of more oil I could use when the towels cooled. In an hour or so, after they'd checked the slides, they'd take him out for another bath.

A little skinny bear brought me another plastic foam slab and some sheets. "How is he?" she asked me quietly as Granite blinked and nodded.

"I'm okay," he said. "How are you?"

"Busy," she said.

The Barcons came back and the biggest one said, "Mites in the ears."

The third eyelid veiled Granite's eyes and he shuddered. I decided not to watch. He stood up and came with them before they went for his elbows. I wondered if backward knees worked better when the creature who had them was frightened and exhausted—he seemed to walk steadily enough.

While they were deep-cleaning his nares and ear holes, I fooled around with the computer, checking on what I could:

Barcons—species with eccentrically orbiting home planet. Weather varies immensely. Long winters. Longer summers. Extremely ecologically various. Includes among parasites a sapient, without space capacity. Barcons mildly xenoreactive to physical contact by species with null social distances. Hard-wired fear of oral or digital to oral contact with strangers, due to parasite spread. First contacted 4,000 years ago. Further information restricted.

*   *   *

Granite came back without the Barcons. His ear hole had been scrubbed red; one of the nares bled a little. He crouched down and pulled the towels around himself again. I poured on the hot oil while he asked, "And you went through this? You had a xenophobic reaction?"

"Yes."

"Mites and aliens. What combinations. I should have thought about mites." He'd had a rough day. "Did the Rector's Man talk to you like that when you were upset?"

"Um, kinda." I thought about how Tesseract played to the species differences even though the Federation wanted us to ignore them. Talk and get the sedative down, but the talk's content depended on the species of the freaked. "We'll both survive and get our blues," I told Granite.

"All the creatures look more like you, Red Clay. My kind is so outnumbered." He looked at the bed pad and said, "I think I'll unwrap these towels and go to sleep, even if it isn't a nice high bed. When will we have the third meal?"

"They'll bring you something. I'm going to see if I can't just go to the cafeteria."

"Come back tonight."

"No problem."

"Are you afraid of me still, in your mammal squishy way?"

"I guess not."

"Guess? Mammal answer. Was the Rector's Man serious about the invitation? If that was said just to calm me down, I wouldn't come with you, but I'd like to run."

"I'll check. But I want you to come with me, too. I don't have many friends here."

"Isn't Tesseract your kind?"

"No."

"I thought maybe you'd grow a crest and thicker jaws when you matured," Granite said as he lay breast-down on the foam pad. He looked at it, then prodded the foam with his beak, a little nervous again. "I'm sorry I thought of you as a lactating monstrosity. Your sex doesn't lactate, does it?" He pulled the covers over his head, going with the quill grain.

"No, we don't lactate," I said.

Slowly, his bottom eyelid raised again, this time, I suspected, more worn out than sedated. When he laid his beak down on his hands, I left quietly to meet my schedule.

The next morning, I woke up on my strange mattress and looked over at Granite Grit sleeping on his pad. Funny, when he was asleep, he looked more alien—as though talking drugged the brain's visual functions. Silent, he was a heap of yellow skin studded with feather pins, a beak with a tiny hook on the end of it, and muscles that slanted differently than mine. I got up quietly and dressed while a Barcon came in to check. The Barcon waited until I was dressed, then followed me out in the hall.

"We'll keep him here until tomorrow, then he can go back to classes. And how are you?"

"I'm fine."

"Lonely for your own kind? We wondered about you tagging along with the bird."

"I'm all right," I said.

"We can get you a female from the other culture group of your species, if you need."

"Everyone seems so surprised that I'm doing so well," I said, going toward their computer to get my schedule. I was a bit annoyed, a bit worried. Maybe something always hit isolates eventually.

"I couldn't live without my mate," the Barcon said. I printed my schedule and left, not sure what to say.

Two days later, when I got back from classes, Granite was talking to Tesseract. "I'm not afraid of anyone, exactly," Granite said, "but I'm afraid of . . ."

"Well, don't be afraid of me," Tesseract said. "You don't like being odd here?"

"Not at all," Granite said quickly. "But our home planet officials . . . I don't want to be in precisely the position I'm in."

I came on in and asked, "Should I go back out and eat?"

"Take Granite with you. I'll give you passes for outside, and movie tickets. Semi-illegal movie, but I thought you both ought to see it."

Granite rose and said, "What happens next, to us, to Sulphur?"

Tesseract said, "We could maintain him until the feathers grow back. Then . . . As for you, we'll talk to your people."

"You'll decide *then*."

"He won't go back all ugly," Tesseract replied. He handed me the movie tickets, drew out a little map so we could find the place, and gave us off-Academy passes. "Blue bus number 3 will always get you back here," he said.

"I can't distinguish blue from violet," Granite said, "but then you can't see shades below violet, can you?"

"Some can. I can't," Tesseract said.

I said, "I can tell blue from violet, Granite."

After dinner, we started out. Granite asked, "Have you been outside the Academy grounds before?"

"Yes, several times, but not around here."

He slowed down his strides and I half jogged to keep up with him. We showed our passes at the gate and looked out at the city, peddlers, tremendous numbers of aliens in all sorts of clothes, all sorts of colors. Hairy, not hairy, feathered, naked skins of all sorts of textures. Aliens, walking along, buying from other aliens, getting on alien buses, all totally calm.

"I hope," Granite Grit said, "we don't meet anything that's afraid of me tonight."

I opened Tesseract's map and looked for the bus that would take us to the movies he recommended. Are we being followed? I wondered, but I didn't mention my suspicion to Granite. What could I do if Granite went xeno again?

We went to the back of the bus so Granite could hunker down on the floor without getting in anyone's way. "They didn't design these for us," he said, holding on to my knee. As the bus pulled back into traffic, he swiveled his head around at all the people. "We've been followed. I'm glad, actually."

About ten blocks later, Granite looked at my map and pushed a button. The bus stopped and we got off, three doors from the building. It didn't look like a movie house, but when we showed the man at the door our tickets, he let us in. *Semi*-illegal movies? I thought as we walked into the screening room.

Granite managed to wiggle up on the seat by me, near the

aisle. Before the lights went down, I noticed that most of the people in the audience were in blue uniforms.

Three giant Ahrams with elephantine legs stalked across the screen. My heart jolted; this was an alien horror film. The audience screamed, laughed, told the filmed Ahrams that the digital distortions were biophysically incorrect. As Granite, beak parted slightly, watched the movie, the pin feathers on his face writhed.

"You watch so I can look at you," he said about midway through one Ahram's attack on a Gwyng, seemingly tickling the smaller sapient to death.

"Okay." I laughed nervously.

"Laughing. Is this funny? Split between xenophobia and mock of xenophobes."

As we walked out of the movie theater, Granite Grit looked at the various aliens, furred, naked-skinned, feathered, and said, "I guess Tesseract wanted me to know mild xenophobia is accepted. We can deal with it."

"It was a very strange movie," I said.

As we waited for the bus, Granite said, "We thought force held the Federation together, that some one species was dominant. What force?"

"Maybe," I said, somewhat reluctant to voice what I was thinking, "all the species' mutual jealousies keep the system honest. And new species can't afford not to buy in."

"Such a bait for joining—a five-thousand-year-old collection of all the stars' thinking."

" 'Curiosity drives intelligence,' " I quoted from somewhere.

"But the tension!"

The next morning, we went to the country in Tesseract's little flier. As Granite Grit boarded, he apologized for being troublesome.

Tesseract took Granite's hands and accepted the apology.

"I'm even glad you made us see that movie," Granite added as he looked for a convenient place to sit.

Then up we flew over Karst City into the interior. The ancients who built Karst with the transformed energies of space war knew beautiful geography: plains enough to rest a plainsman's eyes and fatigue my mountain-bred ones, then a river and mountains with forested foothills merging into plains again.

"This river's tributaries go up into country made to look like an old continental surface," Tesseract said. He turned the flier and went up a river that looked like the Dan, bouncing on its rocks.

"One side of my farm faces scrublands, where, Granite, you can run all day if it isn't too hot. Tom, the other side is close to mountains rather near in height to the ones you were born in."

Until he said that, I hadn't imagined how much I missed the mountains. I leaned back and sighed.

Tesseract's wife, Ammalla, bigger-boned than an Earthwoman, but still slimmer than Tesseract, with just a hint of a skull crest, called us to dinner. Granite Grit was still running near the farm. Ammalla saw that I was worried and said, "We put a satellite on him when he left the house. But don't tell him."

Tesseract put his finger against an ivory-colored plug in his ear and listened. "He's coming back now," he told us, "he went swimming."

Soon Granite Grit, who'd run bare-quilled, came padding onto the porch behind Tesseract's house. "Towel?" he asked. Ammalla went to help him.

"I got almost overheated," he said when he came in, "so I went into the water a bit. My feathers—you can see the colors now." He dropped the big towel from his shoulders to let us see greens, reds, and golds in the quills.

Ammalla put her arm gently around his prickly shoulder. "Dress and join us for dinner." She arranged a low table for him to sit on and passed me something that looked like potatoes, but wasn't.

"Sir," Granite said to Tesseract when he came back, "being re-fledged is a good metaphor for what happens to aliens who come here."

"So you're less upset about the feather stripping. It makes people odd to themselves so they're less concerned about the oddity of the others. And it puts you all through a common ordeal."

"But uniforms still break feathers," Granite said. "Being

re-fledged is one thing. Trying to live as a mammal is another.'' Granite reared back a little, then eased his beak down
toward his food and dabbed at it. After swallowing, he asked,
''Do movies like that ease mammal tensions, too, by playing
with xenophobia?''

''Yes. The Federation is full of tensions. But I don't want
any sapient hurt.''

''I can't hurt you, or Tom, or your wife. You trust me?''

Thinking about the melted walls, only five hundred years
ago, I said, ''Karriaagzh says that the Federation has to be
maintained every day.''

Granite turned slowly and looked at me as though seeing
me for the first time.

Since Granite and I were roommates, Ammalla put us in
the same room. Granite woke up when I began shaving at the
sink and came walking carefully toward me.

''I do this every morning,'' I told his reflection.

''Tesseract also?''

''I don't think he grows face hairs.''

Granite bobbed his body slightly, then went out to see if he
could use the toilet.

''They let me use Karriaagzh's,'' he said proudly when he
came back.

After breakfast, Tesseract and I rode horse-patterned things,
with a touch of analog-antelope, while Granite in his quills
took giant bounds through the grass, over steppe brush, snatching at low-flying birds. We stopped by a stream where he
danced around, quills twitching.

''Are you happier?'' Tesseract asked.

''Yes.'' Granite tried to come closer to the riding beasts
but they backed off. ''You do care?''

''Safer for me if I don't have to fear my charges,'' Tesseract said.

''No jokes,'' Granite said stiffly.

''Yes, I do care.''

''Sense of humor seems to relieve mammal tension by
playing with stresses. We don't do that.''

''Better get an intellectual understanding of it, Granite
Grit,'' Tesseract said. ''I'm a fairly humorous guy.''

We tied the riding stock and went up into the hills on foot.

They weren't like my home mountains except for the air—after we got up to two thousand feet on the trail, we breathed real mountain air, moist yet electric.

Granite stepped along awkwardly, not really at home in mountains. How sad, I thought, that this air meant nothing to him. But when we scrambled up a rock fall, his backward knees gave him better climbing balance than we had with our knees that banged the rock face.

"Born climber," Tesseract commented.

"No, biomechanical accident," Granite said tensely, reaching for a hold.

"You have a looser hip structure than I thought," Tesseract observed as Granite hung one foot way left, bending both his backward knee and another joint which was almost concealed in his upper leg muscles.

Granite grunted and strained for a ledge with his right foot, clinging with both hands to his hold. Then he put his left foot where his hands were and levered up.

"I'll help you people up," he said, reaching down for us. He main-hauled me up—we both helped Tesseract.

At the top we saw Tesseract's house and the plains with another ridge and river beyond that. We sat—the bird crouched down on his shins, me and Tesseract cross-legged.

"Thanks," I told Tesseract.

As we packed to leave, Ammalla said, "You must come back when we have more young guests. Sometimes elders are boring."

"Oh, no," I said. "You and Tesseract aren't boring."

"I must come back when my feathers are out," Granite said. "I'm more colorful than any flying bird I've seen here—or any other bird sapient."

"Granite Grit," she said, embracing him, not so firmly she'd risk bruising a quill, "I'll be very happy to see you in full color." Then she tickled the horny skin around his nostrils.

"You know about our nares?" he said, obviously delighted. Delicately, he ran his tongue around her nose and lips.

"I try to learn the friendly gestures of all my guests," she said. "And now, Tom," she said, opening her arms. We hugged.

"What happens now?" Granite asked, shifting his weight from one leg to the other.

"Granite Grit, we asked your species to join us more honestly. We can stop anything you throw at us, but we've no plans to harm any of your nations. Would you have attacked us if so ordered? Seized the Rector, say, as a hostage?"

"The Rector, yes. If those were my orders." Granite edged back and cocked his head, staring at Tesseract with one eye.

"Federation Council would have replaced him before Karst rotated a quarter. They've let the whole place get bombed away on occasion."

"Is it that cruel an organization?"

"Has to be sometimes."

Granite's people re-negotiated with the Federation. And the Academy made uniforms optional for heavily feathered birds, so Granite's kind and other birds could wear fiber torcs instead. But Karriaagzh wore his mammal clothes, and the two other bird species were divided.

"This is difficult for us," Granite said about a month later. "Fledging." He tried to pull off a split feather sheath behind a shoulder blade.

"Can I help?" I asked. We were listening to music in the central square, Gypsum gone as usual. The Rector's People wouldn't give him a new room, but he only slept here.

Granite backed around to me. "Be careful." I gently pulled off a horny sheath and watched the new feather unfurl like a butterfly. Then another.

"Better to be reciprocal. Can I shave you?"

"I shave every morning. You're not going to need this done every morning, are you?"

"Afraid of letting me touch you? With the electric razor?"

I pulled another sheath away from a green feather and saw a tiny bit of mite damage on the tip. "Well, some people used to get shaved at hair-cutting, *barber*, shops." After I pulled off all the loose sheaths, I got out my electric razor and a lotion Barcons gave me to soften my beard.

Granite got me to lie down, with his feet curled around my head. I looked up at the pin feathers around his falcon eyes and giggled.

"Be calm," he said, rubbing lotion into my skin, his fingers curiously prodding. "Why don't you just grow the face hairs out?"

"My kind doesn't."

"Your kind isn't here," he said, carefully moving the razor over my face. "Are any *humans* here?"

"Some primitives."

"Listen, Tom Red Clay, some of my people are primitives. If they were here, and no one else civilized of my kind, I'd take comfort from my primitives."

"Are you tired of going to movies and music with me?" I asked, suddenly feeling terribly lonesome as the bird shaved my chin. He loved both fighting movies and music—like the mountain guys.

"You don't want to be another creature's pet."

"I'm not your pet. They've promised me that they'd bring me a breeding group in a year."

"Tom," he said, pulling the razor back and blinking his eyes before continuing, "do you want your own people kidnapped from your planet?"

I hadn't thought of how they'd bring in a breeding group. "Kidnapped?"

"Tom, don't you have to mate? I can't imagine you missing that."

When I came back from classes a couple days later, Granite and another half-feathered bird, but a solid color—*female*, I realized—were gravely studying charts spread out on a low table.

"The feathers link with gene structures for other things," Granite explained. "So the females bring family line genetic maps and check to see what males are worth fighting for."

Over the next few weeks, lots of female birds, all different solid colors, all as big as Granite or bigger, came cruising by with their genetic charts.

When spring came, Granite sprouted streamers from his shoulders and began displaying against others of his kind. Only twenty-five of them—but they seemed to be everywhere, colorful and quarrelsome. As the displays got violent, the Academy sent small groups off to various Rector's People's farms.

Granite, his potential ladies, and present rivals went to Tesseract's, and I asked if I could visit on weekends.

When I got to the airport, Karriaagzh, in mammal clothes, and two new birds motioned for me to join them.

"I was going up to Tesseract's," I said.

"I'm taking these people there," he said. "We want all Granite's kind to have mates." The two new birds, both solid colors, seemed nervous, breeding plumes shorter than the female breeding plumes I'd seen sprouted here.

No one spoke on the flight out, until we were over Tesseract's. From the air, I saw four birds, three males and one female. "There's another female there, but I don't see her," Karriaagzh said.

The two young bird females in the flier watched the guys throw their colored feathers around and talked to each other in bird.

When I was getting out of the flier, I saw Granite bound ten feet or more off the prairie and lash out at the other bird with his strange feet, both their feathers streaming around them, flame-colored, glinting. *What rules,* I wondered, *or could they kill each other?*

Tesseract leaned over the porch rail and called to them in their own language. They bounced apart and turned, panting, eyes protected by the transparent shields, to watch us walk up.

"More females," Karriaagzh said. "And might I spar with you? It's been a long time. Heel punches?"

Granite, eyes still veiled, bobbed his body.

"But don't insult me," Karriaagzh said, pulling off his mammal clothes, then hopping in his matted feathers. Granite stared at Karriaagzh, then feinted a kick experimentally at him.

"Insult," Karriaagzh said, clipping him soundly on the upper leg.

The hens began their sparring, all four of them, a whirl of blue, purple, and brown.

"Amazing lot of tendon spring," Tesseract said.

Ammalla smiled. "They *are* beautiful."

Karriaagzh stopped and joined his Rector's People, holding his green and gold uniform in his hands. "And they do well in gath-math and molecular chemistry," the Rector said, handing Ammalla his clothes. "Now I must cool off." He went down to Tesseract's pool and swam, a large wet grey-feathered dinosaur.

Granite scored three quick hits on his opponent, who dropped to a crouch. Then they both stood up and unveiled their eyes, ruffled their feathers and laid them down. Granite bounced up to us, hopping like a giant skinny fighting cock. "We like it here. Other species can admire us without jealousy."

Tesseract looked from bouncing Granite to his boss swimming slowly, head only above water, in his pool. "By the way, Granite Grit, how long do you people live? And how does your year compare to Karst's?"

Between high leaps, Granite said, "About 120 . . . about the same, longer maybe."

Tesseract looked from the young bird to the old. "You'll be around a long time then."

Ammalla said, "Wonder if they'll get as grey as the Rector?"

"It was the feather-stripping," Tesseract told her. "He'll outlive Black Amber. She won't like hearing that."

Karriaagzh climbed out of the pool and shook himself like a dog. His feathers were thin—most of his bulk was body mass.

Looking at me, he said, "Tesseract, Tom is to spend the break time at Black Amber's."

"You know what's going on there. Why not here?"

"You'll be busy. I'm putting a species group here."

Most sapient species with seasonal breeding have the main rut in the spring. And if they didn't, the Barcons adjusted them so the classes could stop for the breeding season.

In species unaffected by the season, older cadets joined a trade or diplomatic crew. First-year cadets went to the country in species groups. I was alone—so I had to go to Black Amber's. Black Amber was pregnant. Unless the larva lived, which wasn't likely, she'd come into heat after delivery.

$$= 7 =$$

Body Bribe

When I met Black Amber at the docks, she looked only a bit thicker in the lower abdomen. "Red Clay (testosterone-fumed)," she said, sprawled across the bow of a rental hydrofoil, "come ride to Gwyng-owned islands, archipelago most like Gwyng Home."

The hydrofoil skimmed across ocean that had barely gotten salty since aliens cooked the water out of gas-giants. At the island, the dock had no groove-way ratchets for the boat, so we tied up with real ropes. The Gwyng island looked tropical, with artificial cliffs crumbling behind the houses and strips of pasture.

More relaxed than I'd ever seen her, Amber hummed and swayed in the driver's seat as I put our bags on the roof of our borrowed car. She called me Mica, oo'ed and corrected herself, but my skull computer still caught glitter on my Academy name.

Black Amber, still swaying, drove the car slowly up a coral-graveled road, until a Holstein-colored pouch beast, bigger than a rhino, lumbered into the road, followed by two more pouch hosts and a smaller black and brown blood beast with ropy veins dangling from its neck like dewlaps. Six baby Gwyngs followed them, two hauling up the beasts' tails into the pouches. They poked their heads out around the tails to stare at us.

We stopped. Gwyng kids giggled like a pigeon roost, while I wondered when Black Amber would hit the horn. Finally the beasts lumbered off the road. Black Amber hugged herself, then drove on to a basketwork house like her beach house. The cliffs were close behind, a white limestone planet-sized stage set.

I carried the bags up the steps. "You know these," Amber said, swinging a long arm at Rhyodolite and Cadmium.

They leaned against each other. "Dead-animal-eating-ape still studying the Barcon cut-up business?" Rhyodolite said. "I bet you know about our breeding habits, but did they explain body bribes?"

"Shut up," Cadmium told him. "Black Amber, it is open, isn't it? You've invited a proper number?"

She didn't answer, so Cadmium turned to me as I passed with the duffels, and said, "Doing eye dissection, I see."

A muscled cloaca excretes their soft wastes. I didn't answer, but started remembering more Gwyng biology, the bones in their arms which gave them more grip than I had. How they hooked their hands around their shoulders so easily—as Rhyodolite and Cadmium did now, staring at me through alien eyes that saw polarized light.

"Come to witness Gwyng mating ritual? Like the film?" Cadmium said. "You do look at us like we were biological cut-ups?"

The heat pheromone molecule is sluggish in the air. It affects both male and female behavior. Black Amber twitched her shoulders and went through into another room. The walls were padded with grass mats.

"Stinky armpits, we like you well enough," Rhyo said. Cadmium interrupted and Gwyng-talked a language my computer couldn't handle. Rhyo said, "Cadmium wants you to sleep on the beach."

I looked at their hands to see if the thumb-base glands were swollen—a sign that a Gwyng was angry.

"Our glands are empty," Rhyodolite said. "We are waiting for Black Amber's season. Not angry, tense."

"Much stinky armpit sex-organ hairs odor from *his* glands," Cadmium commented. "But no nose to tell him much openly/consciously."

"I don't have glands in my armpits."

"Better to learn own biologic than other people's," Cadmium said. "We'll swim/cool off before we eat."

"Can I go with you?" I asked.

"Black Amber swaying from side to side and humming as you came here?" Rhyodolite asked.

"Yes."

"Absolutely come with us," Rhyodolite said.

"He'll stink up the whole ocean," Cadmium said, then launched into impassioned Gwyng that I couldn't follow.

We trudged down to the water. After I'd had enough, I hauled out and sat on the beach watching them. Flight neuro-wiring gave Gwyngs mean butterfly strokes, boosted by their armpit webs. I wondered if eventually Gwyngs would evolve into aquatic creatures, swimming off with those long water-bug arms.

Cadmium and Rhyodolite disappeared into the sun glitter. I finally spotted them, lost them again. After about two hours, they came rolling in on the surf, tired.

We were all resting in shallow water, letting the waves lift us up and down while our hands grabbed the bottom against the undertow, when Black Amber stepped out onto the deck. She only wore a short shift cut out under the arms so the webs were bare. Like a cat, she rubbed her lips against the deck roof posts.

Rhyodolite and Cadmium hurried out of the water to her, questioning her in Gwyng. She appeared dazed, but she finally asked me to approach and explained, "My womb cleared, but the nymph didn't pouch. I'll be attractive in a few days." She sniffed. "Red Clay (glitter), your web glands *will* be a problem. We become even more nose-sensitive during season."

Then she pulled herself up by the post while Rhyodolite and Cadmium told me, as I'd heard in class, that the nymph was no more to them than a nocturnal emission was to me. "Her friends want a viable Black Amber child to raise as pouch kin," Cadmium said. "She'll try until they get one."

"His odor is impossible," Rhyodolite said.

Black Amber said, "(One of you) take him to the city for a Barcon armpit job."

Rhyo called the Barcons to explain what they wanted done to me. Then a Barcon spoke and Rhyo pulled the receiver back and stared at it.

"A (female) *h'mn* is looking for you," he said.

I felt coldly startled. "*Human?*"

"That noise." He talked to the Barcons some more, and then said to me, "Female con-specific primitive."

I felt bewildered. One of those people? "How did she find out about me?"

"She asked for a cadet *h'mn*. Only one." Rhyodolite's lips pursed, the wrinkles deepening, and his nostrils flared a bit at the top.

Cadmium leaned against Black Amber and tried to rub her tummy, but she swatted his hand away. "Cadmium, you take him in," she said.

After the Barcons scraped my armpits, they showed me into a room with a low table, which was set with handleless cups, an electric kettle, and leaves compressed in a brick. I picked up the brick and sniffed—tea!

An Oriental woman, dressed in a brown tunic and pants, a plaid scarf and embroidered boots, came in with a tray of cakes and butter. She stared at the bed, which I hadn't noticed before—*my sheets on it and some furs which must come from her custom*, I thought, suddenly shy.

A Barcon introduced us, "Cadet Red Clay, *Tom*, this is Free Trader *Yanchela*."

She had an impassive, almost flat face, a woman of about twenty-five or so, I guessed, with her hair long. Washed, but not cut. "*Tum*," she said with a bow.

"Tom," I corrected. "Yanchela?"

"Not to talk as out-species. Yangchenla."

"Yangchenla?"

"Tom."

"We'll leave you both here, if you want."

She nodded curtly. I showed her to a cushion by the table and began trying to fix the weird brick tea. I was a bit intimidated by her.

"Here, let me," she said, crumbling off a bit of the brick and setting it up to boil in an electric teakettle. "These kettles are very convenient, don't you think? Cleaner than a fire."

"How long have you been here?"

"I was born in the city. My parents had me educated in the language of most of these creatures, my brother also." She had an accent, the tongue and larynx hadn't been re-built, but she spoke like she thought, in Karst. "The old guys think

Karst is a supernatural punishment region. This place doesn't seem supernatural to me."

"You did come from someplace else, originally, if you're the same kind of people that I am."

She looked at me, then checked the tea. "So you're a cadet here when none of my kin are given a chance."

"Why can't your people become cadets?"

"Something about sponsorship. You say we came off another planet? What happened between when we came off and now, when you came off?"

"Parts of *Earth* are almost like here. We've got electric *tea* pots, cars, buses, airplanes, but we don't use the transformation gates."

"You will explain the transformation gates sometime. So *you* say we didn't evolve here?"

"No."

"And that the people on the original planet are now almost like the creatures here." She used the word for non-differentiated animal for *aliens*. "The old men say many cycles of cycles, grandfathers of grandfathers."

"I bet the Academy or Federation has records."

She poured tea. "Many more of us?"

"Yeah, on the other planet."

"Is their breeding controlled by creatures?"

"No."

"The Barcons told me I could have a child by you. They'd pull this out." She showed me a long hard ridge in her arm.

I wondered what their country was now—most of Asia was Russian or Chinese. "What should I do? My sponsor says she'll send me to live with your people if I don't do well."

"Become an officer. Officers in the Federation live well."

"Sometimes, I get very lonely. My roommate warned me not to become these creatures' pet."

"Roommate's a wise creature."

I sipped the tea and saw oil, butter, floating on top of it. Buttered tea, not too bad. We sat quietly drinking. Sexual tension built, until I leaned back from the table. She looked away, something subtle and fine broke, as though I'd exposed myself. Maybe it was how I leaned back. I winced.

"Yangchenla," I said.

"*Chenla* is a name, too."

"Chenla, I'd like to see more of you. I want . . ."

"Perhaps when you are an officer, you can sponsor one of us into the Academy. And if seeing me again will help you survive to become an officer, I'll see you again."

"It would keep me sane," I said.

"I would like to see the records on my people," she said. "If . . ."

"I couldn't find out anything about the planet we're originally from," I said.

"Do they let you off the Academy grounds?"

"Yes."

"Come visit me at my shop."

She stood up. I didn't know where her shop was, so I asked, "Can you write down your shop address?"

She handed me a card, bigger than an Earth business card. "If you liked the animal milk oil/fat, I have it too. The creatures who can't talk language love it."

"Gwyngs. My sponsor's a Gwyng. My skull computer transforms their languages into one I can understand."

"Do we have skull computers on our planet now?"

"No, these guys implanted it in me."

"Invent something. I don't always want to be from backward people."

I couldn't tell if she was joking or not. "We'll help each other," I said.

"Tom, then? You will help us?"

"I thought I had to choose between being with the *humans* in the primitive range or being a cadet."

She froze when I said *primitive range*, bowed slightly, and began to leave. At the door, she said, "Stay with the Academy. Be a very good cadet. Don't call the waste that name."

"So you didn't mate," the Barcon technician said as he cleaned out my armpits and handed the swabs to another Barcon for freezing. "We'll make you sweet-smelling for Black Amber, but your woman might miss your scent, so afterward, we'll give you back the bacteria that contribute. Black Amber doing a body bribe again, or has she invited more than Wy'um?"

"Open," I said.

"Well, we've made changes in Gwyng matings," the Barcon

said, "with suppression drugs and chemical attractants. Corrupted a whole species, I guess."

All the Barcon noses wiggled. The Barcon who'd been talking depilated me in the armpits and gave me spray cans of deodorants and pheromone disrupters.

Feeling almost like I did after they first stripped off all my hair and put me in cadet black, I re-joined Cadmium, who sniffed and oo'ed.

"Good-for-sex female?" he asked.

"No. We just want to be friends."

"Be friends with Black Amber, have sex with your female," he said. "I'd rather not be friends with Black Amber now, but she has no Mica (glittering in Red Clay) young friend/helper during matings."

After a bus dropped us off at the marina we hydrofoiled it off to the island. "So," Cadmium finally asked, "what did the female want?"

"She wants me to sponsor them when I can afford it."

"Might lose on that. You have to make some linguistics teams, first-contact teams, trade missions, first. Get your own money, then sponsor people who'll make money for you, not primitives."

I'd never thought much about this side of the Federation before. Black Amber would get a cut from deals I made—for sponsoring me. "Black Amber isn't sure I'll make her money, either, is she?"

"You'll be going on a linguistics team to the people who captured you—and you have a first-contact trade share. Your kind's female is a free trader, she can explain much, your female-not-for-sex (you'll be sorry)."

We tied up at the dock and drove the car to Black Amber's borrowed house-and-herds. Even in the short time we'd been away, Black Amber'd collected an entourage. Wy'um of the History Committee was standing almost belly to belly with her when Cadmium and I came dragging clothes, deodorants, and part of a tea brick into the main room.

While her dazed eyes looked down, he reached up to tickle her birth hairs. She leaned forward to trap his hand between their bodies.

Cadmium grunted. "Open mating?" he asked, stopping beyond them at the threshold of the next room.

The other male Gwyngs looked from Wy'um and Amber to Cadmium. Cadmium grunted again and quickly went into the depths of the house.

That night, the other males threw Rhyodolite out of Black Amber's room. He screamed at her and tried to shove the door down, but Wy'um and another male, Wy'um's pouch kin, pinned Rhyodolite to the floor and watched his neck vein throb before they tossed him out on deck. Then Wy'um came over to me while his pouch kin wrestled with the other male Gwyngs.

"This is like First Contact Parties," Wy'um said. "Never talk about it to others."

Then while his kin blocked the other suitors, Wy'um slipped into Black Amber's room.

Cadmium pulled me out to the veranda. "Try to keep them from tearing at her. Be junior, pre-maturity, pouch kin. We love her, but . . ."

"Fuck it."

One of the suitors overheard. "Odd thing to say, as though it were a curse."

Later that day, neither Cadmium nor Rhyodolite could get near Black Amber as the older male Gwyngs swarmed over her, talking so intensely my computer only gave me phrases.

I worked my way up to her and asked what I should do. Her hormone-dazed eyes, huge and alien, roved over me. Before she could answer, Wy'um's pouch kin grabbed me.

Me shocked enough to fight back, we rolled to the floor, his funny muscles twisting under me. My elbow hit a web. A chill, feeling that skin give and recoil. We gripped each other hard, bodies rigid.

The male Gwyng sniffed once—no Barcon magic could cut all the ape smell—and koo'ed. We both relaxed and let each other go. "Fix us tea and food," he said.

Rhyodolite and Cadmium gnawed stones outside, too young for a dominant female, too attached to leave. But they waded back in and got shoved out by the older males, again and again. They never turned on each other. Pouch kin didn't.

I fixed tea, cheese, and oil drinks. All the Gwyngs in the house went naked now. Amber, looking sleepy and slightly scratched, came out and sniffed at me. Remembering female cats who'd approach anything male, I got flustered. She winced, squeezed her nostrils shut—residual ape odor—and took the tea.

I stared at her oval pouch slit, a little lower than the navel was on us, and at stiff hairs between that and the crotch. Moodily, she sat down and sipped her tea slowly; the males didn't molest her when she was sitting.

Black Amber's heat went on and on. After five days, my groin ached and I spent most of my time on the beach when I wasn't needed in the kitchen. Cadmium, Rhyodolite, and I ate clams, commenting on the resemblance to female sex parts. *Why didn't I try something with the human woman?*

One afternoon, Rhyodolite, lying utterly disspirited on the sand beside me, said, "Raw aching cock."

Cadmium, sitting, arms wrapped around himself, said, "Two or three raw aching cocks."

I got up to play with the younger Gwyngs, but they koo'ed and ran off. Little fuzzy kids about two and a half feet tall, with huge eyes, hopped up on the brood beasts' pouch necks, holding the pouch openings spread, watching me.

Older Gwyng children looked pointedly at the house and at me and talked about the situation.

Poor old Tom-meat-eating-ape, too smelly to get some.

Cadmium said, "Red Clay (without Mica), you're letting Black Amber get scratched."

"They'll beat me up if I try to interfere."

Cadmium said, "They haven't broken our bones."

At night, pebbles rattled against Black Amber's windows, and cars scratched off down the coral rubble road. I could relate to that.

Wy'um and his pouch kin took over in Black Amber's bedroom. Another suitor, a grizzled blond like Cadmium, but with blond hairs more mixed in the brown, like a roan, asked me, "You were supposed to be the non-mature kin?"

"Yes," I said, being utterly careful not to nod.

"It's just the show of being open. We're leaving." He'd been bruised and scratched, as had they all, some from Wy'um and his kin, but more from Amber herself. "Help me dress."

The Gwyng leaned heavily against me as he pulled on briefs. Other suitors, groggy and unhappy, with dilated and spongy webs, some torn, got dressed too. "Wy'um should know better," one said.

That night, after the other suitors had left Black Amber to Wy'um and his pouch kin, a hugely swollen brood beast came up to the house and bleated. Black Amber and the two males came out on the deck as Cadmium, Rhyodolite, and I came up from the beach.

The brood beast lay down on the sand and expelled a deformed, almost adult-sized Gwyng. The grey-headed thing scrabbled at the sand with bony hands and drooled milk. Its eyes were white. *Blind*. But the nostrils clapped and fluttered and the head turned toward the deck.

Black Amber hissed.

The brood beast climbed to her feet, nudged the creature, and lowed at us. As the Gwyngs looked at the creatures mewling in the sand, they sobered up from their sexual daze.

"Reminder of death for us both," Wy'um said.

Black Amber grabbed a deck post and nodded. Then she said, "Tom, sometimes a Gwyng, when changing into a near-corpse, gets into a pouch mother, who takes care of it. Misplaced maternal instinct. Near-corpses are like nymphs to us, but other species find our attitude cold-unfeeling, heartless."

The thing squirmed toward us, twisted fingers clawing through the beach grass.

"It is a Gwyng, then?"

Wy'um said, "It was on the History Committee when it was alive/social."

"Why doesn't this happen to Karriaagzh?" Black Amber asked.

"Wy'um, may not be directed against you," his pouch kin said. Rhyodolite and Cadmium stared at the creature and made strangled noises.

"My pouch sister's beast," Wy'um said. "She couldn't have had anything to do with this." Wy'um leaned over the veranda rail and vomited.

The old Gwyng opened a toothless mouth and squealed, then shuddered. The host beast stamped her feet, then nuzzled the old Gwyng and tried to roll it toward her tail. The body moved limply, utterly inert now.

I went up to check the pulse. After a minute and a half, I

found nothing. The pouch mother butted at me, then moaned before shuffling down the beach.

The old Gwyng was dead. Wy'um went in to call his sister as Black Amber eased me away from the corpse.

"Are you shocked?" she asked me.

I felt numb. "If a Gwyng's senile, what happens?"

She stared out over the ocean. "They cool down and die of lung mold. Or they swim and lose track of land." I hated seeing how she stared at the waves after she'd said that, as though she expected to die in them. "Or," she continued, "they crawl into caves, under houses, and die."

"That's horrible."

"Lingering as a near-corpse must be dreadful—to hear without being able to speak . . . better to go quickly." She looked back at me thoughtfully, but began drifting back into the heat spell. As she rubbed her head against the veranda rails, she said, "Perhaps the near-corpse brought us a new life."

Her rear got itchy; she scooted it over the board flooring. "You seem very alien to me now," I said.

She put her fingers to her mouth and pulled her lips into an imitation smile. "I *am* alien to you. Karriaagzh is wrong. Not all minds have the same plan."

In another three days, Black Amber settled. She dragged out a battered box of Gwyng beach things, pulled on a pair of green rubber hand fins, shrugged at Wy'um, and took a long swim in the ocean. Wy'um and his kin left while she was swimming.

When she came back, she said, "It's over. Help me clean and spray."

While I sprayed Gwyng heat pheromone disrupter around, she crawled into her tubular padded sofa. "Wash my bed-clothes and shifts with more pheromone disrupter," she told me as she was falling asleep. Cadmium and Rhyodolite were gone.

After I finished, she dragged herself out of the tube and put on a fresh shift. "We have to have a reconciliant social gathering for everyone. I promise I will help prepare the meal." She held out long thin trembling fingers to me. "Hold me, *Tom*."

I looked at her legs, the webs collapsed along her sides, the wrinkled face and nostril slits. *Delicate nostril slits*, I decided, still uneasy, not sure what she wanted. She moved toward me, then stopped, aware of my nervousness.

"I'm supposed . . . to reassure you . . . that it was fun . . . if you were a real immature Gwyng," she said. "But it's a bit frightening, too."

I took her fur-backed fingers. She moved up and leaned sideways against me. Looking up at me, she said, "Male, taller than I am. Are you driven like we are?"

"It's different."

"Like Karriaagzh? I need to eat," she said. "Come with me to the herds. Or the cooler room," she added when she saw me flinch. "Is Karriaagzh really going to outlive me?"

"I don't know."

"I can get Wy'um to set you up in Rector candidate progression. You're not from a Federation species—you can be Rector without waiting four hundred years for your species to be trusted not to use your position." She was trembling from exhaustion, yet still obsessed with Karriaagzh.

"If he lives to be 150, then I'll be an old man when he dies. Or dead myself."

She didn't reply, just poured blood and oil into a large glass and looked through a drawer until she found one of their broad straws. Then she looked at me while the tongue muscles pumped away. When she was through, she said, "I don't want the History Committee forgetting me."

"The Gwyngs will, won't they?"

"You other sapients have contaminated us." She was Gwyng-planet born; she knew what her people were like in a pure Gwyng culture. Maybe all of us did mess each other up. "We need to bring in new species gradually. Too confusing/brain dilations/reductions."

"Want me to help wash out the scrapes and cuts?"

"Rub out muscles," she said, oo'ing.

It's just like rubbing down a horse, I kept telling myself as I knelt over Black Amber, who sprawled out on a floor mat. The mucles were not quite human. Her reddish black hair wasn't quite as coarse as a terrier's. "You were going to fix the party food?" I asked as she dozed off.

"Sleep some first," she said. "Sit by me."

"I'd better work on the party food."

"*My* heat is over," she said, catching something in my tone.

All the male Gwyngs who'd been shoving for Black Amber's cunt earlier, their female pouch kin, Rhyodolite and Cadmium—all showed up for this party. Black Amber greeted them on the veranda, even though one of them must have sent us the dying Gwyng.

But she hugged side to side with everyone, fed them oil drinks, and soon everyone bumped shoulders and told each other what a good time they'd had—as though they'd forgotten the scratches and bruises—and what a good Gwyng woman Black Amber was.

Gwyng hypocrites—I couldn't believe them. Wy'um bent Rhyodolite over his knees and sang in Rhyodolite's mouth until Rhyo relaxed completely, letting his vocal cords vibrate sympathetically to Wy'um's. Each began pairing off to sing each other's vocal cords, and Wy'um finally leaned back utterly limp across Cadmium's knees, song and under-song vibrating through the room. They all sang that the life/net of dancing patterns was wonderful.

Wy'um finally pulled himself up off Cadmium's knees and said, "I'll leave early."

"Fair enough," said the older blond-grizzled Gwyng who talked to me during the event. "We left early before."

Finally, well after midnight, the party ended with a heap of talked-out, socially reassured Gwyngs dozing on floor cushions—Black Amber and her pouch kin twined in among the rest.

My crotch still ached. Alone I crawled into the tubular sofa which smelled of Gwyng. Wondering why I didn't try to get that human woman, I konked out.

When I woke up, the house owners were talking to Amber, who told them she'd try again.

One female said, "Sorry I threw gravel at the windows, Sub-Rector, but my pouch brother was with you and I worried that he'd have a hard time."

As we hydrofoiled back to Black Amber's own house, Cadmium asked, "Why do you have glands that signal anxiety? I can understand the biological survival value of signaling anger. Knowing who to avoid preserves social relationships for when the angry one is calmer. But anxiety?''

Rhyodolite, still sounding sleepy, said, ''Don't try to figure it out. He's alien.'' He yawned and oo'ed at me.

''It's so the boss ape won't have to hit you,'' I said.

''He's really alien,'' Cadmium murmured, so weirdly my computer barely processed it. Black Amber coughed and began to work the hydrofoil around toward her beach house dock.

The pouch babies—now I understood what they were, other Gwyngs' children that Black Amber was raising—greeted me with a big Cheddar cheese they'd figured out how to make. I suppose they also knew I was too stinky to get laid by a bat, but they still liked me.

I unpacked and came back to the main sitting room. Cadmium and Rhyodolite had gone on, but Black Amber was sitting there, yawning so wide I saw the little teeth, the muscular ring at the base of the tongue.

''How do you get any work done with all these heats a year?'' I asked, almost angry. I hadn't really wanted to sleep with a Gwyng, but my dreams tore me up.

She shut her mouth and looked hurt, nostrils pinched shut, eyes closed. Then she rolled back in her cushions and koo'ed like a fool. ''But your people . . . I was there. They constantly . . . but . . . oh, Red Clay.''

I blushed and went out for a swim. When I came back she was straightening up in the kitchen. ''What I did,'' I asked, ''helping with the tea, was that what Mica did?''

She turned around, tears in her eyes. I gently embraced her, and we rocked side to side a bit. ''You must learn to be sung,'' she said, ''and not to be bluffed away, to keep me from being pulled too much between males. I am better as a politician than a breeder. Sit down by me now.''

I sat down beside her. ''Red Clay,'' she softly said, ''relax your throat. Just open it and relax it. Lean against my arms and close your eyes, it's easier.''

Vampire movies flashed through my mind. She stroked my throat and said, almost irritated, ''Loosen.'' Then she began singing, going up and down some Gwyng scales. At first it was like someone breathing down my mouth, then I relaxed and felt my own voice singing without me doing anything. Only for a second—I tightened up again. She stroked my face. "It is possible. Try with me." She rolled over onto my lap, utterly loose.

I bent down over her wrinkled face, the nostril slits, the bone curves around the eyes, eyes closed now, and sang "Happy Birthday to You," with her vocal cords humming along.

Nothing that happened to me so far was odder—to sing and be sung Gwyng-style. I leaned back and she reached up and stroked my face. "You must do well in the Academy for me," she said.

I got a call the next day from the Rector's office. One of his Barcon clerk-medics told me Karriaagzh wanted to see me in the morning. Black Amber showed me how to drive her car on the beach.

The controls made sense, so we decided I wouldn't have any trouble, as long as I followed the map computer and stopped for the lights.

I drove up to the Rector's office and parked in a lot beside the entrance. A Barcon stopped me when I got to the screening desk and took a blood sample. I asked why, but he just swabbed the puncture with an icy chemical which stopped the bleeding instantly. Then he took me to the Rector's outer office. Karriaagzh, in his green and gold, came out and asked me to follow him in.

He had an odd inner office—huge chandelier which dangled from a ceiling so high he didn't brush the lowest crystal as he passed under it and settled to the floor beside a low boomerang-shaped table of highly figured dark wood. The only thing on the table was a chrome-cased terminal with keyboard and writing pad.

As he looked me over, his facial feathers twitched in disconcerting patterns, so I looked down, away from his weird yellow eyes with those fierce bony ridges over them.

"How was the Sub-Rector Black Amber?" he asked curtly.

"That was a strange experience, *sir*," I said. Feather tufts at the side of his head pricked forward at the English word. "An *English* honorific, *sir*," I said. He twitched some feathers at his beak corners—imitation smile? Real smile? "An old

Gwyng died," I continued. "It had been living in a pouch host. And the mating—weird. But I guess I shouldn't judge."

He just looked at me, then some feathers shifted up and down on his neck. "Was the mating open?"

"Rector Karriaagzh, among my people, such things are private."

"Not among Gwyngs," he replied. "Don't pick up her weird attitudes about me." He sat for a moment, calling up displays on his terminal, looking at them, calling up others. Then he said, "We'd like to prepare you now for your trip to Yauntra. Basically, you'll be tested on how quickly you learn another language in the sequential group. The linguistics team feels confident that they've mastered the main grammar structure and have adequate function-word vocabularies, know the major bound morphemes. Black Amber doesn't want you to go now. Perhaps she wants you for company."

He stared me straight in the eyes as if he knew what Granite Grit had told me about becoming another alien's pet.

"If I didn't go, how long would I be at Amber's?"

"Another month. Cadmium and Rhyodolite have gone out on other missions. Your mission's simple. And you might like being among people similar to you. Sometimes Karst seems like a movie studio where too many films are being made at once, with overly ambitious casts. A rest, perhaps, with some work, exploration of a new planet and species. You were able to talk without fuss with the Yauntry delegate at the First Contact Party."

The Barcon tech came in and cocked his finger at Karriaagzh, who said to me, "Or you could visit your bird friends— Granite Grit and his new mate?"

"Being among all those mated types just makes me feel lonely."

"And the *human* woman is out of contact now, off buying goods from the *primitive* humans. The Yauntra women might be appealing." He typed into his terminal and signed with a light pen.

"What was that finger wiggle about?" I asked, squirming slightly in the sudden silence.

"Report on various hormone levels. Nothing to worry about," Karriaagzh said distantly, clamping down all his head and face feathers. "You'll have an eight-day introduction to linguistics at the Institute for Sound Communication Studies, and then join the team on Yauntra to finish learning linguistics and linguistic contact procedures. We've sent to Black Amber's for your luggage there.'' He looked up, feathers still flattened, and said, ''I hope all goes well for us.''

The Barcons escorted me out.

= 8 =

Brain Wishes

The first time I'd landed on Yauntra, I'd been chained. Now, I waited above the planet in an observation satellite for a shuttle, since Yauntra gravity nets blocked direct gating to planet surface. I plugged in holograms and waited, then reviewed information on Yauntry grammar and waited some more. *Alone again, almost here.*

Finally, a Yauntry came in, round chin tucked down, and said, "Red Clay, you're wanted." I followed him to the main deck and saw a new alien, who looked as though someone had depilated and polished a black T across his eyes and down his pointed nose. Otherwise, he was furry, face covered with black hair like eyebrow hair, the other fur chocolate brown and dense. He said, "Placental male." I kept looking at him. "I'm Carbon-jet, a Jerek, and the Federation's junior linguistics officer here. Karriaagzh sent a message pod about you. You're Black Amber's protégé."

"Jereks were checking out my roommate when he was trying to do weird spy things to the computer," I said, remembering out loud.

The Jerek tucked his nose down, seemingly annoyed. "That has nothing to do with my function here. We've had twenty-seven Federation people on Yauntra for about half a year, all studying Yauntro." He paused, then said, "Let's go." We crawled into a shuttle.

Finally we dropped out of orbit to Uzir, one of Yauntra's main cities, and touched down on the field where I'd landed months ago. This time I saw no curious Yauntry press photographers, just a car and driver who took us both to a dinky apartment near Uzir's university, in the building Yauntra reserved for aliens. The apartment was cold.

"So I'm back," I said.

Carbon-jet asked, "Can you take near-freezing at night, or are we going to have to have separate air temperature systems?"

"I'd rather have it warmer."

He closed his little shoe-button eyes and sighed. The black lids were shiny—from a distance you wouldn't have known whether the eyes were open or not.

The Yauntries in charge of our various alien comforts sent some guy over to install a heater in my room, while Carbon-jet and I hung insulating drapes. The rest of the apartment was cold, about 45 degrees. I ordered the Yauntry equivalent of sweaters.

Carbon-jet said, "Why don't you grow out your face hair while we share this space? You'd be warmer."

We went each morning through what Carbon-jet called sweltering heat, to a battered sub-basement library room where Yauntra linguists and us aliens translated cultural materials. As soon as I mastered the basic morphemes and could give a grammar scan, I'd interline a Yauntra text printout with the corresponding Karst I grammar and all the words I could construe. Carbon-jet, stripped to briefs, argued with a Yauntry scholar for hours about the precise implications of idioms while I doodled cows, hens, and pilling machines.

We must have bored the computers. Yauntra—the planet; Yauntre'h—a (mid-politeness level) native(s); Yauntro—the language (null-polite).

And when we went back to the apartment, Carbon-jet talked only in Yauntro, stumbling after meaning since he was still learning it himself.

My first free day, I took a bus tour of the Yauntra capital with a Yauntry student who was learning Karst I. Slowly, with great aching pauses as we fumbled through each other's languages, he told me about the wife his corporation found for him. The whole Galaxy was obsessed with sex.

The next free day, the Yauntra scholars invited me and the other Karst aliens to the country for a late summer festival picnic. Unlike Karst, it was honest country on a normal planet, really old and eroded, not cobbled together with alien plants still hustling for ecological niches.

I lay back on the grass, green like grass is, good structure for a creeping rhizome plant. Yeah, Karriaagzh was right; Karst was constructed for aliens to gesture from. Yauntra just had one sapient species under a hundred-year-old world government, but the land was fabulously complex, old.

Carbon-jet was relentlessly swimming, trying to stay cool. He climbed out of the river and said to me, "They took away the cooling belt I generally wear. Didn't know what it was and didn't trust it."

"He was trying to smuggle high-technology embarrassments onto the planet," one of the Yauntry said. "We stopped the entry of disruptive systems."

Carbon-jet dried off with his uniform top and slung it across his narrow fuzzy shoulders, and told them, "Technology goes where it will."

The next day I came from blinding myself on Yauntra script and green-screened terminals, to find I'd been invited to dinner with Edwir Hargun. Since he was Ambassador to the Federation, he wanted to meet us all.

An old crotchety person, Federation protocol officer, a stringy-haired ape, warned me not to discuss my captivity. "Say you were warmly welcomed after the initial misunderstanding and that you much appreciate his kindness."

I remembered the electric blanket that Rhyo used to warm with and smiled. The old protocol officer continued, "Their government tried to destroy all the tapes of your cursing their cheese. And they wonder why you taught them English and not Karst I."

"I thought they were the bad guys."

Despite the uniforms and various cuts of suits, all the Yauntries I got introduced to blurred in my mind—round wide eyes, dark skin, short round noses, high cheekbones, and round jaws—short head hair even on their women. I started sorting them, finally, by eye color and the clothes. Lots of the same uniform here—with different embroideries. Uniforms, cops?

One of those uniformed guys came to my apartment to take me to Hargun's and asked, in Karst I, "How did you feel when you landed at the same place where you'd been brought down earlier in chains?''

I tried to figure out his rank—young, junior officer?—and smiled into the earnest blue-grey eyes. "Other than the initial accident, my first meeting with the Yauntry people was pleasant.''

"Why, then, were you in restraints?'' He opened his car door up, like a gull-wing DeLorean. I got in beside him and he looked over at me as though he rather wished he could put restraints on me again. Xenophobes, but just moderately.

"Perhaps the officers in charge wondered what we planned, sneaking into your space. Of course, I thought we were picking up a satellite that bore messages for aliens.''

"I heard one of your companions was a real monster—giant feathered fanged bird who could kick open a man's belly. I've heard that birds rule you.''

"No.''

"Wasn't a bird alien shot?''

"Yes. He and one of your people stumbled against each other in the initial boarding. A weapon went off. We accepted your apologies for the accident.''

"*Mursha* Hargun says a huge grey bird rules you.'' The guy seemed to become more afraid of me as we talked, but he asked his questions mechanically, like he was ticking them off a list. "Your Federation will let us alone if we wish? Plans no reprisals?''

"No offense taken. Listen, I *was* angry to be brought down in chains.''

He smiled or grimaced. "I would have been.''

"I'm just a student, trying to learn your language. I don't make policy.''

"Our attitude toward you strange ones doesn't offend?'' That felt like his own question.

"We seem to be on decent terms now.''

"What are your Federation's intentions toward our lithium?'' We pulled up to another apartment building with a Yauntra globe in front. The driver picked up his car radio-phone and said, "Good evening, *Mursha* Hargun.''

Mursha was one of their ranks, I guessed. "I don't know anything about your lithium,'' I said as I got out. The driver led me up to Hargun's apartment and put his hand and mine on a door plate.

Hargun came to the door and invited us in. "Well, and how did you find your conversation with this young alien?" Hargun said to the other Yauntry. "He looks almost like a real person, doesn't he?"

"He admits he didn't like the restraints," the other Yauntry said as he moved off.

"Thank you for inviting me to dinner, Ambassador Hargun. What does *Mursha* mean? Is it a rank or what?"

I must have fractured their idiom. Hargun shook his head slightly and said, "Mursha—trusted . . . I can't quite explain it. And how is your intimidating rector?" We went into a room with a camera pointed at two big armchairs with small red-lacquer tables set beside them.

"He seems well. You don't think, really, that he rules us, do you?"

He stared at me strangely, eyes almost rigid in his head, and pulsebeats began echoing in my own skull—as though we'd just encountered each other for the first time, dangerously. Then he said softly, in Karst I, "Your people came to rescue you and the other one very intensely. Very much pressure on us."

"Fanged giant man-killer?" Hargun didn't reply. "I told that guy the bird stumbled against one of the boarding party."

Hargun's eyes fluttered. He looked up at the camera, then called in another Yauntry, who put a covered tray on each table. "Reasonable," he finally said. Then he looked back at me and said, more brightly, "I saw no intelligent animals on Karst who looked as much like us as you do. How many of your people study there?"

"I'm the only *human* in the Academy. My planet doesn't have connections with the Federation."

"No? How did they avoid the Federation?"

"Since they don't have space drive, Karst didn't contact them. I tried to help someone who was stranded on *Earth*, my planet—didn't work out well. Although he died, the rescue team took me back with them."

Hargun steered me over to the chair most exposed to the camera. I lifted the tray lid. The Yauntries had prepared a local imitation of Gwyng blood cakes, Yauntry fruits and breads. "Do many of your people know about the other intelligent animals landing?"

"My brother, who went crazy. That's all I know about. Federation crews landed at least once in the past and brought other *humans* to Karst with them. I met two other *humans*, one a woman, other people like me, but . . . I want to get to know her better. My Academy roommate thought I ought to, to avoid becoming just a pet of other intelligent animals. Your language doesn't have a word like *alien*?"

"We didn't imagine. We could use *murshi*, but we try not to make racial distinctions among Yauntry too often, and you are not Yauntry." He stopped talking a moment, then said, "Perhaps *you* are a hostage?"

"Well, not exactly." I almost explained about the aliens being surgically transformed to look like humans, but decided that would scare Hargun. "The *alien* I helped wanted me to take his place. And the Rector agreed."

"So they don't have special mind tools to make you forget? To learn languages fast?" Hargun asked, his breaths getting faster and shallower.

"Yeah, I learned Karst language through mind work."

Hargun looked at me so hard I looked away from those strange green round eyes with the slightly oval pupils. Offputting eyes. He swayed back as though he didn't want to be standing close to me. "Very interesting," he said. "So the Rector brought you to Karst, sent you here? And your planet isn't officially part of the Federation?" He ate a vegetable stalk slowly, then continued, "So you have no companions, no mates, lovers of your species?"

The whole universe, I swear, all mated except poor me. "No, although I almost had a lover from a species that resembled me, more than yours." Poor Calcite—totally alone. "She got sick."

"I'm sorry." He was genuinely sorry, for a second. "I forget that an isolated person might find such talk disturbing. And you, an intelligent animal twice removed from your home. If it wouldn't upset you, tell me about your home, how you lived, what you liked about it?"

Talking about Floyd County and humans for an hour was both neat and a strain. Finally, I asked, "Why are you giving me so much attention?"

"Ah, I'm a fatherly type. You're just a lonely person, needing to talk, perhaps. Not too stressful?"

"No," this little intelligent animal said, twice removed from home, to the alien Ambassador to a Federation neither understood. "Why is that camera there?"

"I must document myself," Hargun answered, "to prove my loyalty." The driver came for me then.

When I got back, Carbon-jet was curled around his notepad with the air conditioner going full blast. He looked up and asked, "What did Hargun want?"

I put on a coat and an extra pair of pants and said, "He asked me about my Earth home. And whether birds had conquered us."

"Um," Carbon-jet said as he hurriedly scrawled me a note that said, *Write, in English, everything you both said tonight. Don't speak any more about it.*

I wrote and then Carbon-jet took what we'd both written into the bathroom with a microscope and a camera.

As I curled up in my imported sheets, I tried to remember when I'd just been me among people, on Earth, without aliens, before Mica.

A couple of days later, we got a new linguist, Filla, a shy-seeming girl Yauntry who had a body shape like a human woman's, breasts lower than they tended to be on Yauntry women. Eyes like mine, as Carbon-jet pointed out, with hair longer than most Yauntries, who generally grew it only down the backs of their necks. Hers was dark blond, with reddish tints, curled below her nape and fluffed up over her ears.

That night, tucked in a sleeping bag, reading, I said to Carbon-jet, "I *know* what she is . . ."

He covered my mouth with his muscular dark hand and handed me a pad and pen.

I know she must be a spy, Carbon-jet, but can I sleep with her anyway?

Carbon-jet rolled his eyes, flashes of whites vivid against the black T of face skin. *Keep me informed. Don't go anywhere, away, with her.*

One afternoon, in the computer vault below the Yauntra library, Filla arranged that we run out of texts early.

"*Tom* Red Clay, come walk in the park with me," she said, smiling.

Carbon-jet leaned down on his elbows—tense, alien about to spring—then jerked upright to snap off a computer. He began to sleek down his forearm fur and play with the fuzz that ran up the back of his hands onto his fingers.

"If you want, come with us," she said, in a voice that was fake for any species.

"Have a good time," he said. "I'm tired of this heat. I'll go back to quarters and chill myself."

She and I walked out and took a Yauntry bus, dirty metal painted flake blue, to their biggest park. Musicians played under little porches, and vendors with trays like movie cigarette girls sold sweets that I tried nervously and found instantly delicious.

"What is your home planet like?" she asked.

"I don't really know. I didn't see much other than where I was born."

"Teach me words of your home. Yes, No, Maybe?" she asked in Karst. We walked through the gardens eating sweets and practicing *yes*, *no*, and *maybe* in English and the three politeness levels of Yauntro.

"And your birthplace? How is it called?"

"*Floyd.*"

Floyd on her lips sounded hilarious. "Big city," she asked in Karst, "this *Floyd*?"

Something disarming about women who speak with accents, I thought. "No, hill country with very few people," I answered in polite but distant Yauntro.

"We have all angles of land," she said. "Anything you want. I would like to get out of the city myself."

"If Carbon-jet can come, too," I said.

"Poisonous thing, but yes," she answered.

I took her in my arms, stared briefly at her oval pupils, and kissed her once for the country. *They're oval up and down*, I thought, *not sideways like Calcite's.*

"You want to go?" Carbon-jet asked, stretched out on his bed. He'd rigged a vest to wear instead of a full uniform tunic. "And I'm invited?" He rolled over, picked up his pad, and wrote, *Be very careful.*

"Well, can we go?"

"*Where* are we going?"

Filla gave me a map, which Carbon-jet duplicated and gave to the protocol officer.

We went ninety miles south, then followed a switchback road up a scarp rise and onto the rolling country back of it, on the mountain as we say in Virginia. The trees bore alien fruit, not apples, but the orchards were still laid out in those two-way rows—double symmetries up and down the slopes. High country, maybe six to seven thousand feet up. The houses weren't so ramshackle—more stone than frame, no brick, but the air was cool, softly windy—that eternal mountain air.

"We didn't turn the way you said we'd turn on the map," Carbon-jet said, gripping the back of the front seat.

"Oh, I found a better house," Filla said.

"We're *off* the map," Carbon-jet added a few miles later.

"Better house. Two bedrooms, one with a massive air cooler. Better for you." Filla smiled at him through the rearview mirror.

Carbon-jet folded the map and stared out the windows. Filla drove through a few more switchbacks and turned off down a dirt road that led to a little wooden house on the first shelf above a creek bottom, built like mountain people did before tourists put hexagonal solar things on ridge tops.

"Do you remember the logging camp we passed back about fifteen minutes ago?" Filla asked Carbon-jet.

"Yes," he said dubiously.

"Well, Red Clay and I are going back there for firewood. The air cooler for your room is like the one in your quarters back at Uzir. I won't steal him."

She was nervous, here with two aliens, but something gave her confidence. We must be covered by at least ten secret guns.

Carbon-jet's shoulder fur flared out just a bit and he lowered his nose at her, presenting the T face skin directly vertical. Then he lowered his fur, reaching up under his vest to smooth it, and trudged on short little legs to the house.

I was nervous, myself. We stopped by the trash pile and loaded the back of the car with cut-off limbs and slabs, only saying Yauntro words for "here's one we won't have to cut" and "here's a good one."

When we got back to the house, I took an armful of wood in to the stove. A new schoolhouse box heater, I noticed, just like the one I described to Hargun, but with Yauntry foundry labels instead of English ones. Sawdust under the pipe hole looked fresh. Wood stoves on Yauntra?

Carbon-jet came out of his room, saw me setting a fire, said, in Karst I, "You've got to be kidding," and went back to the roaring air conditioner in his room. The weather didn't make us build a fire—but I've always liked wood heat's feel, smoother to the skin than oil heat. While I got the fire going, Filla curled up on an Earth-style couch by the heater, watching me.

Then I opened a window a crack and we just sat quietly—me thinking about winter days before the family had oil, using wood stoves, and a feather duster to skim that fine ash off the furniture. I'd watch Mom, who'd intently look into the wood grain, whisking the feathers over, looking, whisking again.

Filla cooked eggs on the stove when the fire got hot enough—just like my mother had done. The way that alien girl fed eggs to me was downright provocative—spooning them into my mouth and hers alternately, curled by me. "It is our custom," she said. Having her body up by mine felt good—alien spy or whatever. I put my arm around her.

"I'd like to stay like this forever, you and me," I said. "No more getting shot at or seeing shipmates die. No more hours studying crazy languages that don't sit right on my tongue."

"I sit on your tongue?" Halfway between misunderstanding me and propositioning me, she reached under my tunic, then froze. "We can . . ." Her fingers tugged my chest hairs, then drew back.

"Filla?" I looked very closely at her and saw her hands do a fine tremble that wasn't for sex.

"This is all very strange."

"I imagine it is," I said as I got up and put more sticks in the fire box. "You can sleep in the bedroom. I'll sleep on the couch." I laid my hand on her shoulder. It quivered, so I jerked my arm away from her. "Not quite like sex with another Yauntry, is it?" She made me feel alien. Xenofreaking bitch, and I didn't even have a little relax-'um pill, nor the boring but species-appropriate talk to get the pill down her. "Seducing me probably seemed like a good idea back in town. Now you can't follow through, can you?"

"You're not supposed to be so different from us."

She wasn't sure what she was supposed to do. That flashed in English. I remembered all the story behind it—one of the dealers in Martinsville told Warren how some bitch trapped him, and he should have known because when he tried to make her, she didn't know what she was supposed to do. But I'd *known* this was a setup for the spy bitch. Why was I doing this with her? I felt sick inside.

I looked closer at the wood heater. *About as long as my arm . . .* that's how I'd described the heater we'd had when I was a boy. "Filla, your people made this heater for me. They sent you here to talk to me."

She looked at Carbon-jet's room and back at me, quivering.

"*Damn*, stop shaking, Filla. Let's at least treat each other like reasonable beings."

"I'm happy if you say we can see again," she said in miserable Karst which made her seem fluffy and cute, but I wondered about a species that sent a girl for spy sex with aliens who terrified her.

And I knew it all—she was a spy, she was afraid of me—but I still wanted to see more of her. Too lonely, that's why. When I sat down on the couch, she sidled off to the bedroom. The lock clicked. Pissed me off, this alien neurosis, with the door locked against me. I stretched out on the couch and wondered how many Yauntries surrounded the house.

I dreamed I got her to see things the Federation way, my way.

When I woke up, Carbon-jet and Filla were fixing separate breakfasts. He whistled when he saw me stumble up to a sink to shave after I'd used the john. "Still has to scrape off the hairs that grow in the night," Carbon-jet said. "Some weird tribal ritual." His black face skin crinkled as he explained to Filla, "I suggested, since we shared quarters, that Tom just grow the face hair out for warmth. Or let the Barcons depilate him permanently, but he likes to fuss with his little electric machine."

"We don't grow animal body hair like either of you," Filla said primly.

"From pictures I've seen, he could grow face hair down to his toes. Right, Red Clay?"

"No, just to my nipples." Killing off my face hairs seemed unmanly. I wasn't the only creature on Karst who shaved daily—me the face, others other things, some backs of hands, fingers, foreheads, whatever. And the jerk was making Filla nervous. "Filla, how are you doing?"

"Fine, Red Clay. Do you think I'm a spy?"

Carbon-jet whistled again and put his hands over his face.

"Filla, I told Hargun I was lonely and you got assigned to our study group, with your almost Earthwoman's tits, long hair for a Yauntry."

She looked from the short fur on Carbon-jet's head to my razored-clean chin. "Perhaps I thought I'd be appreciated by you, for having such features? Do all space people have fur or bristles?"

Carbon-jet lowered his nose slightly at Filla as I sat down cross-legged on the kitchen table and glared at her. "Some have feathers. Your guys shot one of those."

"So odd to see hair coming out from your face last night," Filla said softly. "Then to feel the chest. I couldn't."

Carbon-jet's teeth came together in a click. "Red Clay, you didn't scrape off those barbaric bristles before taking this smooth-skinned *thing* to sex?"

"Maybe we should come back," I said, "with more of her people, so she won't feel so isolated among aliens."

"Sure, wonderful. Do it Gwyng-style." Then Carbon-jet changed to the language we hear when the computer transmutes Karst II, *"Was she about to freak?"*

"She was trembling."

"Speak Yauntro, young man, we can't hear you," Carbon-jet said. "Slick-skinned Filla, you may be a wonderful spy here on Yauntra, but you're a fucking amateur when it comes to aliens." Carbon-jet looked from her to me and back again, then went to his room, came out wearing a pocket vest, and walked outside.

I fixed eggs for breakfast while Filla watched. Since coming to space, I realized as I watched her back, I hadn't really been angry until now. Alien angry. I was pissed that the bitch Yauntry flinched—like I was weird with my beard, body hair, and straight jawbones. I breathed deeply, and she flinched, damn her, again. "I want to just get back to Uzir now," I told her.

"I'm sorry if I upset you by being startled."

"*Bullshit.*"

"What?"

"Excrement from a lactating monster, male, *Earth* species, with horns. Big."

"A curse? Why?" she asked humbly.

"Why are you trying so hard to be friendly when I terrify you?"

"I feel conflict over this," she said in Karst. She folded her hands over her chest and leaned against a cabinet.

"*Fuck it*, Filla."

"Did you ever consider that I might want to contact aliens intellectually, privately?"

Maybe she wasn't Hargun's spy. Carbon-jet came back then, as I was considering asking her more, and said, "Why don't we just go back to the university?"

"Great idea," I said, moving on to pack up. Filla stood in the middle of the living room, staring at us both as we neatened up the place and loaded the car.

Carbon-jet came out of her room with a walkie-talkie. He tossed it to her and suggested, "You go out and make your report to your people, too."

She turned red. "Jerek, named Carbon-jet," she said like she'd memorized it.

When we got back, I headed for the library, and Filla tagged along. We walked toward the cement buildings, me striding fast, she almost running to keep up, passing Yauntra students hung with typical student rigs—backpacks, computer disc satchels, and calculators.

"Wait, *Tom.*"

The Yauntries stared at me as she called. They were the moderately xenophobic Yauntries, who shot nervous gentle birds, who tried to make me into a mysterious space alien. As they pointed their round alien eyes at me, I resented them intensely. Not looking back at her, I stopped. "Tom, Red Clay, we need to know . . ." Her voice faded.

More horrible yet—if she had gone to bed with me, not even that, if she'd relaxed with me, I'd have volunteered the few Karst secrets I'd known to have a quiet month in the country with her.

She came up and touched my hands gently. But I noticed three of her kind watching intently from a short distance, cop-like. My cock withered. "Filla, I'll see you at work. I'm going back to talk to Carbon-jet."

She muttered a farewell and walked straight up to a Yauntry cop. Dumb bitch, I almost fell in love with her again, an amateur, not a pro, spying for her people.

I decided I should talk to the senior Federation guy here, the protocol officer, and walked back to my quarters, shoulders hunched against all the Yauntry stares.

The old ape smiled after I explained what had happened. "The boy's here," he said into his intercom.

Carbon-jet entered, all snippy-nosed, through a side door. The ape introduced him as the resident officer from the Institute of Analytics and Tactics.

"I'm not surprised, Carbon-jet," I said.

He pulled his thin lips back from considerable teeth and punched code on a terminal. He looked from the terminal to me. "Find out what she wants to know. We'll take you on as an Institute trainee. You won't be under Karriaagzh directly. We're pretty independent."

"She's just some amateur fool. And I'm no spy, either."

"You lived illegally on your home planet." He tucked his nose down, but didn't let his eyes meet mine. "Many newly contacted species try, however clumsily, to see if the Federation is an agency of empire rather than free association. We let them investigate, so long as no one's hurt. The Yauntries approached me sexually, but I'm faithful to my own."

"So you—Karriaagzh—thought I'd respond to an alien woman, because I got hot at Black Amber's. *Like a jack without jennies? Making mules.*"

"Explain that alien noise," Carbon-jet said.

"Pen up a male without his females. He'll fuck anything."

Carbon-jet sat down. "That *was* the general idea. If you join our Institute, we can use you *with* your consent. You'll know what we want to know."

"But she's scared of me. I slept with a girl once on

Earth—I know how it's supposed to go. I don't want to sleep with some alien *bitch* who thinks *I'm* a monster.''

"Well, if he's not genuinely attracted, then I doubt he'll have sexual reflexes,'' the old protocol ape said.

"No. And I won't let the Barcons tamper with those.''

Whistling faintly, Carbon-jet seemed to count parquet bits in the floor. "Please see this woman again, if she wants,'' he finally said. "We need to assure Yauntra that the Federation doesn't initiate violence, but can defend itself. You got along well with Granite Grit. Why don't you help us here?''

"How could one species attack one-hundred-plus species?''

"The birds didn't believe the Federation had so many species in the alliance. The Rector showed one of their war presidents enough different species to convince them that we weren't lying.''

"Okay. But I'm not joining your Institute.''

"Just volunteer to help. This device aids memory.'' Carbon-jet pulled out a curved grey slab like a big skull bone, and a jar of gritty jelly. He smeared the inside curve of the slab with a fingerful of jelly, then fitted it to the back of my head and guided my hands to hold the slab while he plugged a cord into it. "Think about this morning,'' Carbon-jet told me, steadying the slab with his own hands, alien thick fingers up against mine.

Suddenly, I saw the exact muscles quivering in Filla's face, arms, the Yauntry cops in brown and yellow suits. The cop on my left had an insect bite on his jaw, grass stains on one knee.

Snap—gone. Carbon-jet had pulled the thing off my head. "Very interesting device, Jerek,'' I said. "So I don't have to take notes?''

"And your skull computer records, also. Wash and dry your hair before you leave.''

And if I got killed, they could read out my last minutes. "How many bytes does the skull computer store?''

"Hour loops of what you hear and an equivalent amount of biodata, without disturbing the translator program.''

Filla and I worked for a couple of weeks without speaking to each other more than linguistics work required—more, actually, than I wanted to talk to her.

And she got paler and paler. Finally, I noticed her hair begin to turn light blond. After we finished for the morning one day, she begged me, third-degree-formality Yauntro, to have lunch with her.

Carbon-jet fleered his lips and told me to go ahead.

Filla took me to a small restaurant, into a back room with separate chairs and individual little tables, so we sat apart. A waiter brought us dishes of jellied starch with meat and strips of vegetables.

She said, still being most polite, "I'm sorry if I insulted you by taking exception to your appearance. It has its charms."

"*Fuck it*. Your people and my people are using us. Let's discuss how to deal with that." I used bare forms, without politeness affixes, business talk.

She looked at me with great shock. "I didn't tell them I'd failed. I couldn't." Hastily, she began eating as I picked among the strange vegetables, watching her look up nervously from time to time. "Perhaps," she finally said, not as politely, but not sheer business either, "I'll bring my brother with us. Leave the Jerek here—too mocking."

"Well, I can't protect you this fast against brain games," Carbon-jet said, "or truth drugs and scanners, if they've got such stuff, but we can always trace you through your computer if we're above the local horizon."

"You want me to go ahead, then," I said, rather wishing he'd say no.

"We know who you're supposed to be with and when you're supposed to return. Why would they link you with Filla if they were arranging an accident?"

As Filla drove up the scarp road, I realized, mountainous or not, the countryside didn't look like rural Virginia, but was really sub-tropical. That earlier weekend, my eyes had done the brain's own wish-landscaping.

And the little house on the second terrace above the creek was the Yauntry miniature of the Karst planet stage-set business. When we got to the house built for me, I saw another Yauntry car, bigger than Filla's, parked by the woodshed. Her "brother," a huge Yauntry the size of Tesseract, opened the door, peered out suspiciously, then helped Filla with her bags.

I started in, but the brother-type said, "Stand and spread your arms."

As he moved a metal disc over me, I said, "What makes me mad is how casual my people are about this. I think the fact that a spy female—so obvious—picked me up would have caused more excitement. They didn't give me any advice or anything."

The disc paused up side of my head. "Shut up."

My head exploded in a hideous screech, like forty million fingernails on real slate blackboards. As soon as I could hear again, the man asked, "That?"

"Tr-translates Gwyng, Karst II languages for me."

Nervous about touching me, he twisted my head to the side with his fingertips, then tapped the artificial bone. "Would it kill you to take it out?"

Suddenly, I had to try very hard not to piss in my pants. "It's just a language computer for Karst II." I thought about how isolated I was. *Oh, so sorry. Accident on mountain road claims alien life. Filla mourns.*

"You don't need it to talk to us?" he asked, watching me sweat. "Come in, now."

"No," I answered, stepping inside.

Sitting at a table, he opened a grey anodized box with black dials with white lettering and pulled out two electrodes. "Come here." I did and he pasted the two electrodes on my skull. My ears rang; I saw a dial move, stop. "Well," he said, "if your skull computer *did* have any other functions you didn't mention . . ."

"What do you want to know?"

"We want a contact with our cadets, if we send cadets. A non-Yauntry could transmit messages less conspicuously." He turned my skull in his hands again and spoke to Filla in a language I didn't understand. "Do species conspire against each other by type group? We're both from tropical brachiators so we should be allies."

"I don't know anything about that. I'm new there." The Yauntries stank, of sweat and rotten flowers. Slowly, I got up and walked out. The brother followed me to the woodpile, which had been covered with clear plastic since Filla'd taken me and Carbon-jet up here.

"She says," the brother told me, "that you were shy, so we lightened her skin and hair to make her more like you."

I dropped a heap of little branches in his arms, and said, "*Is that a fact?*" in English, watching carefully to see if he was going to drop the wood and hit me. "She lied. She's terrified of me. It hurts."

After I picked up more wood, we went back inside and I stacked the wood away from the stove.

The two aliens watched me build the fire, stabbing inside the counterfeit stove with an imitation Earth poker. Finally, I said, "What do you want to know? I'll tell my guys and report back on how they react."

They seemed to be calculating the poker's length, checking me for strange sprouting hairs, or, God knows, sudden tentacles.

"You make me feel alien," I told them, hating feeling so alone. "You guys made me feel horrible from the first day your troops pinned us down with your gravity jerking."

"Monsters for companions," the man said.

I started to pace the floor, swinging the poker until I saw sheer terror on their faces, the hands inside their clothes. This was how Xenon died. He was scared and they were scared. Slowly, as if they had their guns trained on me already, I put the poker down, and sat down on the floor, leg tucked up tailor-style. "The Gwyngs don't make me feel alien. It's bad enough being the intelligent talking creature who fixes tea when the guests come. But a makes-you-nervous alien? Your eyes are round enough, don't stare at me like that. I don't have any weapons on me. I'm sitting down. Okay, I'll lean back on my hands." I did precisely that, wondering if they could follow all that Karst.

Suddenly, I floated outside the scene, outside my body—as one intelligent ape of one species talked to two of another—all of us alien. Tufts of hair marked my armpit and groin glands—not like a chimpanzee. I could grow face hair to my hairy chest, with only a strip of slick forehead, nose, and cheek skin bare. Not too different from Carbon-jet, after all.

Sure was a weird alien sitting in front of them. Filla looked like she was going to have hysterics, but the universe never uses exactly the same pattern each time it forces a beast to think.

What burdens thoughts could be, I decided as I choked on a laugh. Monkeys. And the Gwyngs were such perfect bats—if you're into thoughtful mob sociability, then you've got to be a Gwyng.

Finally, I got myself under control, leaned up, hands to my face, almost in tears. The Yauntries still had their hands on concealed weapons, but they seemed to recognize tears as a reasonable reaction to the situation. "We don't understand all you spoke," the male said.

"No, I understand," Filla countered, which touched off a spate of talking in a language I couldn't follow.

"So I grow face hairs," I muttered dumbly.

"Filla, take him for a walk."

They must have given her a good weapon because she looked more confident about being alone with me than the last time. She stayed five paces or so behind me, so I just rambled around, going down to the spring, while I thought about how badly I wanted to see resemblances to Virginia to have imagined myself back in similar country. But then, I could never go home again, despite Yauntry armed women and spies radioing back and forth for instructions.

"You smell odd," Filla said behind me.

"You stink, of dead flowers."

Back at the house, the whole scene seemed ridiculous—all us sweating in fear of each other while the big guys . . . what were the big guys really doing? Filla looked at her brother Yauntry, who smiled faintly.

"I'm not trained for this," I told him. "If Filla wasn't trained either, the whole incident is absolutely stupid."

"Perhaps your Karst masters chose you because you're not so valuable."

I had no planet to back me, that was true. "What about Filla? What if I'd just eaten her?" I lowered my arms and shambled, ape-style, toward her. She pulled out her weapon, all nice and chromed, and grinned, teeth bare. "*Shit*," I said. "You're supposed to have fallen in love with me?"

The male motioned for her to put the weapon away. It looked like a 9mm automatic—big. "Filla admitted last night that she finds the idea of sex with aliens revolting."

"I'd have slept with her, but she obviously doesn't like to be around me except with her killing thing."

"Sit down," the brother said in rudest Yauntro. Low business. "What do you know about the tribute the Federation wants us to pay?"

"Tribute?" I hadn't thought about that, but the Academy and Institutes couldn't be cheap to run.

"Yes," he said, standing in front of me. "They want us to pay tribute on interstellar commerce in Federation ships, or through Federation gates. Your Federation monopolizes the known geometries to force money from us."

"All I knew was that I'd get a share of duties since I was one of those who first-contacted Yauntra. I don't know anything more."

"Plus charges on all things your many species claim to have invented first. I suspect honest independent discoveries aren't allowed in your Federation universe."

"I really don't know what you're talking about."

"Are we supposed to kill you and then be made guilty?" He stared at me, suddenly nervous. Maybe he'd taken an alien bait? "Just how long have you been with these people?"

"Around two years. Less."

"What cargoes fly between planets?"

"Art things. Computer discs. Some minerals . . . lithium. Ideas are the main trade item," I said, remembering the bit about ideas from a history lesson.

"We have lithium, also hydrocarbons." He sat down heavily and leaned toward me. "Can you appreciate our position?" One grade of politeness.

"You've got me curious," I said. "I appreciate your reluctance to trust the Federation and I hope you understand why I can't trust you."

"Personal or political mistrust?"

"Personal, because you look at me as if I was a monster, armed as you are."

"We have xenophobia, as your people reported to Karst," he said. "Do you understand us now?"

A denial would have been more soothing. Filla had just sat there, listening. Now she got up, stretched, and said, "*Tom*, Red Clay, I am sorry. But my experiences didn't include sex with hairy creatures."

The phrase *So human an animal* drifted through my roiled brain.

"We'll eat now," Filla said.

The male and I watched each other while Filla cooked. "What is your Rector?" he said suddenly.

"A solitary bird. But his kind has space capacities, just doesn't use them."

"Tell Carbon-jet we plan to subvert the bird control of the Federation by organizing a tropical-species resistance group, ex-brachiators."

"Apes," I said in the Karst slang for our stock.

"Yes, we will pit apes against feathered lizards."

"It doesn't work that way. I'll have to tell them all about our conversations."

"We understand that." He smiled. I wondered if he knew how fully I could reconstruct the conversations. Filla came in with dinner and we ate out of bowls held in our various laps, each watching each for bad manners or totally alien weirdnesses.

Then I wondered if they'd given me more than an hour of pure silence.

Back with the pointed-nose Carbon-jet, memory-jogging plate to my skull, I asked, "Do you want to know what color his clothes were?"

"Just tell me exactly what was said, including foreign-language statements." He reached over my shoulder to punch on a recorder, then stood behind me, holding the plate steady.

Exactly. Down the time line. I could even taste the food I'd eaten when we'd finished talking. After I'd told all my memory held, Carbon-jet tugged the plate—wet plop as it pulled away from my jellied hair and scalp. "We undid what they did to your skull computer, also," Carbon-jet said. *Weird.* I went to wash my hair and dried it before I came back to Carbon-jet.

When I returned, C-j was entering data furiously on his terminal. The display changed and he wrote strange characters with a light pen before saying, "I wish I could meet the Yauntry responsible for this move, especially since they knew I sent you."

I was caught between two young intelligence officers strutting their stuff—elaborating lies and honesties for pure cleverness. Agile minds—I almost suspected Carbon-jet of being yet another ape.

The next day, Yauntry cops with big smiles came to the library room where Carbon-jet and I were working and told us, "No Federation creatures or message pods can leave Yauntra until the Xi'isisom files are returned."

Carbon-jet stared at them with his challenge face, nose tucked down, the whole T of naked face skin even shinier. His microfilms for Karst—not going. Since nobody got radio waves to beat Einstein, Tykwing, *et al.*, C-j's information was stuck on Yauntra. Unmanned message pods were easy to trap in gravity nets.

We couldn't find a data entry for the missing materials under the title they'd given us.

Next morning when we woke up, Carbon-jet and I debated whether to go back to the sub-basement or not. We went, thinking that since we weren't guilty, we might as well keep working.

Filla and the male Yauntry who'd been at the cabin last time were both there, looking at me as if they knew I was bait, but still, hook and all, they had to take me.

"Would you like to go back to the country?" Filla asked, her hair back to a more normal Yauntry color.

"No," I said.

Carbon-jet looked up at the silent male and lowered his nose slightly, then raised it when the male smiled and moved a hand to his waistband. Where human pants had pockets, the Yauntry pants had a fold and a lump . . . *there, that's where the gun is.* Carbon-jet said, "Tom, maybe you'd better go with them."

"Come on, Red Clay *Tum*, we won't hurt you."

"Why is everyone doing this to me?" I gripped the chair, then saw Carbon-jet's rigid face and went with them.

The country we drove through looked less and less Earthy. We went to a different cabin, stone and cold, up in their tropical highlands.

I'd come only with the clothes I had on, but they produced other things of mine someone must have snagged from the apartment.

At first, I was really scared, thought they'd kill me, or bring me up on spy charges and pen me here alone on Yauntra forever. Or maybe, I figured when they didn't speak to me but locked me in a stone room with an iron door, they were waiting to see what Karst would do.

Since they'd forgotten my razor, I grew stubble, which exasperated Filla. The two Yauntries were so damn wary around me, either keeping a jump away or crowding in close, sweating through the old parallel armpit glands. Stink glands. They'd both walk me outside by a little creek where I'd flip stones over to uncover flat crabs that were Yauntra analogs to crayfish.

The third day, the male said, "So far, they've done nothing for you, animal."

I sat hunched up against my room's stone wall, staring at him. It seemed we sat for days, them watching my face hair grow, my mind tightening up in a knot, blanking out the alien people, landscape.

"You're destroying me," I finally said.

"Take him outside," he told Filla.

As she walked behind me, I wondered what I could eat to make myself sick, force them to take me to a hospital, something. But they might let me die. *Alien should have known fuji was poison.*

Finally, one day, a phone buzzed. The brother took it off the wall and into a separate room, then came back, scowling, talking with Filla in their strange language.

"We'll have company soon," she said to me.

After about an hour, we heard cars driving toward the house. Then I saw, out the window, at least a dozen Barcons and Jereks. The Rector Karriaagzh ducked through the door, with a needle-gun in his four-fingered hand, crest erect and quivering, followed by Carbon-jet, Black Amber, and Edwir Hargun.

"He tried to disgust us by the neglect of his personal grooming," Filla said in Karst. Black Amber's nostrils clapped, but then she oo'ed at me.

"Shut up," Karriaagzh said in Yauntro. He invaded the Yauntries' personal space with beak and toes. Filla backed against the farthest wall.

"*Sir,*" I said, "they think you're the Federation's ruler."

Karriaagzh looked at the frightened Yauntries and at Black Amber, who kept her own distance. He coughed, then said, "If I were, I wouldn't be here." Looking at Hargun, he asked, "Does my height affect your judgment so adversely?"

Hargun studied the cold stone floor and his own people's faces.

I wasn't sure what was happening, but Edwir Hargun didn't give me or C-j any eye contact. Occasionally, he'd squint at the Rector as we all got into various cars, including one without a rear seat for Karriaagzh.

We drove back down the mountain to a landing grid outside Uzir. When the cars emptied out, we all stood around the blue light bringing in another Karst ship. Hargun looked at all the Barcons and Jereks with guns, miniature robot cannons cruising like vicious high-tech turtles, while Black Amber watched Karriaagzh as if he were the dangerous one.

"The blockade will continue, for your own good," Karriaagzh told Hargun. "Only the medics and the young cadet will accompany us, so we're trading hostages. The others will stay."

Karriaagzh's transport materialized on the grid, and a crew of the most mixed aliens—pug-faces, birds, the skinny shiny blacks—rushed down the ramp while the transport was still rolling off the cables. Carbon-jet, who'd been the weirdest alien previously on Yauntra, talked with Karriaagzh in a strange language, then left, sounding querulous, with a troop of Barcons and five robot guns.

"You will get in, Ambassador," Karriaagzh said to Hargun. "Then you can call for whoever you want to have come with you. Would one of the people who held Red Clay hostage do?" Karriaagzh asked in Karst.

"Sir, we take this as a kidnapping," Hargun said, looking back at the other Yauntries.

"Fine. Shall I drag you? You kidnapped Red Clay."

"I have to have witnesses," he said. "The ones who should come with me had experience in handling aliens earlier."

"Can Black Amber ride with us?" I asked.

Karriaagzh pulled nictitating membranes over his eyes and spat air—bird disgust. "Go talk to her, if you must. She's going back in another transport."

Before she got in her transport, we embraced, first Gwyng-style, then human. "Karr'aggzh uses," she said, brushing the fuzzy backs of her fingers over my stubble beard.

Surprising how glad I was to see her, her to see me. She tried to smooth down my new beard, oo'ing and koo'ing softly. "What happened?" I asked.

"I did what I had to do/was forced by my concerns to do. But the bird bent me with that. Come to rest at my house after. Or at Tesseract's . . . might be politically more expedient/less . . ."

She stopped mid-pattern, holding my head gently with her fingertips, and kissed me on the eyelids, strange dry little kisses. "Go now, to the bird," she said.

After her ship disappeared in a shimmer of blue, the Rector's transport rolled back onto the net. Hargun's witnesses arrived in a Yauntry helicopter flown by Barcons who hustled them up into the transport.

We didn't gate far, just to a Yauntry space net station the Federation people had seized and encircled with Karst cargo bellies.

As we sat in the Rector's salon, Hargun in a chair, Karriaagzh on a leather pad, and me on the floor, Karriaagzh explained to Hargun, "We camouflaged most of our ships. Yauntry panic wasn't considered useful."

Then we swung by the first of their four moons, not as big as Earth's moon, but still none too tiny. On the blind side of the moon, I saw Karst ships, glittering side by side, like wasps on a nest.

Even though Yauntra wasn't my planet, I felt cold and scared. "I hate xenophobes," Karriaagzh said. Edwir Hargun finally drew in a breath and blinked rapidly as he looked at the ships. Karriaagzh continued in Yauntro, "All of our representatives obeyed your restrictions. None deserved to be tempted to desert us."

I wondered if I was in trouble now.

"Sir, you violate my goodwill," Hargun said. He stared, silent, almost quivering, out the glass viewport as we passed the third moon. An eighth of the moon's outside hemisphere was shiny with transports, an eerie sight even for me.

Hargun didn't speak again. Karriaagzh ordered his ship to begin gate hops to Karst.

The viewports turned to perfect mirrors in the jump fields—no "out" for light to escape to. The Rector watched Hargun's reflection flicker on and off, then spoke again, in Karst but slowly. "Once we have five hundred planets in our Federation, no species or group of species could possibly think of trying to dominate. Although we are relatively smaller than I'd prefer, I let new species test the Federation before joining. But it's a waste of energy."

"Would we be exterminated if we attacked?"

Karriaagzh faced Hargun directly. "Ambassador, we don't want to destroy any uniqueness."

"Don't *want* to," Hargun echoed with his own emphasis.

We entered the gravity net near the Karst sun's outermost planet. The Rector's ship cruised around the space yards, so he could point out the freight capacity of cargo bellies, and note the anti-piracy vessels, and the gravity warp capacities of the reserve nets. "If you believe me," he told Hargun gravely.

The viewport flashed into a mirror again, then turned transparent to show Karst rolling through space beside us. Karriaagzh said, "Rotate to Ah-5," and we turned, gas hissing, to face a huge satellite that looked like two dragonflies fighting—metal gauzy wings and crystal ports.

"Lasers and particle beams," Karriaagzh told Hargun. "Two thousand of them in the area from here to the next planet out. Just that type alone. Watch."

We saw three dots of light coming up over the disc of the planet. Then they weren't there.

"Particle beams and lasers are invisible in space," Karriaagzh said matter-of-factly. "Next, Zh-13."

The pilot adjusted the orbit and we came on a squat spherical satellite. "Gravity net—can mass a tenth of an average neutron star—generally not necessary. You understand I won't show you all Karst's defenses."

Sweat beaded on Hargun's short nose. Karriaagzh ordered tea and suggested we just sit for a while.

"Obviously, I'll be returned to Yauntra to tell about this. You understand they won't believe me, since I'm suspected of being an alien sympathizer."

"So you had Red Clay captured? *Other* Yauntry people will see what you saw. Perhaps their reports will be more trusted."

Hargun's eyes drifted toward the pug-face who'd come in

with the tea. As he cringed, I realized each species on board, one at a time, had been coming into our cabin. If all us aliens had suddenly surrounded the Yauntry and friendly-gestured in our different styles, the Barcons would have had to pull Hargun off the bulkheads. But Karriaagzh was giving Hargun manageable jolts every five minutes or so.

I didn't think Hargun noticed a pattern, but I did and looked sharply at Karriaagzh. No high-strung types like Gwyngs served on the ship. Now, an olive-colored bird like Xenon ambled in and looked in Hargun's teacup.

"Hope you like that tea," it said and went out.

Hargun tightened his lips. He never mentioned pitting stock against stock again.

A Barcon entered and said that the other ship had returned to the outer well and would be taking Yauntry observers back to their planet—all except the ones Hargun wanted with him.

"I know this must seem like a zoo," the Barcon told Hargun, "but we're certified tame."

The ship dropped out of orbit and flew over Karst, but Hargun said he'd seen that before and turned away from the viewport, staring at his hands folded on his lap.

When we landed, Hargun's breathing was erratic—I saw the Barcons about to pounce with the tranquilizers—and he kept looking toward his men as they were loaded onto a bus. "Please, Rector, I'd feel better if they were with me."

"We'll have their bus travel in front so you can see them, Edwir Hargun," one of the Barcons said.

Hargun said "hum" faintly, then held his body stiff, tremors breaking through the rigidity every few seconds. I wanted to say something to calm him down, but he seemed so very alien now, face slick with sweat.

"Cadet Red Clay, you'll come with us," Karriaagzh said.

"I'd prefer to be with ranking officials, if I can't be with my own," Hargun said before I could protest.

"Ambassador, he's trained in Yauntro now and has experience with how you deal. He'll continue working with you throughout his career with the Federation."

"Sir?" I asked, not liking that at all.

"Come along, then, you bristly-faced thing," Hargun said as he slid into Karriaagzh's car.

"Perhaps Hargun would prefer that you shaved, Tom,"

Karriaagzh said mildly. "When we get to the lodge, cut the face hair, then join us. Take a nerve tea if you have to."

I had no idea of how long I'd been awake—Karst and Yauntra weren't on the same day cycles—but I was feeling terribly tired. "Sir, perhaps we should sleep," I suggested.

"Reasonable idea. The lodge has rooms enough. Air-cooled, heated—whatever makes a sapient comfortable."

"And if you have trouble sleeping, Edwir Hargun," the Barcon with us said, "we ran tests on your species and can recommend a very safe soporific."

"Shit on your soporific," Hargun said, trembling.

"Could you get a soporific for me, too?" I asked.

Karriaagzh said, "I don't quite trust mammals to prescribe for me, but I found one medicine that helped me fall asleep better, too, when life was stressful."

"I refuse your drug stupor," Hargun said. "You've infected my mind enough with your hideous language."

"But I'm serious," I said, "about having a soporific."

Karriaagzh raised his crest slightly while the Barcon flexed his nose. Hargun almost laughed, but squelched it, maybe to prevent hysterics, and settled back against the seat, intently watching the bus ahead of us.

At the lodge, Hargun and the other Yauntries followed a Barcon to a guarded wing, while a serving bear led me to a small room full of lacquered wood and homespun upholstery. After I showered and shaved, I dressed in a fresh black uniform and asked the room communicator if I could speak to Edwir Hargun.

"Who's calling?" Hargun asked in Karst.

"Sir," I said in Yauntro, "Red Clay."

"You sound as though *you* feel sorry for *me*. Unbearable! Shut up."

I clicked off and felt sorry for him. Taking my uniform off again, I changed to Earth-style pajamas and crawled between my alien polyester sheets.

In the morning, the bear servant coughed several times politely in front of my bed. When I sat up, it said, "Karriaagzh invites you to breakfast with himself and Edwir Hargun, dressed casually or not as is your custom."

The bear waited while I dressed. All I had were pajamas or blacks, so I put myself in uniform. "Where?" I asked.

"Follow," it said.

We went up to a turret room with an airy view, perhaps the same room where Karriaagzh and Black Amber told their myths. Hargun stood by the window, looking out. When he heard me behind him, he turned abruptly, and I saw that he was paler than usual, Yauntry clothes all rumpled.

"Both awake," Karriaagzh said as he, in feathers only, went over to a buffet table and started lifting pot lids and tasting various curds and breads. Karriaagzh's feathers were partly matted, broken—like a sick hen's.

Neither Hargun nor I had noticed the buffet when we came in—I hadn't thought about breakfast in terms of food, more in terms of being with Hargun and Karriaagzh.

"We have eggs, Tom," the bird said. "I think *scrambled* Earth-style. Hargun, we hope you like fish, or perhaps you'd like to try Red Clay's eggs, rich in all sorts of amino acids and fats."

Hargun didn't move. "One of my men was sedated with a drug stronger than a 'mild soporific.' Your Barcons are rather fearsome animals."

" 'Animals' in this language implies non-sapient. 'Creatures' is more general," Karriaagzh said as he dished up my eggs and handed them to me. "And Hargun, you find us all fearsome. They're making your man as comfortable as possible. He's suffering from alien contact disorder. It affects some creatures, sapient or not."

The eggs tasted just like hen's eggs, scrambled in butter, and sprinkled with chives which I'd never had back on Earth. There was also toast and jam. And tea—infusions of dried medicinal leaves, which kept many going on Karst. "Have some tea, Edwir Hargun," I said. "We have our creature differences, but a teacup's a teacup." I was hoping he'd drink it; it smelled like Tesseract's calming tea.

Hargun stood by the window, as though locked in place. "How long am I going to be held hostage?"

"We're studying you," Karriaagzh said. "We wonder why your kind recoils when a species that looks like yours grows heavy facial hair. One strain of Tom's people doesn't do this—perhaps you'd . . ."

"No one on my planet grows facial *fur*—nothing that thinks."

"On my planet, hairy lactating creatures are vermin. I never expected a galaxy of sapient milk rats. Normal for me, Hargun, is my shape, but the universe seems to find growing intelligences in this shape difficult. Still, should I decide *I'm* a monster?"

"Intelligence . . . you trick me with it into relationship." Hargun sighed and came to the end of the serving table. Karriaagzh backed away while the Yauntry looked suspiciously at all the dishes. Finally, he took bread and fish to nibble on.

"I'm sorry you feel tricked," Karriaagzh replied as he settled down on his hocks to watch Hargun while sipping tea from his spouted bird cup—some differences can't hide in a uniform teacup.

I wondered what Karriaagzh had been like before he became the intimidating, tricky Rector who'd set me out as bait for Yauntry spies. Karriaagzh closed his eyes when he saw me looking at him—slowly pulling that strange bottom lid up. Clothes had twisted and frayed his feathers. I thought of how horrified Granite Grit had been about clothes, how feather-proud.

Hargun also looked at Karriaagzh—our eyes met around the bird—while the Rector gave us time for a long look before he slowly dropped his bottom lid and said, "I'm due a molt soon, but mammal clothes are rough on feathers."

"Yet, you wear them," Hargun said.

"When I came here, I was unique. We knew of no other bird sapients until after I became Rector and expanded the exploration service."

"And so now you have company," Hargun said, somewhat bitterly.

"No, Hargun, not unless you have company with the Gwyngs. Perhaps not with Gwyngs, but Barcons. You both are placental mammals; the Gwyngs aren't even that." The Rector levered himself up and walked toward Hargun. Silently, the bird raised a plate of fish to his beak and hooked off pieces, his bird tongue working like a flexible knife. Karriaagzh bolted the fish down and said, "Tom, call up Yauntra history on the computer."

I did. A few more lines had been added—some confusion over requirements for Federation membership, questions about the linguistics team's role. "Show it to Hargun."

Hargun came up, sweating his stale flower smell, so I stepped away from the terminal. "*Mildly* xenophobic," he said to Karriaagzh, "you're very diplomatic."

"Diplomacy has a bad name on many planets," Karriaagzh replied.

"Sir, what do you want from Ambassador Hargun?" I felt sorry for Hargun, despite what he'd done to me.

Karriaagzh's crest rose. "If he'd just stop acting as though we were monsters. If we let Yauntry cadets in, are they going to panic all the time? Over me? Over you?"

"Your Federation could exterminate my whole species."

"Hargun, that's your xenophobia." Karriaagzh's crest jerked and he puffed up other feathers. "Your little cadets will drive us crazy if they're as xenophobic as you. We're barely containing you, right now."

"What about creatures who flop over unconscious when strangers approach them? That's not too xenophilic. And one of them tried to kick me."

The feathers smoothed down, but the crest stayed erect. "Oh, Gwyngs," Karriaagzh said. "They evolved voluntary comas to survive each other's savagery. Works, too. Frequently, one sleeping Gwyng is all we can rescue from a mistaken landing or crash. I don't like them—I evoke their hard-wired compulsion to kick me off with their little feet. But we work together, fairly well. Their intelligence checks those exasperating fears, most of the time."

"They're really nice people," I said. "If you can relax with them, they'll sing your vocal cords for you."

Karriaagzh gagged on air; Hargun looked at me as though I'd sprouted a full beard in that sentence's speaking time.

"Some individuals," Karriaagzh said after a long pause, "get along with anything."

"Why are you hostile because I'm uncomfortable around non-Yauntrou?" Hargun asked in a monotone. "Why *hostile*?"

"I wake up normal, then for the rest of the day, and until I die, for all my working days, I'm a solitary. To be rebuffed offends me, because I identify with all social creatures. Life reflects the overall structure of cosmic mind. Some think I'm a mystic." His cheek feathers raised up and trembled slightly.

"I've heard that solitaries don't do well," I said, feeling chilled. "But most cadets call me a trash-kid."

Karriaagzh looked at me as if he'd just noticed me. "You're not completely isolated, Tom. The primitives."

"Isolated from my time and my culture."

Hargun looked at me, then slumped on a floor cushion. "I'm sorry, Tom, that I tried to use you," he said. "Why all the military pressure?" he asked Karriaagzh, voice less strained and flat than before.

"Drills are good. We might run into a truly dangerous species," Karriaagzh said mildly before he called a servant to take the meal remains away. Then the Rector sat crouched, elbows on the floor. "Karst would go out fighting if it had to. I believe in our system here, its potentials. But for you? We'll wait until your colleagues decide. Perhaps you will be more comfortable with the Rector's Man, Tesseract. He has a charming farm and a sympathetic wife, primate-placental-mother-style. And Tom, you'll stay with Hargun and return to Yauntra if his people continue talking to us."

"Sir?" I asked, not at all happy to be working more with Yauntries. "Can I talk to you alone?"

He moved his hand in assent, then patted both hands against the floor as he watched Hargun.

"I thought," Hargun said slowly, "that I was a hostage when I first came here."

"Misunderstanding. No, Hargun, *then* you were definitely not a hostage."

The servant came to show Hargun out while the Rector watched from his crouch. As soon as the door closed, Karriaagzh said, "Tom, Rhyodolite will be at Tesseract's also. His legs were broken during a Gwyng secret visit to an undeveloped marsupial planet—not fit company for other Gwyngs, that nastiness toward the weak they have." He stood and dusted his breast feathers. "That Hargun is a decent creature for a xenophobe."

= 9 =
Alien Manners

Nostrils huffing, Rhyodolite sat on Tesseract's front porch watching the Yauntries coming in. Both legs, bruised, splinted from thigh to toe in transparent plastic, stuck stiffly out, propped up on a hassock. When I got up close, I saw that the shins looked pulpy and cut in patches, and asked, "Someone smash an ax handle against them?"

As though he'd had to explain his stupidity too often, but was too polite to refuse to tell me, Rhyo squinched his nostril slits shut and spoke slowly. "No contact intended, just watched marsupials/parallel evolvers for years—so few like us. But they caught us. One Gwyng (not me) began pre-sleep gasps so they just broke all our legs. Very parallel, those creatures. Knew we couldn't use evasion coma with major injuries—rot sets in."

Edwir Hargun came up, unable to understand Rhyo without a transforming computer. I didn't translate.

"And civilized Gwyngs would never," Rhyo continued, "break each other's bones. Bruises and insults, yes, not bone breaks. So not all that parallel."

"This is the one who kicked me?" Hargun asked, half circling Rhyo to get a good look as his men went into the house.

Rhyodolite's shoulder fur puffed up, but he continued as if Hargun weren't there. "Horrifying. They talked Gwyng-style, more sensitive to high frequency than us." Finally, he turned to Hargun and nodded. "I couldn't stay at Black Amber's, embarrassment to her. She wants Karriaagzh's crest for his

234

move on Yauntra.'' Rhyodolite mangled *Karriaagzh* and *Yauntra*, but Hargun looked sharply at me.

Tesseract walked onto the porch as Rhyodolite talked. When Rhyo paused, Tesseract said to Hargun, ''Some Federation people think our Rector overreacted to your hostage-taking. I tell you this to make you feel better; don't try to use it as a wedge against us.''

''I'm crippled,'' Rhyo continued. ''No Gwyngs to sleep with me, suffocated by three different ape stinks. Tell Hargun his armpits stink like any other ape.''

''What did he say about me?'' Hargun asked.

''He smells all of us since we have scent glands in our armpits, and he has delicate nostrils,'' I said.

''Dump, spoiled translation.''

''Rhyodolite!'' Ammalla said as she brought out lunch— steamed vegetables, protein curds, eggs, and a flagon of whipped blood and oil for Rhyodolite. She ruffled his head hair as he took his blood and oil.

''Straw?'' Rhyo asked. She handed him an oval straw. ''Looks like a cast,'' he said before he jammed it down his throat and pumped up blood and oil with his tongue and throat muscles. Hargun shuddered.

''Ambassador Hargun,'' Ammalla said gently, ''we have clothes for you, styled to your custom. And we have four types of baths here—dust and three kinds of water delivery systems.'' She gently touched his arm.

Hargun looked Rhyodolite over from casts to head hair. As Ammalla eased him into the house, he said to her, ''He's a rude whatever he is. I'm glad something kicked first.''

''He's a Gwyng,'' we heard Ammalla say before their footsteps and voices faded in Tesseract's large house.

I fixed myself a plate and sat down by Rhyodolite. ''So, who rescued you?''

''Your fault. Granite Grit. The Rector told him how to terrify primitives—Rector terrified as a young officer. Scared me dreadfully—hard to do at that point—thought I'd died anyway, hurt by bats. Puffed feathers and Barcons, gun robots. Whirling. People like me screaming, stunned by sonics, falling down. Huge leaping terrors—birds with whips and torcs, firebrands and laser flashes. Absurdly scary. Heart-stopping if not for broken legs. Your birds are determined to 'cure' me of hard-wired bird fear.''

"Granite Grit and his lady Feldspar are coming up later,'' Tesseract added.

Rhyodolite looked at his mangled legs. "I might owe him my life. But he loved frightening us/them.''

The Barcon pair who tended the Yauntry shock case and these bat-broken legs told Rhyodolite to get up and walk. Rhyodolite gripped his chair arms and glared up at the huge Barcons. "No. I almost died. Do you understand that?''

So Rhyodolite sat. Later that afternoon, Ammalla put yogurt and more oiled blood just out of his reach. He turned distressed eyes to her, then hobbled to the dishes, sighing for every tiny step he took.

"Rhyodolite, you can get over this,'' she said.

Rhyodolite was being a snit; I'd just had aliens trying seductions and guns on me and I wasn't fussing. Rhyo scooped up two yogurts and three flagons of blood and hobbled back to the chair, slopping blood all over the place. He put the food around his feet and looked at the Barcons. "When the splints are below my knees, then I'll walk,'' he said, stirring yogurt viciously.

"You didn't even get those legs broken on service time,'' one Barcon said as he looked at his partner. The other Barcon's nose wiggled. Both grabbed a leg each and pinned Rhyodolite in the chair as they twisted his toes.

As one Barcon went inside, Rhyo looked off and clenched his fists. The other Barcon held him loosely, until the first Barcon came back with a wire-bladed tool.

The Barcon with the wire blade zipped off the plastic below Rhyodolite's knee joint, shot something into the exposed tops of the calf muscles, grabbed the other leg and cut that splint—the Gwyng's tiny body pinned by the other Barcon.

His mate eased off Rhyo, ready to grab him again if Rhyo tried to bite or hit.

"Now walk,'' the Barcon with the wire tool said as he wiped the wire and peeled the cut-off plastic away from Rhyo's thighs. "Gwyng, between our bone setting and your healing abilities, you are able to go.''

Rhyodolite beat his hands against the chair arms, smashing sticky anger juice on them.

"And now you've made the chair too smelly for Gwyng sitting, I think," the other Barcon said.

His nostril slits writhing, Rhyodolite stiffly got up and clumped down the porch stairs. He stopped and raised his hands to his temples, dropped them fast. Slowly he walked back, both hands on the stair rail, and said, "Red Clay, I have to wash."

He sounded horrible, expressionless, as though he'd gone mad. As he went inside, the Barcons talked in their own language, then one said, "Red Clay, follow him."

Before I could, Ammalla came out and asked, "What did you do to him? He's standing by the sink washing his hands and crying."

I went in. Rhyodolite seemed to be paralyzed in front of the sink, hands dripping water, eyes full of oily tears. When he heard me, he started trembling. Slowly, I reached for a towel.

"Do you know which *Yangtree* those are?" Rhyodolite asked as he turned slightly and gave me his hands to dry.

"No."

"They killed the bird cadet," he said.

Oh? I ran more water in the sink and gently washed his hands until I only smelled soap. "Is there any way to clean Ammalla's chair? Or do you mind your own smell?"

"Clean it. Barcons have anger-juice odor distrupter. Breaks our pheromone molecules like legs."

I threw the towels I'd used on his hands aside and drew fresh water to wash his face. "Your head hairs are matted. Want me to wash and comb them?" He grabbed me hard, side pressed to mine, the arms squeezing and letting go convulsively.

"Black Amber, you, Mica."

"She kissed me when the Federation people got me back."

"You/Mica. She tries your human gestures . . . We cripple our brains to be among other sapients, so please like us."

"Are you all right?"

"No." Rhyodolite leaned his side against mine. "I'm an officer. Lost a cadet—rescued by first-year bird cadets and Barcons. They twist here—by species. Manipulative."

"Maybe you won't feel too bad about birds now?"

"Always more creatures to mourn . . . mental world stuffed

full of creatures who die/leave me alone." He started for his room; I went along to make sure he didn't fall.

Painfully, he crawled into a padded tube and twisted around to look at me with those bone-shielded eyes, wrinkle-grooves oily with tears. "Nearly died. A Gwyng embarrassment. To everyone else a medical problem, not their medical problem." He breathed deeply a few times. "Walls hold names—the bright creatures are gone. Where's Mica's 'promising-for-Gwyng'? And if you don't make the wall, bring more creatures together over your hurts."

"Do you want to resign your commission?"

"Somehow, nearly dying has to be more." He watched the ceiling as though it might fall, eyes wavering. "Death is completely lonely, I think, worse than being sick/injured. Do your people leave you to live or die with aliens?"

"You're not so sick now."

"Hideous splints."

"I start feeling sorry for you and you go off into a Gwyng snit." I half meant it. "I thought I'd go crazy when the Yauntries held me captive this time. And wasn't I being used, set up as bait?"

He oo'ed faintly. "Set up by Karriaagzh with all the male hormones raging. So you like birds?"

"We were both rescued." I sat down beside him, tired myself now, and stroked his skinny shoulder. "Little Gwyng who loves alien women."

He giggled. "Now I am obligated to birds. You've intensified the quarrel between Black Amber and the Rector. And you must go back to Yauntra—so not to develop serious xenophobia. *Ed'twing Hapoon* may not be trusted on *Yangtree* himself after capture by us disgusting monsters." He closed his eyes firmly and I sat by him until he appeared to be sleeping. Then I went to ask the Barcons for a spray to kill the Gwyng thumb-gland odor.

Ammalla and I wiped up as best we could.

"Nothing more cranky than a Gwyng bullied by his own," she told me. "Those aliens were too closely related for him to accept their violence, as if his own Gwyngs went mad."

When Rhyodolite woke up, he stiffly walked to the porch and announced, "I was/am a terrible officer." He hobbled to his chair, sat and stared into infinity, his big eyes glazed, the facial folds drooping. Hargun came out on the porch, saw Rhyodolite and grunted.

Rhyodolite rolled his eyes toward the Yauntry, saying, "*Ewing Hargin*, we don't need to search space. At Tesseract's, all our nightmares come to visit us."

"Translate that," Hargun said to me.

"He and you probably are both each other's nightmares."

"Not a complete translation," Rhyodolite said. "Ask him how I could have kept the bird Xenon from being killed."

"Rhyodolite?" I asked. Why did he want to aggravate himself and Hargun? He *had* been a shit toward the bird when Xenon was alive.

"Ask him, Red-Clay-dung. Ask."

"He asks how he could have kept the bird from being shot."

A Barcon snarled at me and shouted to Tesseract, who came out at a fast walk.

"Tom translated," Hargun said. He pointed to Rhyodolite. "He wanted to know if he could have saved the bird. He can understand me if I talk Karst?"

"Don't answer him, Hargun," Tesseract said quickly, looking down at the Gwyng. "Rhyodolite, why?"

Slowly, Rhyo explained, his fingers twisting on the chair arms, "I was relieved (guilt now burns) briefly, when they shot him. I'm still terrified (gut-way) of birds. But he was my cadet. I was cruel. The Barcons say my reaction to birds can be muted."

"Oh, Rhyodolite," Tesseract said, then he translated some of this to Hargun, who blinked as if space had complications far beyond simple militaristic ones.

"Red Clay, you should feel bad, too," Rhyodolite said, gripping my hand hard. "You weren't friendly to Xenon either. If we'd been kinder, he might not have panicked. Now I owe my life to Granite, because he likes you."

I felt sick. Tesseract said, "Rhyodolite, we're going to leave you alone for a while. Tom, go in and help Ammalla." He said to Hargun, "I'd like to show you my livestock." The Barcon padded along with them, a medical pouch on its hip.

"Rhyodolite, you should have set a better example on your ship." I felt hideously guilty as soon as I'd said that.

"Go. Help Ammalla," Rhyodolite hissed. I went.

Ammalla, polishing a carved glass tray, smelled of soap and mamahood. I leaned against a cabinet near her and sighed.

"Rhyodolite will be okay," she said. "Bad luck broke his Gwyng cockiness, but once he's social with Gwyngs again, he'll be himself, as irritating as that can be on occasion."

"I don't know about me, Ammalla. I'm so alone. Cadets, officers of the Federation, we're like test *pilots*, aren't we? I had no idea."

"Sapient tamers, young Red Clay. Tom, you don't need to be quite so alone."

"I met a free trader *human* woman. Yangchenla." I was almost crying.

She set her glass tray aside and rolled me around in her arms, half playfully mauling, not too sweetly hugging. "Ah, you need a hug? A woman?" I felt foolish, but Ammalla felt like a mother, smooth-faced, soft. She gave me a real hug as I leaned into her. Awkwardly I pulled back. "Too old for a mother's hug, hey? Like our boys after all, despite not-so-sexy head bones."

I hugged her back. "Thanks, Ammalla."

"Help me get this tray to the shelf, up there, please."

That afternoon, when a light airplane landed, we all, including the Yauntries, went to the porch. Granite Grit stalked off with Feldspar, a purple iridescent female. Both whirled cast-off breeding plumes in their hands, bouncing and swaying as though beauty and analytical genetics could solve all problems. Cadmium followed, looking bemused and one-quarter frightened as he walked his rolling way behind them.

Bird elegance—the two of them, vivid feathers glistening, lifted my spirits. They were *together*.

As Cadmium came up to Rhyodolite, his nostrils fluttered. Rhyodolite dipped his head and spread his arms. Could Cadmium smell residual anger juice, I wondered, or just all the ape sweat?

"The birds insist on being/becoming friends," Cadmium said. "Due to you, Red Clay (full of feathers)."

Granite cocked his head at Cadmium, handed his streamers to Ammalla, and went inside. He brought out raw meat dangling from his bill. Feldspar, already slightly round in the belly, ducked her head and opened her beak. Both crops pulsated as Granite pushed the meat down her throat. After Feldspar swallowed, Granite asked in Karst I if we'd be embarrassed by such displays. "Feeding each other is such a pleasure now."

"Anything life-evoking is lovely," Ammalla said, stroking their breeding plumes through her hands.

Then Granite bent his legs, the way Karriaagzh did to reduce his height, but with his gold and blue feathers undamaged, and sidled up to Rhyodolite. Feldspar settled down by Granite, leaning her breast feathers against his arm.

"Thanks for saving me," Rhyodolite said in a small voice as he trailed a skinny finger over Granite's head feathers. The finger backed up as it came close to the nares.

Hargun, who couldn't understand Rhyodolite's speech, looked at Rhyodolite and Granite and said to Ammalla, "That pretty display of interceptive community doesn't impress me one bit."

"Sir," she said, "what you saw was very hard won."

He walked into the house without saying anything more. The other Yauntries followed.

"What a goo-egg," Granite Grit said.

Cadmium reached into a bag, pulled out the lathed Frisbee, and tossed it to me. He said, "Keep it. We'll play later."

Tesseract and Ammalla's house had a separate wing for people who needed seclusion and Barcon attendants. One of the two Barcons told me, "Hargun wants to see you." The Barcon didn't seem happy to be tending both Rhyo and the Yauntries. "Maybe safer if he came out to the hall."

"I'll go in." I might as well trust them. Karriaagzh was sending me back with them.

When I went in, Hargun was sitting behind a table. "You were bait for us," he said in Yauntro.

"I wasn't aware of it."

He laughed, a bit harshly, then asked, "Why are you with these beasts? You're almost a real person."

"What the hell did you expect to fetch your satellite?" I said in English. "You sent out a probe? Did you expect aliens to look like you?"

"A rational universe would produce creatures like us. But it's 'the accidental coming together,' isn't it? And the Karriaagzh pretends we're all aspects of the same mind."

"Perhaps if you were younger, you'd adapt better to being around other sapients," I replied.

"Don't you miss your own people?" he asked harshly. We had a pleasanter interview after he'd killed Xenon and held me prisoner.

"Ambassador, you know what I miss." I felt quavery inside as I said that, wishing I could be with Yangchenla now, wishing Warren was sane, here, without fuss from Black Amber. "But these are my friends." *Yangchenla and I could be primitive together. Granite has Feldspar.*

"Feathered lizards?"

"Why don't you talk to Granite Grit? His people started out afraid of the Federation also."

Hargun's eyes caught me on face, armpits, and hands, before he said, "I'm no more a xenophobe than you are."

"Probably not," I told Hargun as I walked out. *"See you around."*

Ammalla served meals on the porch, which forced the Yauntries out of their rooms three times a day, before they went back, like lions escaping a circus audience by retreating to their cages.

Cadmium and Granite began playing with the Frisbee out in front of the porch, leaping and snatching it. The Gwyng could tumble better, but Granite had the definite high-jump advantage. Each time Granite made a high jump, though, I saw Cadmium flinch.

Rhyodolite hobbled out on the porch, then one of the younger Yauntries came out, looked at Rhyodolite, then out at the bird and Gwyng playing with the Frisbee, finally at me. Rhyodolite walked down carefully on his splinted legs to join Cadmium, who gently lobbed him the Frisbee.

"We have discs like that on Yauntra," the young stranger told me. I saw his fingers twitch when Rhyo threw to Granite Grit.

"Join them."

"Huh-na. They can't talk, can they?"

"Hum. I'll translate your Yauntro."

"I was on the team—we're all here—that shot your other bird. I remember kneeling down on him out there and feeling the webs give under my knees."

I'd wrestled a Gwyng—had a tactile flash of how web flexed under a knee. Real squishy. "Rhyodolite told me you guys captured the ship." How had Rhyo remembered? Smell? Memory for patterns?

Rhyodolite hobbled back toward us and yelled, "Come down, *Yaungtri* person. Red Clay (sometimes linguistically too plastic), translate honestly for me. Tell him if he hadn't backed off my webs, I couldn't have chilled down. Would have bit."

"He says he remembers and forgives you. Go down."

"Liar. Non-translator. I want to throw one into his neck," Rhyodolite said, catching a toss from Cadmium and waving the Frisbee so wildly I thought he'd topple off his plastic-coated feet.

"But watch your neck," I added.

The Yauntry smiled, just a lip twitch. I yelled for Rhyo to toss me the Frisbee, caught it and handed it to the Yauntry, who turned it over, looking at both sides. "Handmade?" the Yauntry finally said.

"Yes, we cut down some plastic."

"Umph," he said as he went down the stairs to throw a fairly combative curve at the Gwyngs. Both grabbed for it, Rhyodolite almost tumbling into Cadmium, who steadied him before whirling the disc to the birds, who tossed it over the leaping Yauntry's head back to me. I lobbed it, low and easy, to Rhyodolite, to see what he'd really do.

As Rhyodolite threw the Frisbee so that it rose into the Yauntry's chin, a Barcon came out. "The game should move back to the pool where the Gwyng can rest his legs in the water and not have too much throwing leverage," the Barcon said. "Is the Yauntry happy?"

Cadmium and the birds instantly agreed to move around back.

"I'm amused a bit," the Yauntry said when I translated the Barcon's question for him.

Edwir Hargun came hunting his man only to find the younger Yauntry playing around Tesseract's pool with all the enemy aliens. Ammalla followed Hargun and suggested he come inside for tea. Hargun looked at the Yauntry soldier leaping after a Terran-model Frisbee tossed by a swimming bat, cheered on by two monster-show parrots and me, who looked like a deformed Yauntry. Without speaking, he turned and followed Ammalla inside.

The Yauntry cocked the Frisbee toward Granite Grit. "Is he like the bird on the ship?" the Yauntry asked me.

"Not the same species."

"If I was scared, then he was scared, too, wasn't he?" the Yauntry asked me, still holding on to the disc.

"We were all very scared."

"No weapons."

"No. Better the new species should shoot, maybe."

He lobbed the disc to Granite Grit. "You invaded our system. I feel awkward playing with you now." He turned around and left.

The rest of us continued playing in and around the pool until Rhyodolite complained of the cold. Cadmium and Granite reached down to help him out, but he splashed them.

Granite shook, water spraying off his blue head feathers, then stepped closer and crouched. Rhyo heaved water at the bird with his webs. Turning his head, Granite grabbed and caught Rhyo's arm.

Rhyo squalled, as if he were being killed.

Cadium's shoulder hair went erect. Barcons came running. Instantly, Granite dropped Rhyo's arm and sat down at the edge of the pool, lay his wet head on his hands.

"Grabbed him," Cadium told the Barcons. "Rhyodolite was throwing water at us." Nervously, he smoothed down his shoulder fur, while Rhyodolite, gasping, treaded water.

Granite made strangled sounds, then managed to say, "I didn't grab him hard."

The Barcons looked at each other. Tesseract and Ammalla came down behind them. "Gwyng foolishness," the Barcons told them.

Granite shook his wet feathers and told Rhyodolite, in Karst II, "Can't stand being grabbed, don't splash." Rhyodolite looked up at him, shuddered, then swam to the pool rim and held on, bobbing up and down as he breathed in and out, his eyes squeezed shut. "Rhyodolite, I'm sorry if I startled you," Granite added, very quietly.

"Cadmium, help me out," Rhyo said, eyes still closed. I helped Cadmium pull him onto the apron where he lay shivering, water soaked under the plastic splints. Rhyodolite opened his eyes and quivered his pupils at Granite nervously before easing himself to his feet. "Let's go inside and get warm," he said.

As we walked to the house, Rhyo leaned against Cadmium. Granite moved tentatively toward Rhyo, but Feldspar touched his shoulder.

Hargun watched from the porch, a deep smile on his face. As we passed, he said to me in Yauntro, "Not such a loving bunch after all."

After getting Rhyo out of his wet pants, we draped him in towels until Ammalla brought an electric blanket and hot butter. The two birds gingerly nestled down on either side of his chair, talking in bird over his knees.

Rhyo asked wearily, "Why did you birds rescue me? I failed my own bird."

"You're Tom's friend."

"I feel death guilt now." Rhyodolite drew back, arms tensing against the chair. The web veins throbbed once.

Finally, Granite Grit said, "Rhyodolite, your fear instinct is unbecoming of a sapient."

"We want to help you with your fear. Can you stand us in your room at night?" Feldspar said.

Rhyodolite wiggled and looked back over his shoulder at Cadmium, who gave an eye roll. "I suppose so. You're as warm as we are. Cadmium finds my splints uncomfortable (two ways)—very restless/without sleep."

"We will stay with you quietly. You don't splash," Granite said, "and we won't grab."

"I feel terrible about this."

The Barcons came in and re-splinted Rhyodolite's legs with drier plastic.

Before I went to bed, I checked to see how they were managing. Cadmium and the birds were asleep—the blond-streaked Gwyng curled under Feldspar's breast feathers, muzzle touching Rhyodolite's shoulder, one arm slung over him.

Rhyo lay rigid on his back between the birds, his open eyes almost glazed.

"If it's that bad, just wiggle out and sleep in my room."

"I'll be okay." He looked at the birds on either side of him, then lifted Cadmium's arm very gently, and rolled over, closing his eyes.

Feldspar stirred, dropping her eyelids, but with the nictitating membrane half veiling her eyes, barely awake. She rubbed her beak against the two Gwyng heads and rocked forward a few times to smooth her feathers, then looked, a bit more alertly, haws back, at me before settling her head back on her arms.

Rhyo tucked his fingers under Cadmium's shoulder.

I felt odd, isolated, as I went to my room. My sleeping alone seemed almost a prejudice. I envied Gwyngs their ease with each other—no humans I knew had such physical closeness unless they were lovers. Maybe because we slept together after sex, humans, at least my kind of humans, had sexualized the bed.

But, really, sleeping piled together on a mat didn't seem all that comfortable either, I thought as I felt my body twitch that sleep twitch.

I had weird dreams: humans, Warren, Mica screaming. When I woke, I found blankets twisted around my legs. After I untangled the bedclothes, I went to see how the Gwyngs managed under the birds.

Rhyodolite was asleep on his belly, half covered by Feldspar's and Granite's puffed-up feathers. Cadmium, dressed already, was spreading his face wrinkles open and wiping the grooves with a wet swab, watching himself in the mirror. Granite eased away from Rhyo and Feldspar and stretched first one leg and arm, then the others, like a chicken.

Cadmium watched Granite in the mirror as the bird shook his feathers, all puffed up, before twitching them down. Turning back to his own reflection, Cadmium fussed with his service sash.

I sat down beside Rhyo, smelling the faint chlorine Gwyng smell. Feldspar woke up and rubbed her beak through my hair, then looked down at Rhyodolite, who still slept, arms wrapped around himself. She moved her hand as though she wanted to stroke him, but stopped.

Finally he sighed, turned his head toward me, and opened his large dark eyes. I felt a little embarrassed.

"You're not that cold-blooded, Red Clay, cuddle up," Rhyo told me as he wiggled over on his back and looked up at Feldspar, who gently wiped congealed goo away from his eyes.

He only flinched a little.

"You'll be okay with us eventually," she said, rubbing around his ears.

"Then I should tame myself with the Rector," Rhyodolite said as he reached for her hand and pulled himself up. "You can tame Hargun. One Yauntry already fetches our plastic flying toy." Rhyo looked for his luggage, carefully walked over on his splinted legs, and pulled out his uniform tunic. "I'm going to get the Barcons to take off the rest of the splints. I want a long hot salty bath, with bare legs," he told us as he left.

Cadmium stayed with us. "You birds would make great first-contact people or linguistics investigators," he said to Granite, "if you weren't so different from most sapients."

"For a linguistics team, shouldn't matter," Feldspar said in Karst II. We went silent a bit, thinking about first contacts—at least I was.

"This Federation is wonderful," Granite Grit said, preening what feathers he could reach with serrated metal combs and oil mist. "Your kinds (unjealously) admire us for our genetics work. Utterly surprising—we love alien attention."

"Do the other sapient birds admire you?" Cadmium asked.

"Don't know. They never bred for colors." The two birds began to preen each other, and Cadmium and I went out to the porch for breakfast.

"Very odd, Red Clay, sleeping beside great birds."

"Odd sleeping in piles the way you Gwyngs do."

"Why?"

"*Humans* don't," I said before I thought.

"Universe's worst answer. Don't you get lonely, trapped unconscious in your dreams—no one but you moving through them?"

I shrugged at him, trapped in reality fairly well alone. "Non-conspecifics aren't the company I want in bed."

Cadium oo'ed.

*   *   *

At breakfast on the porch, Hargun stood coughing, slowly eating from a bowl. He stared off at the plains, ignoring the birds and Gwyngs chattering in Karst II. The other Yauntries watched him.

I said hello in Yauntro, second politeness, to the Frisbee-playing Yauntry. Instead of replying, he looked down at his food bowl, then at Hargun.

Rhyodolite said, "Rather be fed in a cage than see us."

Granite replied, "Don't be rude," before he dropped a morsel, bill to bill, in Feldspar's mouth.

Edwir Hargun flicked his eyes at the birds before looking back at the horizon. Granite stepped closer to Hargun, bent his backward knees to be on eye level with the Yauntry, and asked in Karst I, "Do you like music, Ambassador?"

Hargun's face softened, then stiffened again. Hoarsely, he said, "You're the birds who thought force held this thing together."

Granite rose stiffly erect. "Fighting between my people's nations may continue—but why fight space? The others are competitive over different things."

Hargun coughed hard, then said, "You like us monsters?"

"Stop. Do you like music?" Granite almost bounced.

"What music could *I* have in common with a feathered lizard?"

Feathers rose on Granite's neck as he drew his head back, eyes covered by nictitating membranes. Feldspar very softly touched his neck. He flashed the third eyelids back into his eye corners and settled his feathers in nervous little jerks. Muscles tight around his eyes, Granite Grit said, "Tesseract's house has lacked music lately, so I've asked for my discs."

"I'd prefer not to discuss music with you, bird."

At the corners of both birds' eyes, membranes twitched. Granite crouched down low on his hocks and looked up at Hargun. "Music goes around walls, sir, so you will be forced to hear."

"Without facing us terrible monsters," Feldspar added. They both stalked away, hocks raised high.

Hargun coughed up phlegm, then asked, "Was I about to get attacked again?"

Rather nervously, Cadmium moved away from Hargun and

said, "Now I know why Rhyodolite kicked. Ask him why he's being so stupidly insulting/insultingly stupid."

"Sir, you insult us, then wonder why we get mad. Why?"

Hargun sat down in a chair, blew his nose, and wadded the napkin up on a plate. "Insults? I'm a prisoner. I hope *you* catch this virus. The Barcons told me 'mild viral infection, best to let run course . . . stress makes disease from resident viruses.' Like I deserved it."

"I know what captivity's like," I told him. "At least you've got other Yauntries here. *We* won't murder *you*."

Tesseract came out and told Hargun, "Ambassador, your species has asked us to send the Rector Karriaagzh to Yauntra for discussions. The History Committee has to decide whether the Rector is expendable."

Hargun sagged and began breathing hard. Then he said, "Expendable?"

"Well . . ." Tesseract fixed his own breakfast and sat down close to Hargun, who backed up against the far chair arm. Tesseract ate some eggs, then asked, "Do your people know anything about Karriaagzh?"

"He's intimidating, stern . . ."

"To you, Hargun. Karriaagzh, as an isolate, depends on mammal social flexibility. His own people won't deal with us, and they're too technologically sophisticated for us to kidnap a social group for him."

"Xenophobic."

"No, initially, they were calm, according to the records. Karriaagzh came back with the first-contact team when his species refused to join the Federation. I'd enjoy seeing him negotiate with you. Birds have one-track minds. Consider how implacably the birds work to cure poor Rhyodolite of his fear of them."

"Am I going back? Soon?"

"We're still talking to your people. And we need to determine how severe your xenophobia is."

"I'm sicker from being held captive than I am afraid of you monsters."

Tesseract's face stiffened, then he said, "Relax, listen to Granite Grit's discs."

"Is the prisoner ordered to do this?"

Tesseract asked me in English, *"Tom, would your people*

still be so hostile? Most students with xenoreactions would be reasonable by now, except hard-wire cases."

"Tesseract, you've been dealing with too many kids. This one's a full grown-up man."

Tesseract smiled at me and said to Hargun, "Karriaagzh is right. One does get tired of being treated as though one were biologically wrong."

"We're trapped here, Rector's Man," Hargun said. "Can we believe anything you'd say?"

Tesseract began eating furiously, the skin over his skull crest flushed, then he threw down his spoon and said, "First I'd agreed to help the birds with the Gwyngs, then I'm assigned your group. Plus Tom . . ."

"Tesseract," I said, shocked to hear him angry.

"Do you know how far away I am from everything I know, love?" Hargun asked. His eyes fluttered in his grey face.

"I'm sorry. But Tom, Red Clay, is infinitely more isolated. Yet you baited him brutally. Then your people ask for Karriaagzh as a negotiator—another isolate. I only feel sorry for your squad men here. Let them fraternize with us monsters."

Suddenly, aliens nauseated me.

Tesseract massaged his crest as if pushing the blood out of it. "I'm sorry, Tom, Edwir, if I was rude."

Granite Grit came out and bobbed down, watching Hargun a moment before he said, "Ambassador, your men are listening to the music. Please come in and hear my discs."

"Surely, Granite Grit," Hargun said. As he passed by, I noticed his eyes were red.

When we heard the music begin again, Tesseract led me to the back of the house, by the pool.

"Yangchenla!" She sat in a deck chair, wearing an American dress the green of old Coke bottles, belted with a brocade scarf. Awh, she looked so good. I ran up to her.

Smelling of musk and warm skin, she took my hand and said, "I was invited to the country for you."

Her hair was up in a bun—very glossy, as though she'd oiled it. "Are you used to these kinds of people?" I asked nervously.

"I sell *yak* milk oils to the wrinkle-faces who can only listen, and handwovens. I'm not such a barbarian as some seem to think, those . . ."

"Free Trader," Tesseract interrupted, "perhaps you and Red Clay would like to take a walk. I'll be in the kitchen when you come back. Let's give Hargun time alone with Granite Grit and the Gwyngs—see what happens."

"Okay," I said, heart jammed in my lungs.

When Tesseract was almost to the house, Yangchenla said, "That one did not make coming here a raw sexual proposition, even if he dressed me like this."

"I didn't ask for you directly, but it's nice seeing you again."

We walked to see the riding stock which was bedded down on dried ferns. She leaned against a wall and smiled slowly, watching my face, her smile deepening as I began to smile, too. "We ride things, too," she said. "So much the same, despite the surface differences."

"Where are you staying tonight?" I asked.

"The rooms are next to each other, yours and mine."

My face heated up. "Oh," I said.

"No double sex bed prepared as the Barcons did."

I had a double bed in my room. "See enough of the riding beasts?"

"Yes, let's go to the house. I've always wanted to see how the Federation authorities live." She fluttered over some things my surgically contrived tongue and vocal cords got correctly.

"Do you feel comfortable with the others?"

"I'll like," she said, "anyone you like."

When we came in through the kitchen, Tesseract was putting squatty red and silver Karst beer cans in the freezer. "Hargun's fine," he said. "They're all eating mid-meal and arguing about music—even the Gwyngs."

I listened from the doorway. Between musical pieces, they whistled, hummed, or sung phrases and re-phrases, discussing what the composers intended.

"Go in without me," Tesseract said. "I don't want Edwir to think I'm scoring points."

"What are the Gwyngs going to say when they see her?"

"Be glad she can't understand." I got flustered, remembering Rhyo going for tits in the pond, but Tesseract put a hand on my back and said, "They'll be *gentlemen*."

"Wrinkle-faces," Chenla said, making a wrinkled face herself.

When we came in, Cadmium glared at Rhyodolite, who spread his arms slightly. I introduced Yangchenla to everyone, not knowing the names of the three other Yauntries or the two attendant Barcons.

The Yauntries tried, it seemed, to examine her eyelids without getting involved with her pupils. "One of my kind here, a different breed. They came a couple centuries ago," I explained.

Chenla lowered her head and looked at them through her eyelashes. "Free trader," she said.

"With the funny oil," Rhyodolite said. "Ask her if she knows a free trader Gwyng who . . ."

Cadmium interrupted, "Rhyodolite, don't get into that."

Granite put another disc in the system. Hargun sat tensely, but as I watched, I realized he was tense now about being right in his musical opinions. Both he and Granite took music seriously, but the Gwyngs complained this music was for different brains than theirs. The Barcons said that was Gwyng-piss-in-ear, but when Granite translated the Gwyng comment for Hargun, he asked Rhyodolite to explain further.

Chenla leaned against me and said, "Yes. How do these minds work? They speak in language I can't understand, although we gesture and sign to each other."

"Why try to explain? Can't even put our real languages into Karst II," Rhyodolite said to Cadmium.

Cadmium replied, "We'll both try."

So Rhyodolite explained how Gwyngs heard music in chords held across time—meaning found in patterns larger than our minds encompassed, non-binary. Then the computer in my skull garbled part. Granite tried to translate what he understood, but all we could figure out was that ultrasonics and polarized light *must* be meaningful if Gwyngs perceived them. But we aliens survived without those senses. Rhyodolite said, "You (not-Gwyngs) have limited minds."

Chenla had her hand to her face, index finger beside her nose; her heart beat against my arm as she looked intently at the Gwyngs. Hargun asked Granite Grit, "Do you perceive like Gwyngs?"

"No," Granite said. "But I can understand Karst II."

"Karst II is synthetic/limited/cut perception," Rhyodolite

said. "Karst II cripples our brains if that's the first language we learn."

"Some Gwyngs wonder if the patterns do have ecological meaning," Cadmium said. "Old Gwyng languages—imperceptibly rich, isolating."

Odd that Gwyngs, in their plain little bodies, had minds that saw polarized sky, that heard across time in some way different than memory.

"What is my planet's sky like, in polarizations?" I asked them shyly.

Rhyodolite and Cadium looked at each other. "Red Clay, different," Cadmium said. "Would rather not, however, re-construct."

I sat there feeling odd. Granite said, "Red Clay, we have some Earth hill music for you. Would you like to hear it?"

Uneasy, afraid of their judgment, I slowly nodded. Chenla took my hand.

The disc held "Shall the Circle Be Unbroken," "Fox on the Run," and "Foggy Mountain Breakdown." I leaned back, tears in my eyes, not grimly miserable, just aching for the company of fiddlers and mandolin guys. I remembered women dancing on cars with their tits hanging out, heels dinging the hoods and tops as they teased the Fourth of July crowds. My own people, the creatures I most craved.

"Don't discuss them songs," I said in English as the music ended. They all stared at me, so I covered my face.

Chenla pulled back from me slightly. I'd stiffened, but none of the others was that subtly aware of my body postures. *She's human, too.*

"Tom, it's all right," Cadmium said.

"I'd prefer that you not discuss this music," I told them in both Karst and Yauntro. "Not right away," I added, wiping tears away and feeling slightly foolish as Granite rubbed my arm. "Thank you for bringing them, though."

"I wonder if I should have," Granite said, putting the disc away.

"No problem," I said. "My mammal kind cries for lots of reasons."

"You mammals have such strange chambered brains," Granite Grit said. "Somehow past mental images change and go on, as though you could erase a made action, live a different reality inside your minds.''

"For you,'' Hargun asked Granite, "what's done is never regretted?''

"It's done,'' Granite said. He turned his head to the side and examined Hargun with one intense brown eye.

Hargun shrugged and said, "I'm glad you didn't have any records from Yauntra playing today.''

"Oh, we do,'' Rhyodolite said in Karst II, grabbing for a disc, finding his wrist firmly held in Granite's big hand, scales glistening yellow at the wrist.

Rhyo yelped.

"You may be my senior officer,'' Granite said in Karst II, so the Yauntries couldn't follow, "but that is not your disc.''

"You want me to be easy with you—yet you grab me?''

Granite didn't let go. "Rhyodolite, stop teasing.''

Feldspar pecked Granite's elbow. He dropped Rhyo's wrist and sat back on his shins. Taking Rhyo's hand gently, Feldspar wiggled it to see if her mate had hurt it, then trailed one of her fingers Gwyng-style down Rhyo's neck. "You do tease, Rhyodolite,'' she said to him.

"Knock my hand away, but don't grab.''

"How? Scales on hand backs don't bother you?'' Granite said, continuing to talk in Karst II.

Rhyo grabbed for the disc again, but Granite batted the Gwyng's hand away with the back of his. "That's better,'' Rhyodolite said, oo'ing, spotting a new game.

"What are they doing?'' Hargun asked me in Yauntro as the two pushed wrists over the laser disc.

"Playing a game they just invented,'' I said, not wanting Hargun to know we had Yauntra music so close. Feldspar put another disc in the machine while the two guys fooled around. When the music came on, she ran a finger along Rhyodolite's shoulder, preened Granite's head, then pecked both of them on the elbows, almost hard.

The Barcons prescribed beers all around. Hargun looked at a can dubiously, tasted, his round eyes vaguely misty, then told his men to limit themselves to two cans.

Chenla sipped, then giggled. "Like from *tsampa*?'' she asked the Barcons, "grain fermented?''

"Yes,'' one said.

"I can have two cans as I'm not religious."

Beer—practically a universal social solvent. The Barcons brought in a tub full of almost frozen beer, and disappeared with a couple of beers each. The rest of us drank and listened to music less detailed and more rhythmic than the serious lunch music. Some rhythms were damn odd, as if to different heartbeats.

Yeah, different heartbeats.

Beers in hand, Tesseract and Ammalla joined us.

"*Considerable strain,*" Tesseract said in English. Crest pallid, he stooped down beside Hargun, who looked up calmly. "I'm sorry, Ambassador, if I was rude earlier. Red Clay and the Rector will return you and your men to Yauntra and negotiate with your officials. Confirmed now."

Rhyodolite made a little face.

Tesseract played the laser disc of hill music again, holding my eyes with his, probing. I felt powerfully moved, but didn't cry. After the tracks finished, he said, "Yangchenla, will you be comfortable with these males and Ammalla if Red Clay comes with me?"

Yangchenla looked around her, smiled back at Ammalla's smile, and said softly, "Yes."

In the kitchen, Tesseract asked in English, "*If you could return to Earth, without legal penalties, would you?*"

"*I don't know.*"

"Yangchenla?" he asked, like was she suitable marriage material.

I switched to Karst, "She's *human* enough . . ."

". . . *but she doesn't speak the language,*" he finished in English. "But does your feeling for *Virginia* mountains rise mostly from your fine imagination which also dreamed of living with aliens while you were in jail?"

"Like Granite Grit said, a thing I've imagined, like an alternate past."

"The bird has insight into us. What, really, can you go back to?"

I thought about half-naked women dancing on the car tops that Fourth of July: one pregnant, another killed by her lover. And the sheriff's deputies shooting down Warren, hauling him off screaming, wrapped in bloody wet sheets.

And the cold steel handcuffs heavy on my own wrists.

"*Think on it?*" Tesseract suggested, aping my old dialect. Sub-standard dialect. I thought about how boring linguistics work was, then how much worse it was to muck out chicken sheds and tab pills. My Karst cadet room was much nicer than my Earth house. But I paid for it by dangling unarmed in space until strange new aliens calmed down.

"Could Barcons make Warren well without burning out his personality? Bring him here?"

"I don't know, Tom. Would you want to lose Black Amber's favor?" He took beers on a tray back to the other room, leaving me in the kitchen, thinking. Hargun came in, obviously looking for me. I shrugged hugely, like the Jewish comics I'd seen on TV.

He grinned, as though he understood. "I'm as sorry as I can afford to be," he said finally, before reaching into the freezer for a beer, jerking the can out when he felt how cold it was. "Odd way to do it," he muttered in Yauntro. He plucked out another beer, shook both gently to see that they weren't frozen, and offered me one.

I took the beer to be sociable, and he opened his, taking small sips so as not to get freezer burn. "Your Federation is just a trading union, isn't it? Not so mysterious after all?"

"Not quite *just* a trading union," I said.

"To have you look so much like us and then have face hair." His round eyes narrowed, flesh around them crinkled, then he gently touched my chin. "Your woman says her breed's males don't grow such hairs, generally."

"She has weird eyes, doesn't she?" I said.

His shoulders jerked up and down slightly, before he answered, "Yes."

They're not totally over xenophobia, I thought, *but then, am I?*

That afternoon, Chenla and I rode Tesseract's animals away from the others, she dressed in wide skirts that she'd brought with her, me in pants and borrowed boots.

We rode grass that stretched on and on, with brush in it, gold and green, toward a sunset through high cumulus—more pink than purple.

Then Chenla laughed, at what I wasn't sure.

We raced back—she was good with the riding beast, hips

rolling with the gallop, back straight, wrists flexing with the thing's neck.

After we'd cooled them down, she patted hers and said, "What are they?"

"I never asked," I said.

"You don't ask questions, do you?" she said.

I dismounted. "May I?" I asked, reaching for her waist to whisk her off the riding beast.

Very light, but not so soft as the girl I'd slept with when I was fourteen. When I set her down, I held her waist—we were poised like dancers—then she moved away from my fingers, to stable her riding beast.

I followed with my animal. "The ride was so beautiful," I said. "I'm glad they invited you." My cock felt embarrassingly heavy.

With her chin tucked down, she turned her face away slightly, but kept her slitted eyes on me. "We must talk more," she said.

Back at the house, the Yauntries had gone considerably over their planned two beers each. Even the birds and the Gwyngs were giddy, watching little three-dimensional-seeming holographic actors in a round glass tank.

"The primitives returned," Rhyodolite said, madly waving a beer can. "Primitive sexual behavior! Primitive staring at cheap holos!"

"Shut up, piss-brain," Cadmium said.

"Oh, no species loyalty here," Rhyodolite said, standing unsteadily and walking out. Cadmium groaned and followed him, as Chenla and I sat down.

Tesseract pulled out one of the semi-illicit xenophobia films, and we all, even the Yauntries, giggled madly as various small creatures ran screaming from a cargo belly.

Then Karriaagzh got out. Karriaagzh, but younger. We stopped laughing and stared at Tesseract.

"A classic," he said. "Karriaagzh had his own reasons for making it—to work through his feelings about Gwyng fear, Jereks who took away his Jerek lover."

"A bit crude to show it to us," Hargun said.

"Most mammals tend to be in awe of him. He's just a creature."

"Your Rector," Hargun said.

"Your opposite in negotiations—so you want him to be big and severe?"

On screen, the young Karriaagzh stalked a screaming Jerek, feathers clamped tight on his skull.

"Granite Grit," Ammalla said. Granite and Feldspar had squeezed their eyes shut.

"Sometimes," he said, dropping his lids, but guarding his eyes with the nictitating membranes, "fear makes me angry. But mostly I'm scared—terrified creatures can be so dangerous."

Feldspar touched him, bent down more, and gaped her beak. He looked around, found a bit of cheese, and dropped it in her mouth. They sat beak to beak while she reached up and rubbed his nares.

We watched as much of Karriaagzh's rebellious youth movie as we could take, then switched to something really funny when the Gwyngs came back, desperate for more company.

Chenla and I looked at each other, not as drunk as the others—not really drunk at all, but I was half tense and half lethargic, an odd combination. "I'm going to bed," I said.

"Alone?" Rhyodolite asked.

As if she'd understood, Chenla stared coldly at the Gwyng before we got up and walked down the hall toward our side-by-side rooms, me thinking about my double bed.

But she went into her room and I went into mine, wondering if I should have at least kissed her. I should have, but I was afraid to reach for her.

I heard her shower, and footsteps back and forth as she muttered in her language. Then she walked to my door. My cock began rousing itself as I went to open it.

"So don't ask," she said, dressed in a bath sheet. "Let me in quick before the wrinkle-faces find me here."

We both giggled like kids—she found the double bed hilarious. I grabbed her and bounced her onto it, then slowly unwrapped the sheet from her as she giggled behind her hands, eyes slits.

Human female. Human. Female. She sat up and undid my pants' drawstring. Almost hurt as she pulled them down.

After I recovered from the first time, she tickled me. "This time, slow."

* * *

As we lay in bed together in the morning, I touched the birth control implant ridge. *Not the dominant species here,* I thought, still glad to be human, with her, warm in a bed we'd made sticky.

Her Oriental eyes opened slowly and I rubbed the sleep out of the corners the way Feldspar had rubbed Rhyodolite's eyes, only Yangchenla didn't flinch. "I never slept with anyone after," I said. "You know, after . . ."

"With non-species women?"

"No. Close, but never."

"Faithful to kind, at least. How did you get here?"

"I tried to help a Gwyng, one of the wrinkle-faces. My brother caught us trying to escape and killed him. Very complicated story."

"We were supposed to be trained—my father's seen the old records."

Did she expect me *to do something?* I explained, "I had trouble finding a sponsor. Finally, the female Gwyng whose pouch kin I tried to help took me. Now I'm in the middle of her quarrel with the Rector."

"Pick a side, make sure it wins," she said. "Then come help us. My brother wants to be a cadet."

"How did you get to be free traders?"

"My grandfather and grandmother—very ambitious. Sent my father to school—weaving night and day for a handwoven dealer. Handwoven is like live servants with the Federation people. Machines are quicker, but pay to creatures is calculated on city living, so the rich wear live-made cloth to prove their money. But the dealers think they can cheat primitives." She leaned up on her elbow and said, "And you *can* cheat most primitives. Most *are* stupid. But when *we* found out *we* were being cheated, we sued the handwoven dealer. From the settlement, we bought a shop."

"Do you cheat primitives, yourself?"

She laughed.

"Yangchenla!"

I'd have asked her more but the Gwyngs burst into the room, saying, "Your female, not in her room/missing." Then they twined around each other in mock shock as she slowly pulled the sheet up over her breasts.

"Tom, you lied. You sleep together," Rhyo said.

"Only pairs," I said. "Get out so we can dress."

Cadmium brought in a box from the hall. "New clothes for Red Clay," he said as he dumped the box out on the bed. Rhyodolite went out for two more boxes.

"We tried to trick Hargun into coming in," Rhyodolite said, "but he was very cagey/non-cooperative. Since you've seen Black Amber mate, then we should see you."

"I didn't watch Black Amber mate," I said. Yangchenla looked like she was trapped under the sheet. "They won't hurt you," I told her. "I'll get your things."

"Hurt you? No," Rhyodolite said, hopping up by her feet. "We'll keep off the *Yangies*. Protect ape-eating-ape/ female who calls us names."

"They tease, especially the little one, but . . ."

"Bring me my bag," she said. "Under the other bed."

I got up and Rhyodolite crowed, "Used, a male used organ."

Furious, worried about what they might do to Yangchenla, I pulled on my pants and rushed to her room. She'd brought a scuffed leather satchel, full of clothes, papers, and a hand calculator. Something like a metal penis on a chain dangled off the handle.

When I got back, they were sitting on the foot of the bed, humming at Yangchenla, who giggled when she saw me.

"Are you okay?" I asked her.

"Get them out of here," she said.

Rhyodolite moaned. Cadmium Gwyng-talked sternly, and Rhyo said, "But, Tom. Only fun. Shy ape shit."

Cadmium spoke again. Rhyodolite stiffly put his legs on the floor and said, "Had almost forgotten pain and death agonies until you hurt my feelings." His nostrils clapped open and shut as he hobbled out.

"Is he serious?" I asked Cadmium.

"We don't like being excluded from our friends' social lives," Cadmium said stiffly, "but if your primitive woman is a xenophobe, then we'll release our tensions by mobbing the Yauntry."

"Cadmium, please. She can't understand you, so . . ."

"Not *that* serious. Don't become upset, lose erection. But remember, you watched Gwyngs."

"No, I didn't. Black Amber took them to another room. *Shit*." I explained to Yangchenla, "To them, sex is a social occasion. Since they're my friends, they think we should include them. I was at another Gwyng's house during her breeding season. But, of course, the Rector was trying to get me so I'd sleep with a Yauntry woman, be bait for the Yauntries."

"You need frien̲ she said, "on the History Committee."

The Gwyngs ed in the hall about Red Clay and *Yaungcho* sex. Yangchenla, suddenly shy, around me eet up around her collarbones as she s, brown cotton-looking, and a stretchy kni̲ led them under the sheet and wiggled around, then s to straighten the dress and find the right belt for it. I realize she'd wrapped the knitted band around her breasts, and blushed some.

"Do you plan to re-pay your sponsor quickly?" she asked, tying the belt.

"I didn't even know I was going to get a cut in Yauntry tariffs for being in the first-contact group until Hargun told me."

"You must ask questions," she said.

I began going through the clothes the Gwyngs had brought in. "Do your people make clothes like this?" I said, holding up a corduroy suit.

"You can buy cloth like that all over Karst City," she said, "but I guess they don't let cadets out much."

The Gwyngs had brought in suits, jeans, tops, belts, two coats, underclothes—all from Berkeley, California, stores. I felt weird that some alien in surgically shifted human face had gone around shopping for me.

Yangchenla pulled out her pocket calculator and totaled the prices, me translating them to Karst numbers. She asked, "How much is 3,698 *dollas* in Karst credit?"

"I could have lived for a year on 3,000 *dollars* if I'd owned my farm and didn't wear anything but jeans," I said.

"What budget does *this* come from?" she asked, spreading her hands over the clothes.

I couldn't answer her. After I dressed in jeans and a Lacoste shirt, I slipped on the Swiss shoes as Tesseract knocked on the door and asked, "Are you both dressed?"

"Tesseract? No Gwyngs? Come in."

"Karst is trying to seem less militaristic to Yauntra," he said when he came in, "so we're sending you out in species costume."

"I'm not familiar with this," Yangchenla said.

"Chenla, you might want to go out to the porch and have breakfast with Ammalla. I'd like to talk privately to Tom."

She picked up her bag as she left.

"Well," Tesseract said, "was it too embarrassing?"

"She thinks I'm naive." I sat down on the bed and stroked the satin lining of one of the suit vests. "I guess I am. I want to ask you some pretty hard questions about Karst, Yauntra, about what cadets and officers do."

"Most of our work is less exciting than what you've been going through."

"Hum."

He smiled, knowing that much Yauntro, and rubbed his crest, which was still pale. "Hargun's decent, if the Yauntra governing group trusts him now . . ."

"Chenla said I should support Karriaagzh or Black Amber, pick a side and make sure it won."

"Tom, if you must pick a side, help us keep two very intelligent, capable individuals from destroying each other. Karriaagzh and Black Amber . . ."

"I feel odd about Yangchenla."

"We wanted it to be a pleasure for you."

"Well, it was . . ."

". . . *and it wasn't*," he finished in English.

"She makes me nervous. But I feel more *human*," I admitted.

We went out to the porch for breakfast and found Yangchenla talking gravely to Edwir Hargun, who looked over at me with his round inhuman eyes before turning back to her and answering, "We've been told we could send cadets if we join the Federation. Perhaps your species hasn't joined the Federation yet," Hargun said to her.

"So polite," Rhyodolite said, pulling his straw out of his throat.

Yangchenla and Hargun seemed pleased not to be able to understand. Granite and Feldspar came out, seeming sleepy.

"Would you have preferred privacy, Red Clay?" Granite asked in Karst II, looking at Yangchenla.

"It would have been nice," I said.

Cadmium said, "We meant no harm."

Yangchenla and Hargun discussed various oils, butters, and the flavors of grains. Yauntra had much cold land, so she thought *tsampa*, whatever that was, might grow there.

"Perhaps I can sell you seed stock," she said.

"Free traders," Rhyodolite commented, "are always freeing trade." He stuck his broad straw back down his mouth and began pumping away with his tongue muscles.

"We're leaving this afternoon," Granite Grit said, "all of us except you and Yangchenla." He spoke in Karst I this time so she understood.

Mid-morning, I stood with Yangchenla and Ammalla on the veranda to watch the planes rise up into the engineered air.

"Tom just came from the planet you say my people came from years ago?" Yangchenla asked Ammalla.

"Five hundred years ago, to be exact."

"He's in the Academy. Not one of us who has been here for five hundred years has been accepted." Yangchenla's dress fluttered as the plane carrying the birds and Gwyngs took off.

"Tom is a test of *humans*. Your family is another test. We don't take the murder of Rector's People lightly—even if it happened five hundred years ago and the killers were terrified. *Humans* were lethally xenophobic then. Tom, I'm sorry."

"Did Tesseract know a *human* had killed a Rector's Person when he came to Earth?" I asked.

"He knew when you came in with Granite Grit that time." Ammalla smiled slightly.

Poor Tesseract—Granite freaking and me from a species with a history of lethal xenophobia.

"Murder's against our religion," Yangchenla said.

"We've heard *that* before. Karriaagzh wants to contact all language-users, but so many would die—cadets, officers, Rector's People, terrified primitives themselves."

Some near-lethal xenofreaks lived right down the road from our old farm, I thought.

Yangchenla sullenly sat there, staring down. "But," she said, "we have no status, no place." She got up and stretched, displaying her body to me, I sensed. The body was wonderful, so wise on its own terms, that I wished a bit that little, complex Chenla wasn't so much in control of it.

"Cold, Tom?" Ammalla asked gently.

I *was* shivering.

"All that distance between here and our planet," I said, although that didn't really explain things.

Yangchenla went to the porch rail, grabbed it, and hissed through her teeth. Ammalla touched her gingerly. "I hate pass-carrying," she said. "Slimy come-ons."

"I'm sorry," Ammalla said, rubbing the human girl's back.

"Him. You only feel sorry for him. Prize cadet."

"Tom *is* our first concern," Ammalla said, "but perhaps sex-giving makes you feel vulnerable." She turned Chenla around carefully—half afraid for herself, I thought, embarrassed that my species had such a xenofreak record. But had *I* hurt Yangchenla?

Yangchenla stared rigidly at Ammalla and whispered, "Tell Tom to go away."

I nodded to Ammalla and slipped into the house, hearing Yangchenla weeping as I crossed the entry room.

God, let there be beer. I went to the kitchen freezer, pulled one out, popped it open, and drank. Yangchenla and Ammalla came after I'd drained it. "I'm sorry, Tom," Yangchenla said. She went to the sink and dialed cold water to wash her eyes.

"Maybe we should have eased into this."

Yangchenla got her eyes back in the shape she wanted them and turned to look at me. She looked older than early twenties then. "I never wanted to *use* my sex-giving, but you were so tempting."

"Naive? And sexually lonely?"

"The Barcons put in the child-preventive sticks, but I don't have my children anymore," Yangchenla said.

"Didn't your ex-husband take them when he left you?" Ammalla asked.

"Worse for our men in Karst City," Yangchenla said. "Tom, help me."

"He can't help you yet," Ammalla said.

Yangchenla crossed her arms in front of her and gripped

each upper arm with the opposite hand. "I should have gone back with the others."

"Tesseract's coming back tonight," Ammalla said, leaning against a counter. "My poor sink has seen lots of tears—yours, Rhyodolite's—these few days."

"What does a wrinkle-face have to cry over?" Yangchenla said, loosening her fierce handholds on her arms.

"Some near-kin broke his legs—and none of us had *any* idea that the *Gwyngs* were trying to poach a contact."

"Poach a contact?" I asked.

"Some Federation sapients feed primitive cultures scientific information—get them out into space and make the first contact, get the first-contact shares and sometimes even the linguistics team shares."

"Oh," I said. "He told me they were just watching."

"Naive," Yangchenla said.

That afternoon, we heard a plane coming in. Ammalla smiled and fixed a tray of beers and nut cookies loaded with vitamins that Ahrams needed—whether humans needed them or not. Before she carried the tray to the porch, she rubbed her small crest ridge and said, "We need time alone."

Yangchenla and I began talking as if we'd just met and weren't sure the date arranger had paired us up intelligently. "So you were born in a free-trader family?"

Yangchenla nodded as she groped around the freezer, asking, "Have you heard of the Gwyngs who lure stray males into robberies using an in-heat female and her consorts?" She handed me a beer.

"I like Gwyngs," I said, hoping Ammalla and Tesseract were having more fun than we were.

"And you're going to another planet, with those people who were prisoners here."

Slowly, I sipped the beer, dodging any attempt to even think out an answer to myself. Finally, I said, "I'm assigned to do it. Being a cadet's not as neat as you think, Free Trader. We get shot at."

"Transfer to Institutes if you're afraid," she said.

I felt odd, standing there in my human jeans and Lacoste shirt like I was a college kid. I remembered Hargun's eyes watching me in the van from the free side of stout wire mesh. "But they're more afraid of us."

Yeah, we're out here and we do not look like you.

Yangchenla re-folded her arms in front of her breasts and said, "Some individuals, species aside, are problem characters."

That afternoon, we played chess with folded paper chessmen and a board Yangchenla drew up. The rules had changed somewhat in five hundred years, if I'd remembered correctly what I'd read earlier, bored and fiddling through the Floyd County high school's encyclopedia. She beat me until I learned to think out moves in advance.

Tesseract and Ammalla came out briefly to make sure we weren't killing each other. But we stayed polite, sexual energies drained off by both my tension over returning to Yauntra and the mad one night we'd already had together.

In the morning, Tesseract, wearing a shift that seemed to be the uniform tunic's ancestor, looked at me as though he hadn't quite planned for me to be there. He looked more alien, as though he'd never talked English. "Ammalla told you we had trouble with *humans* earlier."

"Yes, I'm sorry," I said. Yangchenla looked tensely from the chessboard, crouched over it.

He sat down heavily on the sofa. "When you came in with Granite Grit . . ." His voice faded.

"After I'd cut classes. Bet you wanted to deal with one crazy cadet at a time."

He smiled. "I talked a long time with Hargun. We're three different social types, you, me, and the Yauntries, regardless of how much we look alike. They beat each other up, by groups like your nations, but then assimilate very quickly. Ahrams—we're more independent even than humans. Odd."

I thought about the Civil War—blacks. *Yeah, we're not good assimilators.* "If you Ahrams are less social, then how come you got to space before we did?"

"Accident." He laughed slightly. "Let's not talk about species. Tell you this, though. Black Amber thinks you're good luck. She pouched a nymph."

"Has it been fifteen weeks?"

"Five months. You were on Yauntra quite a while."

"Cadmium and Rhyodolite must have been excluded from the mating scene again. That's why they were such assholes."

"Is it hard to keep up with all the different manners?" Tesseract asked, sinking deeper into his chair.

"Yeah. Want a beer?" I replied.

"You *humans* read minds?" he asked. Ammalla came out in a long shift, looking tired and sleepy.

I got out four beers and we all sat around the frosted-glass holo tank watching Ahram movies, the behavior not quite human enough to follow emotionally, but Tesseract and Ammalla looked so wasted I didn't have the heart to ask them to explain the obscure points—why did the heroines trade children when their men were killed?

The next morning, Tesseract, dressed in his Rector's Man clothes, woke me. "Pack all of it," he said. "Here, I'll help you."

When we left the room, Yangchenla was waiting on the porch with her bag. She looked a bit fragile, a lone woman making her way in this world.

Nah, she had family. I was the lone human here, the men of her people wouldn't accept me. That's the way humans and chimps are—hard to break into a new circle.

We loaded our things in the plane and sat down behind Tesseract to go back to Karst City.

Suddenly I was exhausted. I wished I could relax a few days more with people I knew, *human* people.

Yangchenla looked out of the plane windows, her eyes fixing on each hill range, then looking over the plains to the next set of mountains. "I'd like to keep in touch with you," she said to me. "Perhaps you'd tell me what has happened to my people since we left?"

"*Tibet,*" Tesseract said. "Got conquered in a war. Many fled to *India,* became religious leaders in Tom's country, but he probably doesn't know about that."

"No, I don't," I said glumly.

"Does our kind have planes now, computers?" she asked. "I know they don't have space gates, but holo tanks?"

"No holo tanks," I said, "but planes and computers."

"Perhaps I should try for an interplanetary trade contract," Chenla said, almost to herself. Slumped down in her seat, she was quiet awhile. "I think," she finally said, "that other sapients' opinions bother me too much. I'm not like you Ahrams."

"Worse for the Yauntry on that, Yangchenla. For them there's terror in either making us monsters or trying to merge with us," Tesseract said. "Humans can be bothered by alien opinions without wanting to be like all of us."

"You must have a place where you can be an Ahram among Ahrams, but we can't escape being primitives."

"Being a refugee," I added. "Expendable, ripe for the name wall."

He reached back and thumped my shoulder. "Tom, was being a *parolee* better?"

I shut up, body swaying with the little motions of the plane, tired, tired, tired.

When we landed, Yangchenla refused help with her bag and walked by herself toward her bus. A guard asked to see her I.D.—suddenly, I remembered seeing a black guy carded at a bar, no one else, just the black guy.

Primitive . . . refugee . . . nigger. I felt sorry for both of us, but my cadet uniform got me by the guard without a twitchy glance. Tesseract in Rector's Rep colors was right beside me.

Yangchenla waved timidly from the bus steps, as though she wasn't sure waving kept its meaning for five hundred years. I shouted, "I'll see you again." She smiled and waved back more vigorously through the bus window by her seat, and I flapped my arms at her as her bus pulled out. "But what's next?" I asked Tesseract.

"I need to talk to you, in my office."

"Yes, sir," I said in English.

"Don't take that tone with me, son," he replied in the same language. I sort of laughed.

We loaded the bags in the car and drove up to the chrome pillars of the Rector's offices. I wondered what I'd feel if I saw Karriaagzh. Such a monster—no wonder the Yauntries thought he ruled us. "Leave the bags in the car," Tesseract said. I walked with him to his office.

A little bear sapient with short all-over curly body hair had one of Tesseract's relax-'um teas waiting. Tesseract sat down in the armchair near his desk. I sat on a wood seat and pulled a little table close for my teacup.

Tesseract rubbed his crest and then drank, both hands on the cup, a huge draught of tea. "The situation on Yauntra," he began, but didn't say more for a few moments, staring into his teacup until the little bear brought the teapot over, but Tesseract waved him away. "Tom, Yauntra's corporations don't want their trade balances destroyed by new alien technologies. That's what Hargun told me. Be careful. Stay with Hargun or Karriaagzh. Unorthodox the bird may be, but he's not stupid."

"It's gonna be dangerous." I started speaking in English.

"Now come with me, you'll spend the night in the dorm."

By myself? I didn't ask, though, just followed Tesseract out to the car again, feeling like a pawn, from the chess games I'd played with Yangchenla. I must have sighed, because Tesseract patted my shoulder.

He carried one bag; I carried the other, back into empty dorms, our footsteps echoing in the long hallway, no sounds of anyone else around. Seems they could have put me up at the Lodge again, but I guessed Karriaagzh wanted to remind me I was just a cadet.

Alone again. I opened the door.

"Surprise," Rhyodolite and Cadmium said. All sorts of young aliens stood up for me. I came in dazed while Tesseract took my suitcases and pushed through the crowd to put them in my alcove. Gwyngs, birds, Ewits, Jereks, two pairs of shiny black people, and a pair of Barcons with a drug dispenser.

A curly-haired bear-stock person came forward. "I'm Dioran Ferrite 4, your hall monitor. Sorry I didn't help you more, but the authorities around you intimidated me."

All the cadets looked pointedly at Tesseract.

"Have a nice party," Tesseract said, leaving. "We'll pick you up in the morning, Tom."

After Tesseract left, Cadmium said, "We have a song for you. Tesseract suggested."

"Our brains must be overridden, but it's for you," Rhyodolite added. They put curved plastic plates, almost like Carbon-jet's memory enhancer, over the computers in their artificial skull bones, and began singing, in English:

* * *

> Gentlemen songsters out on a spree,
> Lost from here to Eternity,
> Lord, have mercy on such as we,
> Baa, Baa, Baa.

Chills ran up and down my spine—that's what cadets were, and greatly in need of mercy. I wondered if Tesseract had translated the song for these other cadets. "Any others going out?" I asked.

"Gypsum's coming back from Ewit home," another Ewit said archly.

"The rest are friends-of-friends," Feldspar said in Karst II, "or went through the operation with you."

"Or will preserve order," a Barcon on the drug box said.

Cadmium and Rhyodolite twisted together when I came around to them, and Cadmium said, "Black Amber told us you did not witness. She asked that we apologize."

"It's okay."

They rolled me between them, and said to the party at large, "And we can sing his throat."

I looked at Rhyodolite's little wrinkled face, the nostril slits quivering in and out as he breathed, felt both Gwyng hearts beating in their bodies. We're all in this together, I thought, then said in Karst, "We're all aliens together."

Granite and Feldspar came over, their long feathered thighs lifted high, hocks bumping people who weren't used to the way birds walked. Feldspar rubbed her nares against Rhyodolite's chin. He didn't flinch, but reached up to tickle the thick golden flesh around her nostrils. I was proud of him, and felt much less lonely.

> Lost from here to Eternity,
> Lord, have mercy on such as we.

One of the other Gwyngs said, "Bird presence always increases the pulse, but we can re-interpret that physiological reaction."

"They're exciting to be around," Cadmium said.

Gypsum came in, babbling in Karst II and Ewit. He looked

around at the party and threw his baggage on his bed. "We're all refugees here," he said.

"Ewit home do something to you?" another Ewit, dressed in officer blue, asked.

"Yeah, they aren't too fond of 'brain-contaminated colonials.' "

The Barcon at the drug box said, "I recommend Terran hash oil for the Ewits."

We filled all three alcove floors and most of the center section with mats from the vacant rooms. They were covered with sleeping cadets and young officers—too emotional, too wasted, to go back to their separate rooms.

"Red Clay. So they had a seeing-you-off party." The harsh voice didn't seem too thrilled. I opened my eyes—Karriaagzh, with an injection cube in his hand.

"What's that?" I asked.

"Sober you up," he replied, "if you need it." I saw Edwir Hargun standing by the disc player, staring at the alien bodies.

"I only did alcohol last night," I said, blinking. A couple of the others sat up grumbling, but went very quiet when they saw Karriaagzh.

"The Rector," someone in the back murmured.

"Your bags still packed? Shower, change into a uniform, and come with us."

"Could you wait outside?" I asked.

"Yes, we'll wait outside. I remember these parties, dimly."

After I had a shower, I realized I did have a headache, which got worse when I changed to fresh clothes. I found a uniform, my sash folded on top of it, and dressed in the whole works. My dirty clothes—jeans, shorts, shirt—I wrapped in a sheet and stuffed in a suitcase.

When I came out, Karriaagzh said, "Bit much," fingering the sash, "but why not?"

"My head does hurt," I admitted to him.

Squinting his yellow eyes, he pulled up my tunic sleeve. Hargun cringed as Karriaagzh pinched my human flesh in his bird fingers and pushed the cube against it.

"Ready now," he said, throwing the cube into a hall trash can.

"Yes." Hargun and I both looked at Karriaagzh, huge and

grey beside us. Those yellow eyes could have been amused, but they were totally unfathomable to us mammals.

Hargun took one of my bags, which surprised me a second. Karriaagzh ruffled his face feathers slightly, but didn't stop his long strides down the hall toward the exit.

"Everyone else is at the ship," he said when we reached his large grey car with the back seat removed.

= 10 =

Us and Them

After Hargun, Karriaagzh, and I boarded Karriaagzh's ship, Karriaagzh handed me computer cards and bubble storage packs. "Trade possibilities."

"If those are Yauntry *fluist* compatible, we've got weeks of work, Tom," Hargun said.

"Yes," Karriaagzh said, settling down on his hocks and pulling up a tripod for his elbows. "Weeks—probably months—of work."

Mirror—space—mirror—space, then we orbited Yauntra. Near the atmosphere's edge, as we began a planet-fall path, we got an escort of Yauntry shuttles. When the ships had atmosphere enough to fly aerodynamically, the escorts moved in front to lead us to a landing field far north of where I'd been before.

"Remember," Karriaagzh said to me in English, *"what we really are—hostages."*

A cold wind hit us when the ship ramp went down. "Wait," Karriaagzh said. "Let the Yauntries out first."

Under a thousand camera lenses, a boy and girl threw themselves at Hargun, crying in Yauntro, "Daddy! Daddy!"

I felt alien, slightly guilty. Karriaagzh touched my shoulder and nudged me down the ramp, then away from the outrageously happy Yauntries.

A Yauntry officer came up and said, "We say now that Edwir Hargun went to space to clear up a misunderstanding between Yauntra and the Federation of Planets."

I translated. Karriaagzh replied, "This welcome seems to belie that." He added in Yauntro, moderate politeness level, "I understand."

Hargun's wife, face wet with tears, walked up toward Karriaagzh, who told the Barcons to let her through. She froze. He crouched slightly as she said, "Thank you for bringing him back alive."

I translated. "Tell her, very politely, that I had no desire to do otherwise," the bird said.

When Hargun and his children came up, Karriaagzh sat down on the cement runway and eased his arm out of his jacket. The girl, with quivering fingers, traced the scales down to the back of his hand. Karriaagzh murmured, eyes half closed, "Very tactile," and slowly lifted his body up again.

The two children gaped at his height. His crop surged, his crest went slack, and he wiggled his fingers, stroking the air.

"Do my children make him uncomfortable?" Mrs. Hargun asked, her voice tight.

"Tell her I'm used to the investigative ape fingers." He winked his left nictitating membrane, and opened his beak slightly, eyes fixed on the children.

The children skittered to their mother and pressed against her. Karriaagzh sighed, almost bitterly, then said, "Your weather is out of phase with Karst. We have adapting to do."

Winter—so cold I wished I'd worn my wool suit and lined overcoat. The boss Yauntries called for our vehicle—a van—as I shivered beside Karriaagzh, whose clothes puffed out as he raised his feathers under them.

In the back of the van, Carbon-jet sat beside a Yauntry with a gun. "Karriaagzh!" he cried. "Why you? Why here? The planet's hostile."

"Carbon-jet, they think birds rule," Karriaagzh said as he looked at the van's floor and judged how he'd best fit in. The bird grabbed the doorframe and settled, feather to fur, by Carbon-jet. "This proves that I can be ordered around by mammals."

Carbon-jet stuttered, then asked, "Who ordered you?"

Karriaagzh didn't answer, but said, a few miles down the road, "I'll simply outlive her."

C-j caught my eye and pursed his lips in the Gwyng oo— Karriaagzh meant Black Amber. A bit later, Karriaagzh scratched under his feathers. His fingers brought out a thumbnail-sized message pod, pushed it into Carbon-jet's shoulder fur. The Yauntry guards didn't notice.

The Yauntries put us on an estate like a giant landscaped park. I was exhausted—more from being on crazy Yauntra again than from the trip's quick flashes of space and mirrors—but Karriaagzh wanted to walk. A Yauntry official told us, "Walk, then, in the fields by the main house, and don't cross the plowed strip in front of the fences."

Carbon-jet seemed desperate to sleep in a cold room (I suspected he wanted to check his message pod) and the Barcons had to test the local food for Karriaagzh, so the bird and I went out alone. What more would he do to me? I wondered. *Is he really just a fat lonely bird?* Brittle leaves crackled under his claw boots and my Swiss shoes as we walked out to a pond skimmed with ice, broken to show water rippling here and there. Karriaagzh bounced a bit on his big legs as his eyes followed a road to the horizon.

It was almost obscene to think of him as lonely. "Now, you're here, too," I said. The weather suited him, cold air to cool his hollow bones if he ran. His head swayed on his feather-muffled neck, eyelids rising and falling; he seemed ready to bolt now. "Can we check to see if they'd mind your running?" I asked.

"Am I so obvious?" He tightened his neck feathers. "I'd appreciate it if *you* asked."

"Yes, Rector."

He roused feathers under his eyes. "Call me Karriaagzh. Black Amber is Acting Rector while I'm here. She gave Wy'um a son."

We ate dinner buffet-style; some Yauntries used tiny chairside tables. Karriaagzh gorged on meats. "I'm a bit indisposed," he said. The Yauntries wanted one of their medics to help him, but I noticed his crop—*surging a bit, eh, Karriaagzh*—and the slack crest of feathers, and said that the Barcons would help if he needed assistance.

He raised himself unsteadily and left. Hargun stared at me and said, "Shouldn't a Barcon go with him?"

"Don't worry," I said.

Finally, feathers drooping, nictitating membranes edged out in his eyes, Karriaagzh came back. I watched too knowingly as he blinked the eyelids and membranes several times. He tucked three large stones, freshly washed, into a napkin and then into a pocket and waggled cheek feathers at me. *We are both gentlemen of the universe,* he seemed to tell me, *so don't say anything about my disgusting pleasures, and I won't mention that Black Amber sexually aroused you.*

"Do you feel better, Rector Ambassador Karriaagzh?" Edwir Hargun asked.

Karriaagzh filled his bird cup and poured watered wine on his hot crop. "Much better."

After dinner, we all escorted Karriaagzh to his room, which had thick drapes over the windows and a red suede-covered mat, ten feet square, on the floor. Karriaagzh looked sharply at Carbon-jet, who must have told the Yauntries what Karriaagzh slept on. Beside the mat, on a table, was a bowl of gravel and a handmade ceramic bird cup.

Edwir Hargun asked, "Does the room suit you?"

Karriaagzh pulled the drapes aside to expose chain link mesh behind the glass. "Could you arrange," the bird asked, "a dust bath? A sand pit would be adequate, although I do have a heated dust shower in my ship. Or Tom Red Clay could clean me by hand, if you gave us sawdust and my feather combs. And the reading light. I'd be more comfortable with more blue in the spectrum."

Hargun asked, "Is that all?"

"Enough for today," Karriaagzh said, looking away from all the round eyes. He roused his feathers, shook, and leaned awkwardly against the table to get his boots off.

So, after you ran my testosterone up so I'd be good Yauntry bait, I'm to be your servant? Karriaagzh wiggled his strange toes free of his left boot. The Yauntries stared at his feet, like distorted parrot feet—two big club toes in front attached directly to each ankle. The heels were short toes in back—not one, like a Gwyng, but two per foot—only slightly longer than a human heel.

Then he looked at us all, feathers on his head almost helplessly slack, body feathers puffed slightly under his uniform—still Rector's clothes, even if Black Amber was

Acting Rector—and sighed, looking at us mammals as though we all were his captors.

In the morning, I woke up early and stayed in bed, worrying. An hour after sunrise, Hargun buzzed me on an intercom to say, "I need time with my family. When I'm ready to talk to you, I'll let you know."

I got up and found Carbon-jet in an informal kitchen. "Come walk," he said to me. Two Yauntries came with us.

"I hate having my life in that crazy bird's hands," C-j said in the language we get from the computers when we listen to Karst II speakers. One of the Yauntries switched on a recorder.

"He's manipulative, but not crazy. I know crazy."

"No? Black Amber's right; he wastes Federation personnel. Federation pilots died to set up the blockade. The bird rescues you, takes hostages, and leaves twenty-six people behind defended by a Barcon squad and anal-gland non-lethal stun guns."

"The Yauntries didn't kill you. And the Gwyngs have been landing on a pre-tech bat planet. Three got their legs broken—had to be rescued by Barcons and birds."

Carbon-jet stared off into space as if searching for the unlikely planet where this happened. "Gwyngs," he said, ". . . rescued by birds? Karriaagzh's behind that."

"Granite Grit rescued Rhyodolite because Rhyodolite was my friend."

"Black Amber's Rhyodolite?" Carbon-jet squealed and whistled when I cupped my hand.

The two Yauntries said, "No more secret talk," and turned us back around toward the main estate building.

As we came back inside, we passed the negotiators in the hall. Karriaagzh said, "I can show you the display in my ship. It only looks three-dimensional." A Yauntry who spoke Karst translated and all the Yauntries tightened their lips, not quite smiling.

What display?

"Crazy," Carbon-jet said. "Consummate refuse."

That afternoon, five Yauntries rode up on the local horse-parallel, burro-looking but with little nub horns, leading a riderless one. "Karriaagzh runs. You translate," one said, motioning for me to mount the riderless animal.

Karriaagzh ran and we followed as closely as our mounts would go. When we stopped, the bird tried to come up. Finally, after puffing at Karriaagzh from enlarged nostrils, a tough male beast let Karriaagzh touch his neck.

"All brachiator-derived bipedals ride something," he said. "Is it a modified hunt, predator on prey-back? Or re-creation of tree-swinging? You ride long after inventing engines. Red Clay's people say, 'Nothing like the outside of a riding quadruped for the inside of a sapient ape.' "

After I translated, the Yauntries kicked their beasts into a trot and aimed them at the stables. Probably they thought the weird alien bird teased them. But when I looked down at my shadow, tall on a "horse," I thought, *Modified hunting behavior, swinging, why, he's right.*

The beast jerked his head toward my thigh and bared big ugly yellow teeth.

When we got back, we were sore. Karriaagzh called for his Barcons and spoke to them in their language, avoiding their eyes, which seemed to relax them. He sat down and cupped his hands over his mandibles and nares. The senior Barcon began massaging Karriaagzh, reaching in with his fingers around feathers and quills on the bird's upper legs.

"And you?" another Barcon asked. I signaled yes without looking at him and tentatively put my hand over my mouth. The Barcon wiggled his nose. The Yauntries watched uneasily as he pushed an electric deep heater down my thigh. Almost too hot—as if it microwaved my muscles.

Something buzzed and the Yauntries left. Karriaagzh stood, roused all his feathers, and went for a water shower.

When he came back, Karriaagzh stretched one side of his body, then the other, bird-style, drying his shabby feathers in front of his dryer.

A Yauntry came by with Carbon-jet. "He's awfully old, isn't he?" the Yauntry asked.

Carbon-jet whistled softly. "Wearing clothes," I answered, "doesn't help his feathers."

The Yauntries brought in truckloads of native delicacies for our formal reception dinner the second night. I dressed in my wool vested suit, and went to the reception room's double doors. Two Yauntry girls, one giggling slightly, the other stern-faced, swept the doors open toward me. I saw Yauntries, Yauntries, and more Yauntries around braziers and tables of food.

Yauntries, wearing different embroidered badges, stood clumped by badge, staring at Karriaagzh and each other.

Around the edges of the room were chairs and sofas with folding desks on the arms. One Yauntry shifted two chairs experimentally and locked them side to side, then swung them apart again.

"Your servers," the stern girl said, "neutral as to corporation." She pointed to a group of Yauntries built more delicately than most, both sexes, dressed in three different basic silks.

"What are your corporations?" I asked. "They seem to be more than organizations that make goods."

"They organize people," she said. "Manufacturing is only one thing. They educate, treat diseases . . ." She stopped abruptly. "Perhaps you should ask someone more versed in these things than I."

A Yauntry with a sun-on-horizon badge watched the servers' huddle until another Yauntry with a tree crest on his shoulder said something rough to him. A server dressed in the rarest servant costume—white tights and a black slithery tunic—reached for a medallion on his neck chain, but the Sun Crest Yauntry left.

A young server male in brown came up to me. "He'll be your facilitator," the girl said in Karst as she disappeared.

I smiled; he gasped that I could smile. Appealing to his professionalism, I said, "I'm not quite sure what to do here. And what was that argument about?"

"Argument? For a space . . . man, you do speak Yauntro very well. If you eat meat, fried lightly with spice, we're serving four dishes your medical space-hairy-people approved. Let me seat you first, Red Clay." He found a chair and pulled up the little attached table. As Karriaagzh and boss-looking Yauntries came in, he stared at them before taking off in a gliding rush, smoother than a run. He brought back a bowl loaded with strips of fried bird meat. "And what function do you play in this?" he asked, handing me the bowl.

"We followed a satellite into your system." The meat was too spicy, but I managed.

"The Encoral Ragar Sim asked to look at you, after he's served," my waiter said. "He is the Encoral dealing with you space people. Perhaps you should address him as Encoral Sim, but Ragar Sim would be appropriate, too. You seem to understand politeness levels?"

"I hope I do."

"I don't want to embarrass you." He paused.

"Could I ask you which politeness level to use? The most polite forms?"

"You have such good understanding." My waiter took my bowl and extended it out.

I looked over the rim. A white-haired Yauntry looked back at me with extraordinary grey eyes, hammered-steel grey with no black rims to them. He flicked his glance to my waiter, who said, "Let's approach the Encoral Ragar Sim *now*."

Sim stood as we came up. The Encoral was about six foot five, dressed in black tweed, with a fir-tree-in-snow lapel badge. Around his neck was a gold chain—big inch-long links—with a fist-sized medallion. Smaller Yauntries with Secret Service eyes and flesh-colored buttons in their ears flanked him.

"So you were on the first ship. Unarmed in our space! Both corporations and the government argue over what that meant," Sim said. "Sit, sit."

"Yes, Encoral Sim," I said as the Encoral Sim's waiters brought chairs for me and his mean-eyed guards.

"You speak Yauntro well enough," Encoral Sim said, taking a bowl of fried bird strips from one of his waiters. "I imagine your people plan projects for you that would use it." He stabbed bird meat with a skewer and held it by his mouth. "But do you realize how complex this world is, even with one central government?" Then his curved jaw dropped and he nipped the meat off with teeth that seemed too delicate for his face. His nose was almost human, high-bridged. "Wouldn't bother *him* that we eat bird?"

"He wears down jackets sometimes."

"If you had your face hairs removed, you could pass for North Yauntry, if one didn't look closely at the jaw. Some have eyes almost like yours."

I remembered face-shifting; my eyes must have flickered

because Sim collected himself, alert. "Yes," I decided to say, "but don't I have an accent?"

"The DNA's different, isn't it? And the amino acids synthesis in the guts." Ragar Sim's eyes hunted for and found Karriaagzh in the crowd.

They locked eyes briefly, then Sim turned back to me and said, "My Edwir says that your species isn't part of the Federation? That you're alone, very junior?"

"Yes," I said.

"Sometimes, I prefer to talk to the unranked. You say Karst treated you well."

"Yes, Encoral Sim, they've rescued me when they've gotten me into trouble." Yauntry had funny phrasings—that came out a bit too honest.

Sim looked at his guards, ate awhile in silence so absolute the waiters gestured to each other, like deaf-mutes. My waiter filled his lungs, about to talk, but Sim finally asked me, "Would you be offended if I touched you?"

"No." We both put our food aside, and a female waiter brought a finger bowl. Sim prodded along my jawbone with his index finger.

"Little hard specks in there." He ran his finger from my chin to my ear, then felt my nose. "None there." He swirled his finger in the finger bowl.

I said, "Once, when my bird roommate was sick, I rubbed oil on where he was growing feathers—felt like *matchsticks,* thin slivers of wood, under his skin."

"How long would that hair grow, if you let it?"

"Down to my chest."

"Good for cold weather, I think," he said with a smile. "Your Karriaagzh asked to be taught Yauntro, but he knows more than he admits." The Encoral Sim ate more, then looked at me again. "And no sense of humor, except to make very big jokes with planets and blockades."

"Birds say our sense of humor is cruel."

"His is. Mine's not." Sim paused, then said, "Would you play with a flying disc and talk to our young people while we videotape you?"

"For a broadcast television show?"

"We have to make you seem less monstrous. If we can." He smiled again and my waiter took me away.

*   *   *

After dinner, Karriaagzh told me on the intercom, "I'll come by and explain how to clean my feathers."

When he came in, he put a sticky grey plate on the window, then plugged a red plastic cylinder into it. "That should take care of taps through the window or through your skull computer." He spoke in Karst II. "Has Carbon-jet tried to make us look vicious here?"

"I don't know, *sir*. He wanted me to be a link between the Intelligence Institute and Yauntry spies." I sat down on the bed.

Karriaagzh loomed over me, smelling of feathers and dust. "Tell me more." He hunkered down on his shins and looked up at me. "They went to charge you and Carbon-jet with espionage." When I gasped, he added, "The penalties aren't harsh, jail for a few years."

"When Filla approached me, I asked the senior Federation officer what to do. If I was being tested . . ."

"A test, yes. But . . ." He looked down at the floor and flicked out his tongue a few times, a flat-bladed tongue like a Gwyng's, but not as broad.

My leg muscles coiled as if I were going to run. "Sir, Rhyodolite said I'm a token in the quarrel between you and Black Amber. That I owed both my 'testing' and rescue to that."

Karriaagzh jumped up, crest erect, and made a terrible sound with his bills—like two timber slabs crashed together, only repeated. I'd heard a wounded great horned owl make a similar sound, but the owl'd only startled me. This paralyzed me.

With a shaky hand, he touched his mandibles, then smoothed down his crest. "She insulted me when I first saw you, talking like a lactating submissive when neither Gwyng nor bird females need to play such fools."

"I thought she'd insulted you with the fists and by not wearing the uniform you gave her."

"I gave her? I'd *never* have made her a Sub-Rector. Gwyng Wy'um and Warst Runnel did that." He slowly lowered his body again and said, "Body bribes." The yellow eyes blinked slowly, fixed on me. "And who are you, Cadet, that I can't use you? Must you be rude to me?"

"I think I've been polite. You scare me a little."

"You try," he said, somewhat calmer.

I decided never to tell Karriaagzh that Tesseract and Ammalla thought his policies would involve the Federation with people who might genuinely fear they dealt with demons. And what *was* Carbon-jet's attitude toward the bird? I wondered.

Mindful that the Yauntries could hear, I said, "Do you know the Yauntries are going to videotape us, to get their people to see us as less monstrous?"

"That's a good idea," Karriaagzh replied in Yauntro.

But the afternoon I was scheduled to be filmed playing with a Yauntry Frisbee, I got dizzy. The Barcons ran cerebral tests, then Karriaagzh's chief attendant asked, "How do you feel about Yauntries?"

I had a gut-negative reaction about being alone even with Hargun. "Could Carbon-jet come with me?"

We left in a car with a Yauntry driver and two guards. Another car, horn wailing like a siren, led off. I sighed. C-j whistled through his sharp nose and said, "Nothing worse than bureaucracies processing novelties."

The cars swept through the estate gates and drove through the country to a small city electrically glittering in the on-coming dusk.

"Don't use me in your intrigues anymore, Carbon-jet," I told him in the analog Karst II language. "They want to charge us with espionage."

"Talk about intrigues, the Rector manipulates Gwyng death fears. He forced you on Black Amber because you'd remind her of Mica. But she fitted you into her life, even though you have no brain by Gwyng standards. Then he snatched you away."

I managed to keep a slight smile embedded on my face along with my incipient whiskers while a Yauntry woman interviewed me, furry Carbon-jet on my shoulder. Then she asked, "Do you grow face hairs like your companion here?"

But I shaved after dinner. I touched my chin to see if I'd sprouted any since then and she flushed. I explained, "Mine are coarser than Carbon-jet's, so to stay clean, I shave them off."

"When are you broadcasting this?" Carbon-jet asked.

"Soon, if no corporations protest."

The T of bare Jerek face skin crinkled slightly.

An official took Carbon-jet and me aside into a room with

a VCR. He ran the tape of Karriaagzh bending over Hargun's children, crop surging.

"He's perverted," Carbon-jet said, "but he wasn't thinking of eating them."

"He wanted to feed them," I explained. "They gaped at him and they're probably the size of bird babies. Bird stocks, male and female, get pleasure from feeding their mates and young."

The Yauntry said, "We will format this so the throbbing organ doesn't show."

"He really loves little sapients," I said.

"Tried to marry a Jerek woman," Carbon-jet added.

The Yauntry's expression was almost comic—those big eyes, that dumb round chin. He decided we'd go out and tape me and a young Yauntry playing with a plastic flying disc.

"Fantastic idea," Carbon-jet said.

"Do you also play with these discs?"

"No, we didn't specialize in grabbing. My people evolved from diggers and biters."

"He had what ships hidden behind what moons?" Carbon-jet said on the ride back, after I'd explained what I'd seen. The Yauntries continued to tape our weird code-talk.

"Covered an eighth of the big moon's surface."

"That many ships? How far away was the moon?"

"Filled a third of the viewport."

"No wonder they want retroactive waiver of immunity. He faked it. What will they do when they find out?"

"Are you sure he faked it?"

"Offense isn't a Federation specialty. Let me know how he did it, someday, if we survive. You're closer than I am to the devious thing. 'Poor old Karriaagzh, pitied for his loneliness, about to die' for nearly twenty years."

"Tesseract extrapolated from the other bird sapients that he could live to be 150, 200."

"Oh, extrapolation from non-sapient birds is enough. We told the History Committee not to be fooled by rumpled bent feathers and grey old looks."

"Isn't he a good Rector?"

"Is he going to explode the Federation by bringing in too many raw species, xenophobes, primitives? That's the important question."

"So, it isn't just Black Amber he has to worry about?"

"What do you mean, 'worry about'? The Yauntries won't hurt *him*." Carbon-jet shifted nervously in the car seat, and a musky odor filled the car. "Sorry," he said. "He's so sly. He speaks Karst languages without an accent when he's drunk."

"And he feeds toilets?"

"Disgusting. I wish he'd take a baby bird from another species, but he probably suspects we'd consider he took a bribe. His posture is aloof disinterested concern for all species, for the Federation."

I remembered the Rector's awful sighing in the men's room after he'd fed the toilet, Rhyodolite's glazed eyes. Why didn't the Federation let him adopt a baby bird—ease him?

Three days later, the Yauntries showed the TV production. Karriaagzh asked Sim if all the Federation aliens could watch it in his room, without Yauntries present. The Yauntries agreed, so the linguistics people who'd stayed on Yauntra and the people who'd come with Karriaagzh gathered there: Barcons, Jereks, the old ape senior officer, a couple of bears, all sitting on backless Yauntry folding stools or on Karriaagzh's suede-covered mat.

On the screen, Hargun fed me at the landing field, the cheese curse cut. Then the scene shifted: I was trying to rouse Rhyodolite—how odd he looked.

I looked around the room. All the bodies seemed more alien. But when I looked back at the screen, I was unsettled to see myself the odd one, among the Yauntry faces.

When shots of Karriaagzh appeared, we all looked at him, so obviously alien on screen, yet both more and less alien in the flesh. His mandibles parted, Karriaagzh watched himself, keeled breast rising and falling, eyes trembling faintly as if he focused on the screen, then looked inward at his mental images. The Yauntry camera caught him bare-armed, with Hargun's girl touching his scales.

Asked how he felt, negotiating with such a creature, the Encoral Ragar Sim said, "The bird is tough, intelligent, but not like us. But his alien diversions will not disrupt our economy. We promised all the corporations that."

Karriaagzh rocked his body. "Karst can't promise that," he said softly.

On-screen again, I looked dirty-faced and apprehensive, while a voice-over commentary mentioned that I was learning to trust the Yauntries after my initial rudeness. The commentating voice hinted that Rhyodolite and Xenon, who went berserk when the Yauntries stopped our ship, had gated into the Yauntry system without Federation authority.

Damn them. I remembered Xenon's olive hackles swaying in null-gravity, his tense politeness.

Edwir Hargun talked about Tesseract as though he'd been an invited house guest. "The xenophobic crew leader," Hargun told the Yauntries, "has since been learning better manners from birds like Karriaagzh."

"Bird heroes?" Carbon-jet said.

Karriaagzh hushed him, as Hargun explained, "Part of Tom Red Clay's rehabilitation will be helping me hammer out a non-exploitive trade agreement. He, too, is moderately xenophobic."

Carbon-jet lay back and whistled trills. Karriaagzh clacked— that horrid sound again. "You don't think that's funny?" Carbon-jet asked him.

"I have no mammal sense of finding fun in potential dangers."

"Well, you got off looking fabulous and tough. I heard they want me and Red Clay up on espionage charges. Do good, don't give up immunity."

Karriaagzh replied, "If we were slaughtered, Karst would just continue to blockade the planet. The Yauntries could evict us with abusive tactics, but the Federation will still be out there."

I sat rigidly, trying not to be so afraid. Finally, I said, "I kept thinking about how alien I looked."

"Mammals always look abnormal on video," Karriaagzh said as he got up to pour water down his throat.

"I can't expose my people to your technologies yet," Hargun told me over the phone. He said it curtly, no politeness. "They're shaken, so it's too early to talk."

Carbon-jet and I bitched at each other for two months over laser disc music and Yauntry novels while Karriaagzh and the Encoral Ragar Sim disappeared each morning.

When certain guards were on duty, a Yauntry with a

sun-on-horizon crest would visit Carbon-jet. The first time, Carbon-jet told me, "Go ride those damn animals. I'll tell you later what's going on."

But Carbon-jet told me nothing. After weeks of squabbling with him and riding with Yauntries who wouldn't talk to me, I asked Karriaagzh if Carbon-jet and I could sit in on the negotiations.

"Great idea," Carbon-jet said. "Especially since they want to negotiate us into jail here."

The Yauntries would permit us to sit at Karriaagzh's table if we didn't communicate either verbally or by signal to anyone in the room.

The Yauntry guard opened the conference room door; we walked into a funnel-shaped room. "A theater," Carbon-jet murmured, knowing a different kind of theater than the ones I'd seen. The conference tables were deep below tiers of seats. Giant fiber-optic bundles fanned out from the ceiling to spray light all over. Most seats were empty, but we passed two clusters of Yauntries, two different embroidered badges on their shoulders.

"Odd fingernails, besides all that fur," one said.

"They understand Yauntro," his companion hissed. Carbon-jet looked at my hands and at his own, which did have odd nails, thick at the base, with a ridge through the center, as though claws had been flattened.

"Not supposed to think so much about species differences," Carbon-jet said as we passed them.

"You looked first," I replied as we sat down at the end of Karriaagzh's table. Karriaagzh and Sim glared at me, so I quickly shut up and sat very still.

Two tables faced each other across the pit—white hair against grey feathers. As the morning crept on, I found out how boring life-and-death negotiations could be.

Then Sim said, "Your people must know that attempting to suborn Yauntry intelligence is unethical."

Looking at me and C-j, Karriaagzh replied, "I refuse to waive immunity retroactively."

"We suspect contacts with you *will* de-stabilize us. The computer in the first ship was beyond anything we have. And what if a species tries to dominate the others?"

Karriaagzh said, "Only medicine is dominated by one species—the Barcons, who don't use that against the rest of us."

Sim looked for a Barcon, saw one and shuddered slightly, then said, "Can we keep our native physicians?"

"Of course. And species don't always agree along group lines. Close parallels can be most annoying." Karriaagzh added in Yauntro, "Send observers to Karst, from each corporation if they function as semi-independent political units."

The discussions veered off into dull discussion of the nature of the observers on Karst and Yauntra, what Institutes might be observed, etc., etc.

Then Sim said, "And we must discuss retribution for the Federation damages to Yauntra's defenses."

"Define your Yauntro term 'retribution,' " Karriaagzh said. As he listened, he slid his nictitating membranes a quarter way over his eyes and raised his feathers—deep in thought—while Sim explained slowly that the Yauntro term meant money for damages paid by a nation or corporation to another.

Suddenly Karriaagzh seemed to understand. His feathers snapped flat, the eyes opened wide, membranes back. "I believe," he said stiffly, "that this is somewhat like a Karst II term which means, depending on pattern context, something similar to the Karst I word for punitive damages." The crest started rising. "Punitive damages?"

Encoral Sim leaned his chin down on his folded arms as he listened to Karriaagzh.

The bird eased his crest down, all the time staring at Sim with those yellow eyes. "You can't mean that," Karriaagzh said. "Perhaps mutual recompense—we've both suffered from misunderstandings."

Hargun closed his eyes and leaned back up, then suddenly caught Karriaagzh with a full grey stare. "Bird," Sim said, "you're so expressive for a feathered space creature. But not always convincing."

"Perhaps the Federation could give money," Karriaagzh said, "for startling you so badly. We understand your species is afflicted with xenophobia—most of you. Would this be offensive?"

Damn them, they enjoy this. Karriaagzh moved more fluidly than he let himself move on Karst, and he spoke startlingly good Yauntro from so short a study of it.

"We will admit to being startled," Sim said with a smile, "if you pay your debt without disrupting our economy. We don't use your currency, and trade items could hurt our local manufacturers."

"We'll give you training. Your corporations and government can figure out how to use it," Karriaagzh replied. Sim grimaced. Behind me, Yauntries drew in hissing breaths.

We all ate lunch standing around the table Karst-style as Karriaagzh's Barcons and native Yauntry servants brought food in. The two negotiators kept hammering.

"Laws?" Encoral Sim asked, grey eyes slitted. "What laws will your visiting scholars obey? Ours? Yours?"

"Negotiator, except for sexual and eating behavior, we'd obey your laws on your planet. But give us time to learn them. We can't waive immunity until we do. As for your students on Karst, should you send them, we would like to discuss how appropriate *your* laws would be in *that* context. We've given you copies of Federation legal codes and the rules of space claims, interplanetary trading."

Sim looked briefly at me and Carbon-jet, the tokens in this game. "So many regulations. We're still translating. How are we to protect our adjacent system space?"

"We protect any species's title to its solar system—inside that is planetary business," Karriaagzh answered.

Sim considered that as he chewed, then said, "What limits to raw materials? Anything necessary that the universe will run out of soon?"

"Considering the gates, and considering that we control breeding and migration on all systems except systems of origin—Yauntra's solar system for your species—there are almost no limited resources."

"Lithium? Aluminum?"

"Lithium's rare, but no one forces you to sell."

Hargun came up. "Will your creatures be decent among us?" he asked as Karriaagzh gorged on meat. "I've heard bird sapients get sexual pleasure from feeding gaping babies of any species. Will even feed inanimate objects."

Karriaagzh grabbed his lower mandible. Muscles between

his eyes quivered. His crest shot erect and he stared at Carbon-jet, then at me.

I blushed. Eyes fixed on me, motionless even though the membranes slid back and forth across them, Karriaagzh said, "Sirs, I have as part of my mating and bonding behavior such an act. Under stress, the act comforts. Did you not share sex with your female, Hargun, when you came back here?" Karriaagzh seemed to stare into my brain, see me with Yangchenla. "While I've been away from my own kind for over fifty years, these drives are powerful, as much as they amuse sneaky young mammals." He finally looked away from me.

I raised my hands alongside of my nose, trembling.

Karriaagzh continued, "It is not equivalent to your vomit. We have an organ that cleanly grinds food and the bolus is odorless and very nutritious. The babies . . ."

"Hargun's sorry he brought it up," Sim said, "but your food-grinding organ was throbbing over *his* babies."

Karriaagzh, nictitating membranes half covering his eyes, looked stiffly over the Encoral Sim's head. "The Federation brings us knowledge of all the ways that Mind works out life systems. Yet, in our sex acts, we often look foolish. In following instincts that bind matter to mind, perhaps no species is completely intelligent. Between all of us . . ."

"You're saying sex makes us fools?" Sim asked.

"One of my cadets was made a fool here, over sex," Karriaagzh said as he slumped down to the floor, taking his meat plate with him, nibbling away with his beak.

I rushed out into the hall and Carbon-jet followed me out, whistling merrily. "Sneaky young mammal," he said.

"I guess I shouldn't have explained to them about the Rector. *They'd asked about it when he wiggled his crop at the Hargun kids*," I said, slipping into English.

"Karst I, boy, Karst."

"He wiggled his throat organ at Hargun's children. They must have connected what I said with Karriaagzh's going out at the first dinner."

"He made Hargun look prissy."

That night, at a Yauntry-style formal dinner, I dodged my waiter and apologized to Karriaagzh.

He pecked my head almost hard. "For that, you wash the stones."

Yuck, those meat-greasy stones. "Yes, sir," I said.

"Carbon-jet was amused?"

"He thought you made the best of it."

After dinner, I went to the Rector's room. Karriaagzh was crouched on the red suede mat in front of an English falconry book, surrounded by feather-cleaning paraphernalia: sawdust in a big shaker, combs like serrated knives, oils, razors, towels, and plastic pins. Beyond the mat was his feather dryer.

I looked at the tools and Karriaagzh; cleaning him feather by feather could get real old, real fast.

"Sit down beside me. I want you to read this." Nervously, I sat, and he passed me the book, open to a section on feather repair—imping.

As I looked at the photo of a hawk on its back with a wing stretched out, Karriaagzh inspected himself in a three-way mirror and said, "If you cut out the kinks on the bigger feathers and splice the feather segments together, I'd look less like *a dirty old man.*"

I was startled to hear more English, then felt guilty that I'd told the Yauntry about his pleasure reflex.

"Do these tonight," he said, pointing to about ten feathers. "The longer these negotiations last, the better I'll look." He caught my reflected eyes in the mirror. "Your species trained hunting birds—interesting to think about, for me."

Where to begin? I cut and spliced, using glue and plastic needles inside the feather shafts. Down silkier than Granite's came out in my hands and stuck to the glue. The musty feather smell made me gag. "What's happening?" I asked.

"Molt," he said. "It's stressful for us."

I sat behind him, holding the feathers until the glue hardened. After the last splice, Karriaagzh went to shower, taking a bottle of soap with him. I looked through the falconry book until he came padding back, totally sopping wet, the big hoof nails on each foot cut short. He patted himself carefully with a towel and turned on his dryer.

"Tom, what are Gwyngs to you?"

"Black Amber's my sponsor. What else do you mean?"

"Wy'um, her heat. Did she use you to scare away the others?"

"Sir?" I wasn't raised by Warren for nothing. Sometimes, it was better to seem stupid. "I just made tea. Did get tackled by one—I can't tell them all apart."

Silently, since I was supposed to have cleaned him earlier, he showed me how to spread preening oil. This close up, I saw patterns of lighter and darker grey on his body feathers and upper limbs.

"Red Clay, do you like knowing things that no *human* who mocked you as a *parolee* will ever know?"

"That's not why I came to Karst," I said, a bit hotly. "And Amber's right about real primitives. Calcite, another refugee, freaked out. Barcons killed her personality to keep the body alive."

He didn't reply, just combed himself where he could reach, then handed me the combs. "I thought you weren't so tactile," I said when I began to comb his back, him crouched with half-closed eyes between my feet.

"We don't gather information with fingers." He opened his eyes and looked at mine in the mirror again. "Tug on the new feather sheaths, don't force them off," he said, shutting his eyes and crooning softly to himself as I worked.

"I think I've finished."

He opened his eyes, bottom lids dropping slowly, head very heavy, and turned around. "Good work for a novice."

Stiffly, I backed away, sure I'd get the tedious jobs this trip. He asked, "Would reciprocal grooming be polite?"

"I owed you after today."

"Why did you tell them about my pleasure reflex? It made me seem terribly strange."

"They thought you wanted to eat the Hargun children, so I had to explain."

"Rhyodolite took you to spy on me. Gwyngs can be hateful. And *you were* aroused by Black Amber's mating." He took my arm and sat me down between his spread-out toes, poured oil on his hands, which were softer than I'd expected, and chopped the soreness out of my neck.

"I know a bit about mammal back muscles." He rubbed a bit lower. "Many creatures strengthen social units with reciprocal grooming. Only sapients create social grooming analogs— trade, tourism, storytelling."

"Barcons? They're not so social."

"Pairs and families—brain parasites on their home planet make strangers affectionate. We're lucky they don't think us infected with brain worms and kill us." His thumbs mashed down on either side of my spine. Even if a woman had done it, the massage was too rough to be sexy, but it hurt good. "You've been quite tense?"

"Of course," I said.

"I'd like you to stay on Yauntra."

"No." *Yangchenla!*

"If we surrender someone, they'll have proved they're lords of their own planet," he said.

Not me! All my muscles coiled up again, my stomach burning. We both stood up and I wished him good night. He settled back down on his suede-covered mat.

Two days later, Karriaagzh brought the Karst people to his room and told us, "You're now under Yauntra inter-corporate treaty and criminal laws. Contacts with Yauntries who suggest illegal activities must be reported to me and either Edwir Hargun or the Encoral Sim within six hours. No texts can leave Yauntra without releases signed by the Encoral Ragar Sim. Don't speak to each other in analog Karst II."

Carbon-jet leaned back, mouth slightly open, tongue flickering over sharp teeth, face skin crinkled.

"Red Clay, Carbon-jet, Sim suggested immunity for the others if I would surrender you both on past espionage conspiracy. I refused. Hargun was also opposed, on Tom's behalf."

"One question, Rector-who-has-been-suspended," Carbon-jet said. "Why are *you* here? I thought you had clout enough to avoid a potential embarrassment, and Yauntra may be quite embarrassing to you."

"If I did overreact, then I should settle the problem I started, Rector or not. And, Carbon-jet, I save my political credit for really important matters."

"Yes?"

"Carbon-jet, I tell you to stay away from the corporate crests."

Edwir Hargun called to ask me if I was ready to begin trade work. "I hope," he said, "that you weren't offended by what I said on the video."

"*Nah*, I figured that was just politics." I felt weird talking to Hargun; his boss, maybe even mine, wanted me jailed. Jail again—far away and very alone, this time. But Hargun had defended me.

That afternoon, we worked at the estate. Hargun brought a Yauntry computer—old *fluist*—to read our non-graphics trade list. Each offering was current when we left Karst.

The room was plain, white, like an ex-kitchen, with the Yauntry equivalent of roller blinds, a table for the computer, and unpadded wooden chairs for us.

Both of us moved around the room stiffly. Hargun knew almost too much about me: he'd seen me shaking with terror after the Yauntries shot Xenon; he'd been at Tesseract's when Yangchenla visited me. If Tesseract and Ammalla had paid her to fuck me, maybe he knew. After Hargun set up the operating system, I loaded the first non-graphic card. "Push this," Hargun told me. "The operating system varies some from spoken Yauntry."

The list began to scroll—and went scrolling on, our monster. The first day, first Hargun watched it, jotting down frame numbers, then me, mumbling the items, noting whatever caught Hargun's interest. Intimidating Federation—technology beyond my dreams, from planets utterly more advanced than Earth.

That afternoon, Hargun stopped the machine. "We must be primitive! What are Jerek sterile entertainers? What are Llammash space net matrices? Biochips, core-riding plasma containers, deep space mining tori!" He yanked the card out of the computer and stared at it. "Don't be insulted, but I'm glad you're not from one of those planets. How much more primitive are you compared to us?"

I thought a bit—I hadn't seen either Earth's or Yauntra's most advanced technology. "Say, twenty years behind you."

"And our computer," Hargun stabbed viciously toward the computer screen, "doesn't intimidate you?"

"On Karst," I said, "the teaching computer works in our regular languages, one non-linear. And lines per inch, scan dot sizes—all that changes to fit the graphics you want." I sounded dazed.

"What is the capacity of your teaching computer?"

"Main storage is on a crustal discontinuity, semi-liquid

iron crystals, with micro-gates, like the ships. Your computer here looks like *Earth* ones, bit more sophisticated ROM storage.'' I leaned against the wall, suddenly awed by my pet terminal on Karst.

Hargun got up out of the operator's chair and asked me to key in *fluist*/computer. Over thirty planets offered computer plans—molecular chips, crystal discontinuity storage with micro-gates, laser crystal matrixing—more advanced than what Yauntra had.

Hargun yanked the card and asked me to let him have the chair. He ran an economics model program. Let lithium be high—Yauntra would be less affected, but might not get the highest-tech computers. Let lithium be low—local industries were suddenly obsolete. He stared at the screen, stabbing keys.

"You can't tempt us like this. Cruel.''

"You're blaming Karst if the technology tempts you?''

"Impacting technology. Sim asked me to check computers.'' He put the trade list back up and scrolled through computers again, then pulled a printout.

"Not my fault,'' I said.

A night later, Carbon-jet asked me to watch Karriaagzh on television in his room. As I came in with a quilt, C-j lay on his mattress looking up at Karriaagzh's image. The Rector, dressed only in feathers, explained, "I'm really lighter than I appear, about twenty percent lighter per volume area than a mammal would be.''

"Yeah, filled with hot air. And he seems so helpless,'' C-j interjected, "when he closes his eyes, the bottom lid so hurtly sliding up. Red Clay, do you think birds are less calculating because they've got wired-upside-down eyelids and because they weigh twenty percent less than a seven-to-eight-foot mammal would weigh?''

I shrugged and wrapped the quilt around me. On-screen, Karriaagzh and the Encoral Sim agreed that Yauntra would control its own solar system.

"We've always said,'' Sim commented, "that the satellite was not launched to leave our solar system, but was rather a deep probe to investigate our hydrocarbon reserves.'' Karriaagzh, hunkered down on his shins, admitted that the Federation infringed by entering the system.

Neither Karriaagzh nor Sim mentioned the Federation block-ade. "The Encorals promise Yauntra that satellite thieves can't force trade concessions damaging to the local corporations," Sim said.

"Oh, shit," I said as Karriaagzh asked for a translation of the Yauntro term "force concessions." Repeating the phrase, accent shifting across the syllables in several politeness forms, Karriaagzh puffed up his feathers and hauled out his eye shields, much, I guessed, to the utter fascination of all Yauntra.

Settling the feathers back with a jerk, he said, "Karst would be liable under its own laws if it forced Yauntra to buy off-planet products. We don't force you to join the Federation. My own people didn't join."

C-j rolled over and bit his mattress.

"Will we get interstellar space drives?" the interviewer asked Karriaagzh.

"You've developed them since discovering from our ships that they were possible. How much you need our technology, I leave to your corporations and central government to decide." Karriaagzh shuffled face feathers. "We could help you improve."

C-j had buried his head in his mattress cover, but finally he rolled his furry body over and stared, sniffing, at Karriaagzh's image.

Karriaagzh said, "Yauntra seems more civilized than some planets, with wonderful music and fine educational institutions."

"Our computers fascinated Edwir Hargun," I said.

"He'd give away our technology for their stupid music."

"Don't bet on it, Jerek."

The announcer continued, "We see you don't wear clothes these days. Do you feel dressed sufficiently in feathers?"

"I use an arm sheath for papers and currency—the scales keep it from sliding down my arm. I do feel more comfortable this way. On Karst, some mammals fear birds, so we hide our feathers. Fortunately, your people are less prejudiced."

The Encoral Sim spoke: "He's honest with us, shows us what he really is. No more disguises. We're going hunting at my country place, to get to know each other better. My gunsmith fitted a stock for him to one of my finest guns. After months of hard negotiations, we need a break."

"Is this live?" C-j asked.

"They left yesterday," I said.

"So if someone tries to entrap us, where's your Edwir Hargun? Here Karriaagzh is, off-planet, having you fix those poor matted feathers he uses to make Federation mammals feel so guilty. For some xenophobes, he preens? Trash bird."

"Hey, the Federation sent him out during a molt. Molting's stressful, so he needs a break from negotiations."

"He keeps everything from *me*," C-j said before heading for the toilet. When he came back, he circled the room, touching furniture.

"Isn't scent marking a bit primitive?" I asked him as stink filled the room.

"Get out, refugee," C-j said. He fleered back his lips and threw a urine-and-musk-soaked swab at me. "Didn't tell me. Don't know where he is, what he's doing."

A strange Yauntry asked me to come walk with him, "if you're not afraid." He reminded me of the anonymous guys connected to the Atlanta investors—no badge on his shoulder, a Yauntra knit hat pulled down over all his hair, colored contact lenses.

We walked out toward the pond. "We can get you back to your planet," he said. "You liked things on Yauntra that were like it, so you must miss it."

I didn't explain that I'd skipped parole. "I can't talk to you," I said, turning back to the house.

"To know you have faster computers and quicker atmospheric battle planes makes your Federation a challenge and danger to us. I can promise your safety if you help."

"I'm just here to talk to Hargun." The man didn't follow me back to the compound, but Hargun wasn't there. Neither was Carbon-jet.

Karriaagzh and the Encoral Sim slaughtered a quarter ton of mixed birds and mammals between them, shooting some on television. They'd wagered the three Yauntry operas against a Federation molecular data chip over who'd kill the most game.

I finally saw Hargun again in the computer room more than twelve hours after the Yauntry had approached me. "I'm pissed at you, Edwir," I said. "You were obviously gone so

I couldn't report the approach in the time limit. I've had it with Yauntries trying to mess me up with the Federation.''

Hargun pulled his dizzy eyes away from the detailed mobile graphic computer ads from the bubble storage packs and asked, "Is Carbon-jet a special friend of yours?''

"Are you trying to catch Carbon-jet in something illegal?'' I asked. "And me?''

"No,'' he said, but I suspected he could keep as good a face around a lying tongue as any Terran drug dealer.

"Hargun, I don't want to hurt Yauntra, or get hurt.'' I caught myself trembling.

He didn't look at me, but called up a new graphic. "Overwhelming . . .'' he murmured. He seemed to be punching stuff up at random.

"They've just had longer to get all that stuff,'' I said. "They aren't particularly smarter.''

"Have you met them all?'' Hargun asked, eyes on a spun-gold wire basket on a turning pedestal.

C-j started to carry a stick—black dented wood—which he bit from time to time. When certain Yauntries guarded us, he slipped out to talk to the Yauntry who'd visited him earlier.

"There's a strange Yauntry with Carbon-jet now,'' I said to Hargun after lunch. "And Carbon-jet wants to know what we've been doing. I told him we haven't decided anything.''

Hargun yanked out the cartridges we'd been working with and clenched his jaw. "I can't stop this. We're going to the Encoral Sim's. Let him see what alien technology is like, then he'll know why the corporations plot.''

"Should I get my clothes?''

"I've had a plane ready for days. Don't stop for anything. I have snow clothes 'styled to your custom.' ''

"What about Carbon-jet?'' I asked.

"He's safe enough for now.'' Hargun got very polite with me, almost eerily polite, as though he really wanted to be angry. When we left, Hargun walked faster and faster until we were almost running toward the estate garage.

As we started across open space between the main house and the garage, I heard a bullet—that crashing sound—and threw myself flat, twisting. *Keep movin' while they're shootin'*, Warren had taught me.

Out of the corner of my eye, I saw Hargun plant both feet in shooter's stance, raise a gun, and fire. I kept twisting around, terrified, even of him.

"Tom," Hargun said. "Why didn't you shoot?"

"What? What?" I quivered, still moving.

Hargun held the gun up as he took careful steps to a body lying half out of the bushes. I stood up slowly and followed him. "It's the Yauntry who talked to me three days ago," I said as Hargun rolled him over.

Hargun knelt by the body, checked the pulse in the neck. "I killed a Yauntry for an alien." He stared up at me as though I'd just been captured. "Why didn't *you* shoot?"

"I'm not armed!" We were shouting at each other—very dangerous. "You've got a plane waiting. Come on, let's go. Now."

Hargun stood up, blood on his knees, looking like he was going to faint. "Yes, we must," he said.

Hargun and I landed on a rolled snowfield surrounded by dark fine-needled evergreens, shorter than pines, the size of red cedars—millions of them as far as I could see. A Yauntry guard, breath a white cloud, stood by a snow coach, like a large snowmobile, red with black racing stripes, totally enclosed, though, with plastic windows. We got in, and the snow coach whipped us through the Yauntry spruces, down by willow thickets, the coach almost bouncing as the Yauntry driver rushed us across the taiga. The coach noise made talking impossible.

Suddenly, as the coach went over another hill, I saw the lodge—a golden log fantasy, high-pitched roof, big dormers with stained-glass panels in the windows.

The coach pulled up to the lodge and stopped. In sudden silence, Edwir Hargun and I pulled out our bags and stepped on crunchy snow.

Logs can't be machine-laid, so those irregular monster pines, hauled in from considerably farther south, dovetailed and squared off, made a considerable statement to this country boy. If Tesseract's place said money made nice things to share, Sim's lodge sneered, "Permanence isn't important. The Encorals will keep the power to build again."

No one came out to meet us. Hargun waited, hunched

over, breath fog wisping off. He looked terrified, so I knew I should be, too. Finally, almost shivering, he picked up his bag and went into the house.

The main room was a huge hall with a balcony running around three walls, heated by a boiler-sized wood stove in the center. Despite the stove's size, the hall was chilly.

Then, under a balcony, I saw Karriaagzh crouched on a leather pad and Sim sprawled in a hide-covered sofa. "Ah, Edwir-who-belongs-to-me, afraid they'd corrupt you?" Sim said, as though to a child.

Hargun stood, his round eyes blinking at Sim, chin down and shoulder up. Then he said, "I'm not corrupt, Encoral. We needed help. I shot someone trying to kill this alien." He lifted his hand limply toward me.

Karriaagzh said, "Where's Carbon-jet?"

"Relax, Edwir," Sim finally said. "Carbon-jet's safe for now, Karriaagzh. I thought some corporate *ze'eshi* might try to kill *you*, bird, to make an incident. So I brought you to where I run things, not the corporations."

Karriaagzh puffed up his head feathers.

Hargun shuddered and looked around the lodge as though he'd never been there before. Karriaagzh stood up and stretched, thick-feathered now after two weeks of running around in the cold without a uniform. "We can talk in the morning," Karriaagzh said. "You both should unpack now, see your rooms, adjust their temperatures. Carbon-jet would have been happier here, in the cold."

"Karriaagzh," I said, "a Yauntry tried to shoot me after he asked if I'd like to go home."

"I shot a Yauntry to save . . ." Hargun said.

"Go to your rooms, now," Sim said. Hargun's face seemed to shrivel. "On that balcony," Sim added, pointing, "first and second."

After we climbed the stairs, a Barcon came out of another bedroom, clucked, and took our bags. A Yauntry servant brought me a thermos of hot wine.

As I sipped the wine to get warm, I looked at my room, paneled in bird's-eye wood—a waste of cabinet veneer, which was, I guessed, the point. A fur rug covered the floor. My bed, high and fluffy, stood on it. I climbed into the stack of quilts and furs and tried on my Yauntry-made arctic clothes, almost shivering. Padded Yauntry cloth and earth suit styles blended into something a trifle exotic.

Night now, the room was chilly and the wine strong, so I stripped, rolled up in the quilts, and went to sleep.

In the morning, we sat around eating small grilled animals that Sim and Karriaagzh had shot. "There is a cartel of lithium planets," Karriaagzh rumbled. He swallowed his animal whole, followed by coarse gravel to rub the meat off the bones.

"Would we be required to join this cartel?" Hargun asked. He seemed sane again this morning.

"We don't force you to sell your lithium to anyone, at any price. Nor do we force you to join the Federation."

"The list," Hargun said to Sim, "is overwhelming."

"Some species stayed out of space once they saw that list," Karriaagzh said, rubbing his bottom mandible with both hands, then wiping his hands with a hot towel.

"Protected from other species, though?" Sim asked. He looked sleepy, grey hair tousled; even the steely eyes seemed a bit softer.

"Yes, we protect those species," Karriaagzh said.

"I was intimidated by the list, too," I said.

Sim smiled at me and said, "But you're not connected to any space-going species, are you?"

"No."

"They keep a watch on your planet?" I remembered all the clothes that had come from Berkeley. Sim saw my eyes wobble and added, "Very close watch, I'd imagine."

"We can't promise that your economy won't be disrupted," Karriaagzh said. "You'll have to work hard."

Karriaagzh's chief Barcon came shambling up, fur short, still growing out, but thick. He loaded a tray, and said, "Or find a speciality."

"Like the Institute of Medicine," Karriaagzh said.

The Barcon went back with the bones on his tray.

"They're equal members of your Federation?" Sim asked. "I can't tell if you're their pet or master."

"Not either," Karriaagzh said, "but equals."

Sim looked at Hargun and said, "We'll get a computer from the South."

* * *

Sim stared at the computer screen a whole day, switching back and forth from the short descriptions to motion graphics.

Karriaagzh sat away from the fire, reading from a Yauntry module screen, feathers puffed up, staring at me with his yellow eyes from time to time.

Sim called up a chromium-looking spidery industrial robot. As it rotated through its routine, he said, "My people in the North conquered everyone who tried to conquer us. Now the whole universe invades Yauntra." Sim turned his steel-grey eyes to Hargun. "Load the economics program, Edwir."

As Hargun and I worked with the program, Karriaagzh and Sim watched. All the models showed at least one corporation falling. Karriaagzh suggested, "Send your young to train on high-tech computer planets—better to get the computers slowly and really know them than to be dependent on another species. No one will force concessions."

Hargun and Sim flashed their teeth at each other. Hargun looked at the bubble graphics again. Information in illegally acquired systems can be drained or purged, the devices confiscated.

Yauntry had to deal through the Federation for giga-megabit computers, architectures with mini-gates that skipped information around inter-molecular space.

"I hate being inferior. But enough," Sim finally said. "Time to hunt."

Sub-zero out on the taiga, even Karriaagzh wore elbow-length mittens and down mukluks on his lower legs. The snow squeaked under my borrowed boots as I paced to stay warm while Hargun brought the red snow coach around. Karriaagzh puffed up his feathers and blinked rapidly. Only Sim seemed used to the cold, standing in furs smiling at us.

The snow coach engine shattered the silence as it came toward us like a fiberglass bullet, its huge central tread kicking snowballs behind it. When it stopped, Karriaagzh climbed awkwardly in back. I sat beside him while the Encoral climbed in by Hargun. The noise kept us from talking as the machine kicked forward and careered through the short firs.

We drove up through a cleared killing ground to a round stone hut, its walls pierced with slits. Hargun parked the snow coach beside it, and we climbed out. Hargun and I carried the guns in, pushing the quilted leather door flaps aside. Sim listened to the beaters on a radio as I helped Hargun fire up the stove—a huge circular thing with fins on top.

"Karriaagzh," Sim said, "I have no idea what some of those industrial robots do. What cultural level do we appear to be on?"

Karriaagzh hunkered down on his mukluk-covered shins and looked at the gun he'd been given, and didn't answer for so long I wondered if the Rector *would* answer.

"You're a species in transition," Karriaagzh finally said, shifting his two feet out from each other, then pulling them parallel and standing up.

"Come on, bird. Species must always be in transition."

"Early, when intelligence first erupts in a body, the new brain tries to glorify itself. Eventually, the brain settles to being support for just another superior animal. Do we mature? Or do we lose something? Space travel generally evolves in the transition."

"You think we're barbarians," Sim said. "I shouldn't have shown you the hunt." The big Yauntry was teasing, but only slightly. He sat down by the stove, his gun between his outspraddled knees.

"No," Karriaagzh said, voice slighter than usual, "I hunted on my home planet before I left. I'd love to contact species just before the space jump stage—to approach them just when they've realized the universe could be populated by different intelligences, not by gods. To build the Federation into a Family of Mind, with all ages, all cultural levels. Find a way to work even with primitives."

"Yet you'd sacrifice Tom," Sim said as he passed the bullets around, "to make us feel less powerless."

"You want certainty? Tom may be killed by the next first-contact species; I might be assassinated by mad Gwyngs."

Just then the beaters told Sim the game would be driven across the killing ground in three minutes, so we loaded the guns and took positions at the slots.

"By the way," Sim added, "your Carbon-jet Jerek was stupid. We have to arrest him."

Karriaagzh snapped his beak softly. "Jereks are difficult when offended."

"So am I," Sim said. "And you, Karriaagzh, should be the most offended. Silence now, the game's coming."

White animals and birds fleeing the beaters cast shadows on the blue-white snow, fell in red patches as the bullets hit. A large antlered thing, almost white, thrashed through the snow, breaking the crust.

Sim held his fire and touched Karriaagzh's feathered shoulder. The bird shot the big antlered mammal in the throat, but it leaped and ran almost to the woods before collapsing.

The radio told us that the beaters were approaching the clearing, so we set the guns aside. "Everyone's gun used different bullets," Sim explained to me, "so we can tally the game."

Karriaagzh took off his boots and waded through the snow to where the deer-creature lay. He circled it, hocks raised high behind him, then slashed into its neck with his hoof nails.

I heard a gasp and turned around. Hargun, hands stiff on his gunstock, was looking at Sim, whose face seemed icy, lips tucked in.

Karriaagzh wiped the blood off his lower legs with a handful of snow, then walked back to his boots, leaning against the hut wall so he could use both hands to put them on.

Sim said, "You didn't need to do that. The beaters manage the wounded beasts."

"We handled prey like that," said Karriaagzh in a voice that passed beyond being without accent into something flat, almost mechanical. *Alien*. He slid nictitating membranes back and forth across his eyes as though rubbing his eyeballs warm. "How did Carbon-jet fall into a Yauntry trap that Red Clay evaded?"

I saw Hargun look at Sim, heard clothes rustle as the Yauntries shifted, moved closer together. Karriaagzh and I'd both turned into aliens again. Neither answered.

The beaters field-dressed the game, then loaded the carcasses into snowmobiles. Sim stared at Karriaagzh, groaned, and said, "Edwir, snow coach." Hargun unglazed his eyes and went out to start it. We drove back to the garage, and went silently into the lodge to change into other clothes.

Sim and Hargun were downstairs when I finished changing, but Karriaagzh, who didn't wear clothes, came down last, pausing on the stairs to really tower over everyone.

The bird said softly, "You could kill the Federation people here, but that's no matter. Aliens will always be out-there, *k'fang*. A word of my first language." He didn't twitch anything on his eyes or ruffle a feather, but continued awkwardly down the stairs. Then he crouched in front of Sim and said, "Why Carbon-jet? Why not Red Clay?"

Hargun, who'd backed away as Karriaagzh came down the stairs, answered, "I didn't want . . ."

Sim chopped his hands through the air and Hargun stopped, and the Encoral Ragar Sim, all the rank, whatever it meant to Yauntries, spoke: "No, my Edwir, if we're masters in our house, we don't prove it by jailing powerless people. I don't prove my power if I take Red Clay into captivity. Tom is better as our intermediary, no political connections to more advanced species."

"What will this mean to Carbon-jet?" Karriaagzh asked.

Sim said, "We'll allow conjugal visits, keep him in house rather than jail."

Karriaagzh stared at me—an utterly alien stare that seemed to consider me as a potential wall trophy. His feathers went erect, then settled in quivering jerks. "I trust Jereks. I still . . . bonded with one, once."

"Think again, bird," Sim said harshly. "Some Yauntrous convinced the Jerek that you didn't offer honest terms."

"What corporation?" Hargun asked.

"Star-and-Garden," Sim replied in an utterly conversational tone. "Are the rest of you hungry? I'm calling the waiters."

I couldn't eat; how horror-movie alien they all could be.

Later that night Karriaagzh came to my room, bobbing his head, and crouched down on his hocks at the door, hands full of combs and feather oils. I closed the book on Yauntry corporations that I'd been reading.

We stared at each other. Angry, yet afraid, I stood up before him and said, "Rector, you and Sim are such *bastards*."

"Odd creature," Karriaagzh said sadly, "no need for such hostility." As though *I* upset *him*. Suddenly very self-conscious, I pulled my left leg closer to the right—less spraddle-legged fight posture.

"May I come in?" he asked.

"Certainly," I said.

"Am I likely to be attacked?"

He stood, crouched over his hocks, head bent slightly to the side, still in the doorway. "*Oh, my God*, Karriaagzh."

He straightened up slightly, walked in, and spread his combs and oil sprays around on the carpet. Then he sat in the middle of all that feather-cleaning stuff, eyes fixed on me, rolling slightly up as he sank down. "Do I intimidate you?"

"You're bigger than I am. You feel free to send me out to be shot at, jailed." I sprayed him with oil and got to work, feeling under the glossy new feathers the muscles he'd gotten from snow-walking.

He looked over his shoulder with those fierce yellow eyes. "I beat Sim in the shooting." The bony ridges over the eyes, I realized, made him look fierce. I couldn't really judge his expressions.

"Congratulations."

"They'll join the Federation and test us for a few years." He didn't seem to care whether the Yauntries heard that or not, sitting between my feet in that ornate little room surrounded by taiga, Yauntries, and a universe that didn't often make brains in shapes like his.

"Were your first years in the Academy difficult?" I finally asked him. Muscles under my fingers shuddered and loosened, then tightened again as he twitched his feathers.

"More than you can imagine," he said.

"It's very difficult for me, too."

He looked back at me again. "You have your *human* woman. I heard about her." He switched then to Karst II as though Karst I couldn't say what he wanted. "We (all sapients) (and you and me) must not twist nervousnesses between each other, does emotional damage/hurt."

"Black Amber's afraid of you—something innate in Gwyngs," I said. "And Gwyng minds are different, so what overmind do they reflect?"

He took my hand and rubbed it, then gathered the feather-grooming things. "Overmind isn't limited to what we can know, bare-minded, about each other. No one species is as comprehensive as the universe."

After he left, I fell across the bed, face up, and rubbed my eyes, feeling vaguely ashamed.

* * *

In the morning, as the Yauntry servants fried liver from the big animal Karriaagzh had killed, Karriaagzh said to Sim, "I want to be there when you arrest Carbon-jet."

"I can arrange that," Sim said.

After breakfast we left in the snow coach for the airfield. Once we were airborne, the taiga disappeared below us—the snow coaches, the wood castle of a lodge, and all the game animals that had escaped Karriaagzh and Sim. When we landed near the estate, the Yauntries had the van waiting.

Sim rode along with us, talking to Karriaagzh about the way the Yauntries would hold Carbon-jet. "Conjugal visits?" Karriaagzh asked. "Would you mind if they had young?"

"Radio the house to make sure Carbon-jet's indoors," Sim told the driver, then he asked Karriaagzh, "Young? How many at a time?"

"One, eight months gestation."

"I don't know. Conjugal visits are customary, but . . ."

"He'd be more tractable. He nurses the baby, too. Hard to fight with an infant dangling from your tit or with your beak down its throat."

Sim went "hum-ph," almost a laugh. Karriaagzh's head bounced back a bit.

"You don't want the whole Jerek species against you either," Karriaagzh added.

We waited in the hall while one of the Barcons went for Carbon-jet. The Jerek came out dressed in his uniform blues with his awards sash, fur brushed back, dwarfed by the Yauntries and Barcons flanking him. When he saw us, he stopped, nose down, as though he'd expected this.

Sim asked, "Are you Carbon-jet, a Jerek who has been in contact with Tellian Wert of Sun-and-Garden?"

"I am Seezat Rentral Awik, of Tunnel Awikkar. The Federation of Sapient Planets calls me Carbon-jet," Carbon-jet replied, swaying on the balls of his feet, nose tucked down. "I am utterly loyal to that Federation."

Sim looked at Karriaagzh, then told Carbon-jet, "You're under arrest for conspiring against trade negotiations between the Federation of Sapient Planets and Yauntra, a planet that wishes to join that Federation."

"I was trapped!" He swayed faster, then screamed, "Tom!" He leaped as he screamed.

I tried to pin my forearm under his chin, keep him from biting. Horrible to fight a Jerek. They're loose inside their skins, the fur sheds in your hands. We tumbled over and I managed to get on top of him, staring into those dark eyes, at that black crinkled face skin.

His heart fluttered, and he closed his eyes and screamed like a caught rabbit.

"Tom, get off," Karriaagzh said.

As I rose, he whipped his body around and sunk his teeth into my thigh. Barcons pulled us apart and Karriaagzh's big one held Carbon-jet Seezat's head while the Jerek cried "eek, eek, eek," almost choking.

"Seezat," the big Barcon said softly, "we'd like to sedate you. Encoral Sim, would you permit this?"

Sim stared down with his grey eyes at Carbon-jet, who writhed, shedding fur, on the floor. "Yes," he mumbled, realizing that arresting an alien was different from arresting a Yauntry.

Karriaagzh nestled down by Carbon-jet as the Barcons went to get their Jerek sedatives. "You'll have a breeding permit," he told the Jerek, stroking him, fur pulling away on the bird's fingers. "Zharr can join you. Seezat, why didn't you trust me?"

Carbon-jet's musk odor thickened. "My biting stick," he said, body quivering. A Barcon went for it.

"The sentence is not terrible," Sim said. "House confinement." He sounded as though he was apologizing.

The Barcon brought Carbon-jet's biting stick, put it in his mouth. Gritting down on the stick, Carbon-jet rolled to face the wall. Another Barcon pulled out the Jerek's left arm, took his pulse, then injected the sedative.

Moments later, Carbon-jet sat up, slumped against the wall, clots of shed fur around him. He brushed his dark hand against his nose and looked up at Sim. They both gravely regarded each other; Carbon-jet said, "Don't put me anywhere hot. Don't confine me to just one room. I'll die. Or do you want to kill me?"

"My lodge might suit you."

"Long time since a Jerek's felt this way," Carbon-jet said, speech slurred. "Like an alien."

"We'll arrange a quick magistrate court—either Hargun or I can officiate," Sim said. "Do you need a stretcher?"

Carbon-jet looked around the room, then said to Sim, "I'll surrender to you. You're the boss. I'll walk."

A Barcon helped Carbon-jet to his feet. Sim said, "Come with me, then," and led the Barcon and the tiny Jerek down the hall.

"You limp," one of the Barcons said to me, leading me into the kitchen.

I took off my pants and sat on a high table in my shorts as the Barcon and I looked at my thigh where Carbon-jet had got me. Huge bruise—the size of my hand—but the skin was scraped, not punched. "Is he poisonous?" I asked.

The Barcon checked a computer and my skin tightened as I waited for the answer. "No allergic reactions likely. Sit, calm down."

Sim came in and stared at my hairy exposed legs. I resented him and Karriaagzh then and it showed, because he said, "You can't surrender, can you?"

I remembered the bird cadet shot in space and Carbon-jet shrieking in the hall. And how terrified I'd been. "So you think I'm harmless," I said.

He came closer and touched the bruise. "Seezat has sprains. No, what I like about you is that you're honest. But don't try to make Edwir Hargun into a *'uman* . . ."

"Maybe your people don't surrender as neatly as your theory says they do," I said. "Your corporations . . ."

"You have people who haven't joined with others of their species for thousands of years, Karriaagzh said."

"*Yeah*." I felt embarrassed to be sitting there with my hairy legs sticking out at him, so I pulled on my pants.

For the rest of the afternoon, Hargun and I wandered around the estate, picking at books, listening to music and shutting it off, while Sim talked to Carbon-jet. Karriaagzh nestled down on a leather sofa, sitting toes and hocks parallel to the back, eyes rigid and unfocused, as though he were in a trance, as though he were wishing we'd all arrest each other, disappear.

Hargun came up to me at dinner. "Thanks, *man,* for saving my life," I said to him as we served our plates off the buffet. "But you always tried to be kind, didn't you?"

He looked at me as if suddenly aliens overwhelmed him with their cries and resistance to Yauntry ways. I thought about Mica, desperate to leave, with the shotgun in his hand, then dying on our kitchen table.

The next day, Hargun woke me up and stood in my room watching me dress. "We still have work to do," he said. "All the equipment for looking into your fantastic shopping list is here." He sounded kind of puckish. He looked happier today, all glittering round eyes and so-serious round comic chin. "We'll work things out," he said. "And the Jerek seems better and contrite today."

"I was never contrite," I said, "but I had no idea that we were being sent into your space against your wishes."

"You were just suddenly there," he said, "and scared us."

"It's very dangerous to scare creatures." *Mica, oh, Mica, if you'd just not pulled the gun on Warren.*

Hargun and I looked at all the industrial machines, bio-molecular brains, black boxes for gates, and the thousands of varieties of lithium-powered watches and flashlights. Then we worked on a draft of the proposed conversion rates between Yauntry currency and Federation val-unit. "We'll have to sell some of the lithium," Hargun said sadly, as though that would strip a moon from his sky. *Maybe it would.*

Finally, I sighed and pushed myself away from the terminal. Hargun pulled out the bubble memory pack and hefted it in his palm—odd lines on the palm, not like mine. Funny, I hadn't noticed that before. I stood and stretched, sight blurred, seeing letters and numbers when I closed my eyes.

"Your people are twenty years behind mine?" Hargun asked.

I looked over at him. "Actually my own family was behind that."

"I thought becoming involved in our space explorations would give me status. A place where virtues mattered, courage, intelligence. Well, I've become very good with aliens." He put his hands on my shoulders in the Yauntry gesture between an Earth handshake and almost every other creature's body embrace. I raised my hands to his shoulders.

"Good to have met you, Edwir Hargun."

"We'll be working together for many years," he said, "since neither of us was disgraced."

"It was work, wasn't it?"

He smiled, dropped his hands, and went to turn off the computer. "I'm as sorry for the deaths as I can be, considering that I'm most honest with Yauntra."

"Your people were conquered by Sim's?"

"He says we went against them."

"Eventually . . ."

"Dominance and submission fades into order."

I thought about the Jews—nobody'd beaten or assimilated them; killed them, yes, which turned the survivors into the Israeli Army complete with Uzis. I wouldn't want to be conquered and assimilated. "Different from us," I said.

"It seems your species leaders would be tempted to continual cruelty. Yet we do have the corporations," he said with a smile. "Are you hungry yet?"

I was. When we went into the lunchroom, I saw Carbonjet, standing in a leather breechclout, one curved strap of leather low around his hips and softer strips hanging in front and back to his knees, all the leather tooled and painted. He was reading and picking at his food. God, his fur was a mess, clumps out and the rest not combed.

Sim watched him as though he always wanted a Jerek. A Yauntry guard stood beyond both of them holding what looked like a Federation stun gun. Probably the safest thing to use on a prisoner that had to be held alive. Carbon-jet finally looked up from what he'd been reading and said to Sim, "This isn't what I was told would be the treaty."

"Karriaagzh didn't cheat your Federation," Sim said. "That is the treaty we worked out."

Carbon-jet slipped his curved shoulder blades around and hissed faintly. Karriaagzh came stepping in. "I apologize," Carbon-jet said to him, then said to Sim, "This contact will change your planet's economic life, despite all the safeguards we could ever impose."

"Our species is very adaptable, and strong." Sim drained a cup and stared at the Jerek as though challenging him. Carbon-jet shuddered his mobile skin. He had two nipples, just above the hip strap, and he reached down and scratched around them. Breasts like a human woman's 34 double A, smaller around, but there.

Sim touched Carbon-jet's forearm fur. "Nice," he said in his boss-Yauntry tone. "But don't you need to comb it?"

Carbon-jet swayed a bit. "The follicles aren't tight, shock. Don't want to shed more."

"Jerek females," Karriaagzh said, his eyes off-focus again, "have fur like down over the buttocks."

Carbon-jet hissed. The Yauntry guard looked sympathetically at him and asked, "Carbon-jet, would you like to go back to the cooled room?"

"Lead me out."

I didn't see Hargun at the final press conference in the red-velvet theater where camera lenses and optic fibers glittered for hours. I missed him.

When we finally closed the ship doors, Karriaagzh pulled down a mirror and took one long final look at the feathers he'd grown on Yauntra, rousing them, laying them flat. He fluttered his fingers over them, then pulled on the Rector's rust and gold uniform. Leaning against a bulkhead, he closed his eyes.

"How did you get all the ships on the moons?" I asked. "Carbon-jet said it was impossible."

Karriaagzh rippled his crest. "Take us out," he told his pilot. "And stop at the orbiting gate."

We left the gate and went by one of the Yauntry moons. The ships suddenly appeared, and I took a closer look at the thick windows.

"Computer graphics," he said.

"Won't they be mad when they find out?"

"I told them the first day."

We were both falling asleep before the ship reached another gate to jump to Karst. I slumped down in a chair, too tired to get up and go to my bunk. Even the Barcons were yawning. We all looked at each other—a wonderful bounce of eyes looking at alien eyes.

The next morning, I stared at the Karst far-planet freight yard—the transports and cargo bellies sitting in gate nets lit by such tiny lights stabbing against all the black of space. I'd gotten so involved in all this space . . . no, not the space so much as the creatures between the spaces. Karriaagzh came up behind me—I saw his reflection in the thick glass.

The ship surged through another gate and fell into planetary orbit. "I have to do the best I can," I told him, "as honestly as I can. Not be yours, not be Black Amber's."

He turned me around gently. "Ah, I thought you belonged to the Gwyng, to be aroused by her."

"Me, I don't belong to nobody," I said in tough English. "My kind doesn't like belonging to others."

"But will you have contempt for Hargun for his belonging to Sim?" he said.

"No, I can't," I said, remembering the first time I saw Hargun, when he was afraid of me but was trying to be kind. "He is what he is. *Sir,* you acted differently when you talked with the Yauntry. Different with other species. What's the real bird?"

"I've been rather a long time among mammals." He wiped his beak with his hands. "If I'm alone for a few days, then re-join you, it's strange all over again." He shrugged as I would have.

Then jets hissed and turned us into a night re-entry path. Karst City traffic lights below us moved like a galaxy on fast frame. My body surprised me—reacting as though I'd come home, relaxing, the dryness gone from my mouth, my lungs light with alien air. "So we're all Mind together? I don't know if it is true, but I can believe it right now."